Rainy Day Man

W·W·Norton & Company

New York · London

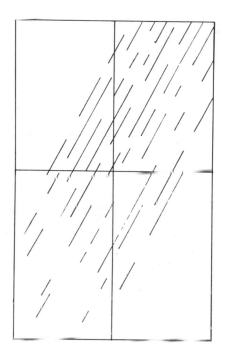

Rainy Day Man

A Novel by Rita Garitano

The text of this book is composed in Divinne, with
display type set in Torino. Composition and
Manufacturing by The Haddon Craftsmen, Inc.
Book design by Antonina Krass

First Edition

Library of Congress Cataloging in Publication Data
Garitano, Rita, 1939-
Rainy day man.
I. Title.
PS3557.A7156R3 1985   813'.54   84-16712

ISBN 0-393-01949-7

W. W. Norton & Company, Inc.
500 Fifth Avenue, New York, N. Y. 10110
W. W. Norton & Company Ltd.
37 Great Russell Street, London WC1B 3NU
1 2 3 4 5 6 7 8 9 0

For Robert

summer | 1972

Chapter **1**

Amy loves rain. And as the end of the school year draws near, Phoenix is experiencing what Mr. Crandall told the sixth graders is "a period of unseasonable rain." The afternoons are whipped into clouds of dust and even in the suburban neighborhood, the air smells of mesquite. Then lightning and thunder rip through the sky like a violent, drunken fight and after a short silence, the rain comes, heavy drops at first, followed by millions of sharp needles. She walks in the rain with her face turned up, mouth open, playing a hopeless game to satisfy her thirst.

This April afternoon, she sloshes along, indulging her whim, for she's already made her visit to the ghostly woman who was Gram Hershey. Daily, Amy runs from the classroom so the other children won't know she goes to the home to see Gram, a self-imposed penance. At first Mom had been surprised by the activity and asked in disbelief, "You went there again?" But now Mom rarely asks about Gram and only goes to visit once a week for shorter and shorter stays.

Today at the home, Amy had difficulty behaving like a good girl. She barely managed her sugary smile for the nurse manning the desk at the entrance, and the skip down the hall passing patients' doorways was a nightmare. Nodding so her curls bounced, she called out, "Hello, Mrs. Rosenbaum; hello, Mr. Hartley; hello, Miss Ashton." She was glad the hall was dim, for her mouth twitched from the strain of her forced smile as she gasped the dizzying odors of rubbing alcohol, stale urine, and death.

She brushed her lips across Gram's cheek and squeezed her bony wrist and sat in the bedside chair. Amy stared at the parchment skin of Gram's forehead to avoid the black, dead eyes. "Today, we studied mythology, and Elizabeth knew all the answers. And Flossie says she wants to visit soon. And she's being a big help to Mom lately, 'cause Mom's working nights again, selling tickets at the theater." Oh, God, keep me from speaking too fast. Keep my wrists in my lap, so Gram won't see the scars. God, make me pause, pretend she can speak, pause as if she can speak. "Yes, and, Hail Mary full of Grace, the Lord, "The Edgar Allan Poe stories are wonderful." The Lord is with thee. "And, yes, and Daddy is . . . is still busy, still selling." Then since there was nothing left to say, she could leave; so she kissed Gram's forehead, and raced down the hall, past the tiny rooms. Tomorrow, Gram's bed might be empty, the mattress stripped of its sheets, the black and white ticking airing.

Short blasts of a car horn stop her. She turns, clutched by her fear of strangers in cars who beg favors, and sees a rain-streaked Mustang the color of her father's when it was new. Embarrassed at being observed, she clasps her hands about her soaked hair and walks toward the slowing car. It might be him. The window rolls down on the passenger's side and Daddy leans toward the opening, asking a question she can't hear. He probably wants to take her home. But before she can answer no because it's out of his way and because it's only three-fifteen when he's supposed to be working, he has opened the door: a commandment she must obey.

Sitting in the passenger's seat, ashamed of the puddle she's creating on the floor, she's too preoccupied to take close inventory of him. When he hammers the steering wheel and smacks the horn as he curses a driver, she looks his way. His hand trembles as he takes the cigarette from his mouth so he can roundly curse the old lady who's made a left turn without signaling. Disgraced for him, Amy watches her own carefully folded hands in her lap until his breathing slows and he begins to talk to her in the forced, cheery voice he uses after one of his explosions. He asks, "Hey, lady, could I buy you a drink?"

In spite of herself, she giggles. Nobody has ever asked her for a date and here's this handsome man picking her up on a rainy day to rescue her from the puddles like the nobleman who spread his cape on the ground for ladies to walk upon. Daddy's such a kidder. She hugs herself, and as she rubs her hands up and down her shivering arms, she realizes how clammy her hands have become. She blows into her palms to warm them and begins to rub them rapidly back and forth.

He slows the car for a stoplight, and she feels him turn to stare at her huddled figure. She's embarrassed to have him witness her rodent-like gestures and drenched curls; she's ugly now. He might not . . . "Lady, I asked you a question. Can I buy you a drink? Can I warm you up?"

He opens the door of the tavern for her, so she can slip into the dark room ahead of him. And it's cold inside, smelling of old beer and cigar smoke and a little like the bathroom at school. Above the bar a brilliantly red and blue neon waterfall appears to flow down exploding into a blue starburst of shattered ice. Her knees are numb and her calves prickle with icicles. Her toes are tiny cubes. He nudges her shoulder. She must close her mouth and stop staring. She takes a tentative step toward the bar and feels him moving behind her. She has to walk faster. Hesitating before the bar stools, she watches as he slides onto one and pats the stool beside it. He's mounted the stool with such ease and rapid-ity, she isn't sure how he negotiated it. He spins the black stool top, patting it with quick slaps. He's getting angry. She sidles up to the spinning blur, knowing even on tiptoe her rear end will miss the mark. He bends forward, sliding his hands beneath her armpits to lift her. She's the snow princess being swept up by the knight to his white horse. His breath is sunlight on her icy cheek, his hands beneath her arms and along the sides of her breasts are lifting her into the blue-white light of sun on snow. In one swoop, he sets her in place, and she opens her eyes as he spins her so she faces the mirror. Her face is small and pale beside the dark man hunched at the bar.

The top of Daddy's hair is a dull gold; he's lifting his head. His face in the shadowy glass is painfully tired. He watches the reflection of a woman leaning on the counter, rhythmically chewing gum as she dries a glass with a soggy towel. Their eyes meet for a moment, then they look at Amy. The woman doesn't smile. With an electric jolt, Daddy's fingers rest on Amy's shoulder. She feels her body soften with ease as warmth flows into her. His breath glazes her cheek as he looks down at her. "Debbie, this is my girl." And as Amy lifts her chin so she may be inspected, she sees a quick half-smile twist the mouth of the woman, but her eyes are a flat stare. Such hatred should be accepted by bowing one's head. Amy drops her chin to her chest, but she can see Daddy sliding his arms across the bar. His elbows sink into the grooves along the edge. "A beer for me. And a Shirley Temple for the lady."

A Shirley Temple sounds silly, but he's not smiling as he rests his chin on the heel of his hand, his face turned toward the end of the bar where a little TV on a shelf on the wall blinks a gray picture. The row of men staring up at it exhale plumes of smoke and lift glasses to their lips in a slow, pump-like motion. The sound of the baseball game is so low they lean forward to hear. If she tries to talk, Daddy won't be able to hear the scores, and he's trying to figure out what's happened in the game. The barmaid sets a beer in front of him, puts a napkin in front of Amy, and sets a bubbly drink on it. A cherry, speared by a toothpick, surrounded by sprigs of mint, bobs at the top of the glass. She pulls out the toothpick. It might bump her mouth when she tries to drink. The barmaid shoves a straw at her. The toothpick belongs in the drink. But it wouldn't be right to put it back. It probably isn't right to eat the cherry before drinking. Maybe it isn't right to ever eat the cherry.

Daddy pleats a five dollar bill and holds it between his forefinger and middle finger. He waves it toward Debbie as if it were a single, long horn. The woman takes the money he's prepared so carefully, slips it into her apron pocket, and pats it against her thigh. She holds some coins toward him. But he raises his hand, refusing the change. He says he wants another drink and now he's looking down, asking if Amy wants one too. She hangs her head and mumbles, "No."

It seems as if they've spent at least three hours inside the dim bar. It must be getting dark outside. Daddy has had a whiskey and another beer and another whiskey. She isn't sure of the number of links in the chain. Each time he orders another, she studies the barroom, so he won't think she's being critical. They both know he's doing something he shouldn't be doing, and since she isn't drinking any more, she must not approve. Three times she's refused him. The last time, he tipped his head, laughed, and said, "Hey, I got a teetotaler on my hands." She giggled because she didn't know what he meant, but he was getting angry. She thought she'd better drink another to keep him happy, but she hadn't drunk the first one and Mom always got mad if they spent money when they didn't have it. And Daddy never had money at home.

He stops asking her if she wants a drink. Now he talks to the barmaid, telling her stories, keeping her laughing. He uses his special voices, making up long involved tales about people Amy doesn't know, using funny words she doesn't understand, laughing so loudly when he finishes that he coughs a little. And in between each story, he reaches for his cigarettes, lighting them and inhaling as if it brings him great pleasure. As he tells his stories with dramatic gestures, a trail of ashes scatters the bar beneath his hands.

She's been silly to come here. She hasn't pleased him. He's sorry he's brought her to this secret place. He's ashamed and wants her to go away. She'd better oblige him as quickly as possible. She'll wait for a quiet time between stories, a time when she can get his attention without interrupting him. But she can't gather her energies to dare to tunnel into his world. Part of her scolds herself for being so plain and so boring now words come to her to attract the attention of others. Part of her burns with a need to race to the end of the bar to the restroom marked "Gals" in big black letters. There she could crouch over the stool and empty her bladder while she planned how to begin again and make this visit into what it should be. But sliding off the stool and walking across the open space will call attention to herself. She might have to give an explanation to him of her intentions: to say "I'm going to the bathroom" out loud would be terribly humiliating. She shreds the toothpick as she tries to focus her energies on an action.

Daddy stares at her, his eyes glazed and dull. He touches her hair and says, "It's almost dry." This means he wants her to leave. She fingers her hair without looking at him and regrets the gesture as she performs it. He might think she questions his judgment. Nodding stupidly as a sign he's right, she slides from the stool, muttering barely loud enough for herself to hear, "I'll go now." Two steps away from the bar, she starts to run. The heavy door is hard to push open. Too embarrassed to turn back when Daddy calls her, she races into the darkening, wet afternoon.

Mom doesn't scold about being late, or seem to notice the smell of a bar, and she's easy to dash past to get to the bathroom. Amy has to look into the mirror to check her face for clues to see why she was invisible to Daddy. It's the same pretty face, except for the rosy places where the skin was broken. The bruises are gone now—she's as pink and blue and golden as a girl in a Breck shampoo ad. She should be thin and pale, a dark-eyed martyr like Anne Frank. Then people would pity and love her. The drenched hair has dried and blown into a filigree of spun gold haloing her head. Daddy would like these curls. He likes fairy-princess prettiness. It would be hard for him not to find her beautiful. She pinches her cheeks as Scarlett O'Hara did in the movie, but they're already flushed and dewy from her run home. She opens the mirrored medicine chest and looks at her mother's cosmetics, but the chance of discovery by Mom, the possibility of the humiliation of a scolding in front of Daddy, keeps her from experimenting. She opens the lipstick, the rouge, the mascara, and is saddened by how thoroughly used and aged the contents are. She puts them back exactly where she got them and bites her lips to bring the blood to them.

He doesn't come home for dinner. And because her mother doesn't ask, Amy doesn't say where he might be. She answers her mother's litany of questions, the ones she asks and gets the same answers to each day. "Yes" and "fine" and "okay" keep Mom talking until she runs down, her conversation for the day finished. As they clear the table, listening for his sounds, no one speaks for a long while. Finally, Mom starts asking questions about school again, but she doesn't wait for answers, and she leaves her cigarette smoldering in the ashtray. Amy stubs it out and takes the smoking tray to the trash.

In the kitchen, Amy works rapidly and well, trying to calm Mom, who is muttering to no one. The poor creature must be cared for; her hand trembles as she holds the match to the end of a cigarette, although another still smokes in the ashtray. When Mom turns back to the sink, her newly lit cigarette between her lips, Amy crushes out the half-smoked one. With Mom washing, Amy drying, and Flossie putting away, they work their way through the clutter of dishes until the crunch of tires on gravel slows their movements. The car door slams. The footsteps on the front porch constrict Amy's throat. She bites her inner cheek to keep from loudly humming. She prays, Oh, Jesus, my God, let me be as beautiful as one of your angels and let Mom not turn to the door but keep her hands in water when he passes by.

God answers her prayer. Mom bends dutifully forward over the sink, her head bowed as he passes through the bright light of the living room, into the darkened dining alcove. As he turns to enter the hall, he looks over his shoulder at Amy. And though he walks with the great care he uses when he's been in the bar too long, he manages a graceful pause and his most winning half-smile, coupled with a perfectly-timed wink intended only for her.

And because Amy's grades are very good, and her mother is very busy, and her father has problems, they trust her to take care of her life. And she thinks she's doing very well, except for a few indulgences. Rainy days are her special days. Alone in the house, she lies in bed, curled on her side beneath the covers, her wrists pressed together between her thighs. Drifting in and out of sleep, she sees herself in a field of green, holding hands with a tall, blonde man who adores her.

fall | 1971

Chapter 2

*Amy doesn't lick her ice cream cone clockwise then counter clock-
wise like a good little girl who is careful; instead, she bites the
ball of melting chocolate so her mouth fills, then swallows a
chunk with an aching throat. She crunches the sugar cone in half
and throws the remains between the slats of the pier. When it
hits the water, the napkin unfurls and floats from the sinking
witch hat. The witchy face of Gram O'Connor flashes for a moment on the murky waters and then the cone swirls out of sight.
If Amy hurries, Gram O. won't be aware she's not being obeyed.
Twenty, even thirty minutes, the old woman will wander the sou-
venir shops along the boardwalk, her daffy green eyes focusing on
the price of dehydrated sea horses and ashtrays stamped "Atlantic City." Amy runs down to the edge of the sea to watch the
blue-gray tongue of water come out of the mouth of the sky. Her
patent-leather Mary Janes make a very satisfactory clunking
sound on the wooden stairs leading to the beach. By the third
step, she corrects the placement of her feet on the stairs so the
rest is a perfect game of hopscotch. When she leaps onto the*

beach, her feet sink in the sand. Hot grains seep into her shoes. She squats to unfasten the buckles of her Mary Janes. Slippers, stuffed with socks, hanging from each forefinger, she walks toward the surf. Foam fringes the edge of the water. She lets her toes touch the froth coming toward her, going away, returning, higher and wilder, lapping at her shins. Soon water will soak the cuffs of the red corduroy trousers Gram H. gave her. The heavy fabric is difficult for her fingers to gather as the tide advances. She cries with frustration as she yanks at her pants legs, trying to lift them, but the sand slides beneath her, and she lands on her bottom in the lukewarm, fishy water. Blinking against the salty spray, she can't immediately recognize the floating objects as her shoes. Her pants look as if they are soaked with pee. Gram O. will see the soggy pants. Her brittle nails will dig into Amy's shoulder and everyone will hear the shrill Brooklynese scream, "Oh, my Gawd."

Amy lifts her face from the pillow. There is no ocean. This is bed. She tentatively touches the mattress: it's dry. Rolling to her side, she feels beneath her. Yes, she's safe. She's only dreamed of warm water. She does need to go to the bathroom, but this time she woke before it happened; she isn't the baby in the dream. She isn't six and living in New York. Now Amy's eleven and living with Flossie and Mom and Dad, not with Gram O. Since Amy turned nine, whenever it happens she can take care of it, can hide the sheets or let them dry and make her bed. For two years, she hasn't waked Mom to ask for help. Because it made them both so sad when Mom got up and quietly changed the sheets, Amy stopped waking her. Sneaking to care for the problem by herself is hard, but it's easier than seeing her mother's sleeping face shake itself awake, watching her hands tuck fresh sheets about the mattress, seeing her carry the wet bundles away. Maybe the problem's solved. She will lie here and say, thank you, thank you, now I lay me down to . . . God, thank you. Or maybe she's just been lucky. This time God rewarded her for being good although she doesn't know what she's done to win His favor. For minutes she lies in bed, watching the lights from passing cars make patterns on the wall through the opening in her curtains, forcing herself to be aware of her full bladder, memorizing the feeling, so she won't, even in the deepest sleep, make another mistake. Maybe this means she will never be in trouble again.

She doesn't turn on the lights when she walks in her room or down the hall or in the bathroom. She lets her fingers trail along the walls. This is the doorjamb. This is the door. Without turning on the light, she finds the stool, hitches up her nightie and pulls down her panties to her knees. She sits on the cool seat and closes her eyes, telling herself, this is what it's like to pee. And starting at the back of the belly button, she feels a can of purple paint turning upside down. It pours like a funnel, big then narrow as a ribbon, a long ribbon passing through her belly, until the color is gone. She reaches for the toilet paper and makes a neat tissue square to blot herself dry. She closes the lid. At sunrise, she'll sneak in the room to flush the toilet, so no one will know how close she came to making the mistake she'd made when she was a baby. She feels secure as she walks back to her bed, so she rarely feels on the walls or walks toe-to-heel to get through the dark.

She wakes again, frightened for a second, trying to remember if she's wet her bed. No, that was a dream. She's been to the bathroom. A door slams. It's not part of a dream. Something crashes. The sound comes from the kitchen. She burrows beneath her covers, dragging her pillow with her, curling her knees toward her, crushing the pillow to her belly. A knocking shakes her. She recognizes her frightened heartbeat. Someone is walking in the kitchen. Something else falls with a whoosh and a clatter. "Ah, Christ," says the drunken voice of her father. A corner of light is purple in the back of her eyes. He has turned on the light. Making an opening for herself in the cave of covers, she looks toward the light, hoping she'll hear better, trying to stop breathing so she'll understand every sound he makes. He's sputtering curses. He must be fumbling with the mess he's made coming into the dark. She wants to go to the kitchen to pick up everything he's spilled, help him sit at the kitchen table, and brush the hair falling across his forehead, so his tired blue eyes will look into hers. She'll massage his shoulders as he sits waiting while the coffee brews, as she's seen her mother do so long ago in the old house in New York. As he sat at the table and Mom stood beside him, they hadn't known Amy watched while Mom, looking pale in her long, white nightgown, brushed his hair aside, kissed his temple and caressed the side of his face with her slender hand. His shoulders had trembled, and Amy knew he was crying, which made her cry. Mom had forgiven him, for doing again what he'd promised never to do. But now Mom doesn't go to the kitchen. Amy imagines her lying in bed staring at the ceiling, refusing to go to him, letting him stumble and curse and fall by himself. Mom is so wrong. He's coughing now, the kind of cough to make his ribs ache. Amy's voice is muffled by the taut rubber band of her throat as she says "Daddy." The light goes out. She hears his measured steps and knows he's feeling his way along the wall to get to the bedroom.

She savagely bites her thumbnail as she listens for what her mother will do when he reaches their bed. There's no sound but the falling of his shoes. He may loosen his tie. He may be lying down beside her, on his side of the bed, fully clothed, his arms beneath his head, his ankles crossed, lying on the blankets and sheets which haven't been turned down. He's there not to sleep but to wait for morning. She wonders if her mother will speak, or turn to him. If Amy could be Mom, she'd touch him. Amy knew, even Gram O. knew, anyone who could feel would know what Mom should do. All she has to do is turn in that tiny space keeping them apart. Just a hand on his arm will make him start to come back to them.

But this silence means there is no touching. She wants to guide her mother's hand toward him. Amy's hand slides from her mouth to her breast. She rubs the bumpy skin around her nipple so it tingles. She pinches the nipple between her thumb and forefinger. If her mother won't touch him, he'll go away. Not just drunk and alone in the house, but drunk and never coming home. Amy feels warm between her thighs. She lets her hand slide from her breast to her secret place. Her fingers find the warm, wet folds. She bites the thumb of her other hand. He'll go away like he did before, but this time he won't come back. Her middle finger, the one the boys use to make the dirty sign, touches her red part, the part like a turkey wattle. She'll ask him tomorrow not to go away, to stay with them and not go to the bars. She'll hide his money, and sit on his lap while he watches TV, and let him pull nickels from her ears. Her finger makes warm, red circles. Her mother can stand in the kitchen with her back to them; let her be the zombie she'd been at Gram O.'s when she'd driven him away before. She'll never have to say another word. Amy will make it okay. Let her mother go away in her long silences with her pale, sagging shoulders. Amy will meet Daddy out on the lawn when he comes home from work and hold his hand all the way to the house. She'll take his rumpled jacket, hang it up, and ask about his day. She sucks the end of her thumb and makes faster and faster circles until the warm fills her belly.

In the morning, she gets up before Flossie to find the best blue shirt. One of the few topics Gram O. and Mom agree on is how good Amy looks in blue. Gram O. says it makes her look like a true O'Connor with the blue of Irish eyes. Mom says it's pretty for a strawberry blonde to be pink and blue, so Amy quietly looks in the back of her rickety dresser in the tangle of T-shirts for the best one she can find. She chooses one of Flossie's with "Sugar and Spice" written in cursive and a gingerbread boy dancing across the chest. It's a baby shirt, but Daddy liked her best when she was a baby. She'll wear her overalls to cover the baby part at school and tie her hair in ponytails with yarn so he'll play with her hair when she sits on his knee.

She goes to the bathroom to dress and to flush the toilet. She smiles at herself in the mirror and admires her face. People say she looks like her father. Except for the freckles scattered across her nose and flushed cheeks, she's a chubby version of how he might have looked had he been a girl. She rubs her nose. Her hands smells like fish. Last night she made herself dirty. She rubs the slip of the bar of soap over and over across her stubby fingernails.

On the way to the kitchen, she passes her parents' room. The door is partially open: it's just as she'd imagined. All she can see are his black socks and the dark cuffs of his pants, for he's stretched on his side, sleeping or pretending to sleep. In the kitchen, her mother fusses at the stove. The yellow bow of the apron of her waitress uniform is a butterfly in flight, her starchy cap pinned on her head above her bun with the invisible net holding everything in place. Amy goes to the refrigerator to get what she needs to eat, then sits at the table. Her mother and she don't speak and rarely glance at one another as Amy slurps her cereal and Mom sips her coffee. Amy wants to ask if she shouldn't wake Daddy: he probably has to drive to Phoenix, or maybe Tucson or even Bisbee, to take orders at the grocery stores for his company. But she can see by the dark rings beneath Mom's eyes and the little lines across her forehead what her answer will be. She sets her coffee cup in the saucer and looks toward the door. Amy opens her mouth so words might tumble out to set Daddy at the head of the table, bright and smiling, and Mom in a housedress bringing pancakes. But the scene is dissolved by Mom's harsh voice, "Call your father. Tell your sister to get out of bed. They're making us late."

Amy loves sixth grade, tolerating, even enjoying, sitting at the desk from eight-thirty until two-thirty, every weekday, because of Mr. Crandall, the only male teacher she's ever had. On the first day, she hadn't liked him. He isn't handsome like her father. Mr. Crandall's eyes aren't the sparkling blue of Daddy's when he tells a joke. Mr. Crandall wears thick glasses, so his eyes are an indefinable darkness. But once when he crouched beside her desk, she had seen around his glasses into his dark chocolate eyes. Studying his straight black lashes and the clear whites of his eyes, she listened as he explained how she might improve her sentence. The blend of his scents of soap, mouthwash, and aftershave were not those of her father. The delicacy of this man was foreign and intriguing. She decided, although he was strange, she'd work for him. Papers she normally finished quickly and neatly, her criteria for schoolwork, became gifts to invest with effort—revelations of herself. His broad hips and slightly lumpy torso are laughable in contrast to Daddy's slim hips and graceful height. And although both men wear long-sleeved white shirts—the kind of shirts she loves because men from back East wear them—Mr. Crandall buttons his at the cuff to hide his skin that is the color of white fish, while Daddy folds his cuffs back twice to show his forearms that are brown and glossy with golden hair. And she's sure Mr. Crandall could never pitch a no-hitter. Daddy was a baseball star in high school and got a college baseball scholarship. When the family first came out West, he had talked about playing in a local league, but he said they were "scrubs." So she and Mom and Flossie had never gone to the games at night, where he could have worn a uniform, standing in the center of the diamond, pitching his fastball, winning for his team. But before Daddy got sick again, he had played catch with her, tossing the ball very gently, since he was so strong. Compared to Daddy, Mr. Crandall is terrible at sports. After playing a game of speed-o with the class, he was breathless and had to tuck in his shirttail and pat his ruffled hair.

Like the rest of the kids in the room, Amy had almost laughed when she'd first heard the teacher speak. He must've sensed their amusement, for he explained that he came from Boston. She was sorry she'd been swept along with the class. They'd probably laugh at Gram O. or maybe even Daddy. They had laughed at Amy when she couldn't pronounce Mexican words. But Mr. Crandall had a wonderful way of reading stories, which he did each day, making his voice change to fit each character. He could almost tell a story as well as Daddy. Of course, Mr. Crandall used a book, while Daddy made his up, but all the same, Mr. Crandall could read so well that he could make her cry. She'd put her fingers beside her nose, so no one could see her tears, but she thought he knew because he looked at her often as he read, yet he kept their secret.

All the parents are invited to the P.T.A.'s open house. Mr. Crandall says it is being held at night so working parents can attend. Asking Daddy is hopeless. He doesn't like to "hang around schools," but nagging Mom to attend is a satisfying game. She finally agrees to come, but Amy doesn't really believe she will. Yet when the day comes, Mom does not beg off when she is reminded.

The classroom looks brighter than usual with all the lights turned on and new bulletin board displays, but the room doesn't seem to perk up Mom. If only she didn't look so tired and serious. If only she'd smile, Mr. Crandall would be able to imagine how pretty she'd once been, but she'll probably say nothing and not even unbutton her ugly coat. As the parents wait in a line snaking around the teacher's desk, Amy prays he'll see the good hidden within her mother.

After they've shaken hands, Mr. Crandall speaks. He watches Amy as he describes her as "cooperative," "intelligent" and "very mature." She feels goosebumpy with pleasure and wants to turn to see what Mom thinks, but this would be so obvious.

Mr. Crandall looks confused by Mom's silence. She doesn't

believe him. She thinks he's what Daddy calls a "bullshit
artist." Amy is angry with her, embarrassed for Mr. Crandall, sorry for herself. He tries to fill the silence with a rush
of words. "Amy is one of the most outstanding students I've
ever had in my eleven years of teaching sixth grade."

On the way back to the car, Amy wants to ask, "Didn't
you like him? He's nice, isn't he?" but decides she's totally
misjudged the man or her mother would've agreed with
what he said. She can't even imagine how Daddy would have
behaved here. Inside the dark car, Mom mutters, "He seems
like a nice enough man. He really seems to like you." But
her voice is so flat and lifeless what she says must not be
true. Amy lets his words tumble within her—beautiful,
beautiful words, which must be totally untrue, words Daddy
would never believe.

Today Mr. Crandall is trying to teach inverting the denominator in fractions. Math is all right, not like reading or
writing or art. It is fun to make neat columns with numbers
to solve little puzzles, and to get back graded papers with
"good" scribbled on them. But she wants to think about tonight with Daddy and must force herself to watch the
teacher. Not that she's afraid of him. He's not like the nuns
who taught her from first grade through fifth, who could
frighten with words or looks or punishments, who kept her
nervous and wary, paying attention so she wouldn't get
hurt. When someone misbehaves in this class, the teacher
makes faces, or shakes his head, or says something funny.
She doesn't want to make him unhappy.

Because she needs glasses, she sits in the second seat in
the first row. After the eye tests, the nurse recommended a
doctor's examination. Mom says they'll go to the doctor
when all their bills are paid, which means there will never be
any glasses. But Amy doesn't mind. She loves her assigned
seat because she can view the hall and can catch Mr. Crandall's eye, so he calls on her more than anyone else. And she
sits in front of Marcy Briggs, whose mom is room mother.

Marcy tries so hard to win attention she waves her arm shouting, "Me, call on me." Being proper and controlled in contrast to Marcy is a pleasure.

But today there has been a change in the seating arrangements. Duane Fenton, the stupidest boy in class, sits in front of Amy. She has watched him since the first day of school. He's at least a foot taller than the other boys and has a face with sharply carved features. She assumed they reflected a sensitive spirit, for he rarely looked up, his downcast eyes revealing a fringe of dark lashes. But yesterday, he propelled his desk around the back of the room. Using his gangly arms and planting the toes of his battered cowboy boots against the walls, he stretched his long legs to travel to a variety of spots. He penciled in the mortar between the bricks, rearranged the books in the bookcase, and moved the plastic horses in the rodeo scene, so the big black one was mounting the small paint. Chuckling to himself, he coupled all the horses in the corral. Ashamed for him, Amy looked away, but his activities caught the attention of the boys nearest him and word spread in loud whispers and giggles. Duane was asked to remain after class.

Now that Duane is seated just a few feet from her, she begins to play Mr. Crandall's making-imaginative-comparisons game. The curls of Duane's neck are like pencil shavings scattered on caramel-apple skin. The profile he reveals when he restlessly shifts in his desk might be a bronze statue of a young noble man. But the beauty of the image is destroyed by his noisy, slack-lipped breathing. Perhaps he breathes through his mouth to avoid smelling the odors of stale sweat, urine-stained underwear, axle grease, and tobacco smoke hovering about him. She must turn aside to breathe, for it is only when he is three feet away that she is free of his odor. But she is always aware of the ceaseless movement of his hands, drumming on the desk, or picking at his warts until they bleed, or sticking straight pins through the first layer of skin on the pads of his fingers to make five daggers on each hand.

At first, he doesn't seem to notice her. Because he doesn't pass back the papers, she has to tap him on the shoulder, so he turns his puppy-dog eyes to her. As she whispers, his eyes narrow. His simple mind is making a connection: the smart girl in class is speaking to him. Even he understands how skillfully she plays the classroom game to win grades, skills he hasn't achieved although he's repeated two years. Shifting from his slump above his desktop to a sideways sprawl, he stares at the large script of her correct answers. She demurely pretends not to notice his copying until their eyes meet and his shamefaced grin makes her blush. He doesn't complete the whole assignment and copies some things wrong. Perhaps this is laziness, or he can't hold the answer in his mind long enough to transfer the answer from her paper to his. Perhaps he's protecting them from discovery. Although he hasn't asked her permission to copy, he may feel grateful and responsible for providing them with an argument if they're accused of cheating.

As the morning passes, she begins to think of Duane as her gigantic baby doll. No one else in class cares for him as she does, making him smile, getting him to mumble a few words. She hasn't charted the course of what they'll accomplish together, yet she knows there are definite possibilities. But this afternoon, he's not cooperating. She's tempted to punch him in the shoulder with a stiff forefinger and to hiss his name, but knows nagging is a terrible approach. She's heard her mother whine and scream at Daddy when he was sick from drinking and seen him turn away. Sitting back in her desk, she sighs. Duane is placing himself in a dangerous position by not even pretending to listen to the explanation of the principles of fractions. Totally absorbed, he cups his hands to catch a fly. With a soft smack, he captures his victim and clasps his big knuckled hands at the edge of his desk. His head bobs as he chuckles. He's probably deciding whether to tear off the wings, or burn it, or mount it on a pin to stick it in some unsuspecting girl's face. Amy looks to the front of the room—too much time has passed as she watched Duane. The lesson will be unclear.

Mr. Crandall is staring at them, a long, cold look. Duane hangs his head, and Amy smiles apologetically as assurance she won't stray again. With a loud sigh, the teacher turns to the board. With dramatic emphasis, he says over his shoulder, "I'm going to put more examples on the board for those who weren't paying attention." The silent room echoes his words as he scrawls the figures on the board.

Duane opens his palms and the fly flutters up and back to Amy's desk. Flapping his arms, his elbow bounces the math book to the floor with a loud smack. Mr. Crandall's back contracts, and he turns. The class gasps as if punched in the belly, yet Duane continues his pursuit. His dirty, chapped hand claps loudly on Amy's desk. The fly must be a bloody smear beneath his palm. She looks up into the glare of Mr. Crandall's glasses. Fists on hips, he stares at Duane, who seems unaware he's the focus of everyone's attention. Lifting his hand from the mutilated fly, he grins foolishly at his victim. The teacher is stepping closer to them. Amy taps Duane's wrist. He looks at her hand on his wrist then slowly shifts his eyes to her face, but Mr. Crandall has reached his destination. He rests his palm on Duane's shoulder in a position where the thumb can dig into the hollow of the collarbone and pinch hard, a technique she has seen the nuns use. She's shocked to see Mr. Crandall do it. Duane rolls his sheep eyes toward heaven. The class chatters in anticipation. Staring down at the stupified face, Mr. Crandall has never looked so powerful, nor Duane so idiotic. The thirty-six students stare silently. As if he doesn't trust his voice, Mr. Crandall shakes his head slowly and lifts his pale, menacing hand from Duane's shoulder.

With his head so low that his chin brushes his chest, Duane turns to his own desk. Amy flushes as she looks at her desktop. To remove the bloody mess will make her filthy. The class remains silent, but their curious stares are tattling on her, telling how she's part of the disturbance. Mr. Crandall is taking a step down the aisle to check why she's not met his eyes. As he towers over her, she senses his disgust at the sight of the tiny, bloody blob. She is filled with regret for the failure he must feel for his ruined lesson. He might lose control and explode in a rage as she's seen the nuns do. He shakes his head in disbelief. The class settles back in anticipation. This is story hour with the teacher improvising. His voice is soft, almost friendly. "Duane, that's a fly."

Breathing softly through his mouth, Duane nods yes.

Excluding Amy, Mr. Crandall looks around the class to focus on the other student leaders. If he has their support, then the rest will follow. "You know, class," his tone is confiding, but his pause is frighteningly lengthy, "all some people know how to do with themselves is take up space and attract flies." The blank-faced response of the class goads him to expand his story. Amy shivers sensing the lashing she will witness. Words are used as weapons in ugly arguments in her home. She warily glances up; Mr. Crandall's finger is pointing directly at Duane, setting him up for the class's loud laughter. His voice is a whip winding around his victim. "Duane, you're not even attractive to flies. You just take up space and kill them."

The kids laugh loudly. A lot of them probably don't get the joke, but they're always glad to escape dull lessons, glad to pick on someone who can't fight back. Duane slumps further into his desk. Now he must really hate the man he calls "fat ass." The class should shut up; they're so stupid and mean ganging up like this. With effort, she looks at Mr. Crandall's face, which is paler than usual, twisted with a little smirk she hasn't seen before, so he looks like a stranger. If she could lead Duane out of this dangerous place, she would take him home, clean him up, teach him to read and do math, then bring him back and show them all, especially Mr. Crandall. But she doesn't dare to touch Duane's hunched shoulders. She's afraid of him, and everyone in this room, especially Mr. Crandall.

The stranger who has become the teacher is waiting for total silence, his face showing a mixture of surprise and satisfaction. The class is his audience; he will get them to do just what he wants. Duane has actually closed his mouth and clasps his big paws in a giant fist. To talk with him, is not possible. She wants to hug him, in spite of his stupidity, and his nastiness. When the teacher looks at Duane's puffed-out lower lip, she inhales sharply. Mr. Crandall says, "Amy tried to help you, but you wouldn't pay attention. Now I know you have problems, but when a pretty girl like Amy tries to get your attention and you ignore her, I know you've got serious problems."

The boys in the back of the class guffaw, and the shortest one calls, "Fag!" yet Mr. Crandall turns his back and begins to write on the board. "Fag" is the worst word they can use against Duane, the one he hates the most, the one he taught the class by teasing the smaller boys, calling them "fag" until they cried. And today the teacher is letting the boys say it. He must want to punish Duane as cruelly as possible. Amy slides a few inches lower in her chair, staring with contempt at the man's back, his rumpled hair, his narrow, sloping shoulders, his broad hips in his sagging trousers. She looks at the angry set of Duane's shoulders. Behind her she hears Marcy Briggs talking in her loud voice to the girls across the aisle. "Isn't he the funniest teacher you've ever had?" Marcy laughs affectedly.

Amy plans not to stay after school to ask Mr. Crandall questions as she usually does; instead, she puts away her materials and gets ready so she'll be first out of the room. She doesn't take her usual walk to the third graders' wing to look for Flossie, who's a dawdler, for Amy doesn't want to run the risk of having to talk to anyone from sixth grade, not even the ones who hadn't laughed or smiled. Mr. Crandall had called her pretty, but it doesn't count because it had been part of his mean game. Duane is stupid and stinky, but he doesn't deserve such cruelty. Her whole insides feel as if they're yawning, the way she felt when she saw Daddy slouched at the table with Gram O. shrieking, "You're a drunk, you're a lousy drunk." Mr. Crandall's pale, smirking face is as scary as her mother's, as the nun's. He can take words and poke holes in people and the words are so sharp and thrown with such skill that the wounds aren't visible at first. How cruel would he be if he knew how she woke lying in a bed she had wet? He could probably be as vicious as Sister Theresa with the moustache who could make her stu dents tremble and cry when she demanded a recital.

To forget, she begins to run and the legs of her overalls rub together with a swishing noise, chafing her thighs. They'll be bloody with a rash when she gets home, where she can be alone. She'll find a carton of milk in the refrigerator, and drink milk and eat Oreos and watch TV. It'll be almost as good as being with Gram Hershey, who baked chocolate chip cookies from scratch and read stories out loud until she was hoarse. Tears fog Amy's eyes as she trudges through the woods of the vacant lot. Mr. Crandall had been like Gram Hershey, making stories come alive, teaching how to make things out of food or yarn or thread. But Amy never gets to see Grammy since the family left New York. Trampling every weed she can, she pushes on, wanting to hurt something. Even before they'd come to Arizona, she'd seen Grammy less and less. Mom and Dad never wanted to take the long drive. They said it would be too crowded in the car. Then Daddy went away. And Grandpa Hershey died, then she never saw Grammy Hershey, then Big Mike died and Gram O. got mad because they moved, and Mr. Crandall might as well be dead. He hasn't died, but he should. He's a liar who isn't who he seems to be. His white, silent face is like her mother's. The words coming out of those mouths mean no laughter, no joy. Their words mean, "Feel bad."

With a stack of Oreos in one hand and the rim of a plastic tumbler full of milk clamped between her teeth, Amy manages to flip on their tired, black and white TV, switching from channel to channel until she finds the "Bugs Bunny Festival." Usually she studies in the bedroom in the afternoons, but she can always hear the peppy tune of the theme of the show in the background. Daily Flossie sits inches from the screen from the time she gets home from school until Dad comes home and switches the channel to the evening news. Flossie always whines about missing her show, but he ignores her, and she stomps out. Then Amy goes to the living room, smiles, and calls him. After he collapses in his chair, she sits on the sagging armrest.

Today she'll get even with Mr. Crandall by not doing her homework. And she mustn't miss a moment of being with Daddy. Bugs Bunny is leaping across the screen, screaming in pain. Porky Pig has accidentally dropped a load of brick on the rabbit's foot and is stuttering his apologies. Amy shakes her head in disgust. Mr. Crandall is right. Most television programs are for idiots. She had laughed when he had described it as "the idiot box," but remembered the small square of light in the darkened room when they lived with Gram O., who turned on the set when she woke in the morning and left it talking to itself all day; sometimes she'd forget to turn it off at night, and it would flicker like a votive candle.

Often Gram O. played the radio while the television hummed. And even though she rarely watched the picture, she kept the curtains drawn in the living room while the set was on and didn't turn on any lights. According to her, it was bad for your eyes to watch TV with the lights on, one of her ideas about good and bad. Grammy Hershey had taught Amy to read when she was five, so she brought books checked out from Sister Theresa and read in the kitchen. But Flossie, who was only three, sat most of the day eating cookies and watching TV.

Amy looks around for one of the worn corduroy pillows Flossie loves. Willing to fight for it, Amy rolls to her side and props her head on the pillow. She watches the gray pictures flicker. The images of Mr. Crandall and Duane and the laughing classmates have faded. She'll be glassy-eyed by five or six when Daddy walks through and tosses his crumpled jacket onto the couch, loosens his tie, and changes the channel, sending Flossie off in a huff. Then he'll pretend to watch the news, but his eyes will close to slits and unless she prods him into conversation during the commercials, he'll fall asleep in five minutes. Mom will get home after six, walk through the living room on her way to the kitchen, look at them and say nothing, but she'll bang around in the kitchen until dinner is ready, and then they'll eat silently at the little table. Lots of times Daddy doesn't join them. And if Amy cleans up the kitchen super fast, and Mom and Flossie are still mad at Daddy, Amy can race back to the living room to be alone with him. Perched on the chair arm beside him, she'll let him use her knees as an arm rest or he'll absently play with her fingers as he watches the screen. Sometimes she'll sit at his feet so he can stroke her thick, wavy hair while they both stare at the flickering picture until her mind becomes hazy and she feels as happy as Gram H.'s old tiger cat that purred when she pet it.

Flossie slams the kitchen door, stomps into the dining alcove, and dumps her workbook on the table, a book she always brings home and rarely opens. She stands silhouetted in the doorway to the living room. Fists on her hips, she yells, "I waited for you."

Amy rolls onto her belly, and mutters, "Sorry." Flossie isn't angry about having to walk home alone, but not having an ice cream bar has made her feel deprived. She never keeps track of her own money and always relies on Amy to treat.

Sinking to her knees beside Amy, Flossie eyes her suspiciously and says, "You're watching TV."

Amy sits up. Careful to hide the remaining Oreos in her bib overalls, she mutters, "I don't have any homework."

"So you're watching my 'idiot show'?"

Her righteousness touches anger. "It's not your show."

As Flossie smiles, Amy recognizes her game. "You're watching it," Flossie fairly sings, "so you're an idiot too."

Amy wants to slap the fat, rosy face, but knows it would crumple and discolor, and loud, uncontrollable hiccuping cries would follow. She clasps her arms across the bib overalls where the last of the Oreos roll, dangerously close to falling. Discovered watching TV, almost caught eating Oreos, she scrambles to her feet. Food can be the bait to distract her sister, who Daddy calls "the cookie monster" because she gobbles up every sweet she can find. Mom even has to hide the sugar cubes from her. Amy asks loudly, "Is there something to eat in this house?" and, realizing Oreos will be the first choice, quickly adds, "I can make honey sandwiches."

Delighted by the suggestion, Flossie bustles toward the kitchen. Amy follows, pleased by her plan. Flossie'll be so groggy, getting to Daddy will be easy.

After three honey sandwiches, and three of her favorite TV shows, Flossie still manages to lift herself from the floor to be the first to greet Daddy at the door. Skipping ahead of Flossie to get to Daddy's side on his route to the bedroom, Amy shakes her head from side to side so her soft shining hair will please him. She manages to slip her hand into his and make him smile and laugh by the time she steers him into his room.

Mom doesn't approve of children in her bedroom, but she's not home yet, and Daddy doesn't know about this rule or doesn't care. Hilarity can distract him. She pulls him to the edge of the bed where she falls backwards in a sprawl and smiles provocatively. He releases her hand, but he laughs, his eyes bright. Ready for fun, he says "Amanda, my panda." She giggles convulsively, delighted to hear him use her nickname from infancy, anxious that maybe he's finished playing for today. But he's removing his tie, which means he's just taking a break. He turns to hang it over the closet doorknob, unaware of Flossie. Hands on hips, mouth pinched, she's ready to blurt out something to get his attention. It's time to get rid of her. Sitting up so her silent command will be focused precisely on target, Amy narrows her eyes, making her most powerful you'd-better-shut-up stare. Flossie's mouth trembles at the corners. Hugging herself, she runs from the room.

Daddy turns toward Amy. He's unbuttoning the top three buttons on his shirt, so the top of his undershirt shows. She loves his tan skin and the fringe of blonde hair at the neckline. He unbuttons the cuff of his left sleeve and rolls the cuff back two times. As he repeats the process on his right sleeve, he whistles softly. She recognizes the tune immediately: the music for his lyric, "Amanda, my panda." When she giggles, he raises his index finger, saying softly, "and-a-one-and-a-two-and-a-three-and-a," so she's able to start singing the chorus with him right on time. Daddy is better than any movie star.

She rolls from the center of the bed, making room for him at the foot. When their song is finished, he'll sit down to take off his shoes. The old bed sags with his weight, so it's easy to roll back beside him and sit up. She sits so closely, she can feel the warmth of his body. Daddy smells like tobacco, whiskey, and soap, and a tiny bit of perspiration. He whispers another chorus as he eases off his heavy, black oxford and tosses it in the closet. Speaking in a fake deep voice, he takes off the other shoe and wriggles his toes for one last chorus, then he leans closer and closer until he kisses the end of her nose.

At the dinner table, Daddy only takes a couple of bites, throws his paper napkin over his food, and begins to smoke. With each puff he takes, Mom gets icier. When the meal ends, she stands abruptly, such an angry movement it might

be the beginning of a scolding for Daddy, but she looks at
Flossie and tells her to bring the dishes to the kitchen, to
help clean up since it was Amy's turn last night. As they
leave, they look sulky and ugly. Even through his cloud of
smoke, Daddy sees their silliness. He winks, crushes his cigarette, and says, "Hey, babe, how about some TV?"

Sitting at his feet, it's easy to slide her arm across his
knee and rest it there. She considers offering him a beer as
she's seen women on TV do for their husbands after a long,
hard day. But beer isn't kept in this house. She politely
waits to make conversation during commercials. Her entertaining evening is a balloon that she's puffing into with all
her might, but it just won't expand. Daddy's eyes are closing, his chin is bobbing; she pushes his knee that wobbles
loosely. "Daddy."

He shakes his head. "Um?"

"Daddy, can I make you some cocoa?"

His throat constricts. He's working to hold his eyelids
open. "No, thanks, baby."

She claps her hands, trying to add a little excitement.
"Could I get you a highball?" She's not sure what it is, but
it sounds sophisticated.

He slaps his hollow belly, and his laugh is almost a moan.
"No, no, I'm fine."

She speaks in a prim manner, a good imitation of how her
mother must speak to customers, "Is there anything I can
get you, sir?"

He makes a strange sound, she guesses is a laugh, and
then he hunches his shoulders, trying to wake up. "Well,
ma'am, there's one item you can bring me." He touches his
empty shirt pocket. "I need some smokes." He tilts her
chin so she looks into his eyes. "Oh, please," he begs, "I
need a fix." In the dim living room, his blue eyes have vio-
let shadows, but they probably glisten teasingly. His
hand on her chin is warm. She should tell him she won't
get up to bring him poison. "I don't know where they

are," she lies. "I don't think Mom has any."

He lifts a lock of her hair, smoothing it behind her ear. "Your Mom'd run away from home if there weren't any cigarettes here."

She scrambles to her feet. He's right. Of course, Mom couldn't get through an hour without a cigarette. She's the one who smokes and smokes and leaves the dirty ashtrays for her children to empty. If she'd stop, then he'd stop. Amy hurries to the kitchen.

Standing on a chair to reach the cabinet over the stove where the cigarettes are stored, she notices there is coffee left over from this morning. Reheated coffee will keep him awake. Coffee is used to cure a drunk. Whether or not he's drunk right now is hard to tell. Maybe he's a little drunk, he always smells a little like whiskey, and he's been singing this evening, something he does when he's been drinking. "Dad," she calls, liking the mature sound of the word, "Could I fix you a cup of coffee?" She listens for his answer, fearful she's lost him to sleep. When she hears "Yeah, why not?" she smiles.

Waiting for the coffee to heat, she doesn't know whether to watch the pot to keep it from boiling, or to stand beside his chair so he won't escape. Grammy H. says reheated coffee always tastes awful. Gram O. says reheated coffee is fine as long as it doesn't come to a boil. Daddy loves his coffee. Just about the only thing Mom fixes that he likes is coffee. This cup had better be perfect. Pacing back and forth from the stove to the door, she keeps track of the state of the coffee and his condition.

In the light from the television picture, he looks like a monster in a horror film. His color is ashen and there are deep circles along the lines of his eyes sockets. He looks sick. Once, late at night, she'd heard her mother go to him when he stumbled in the kitchen. Mom cried and the words she'd sobbed over and over were "You're sick." It was scary and confusing. Maybe Daddy wasn't just drunk, maybe he had some strange disease. But the next afternoon when she saw him, he looked like he usually did. His face was a little pale, and his eyes didn't look snappy and bright. She wanted to ask her mother how he was sick, but was ashamed to confess she'd listened to their conversation. The next day, she finally sputtered, "What's wrong with Daddy?" And Mom had looked so shocked, Amy braced herself for a scolding. But Mom turned away and said, "Your father has a problem," with the finality of snapping shut a purse that wouldn't be opened again.

Mom saying he had a "problem" yet telling him he was "sick," when he acted like he was drunk, didn't make sense. Daddy's problem made him run away. Once, he'd gone away for half a school year. And Mom hadn't said anything at all about him, but she'd cried and been quiet and strange. On the day he left, Gram O. said, "Your father's gone away for a while. He wants to find himself." Over and over during the endless months, Amy had visions of him opening countless doors looking inside for a man who looked like himself.

On their last day in New York, when they threw everything into suitcases to come out West to meet Daddy, Gram O. screamed at Mom, "You made him run away. You'll never catch him. You'll keep him on the run." Mom's face got red as if it had been slapped. They never talked about Gram O.'s tantrum. They didn't even say goodbye to her, and they had to call a cab to take them to the station.

For his job in Phoenix, Daddy drove around to stores in his old Mustang with his sample case. Sometimes he came home smelling like whiskey, so he must go to bars. Whenever she walked by one, she peeked inside to see what it was people did in there, but all she ever saw were the backs of men sitting on stools, looking up at a TV, or a neon beer sign. They were all very quiet.

But once in a while, at home, Daddy loosened his tie, rolled up his sleeves, sang and did his voices. He had special voices for every character in his stories and could make a joke go on forever, twisting his face and his body to make anybody laugh. He could've been an entertainer on TV. Gram O. said he was better than Johnny Carson.

The coffee is boiling furiously. Muttering her mother's swear word, "Damn, damn," Amy turns off the gas and pushes the pot off the burner. Trying to figure Daddy out is hopeless.

She adds tap water to the coffee because once Gram O. said that adding a little water dilutes the bitter boiled taste But even when Amy walks slowly, the cup is so full that is sloshes coffee onto the cigarette pack balanced in the saucer. Nothing is working out right. Daddy has fallen asleep. Swiping the pack across her overalls, then wiping her fingers, she taps his wrist. He jumps a little, the way her knee does when the doctor hits it with a rubber hammer. For a second, he looks as if he might be furious. She could drop to her knees and crawl behind the chair. But he yawns then smiles. Staring at the cup, he asks, "For me?" and reaches for the cigarettes.

She holds the cup toward him with both hands, but still the saucer trembles. He takes the cup from her before she drops it; closes his eyes, sips, swallows, smiles faintly and nods yes.

Her voice is pleading, "It's good?"

He sets the cup on the table. "Mrs. Olson," he sounds just like the TV announcer, "could you teach my wife to make coffee like this?" He slaps the arm of the chair, her signal to sit there. Plunging toward the spot, she crawls over his lap, and arranges herself so her legs dangle over his and her arm is on the back of the chair. He rests his arm across her knees, so she is warm and tingly every place his body touches hers, every place she is close enough to feel his warmth. She wants to lean forward to brush the hair falling across his forehead. But she's only been invited to sit, so she freezes in the awkward position and her arm begins to ache and her feet fall asleep.

He stares at the TV, leaving the coffee cooling on the table. She must've done a horrible job. He lights one of his cigarettes, so the smoke drifts into her face, but she manages not to squirm. In a commercial about a local business, a man recites lines woodenly. Daddy mimics the man's flat, midwestern accent, and as she laughs, says, "A real goon, huh?"

Amy considers sliding slowly into his lap, letting her body rest on his. She slides a little closer, embarrassed by how heavy she must be, yet ecstatic to be so close. His wheezy laughter buzzes through her when he murmurs, "What an idiot." Lots of times they joke about people, imitating them and ridiculing them unmercifully. She likes it when they do. It reminds her of how superior Daddy is to everyone else, with perhaps the exception of Grammy H. But this is probably a silly comparison. Mr. Crandall says apples and oranges can't be added, and lately she's concluded men are oranges and women are apples. Mom says navels are best so that's what Daddy must be. The best apples are Red Delicious, so that must be Gram H. It's obvious Daddy's best. She dares to lean her head against his chest, so as he speaks, she feels the vibrations of his voice through her ear. "Hey, babe, do you want to watch John Wayne, or would you like me to switch the channel?"

Johnny Carson is almost over which means it's really late. Mom and Flossie must've gone to sleep hours ago. Mom would never let them stay up this late on a weeknight. But tonight Mom's in a mood, so she's letting Daddy be the boss. One of the things Amy loves about Daddy is how he never makes rules. He never nags. Mom has a rule for everything, so many rules the family can't remember them, so they do what they want, hoping not to get caught. Chances are they won't unless Mom is in one of her moods when she's trying to get tough. Then she'll probably scream, and threaten, maybe even punish. Mom says spankings are for dogs and cruel parents, but sometimes, when she's really mad, she slaps their hands or tries to slap their faces. But she's always sorry later, and apologizes, her voice trembly and breathless when she tries to explain how she's sorry for losing control. Mom's punishment is being sent to the bedroom for what she calls restriction. But that's not bad, not with the radio, books, papers, and crayons. And it only lasts a couple of days, then she forgets. Amy tries to move her sleeping legs. Daddy rubs her thighs, "Gettin' tired, baby?"

She doesn't want to move although she knows she must look silly sprawled across him with her feet dangling over the armrest. Her weight must be crushing him and this is his plan to get her to move. To ask if she's too heavy is too humiliating, so she mutters, "I'm fine." Gram O. must've been right when she said, "Amy, you're gettin' big," and the emphasis on "big" meant ugly and bad. This year her thighs and hips have become rounder and breasts are beginning to swell beneath her nipples. She wriggles her legs so some of her weight shifts off his lap onto the armrest. Her body looks embarrassingly large in this position, but she doesn't know how to be graceful and remain close to him. She decides to breathe very shallowly and not to relax. A dead weight is the heaviest. Maybe if she never eats again, she'll stop growing and shrink to her little-girl size, so she can sit with Daddy and not feel so frightened of making him so uncomfortable he'll go away.

Chapter 3

Michael studies the tousled head leaning against his shirt pocket. Jesus, Amy's getting to be a damned big kid. She finally brought some smokes after stalling long enough to set off the smoker's guilt trip. The pack isn't mashed against his chest, and the other pocket's empty too. With her crawling all over, he couldn't even wedge them in a pocket. Lately she's been so desperate to get close, that even with the old body feeling like a diesel mowed it down, he hadn't the heart to stop her making her moves. But she's burrowing in like a tick coming home. He's got to shake her loose. Her hot little body is numbing. "Hey, babe, help me find my cigarettes, okay?"

The little nuzzle of the nose into his chest feels like a refusal. He could stand up real fast and she'd bounce right onto the rug. Geez, what a shitty idea. But there oughta be something to get the kid to move. Ah, there she goes, sliding to the floor. Sometimes she's a regular little mindreader. Spooky kid, she can really wring his heart. Wow, she's a real klutz untangling herself to get out of the chair. She's gettin' a real butt on her and chunks for thighs. Poor kid, hasn't got the foggiest of what to do with her new body. She's being careful to keep her eyes on the floor, but she's so wound up in what she looks like, she's blushing at the thought. Could be Barbara. Yeah, it's Barbara all over again when he used to watch her undress. Now the kid's scuttling around, balancing on her hands and knees, groveling on the floor. That butt in the air with its twin moons is mighty tempting: a little pinch or goose would send her end-over-end. But then she'd cry, and an instant of fun would take years to undo. He'll close his eyes and temptation will disappear, just a couple of minutes of sleep and maybe there'll be enough steam to scoot out of this chair and into the bed.

Jesus, that kid could pull a corpse outa the ground. Her moony eyes can shine right through your eyelids. She's kneeling on the floor looking like one a those crazy Catholics who crawl on their knees, but she's found the cigarettes. Mashed the hell out of 'em. Musta knocked 'em off crawling up on the chair. She holds them out to him—this is her little peace offering. Taking hold of her hand and holding it for just a second might ease the tug of those anxious eyes, oh, but Jesus, it would take a lot more than that, so fuckin' much more. She jerks back and sits on her heels. "Thanks, honey," Michael whispers, but the words don't begin to tear away the shyness wrapped around her.

The cigarette pack is as fucked up as their lives. To get out a good one will take a miracle.

Michael watches Amy. His little buddy is growing up, she's not the kid she used to be, somebody to toss a ball to or swing by the hands or tickle. Such a pretty kid. People always stopped, turned, and smiled when they were together. Coulda been a color photo ad in *Life* for the phone company. But big and moody sure ain't cute. Christ, it's great to have another difficult woman around—there's Ma, and Barbara, and Amy, and pretty soon old Floss can join the crew. Amy's trying to squeeze her hands into the pockets of her pants that've gotten too tight. Another three years and she might be fat, a fat homely adolescent—a stranger to never get close to.

Michael fingers his pocket. Where the hell are the matches? Oh, Jesus, she's holding up a match pack like it's some kinda present. Her pants pocket is yanked out, hanging inside out from the squeeze of pulling out the matches. Yeah, his baby has disappeared all right, replaced by a slave. This kid will out-Barbara Barbara in a couple of years. Get the cigarette lit before she starts rubbing sticks together. Got to hand it to her. She's got an ashtray in just the right place to drop the match. Christ, she's like a puppy dog waitin' to get picked at the pound.

Loudly exhaling, he watches the smoke drift to the ceiling —just like life, everything's going away, totally out of control. Amy's growing up. Hell, everyone does, but it's hard to imagine Amy changing. Oh, sure, growing from a baby to a kid, but never a kid to a woman. Just can't seem to see her little face any bigger—her bones stay hidden under baby fat, her eyes keep the look kid's eyes have. But Barbara's face when they'd first met is lost in twisted images. Amy's face might grow into that face. Each year their faces are changing; they're just fading images drifting by on a stream moving swiftly.

He takes a long soothing drag. Squinting through smoke, he tries to look at Amy, but her face is downcast, hidden. Her arms are longer, her body rounder. He should send her to bed. Barbara's going to be mad as hell that he's kept the kid up so late. In this silence, the rawness of his throat and chest and belly is intensified. A toe slid under Amy's knee might tip her over, make her laugh. Nah, she'd cry. Jokes just don't cut it around here any more. This is no laughing matter.

He lets his head fall back on the headrest to watch the smoke spiraling upward until it becomes lost in the air. All the booze in the world couldn't fill this hollow of sorrow, but a little wouldn't hurt right now. Be out in the old Mustang tomorrow. Out on the road selling toilet paper to the nation to wipe their asses. Christ, his shoulders and belly and butt, every part of his body feels like all the interstate traffic passed over it—just like a piece of the road where the Mustang will drive tomorrow with the radio playing softly.

Chapter 4

In the bathroom, Amy squats on the toilet, hugging herself and rocking. If only last night, when Daddy had been so bored by her, could be flushed away. Hiding in the bed all day is what she'd like to do, but her head doesn't ache, her throat isn't sore. If she covered herself with the blankets from her bed and Flossie's, she'd get so hot she'd feel as if she had a fever and get to miss school. But Flossie wouldn't give up her blankets, and she'd tattle. A stomachache might be a good excuse. Clutching her belly, she tries to imagine pain. If she could vomit, Mom would be sure to let her stay home. Mom's so rushed and angry this morning any illness has got to be major or it will be judged as an interruption and might be met with anger.

The best plan of all is to lock the bathroom door and stay where it smells like Daddy's shaving lotion and soap, and it's humid yet warm from his shower. The soggy towels on the floor are the ones he's used to dry his body. She squeezes her eyes closed until she sees red and feels tears roll down her cheeks. Like all the fathers she's read about, he should be in the kitchen eating bacon and eggs, and asking her what she'll be doing today, and wanting to know how she's doing in school, but he's gone because she hadn't been able to make him laugh enough last night and made him terrible coffee, and because her big body crushed his.

Her bottom is getting sore from sitting on the toilet. Soon Mom will be pounding on the door, screaming, "Hurry up." If it's really late, Amy will be tardy to Mr. Crandall's class, something she's never done—the pride of a report card with no tardies will be destroyed. Running to school, she'd be red-faced and sweaty and still late, so when she came into the room, everyone would stare and laugh. Mr. Crandall might make jokes like he had yesterday. Even if she could get there on time, she doesn't want to go back to his room.

While she's brushing her teeth, Mom knocks on the door. "Flossie and I are leaving. You'll have to go alone." Amy looks at her frothy mouth, and begins to make a plan, in spite of the guilt Mom's apologetic voice stirs by adding in a rush, "If you really hurry, you won't be late. I left your lunch money on the table."

Because Flossie had a case of flu earlier in the year, Amy knows the procedure for reporting absences. She paces the kitchen, watching the clock hands crawl closer to bell time. There's no way around it; she'll have to lie. Whispering each number, she dials the school. If no one answers by the tenth ring, she promises the bearded God, whose image lingers from parochial school days and reappears in moments of panic, she'll hang up and go to school. Listening to the long ring and the short beep, she chants, "Answer." Between rings, she counts her heart beat. On the sixth ring, the bossy secretary Mrs. MacArthur answers. Amy's voice sounds sick and shaky saying, "I don't feel good." She is sobbing by the time she hangs up. The woman who usually sees through liars believes her, tells her to take care of herself and come back to school when she feels better.

She crawls back in bed and pulls the covers up to her shoulders. Lying on her belly, she presses her face into the pillow and weeps until there's a wet spot on the case. If she sleeps, the day will vanish as it does when she's sick. But behind her closed eyes, Mom, Mr. Crandall, Mrs. Mac, and even the principal, Mr. Johnson, are appearing in scenes, each busily performing a job, not suspecting she's a liar hiding in bed, tricking the people who trust her. She pulls her knees to her chest like a baby. At noontime, Mr. Crandall might see the principal. They might decide to phone. They might send the secretary to the house, or call Mom at work, or Flossie might tell. But Amy will protect herself by waiting after school at the edge of the playground blending in with the other children, so grownups won't recognize her, and mention what she's done at school, so Flossie won't be suspicious. This morning Amy can leave the house with her lunch money, two pieces of Mom's note-paper, a Big Chief tablet, and a ballpoint pen. She'll trace every letter of Mom's writing until she can imitate it perfectly. The note will be flawless. Amy throws back the covers and hurriedly dresses.

Six months ago, Mom and Flossie and she had gone to the Scottsdale Center for the Performing Arts. Going to the library and all the little shops on that Saturday had been a day with a halo over it. Laughing at the swans by the library, and even spending a quarter to buy peanuts to feed the ornery birds, had been like being with Grammy H.: no-

body got scolded and there had been one thing to do right
after another, a string of perfect, bright beads. Reflecting
on the memory often, she knows the bus to catch. But as she
rides, watching for street names and numbers, feeling
rushes of guilt and fear, she decides God might punish her
by letting her get lost. None of the bored-looking passengers
watch her as if she is a criminal. A little crippled man, sitting across from her, stands for his stop and winks at her,
not a nasty wink, but one for a pretty, nice girl. By the time
she reaches the stop where the brick wall branches, leading
to each of the buildings of the center, her spirits are lifted
from muddy depths to a fleecy, gray cloudcover. As she
walks, following the curving sidewalk made of brick, she
thinks of Dorothy and the yellow brick road to Oz. In a
light-flooded corner of a library reading room, she practices
Mom's signature. Sealing the envelope containing the forged
note, she doesn't feel like a counterfeiter but an accomplished scribe, who has performed well. She feels proud of
how similar her writing is to Mom's. Now the library may be
explored. Because she doesn't have a card, no books can be
taken from the building. If anyone asks, she will tell them
she is Sally Simpson from New York City visiting her sick
grandmother who moved to Arizona to live in the sun. But
no one questions her. A few of the old gentlemen on the second floor, where she wrote her note, glance up from their
newspapers to smile, but most are too busy working at reading and breathing to be aware of her. She's invisible in this
setting, wandering about the stacks, up the stairs, into the
lavatory, into the record room, where people take phono-
graph records and headphones to booths with turntables,
where they sit wearing headphones, smiling at the music no
one else hears. Meekly, she goes to the desk and asks for
Peter and the Wolf and is handed a record with a booklet of
color photgraphs, escorted to a booth, and shown how to op-
erate the machine. She is an honored guest in the beautiful
rooms with paintings, magazines, books, and music: all for

her enjoyment, all for free and for as long as she likes. However, she will be more careful than Cinderella, so the bus won't turn into a pumpkin before it is time to meet her sister.

Flossie is so simple to fool about the day of the adventure, all the careful planning and worrying had been a waste of time. And when Mom asks, "Were you tardy this morning?" Amy answers quickly to mask fear, "No, I made it by the tardy bell."

Frowning, Mom turns from the sink and Amy shudders, sure of discovery, but Mom continues in her nagging voice, "Well, you've got to get up in the morning. I don't want to write notes for you or have to talk to your teacher." Hanging her head, flushed with relief, Amy realizes Mom thinks she's ashamed. To share the secret of the new power of writing notes as well as an adult will never be possible. But Mom returns to the dishes, revealing how easy it could be to have other misadventures.

Daddy is late coming home again, and his slightly dazed expression tells why. If she sat by him in front of the TV, she might be able to tell him how he could check out records and lounge in comfortable chairs to read newspapers from New York, but he's as gray as the TV, lost in its snow, so she only dares to walk by murmuring, "Hi, Dad," and he lifts a finger of acknowledgment.

The next day, Mr. Crandall doesn't instantly open the note she gives him. From her desk, she manages not to squirm as he reads, his face not showing signs of disbelief. By afternoon, she's sure he won't question her, and the rest of the week goes smoothly. Mr. Crandall repeats everything so often, the lessons are easy. On the first day back, she has time to help Duane. Every chance she has, she smiles at Mr. Crandall, being his perfect student, watching him with great curiosity as if his topics are fascinating. He returns her look with affection. Although he says he's a good judge of character, he was easily tricked by the sneaky, bad girl she's become.

She has learned to spin fantasies. She will live as if her life is a movie. Like Dorothy in *The Wizard of Oz,* she will have two lives, one in black and white and one in color. Her recent adventure has taught her how to transform a fuzzy black and white picture into a brightly focused world. The grim picture of black and white she acted within, like the education films she sees at school, becomes only a part of her world. She begins to devise rules for a new life. If she behaves very well according to black and white rules, then she can have the pleasure of color. Having the opportunity for these adventures does involve the sin of lying and sneaking, but it doesn't really hurt people as long as she is convincing and pleasant when she is with them. The lovely part about her new life is no one gets angry, and everyone is pleased. One day a week, every other week, will be color time. This plan delights her: fulfilling wishes is possible. And she's satisfied a wish she's had for a very long time: finally, she has a best friend, a wonderfully imaginative person, herself.

Walking home from class the day after her truancy, Amy decides to serve a penance, an activity the nuns said paid for a sin. She'll listen to Flossie whine, and instead of saying mean things, speak soothingly. When they reach the cluttered house smelling faintly of garbage, she decides to get Flossie to help her surprise their parents with a scene from Walt Disney, their version of *Snow White.* Like the dwarves and animals, they will work together and set the house to sparkling, making a colorful evening at home, starring the family. Mom will probably get home first tonight. It's only three-fifteen. Amy flips on the kitchen radio, turning the dial to find a station with energetic music for the background of their scene. Making Flossie into a worker bee won't be easy, but she'd been fairly happy during their walk home from school. It's worth a try. She's staring into the interior of the refrigerator. The Brownie Troop in New York learned about performing good deeds before anyone in the house was awake, a tale she'd once told Flossie, but it is doubtful her fluffy mind retains the memory. Placing an arm around her sister's shoulder, Amy stares with her into the arctic cavern. "If we got some cookies, would you like to play a game?" Flossie turns and Amy continues energetically, "Start collecting bottles. We're going to go to the store."

Loading up their old wagon with Mom's empty Pepsies and bottles left in the shed by former tenants, they make two trips and finally get $5.06. At the discount market, Amy carefully picks out the goceries, fearful there won't be enough money. But the grouchy cashier checks them through, leaving only nine cents change. With their bulging grocery sack, they hurry home singing. Everything. They got everything. And Flossie is giggly with the promise of two helpings of pudding and the honor of preparing it. Trotting along because she has to go to the bathroom, her face is as flushed as if she had a fever. If Amy isn't the calm, dependable one, the hero in the movie, the surprise will fail. Inside the house, Flossie shoves her packages on the counter and dashes off to pee, leaving everything to put away. Amy reads the directions on the boxes as she puts them on the shelves, calculating her cooking schedule so dinner will be served at six. Preparing the pudding can keep Flossie busy while Amy tries to make the house look clean. Everything must be done in an hour. Mom's approval and Daddy's laughter will be worth sharing the credit with Flossie. Humming loudly, Amy sets the wobbly table in the nook Mom calls the dining room. The surprise will be better if it has several parts, like finding a present inside a present. To make the table prettier, they need a bouquet. When Flossie finishes her only task, she can cross the alley to pick sweet peas and queen's wreath from the vines crawling up the neighbor's back wall.

Only forty-five minutes left and Gram H. would judge the house as messy. They can race through tasks in relays. The clock's hands have flown to five o'clock and Dad's not here.

They will keep building the surprise until Mom walks through the door. Amy starts thinking out loud, plotting a ceremony for Mom. Flossie can greet her with a garland of flowers, a lei of braided queen's wreath and jewels of sweet peas. They can chant, "Surprise, surprise, a merry unbirthday today," a hodge-podge of lines from every Walt Disney movie they've ever seen. Flossie will lead Mom to the living room, make her sit in the easy chair, and Amy will bring her a cocktail. She knows where the cooking sherry is hidden. After taking off Mom's shoes, they'll command her to relax while they prepare the banquet and await the arrival of Daddy, whose happiness will be the best part of the surprise. He'll have to be a spectator since he'll probably refuse to wear flowers, and he might not feel too playful if he hasn't had time to stop by a bar or if he's gone there and stayed too long. Mom can watch TV if she wants, or listen to the radio. They'll give her choices as if she were a queen; and if Mom is queen, then, of course, Daddy is king.

Chapter **5**

Hot and tired from eight hours at work and the three-block walk from the bus stop, Barbara O'Connor's daily tension headache knots her shoulders and leaves her nauseated. Thank God, she won't be working the dinner shift. As she steps on her porch, she worries about whether she's left the hamburger out to thaw, whether there will be enough bread to substitute for buns. Standing on the kitchen stoop, searching for her key, she sees her children through the half-window of the door. She snaps her purse closed and knocks.

Through the door, their laughter is muffled. How nice it would be if they'd started dinner. To have some help would be such a blessed relief. Michael is an unending burden. In the open doorway, the girls are framed, picture-book bright and fresh, sending a wash of affection through her, loosening the tension which is keeping her wound like a robot, providing a reprieve—at least for now—from her fear that the top of her head will snap open, scattering nuts and bolts and springs, so she'll stand before them, a hollow-eyed doll. They seem caught up in the excitement of some hastily prepared ceremony. Flossie approaches, carrying a loop of queen's wreath shedding blossoms on the floor. And Amy's smiling anxiously. Their cheeks, as rosy as the falling flowers, their voices high and birdlike, they chant the message, "Surprise!" Flossie holds up flowers they've woven into a necklace. With a tiny sigh, Barbara drops to her knees and lets her baby Flossie drop the garland about her neck. Rushes of emotion electrify her. If she lifts her face, tears will roll down her cheeks. She opens her arms to blindly embrace them. "We love you," they whisper.

She chokes, "I know." And then, weak with emotion and confused by this drama where she is the focus of attention, thrown off balance by the sudden reversal of her role as waitress and servant to her family, she permits the girls to take her by the hand and lead her about playing their game. They leave her in the livingroom, seated in Michael's chair. If he were to walk in the front door right now, she'd involuntarily jump from his place. She'll try to relax, for the girls' sake, and listen to the radio they've switched on for her entertainment. Static crackles above the syrupy strains of Montovani. She stares at the glass that Amy places in her hand. The odor of sherry wafts up to her nose. Her child has given her a drink with liquor in it—her girls must not know how drinking is ruining all of their lives.

Seated at the table with her daughters on either side, she recalls the triangle of her childhood: Mother, Ann, and Barbara. Although Dad was their financial support, he was excluded from their tight formation. And Mom's remarks about him and to him lost their subtlety as the girls matured. Not only was he an outsider, but the enemy. Hostility toward him bound the women of her family together. But fear of Michael is tearing her family apart.

In spite of everyone's efforts, conversation slows to silence. Obviously, Michael is not coming home for dinner. They'll eat without him. Barbara picks up her fork. To swallow the pasty food requires an act of will. How sad for the girls to believe this is a luxurious meal. Mom would be shocked by their diet. It is surprising the girls maintain good health. Breakfast in this house is sugary cereal. They eat school lunches where they probably gobble the starch and leave the rest. By dinner, they're full of snacks of ice cream bars and cookies. When she had school-age children, Mom's life had centered around the house. Three meals a day were prepared with care and imagination: a luxury Michael's children will never experience. A typical creation of her Mom's was a smiling open-faced cheese sandwich with pickle eyes, an olive nose, and a celery-stick mouth. Their house smelled faintly of yeast, for all their bread was baked at home, as well as cakes, pies, and cookies. The setting for their family life was as immaculate and warm as a hospital nursery, and totally controlled by Mom.

Barbara glances at her children as they stare at their plates. The paper napkin draped on her plate disguises her uneaten food. There might be some coffee to reheat from breakfast. She lights a cigarette, then searches the dim room for an ashtray and drops the burnt-out match on the mound of lipstick-stained cigarette butts. Cigarettes and coffee are her staples. Michael taught her to smoke during their courtship, but the addiction probably began when she got her first job after Flossie started kindergarten. Michael hadn't approved of her working, claiming he could support his family. But the facts were clear: his paycheck couldn't stretch to feed and clothe four people and support the endless rounds of drinks he bought at the Royal Sports Tavern. Always tired before she took her job, she was exhausted after she was employed. Coffee got her started in the mornings. Cigarettes gave her a lift. Her sagging spirits were bolstered through the day with periodic cigarette and coffee breaks to keep from becoming totally numb. Oh, God, this is not what she'd imagined her life would be. She'll never equal Mom's ideal role: room mother, officer in the P.T.A., assistant Girl Scout leader. Only after her daughters were practically grown and Dad's health started to fail, when money became a problem, had Mom renewed her teaching certificate to return to her career before marriage. Through a veil of smoke, Amy's face is anxious, waiting to be dismissed from this painful silence. She and Flossie can clean up. Maybe if Barbara had a few moments alone, she could see a way to pull the family back together.

When Amy reads the wordless command and turns to relay it to Flossie, their insecurity is painfully obvious, a feeling Barbara never wanted them to experience and yet has helped create. As a child she'd always wanted to please, believing if everyone loved her, than she would be happy and the world would be right. Watching the girls clear the table, she tries to refocus the past with her mother. The old fears, the old resentments are fuzzy, but the painful insecurity returns with intensity. Ann had been the brightest, the prettiest, the most popular, the one who made their mother proud. Mom shook her head sadly at the C's and D's sprinkling her youngest child's report cards and said, "As long as you try, it's all we ask of you." Trying meant playing alone in the schoolyard or hurrying home, letting Ann be Mom's "social butterfly." When Ann was high school valedictorian and received a full scholarship to Wellesley, it confirmed what everyone knew. Ann was the best and deserved to be happy. It didn't matter when Mom said she was proud of both children, when she publicly announced, "I don't know what I'd do without Barbara. She's so sweet and dependable." It didn't matter when her mother confided Barbara was Dad's favorite. Mom's judgment was beyond questioning, and she'd taught her children that in spite of her husband's dependability, he was a fool who knew nothing of the world of ideas like his wife and his eldest daughter. If he preferred his youngest child, it was because she was his mirror image.

As Amy and Flossie carry the last plates to the kitchen, they are silent and miserable, reflecting Barbara's failure as a mother, as a wife. She busies herself lighting a cigarette so she won't have to watch them. Failure. A single word summing up her life. By the age of eighteen, she was sure she was a failure. Attending Oneonta State Teachers College was a failure compared to Wellesley, and a major in early childhood education a failure compared to physics. Scholastic probation in the College of Education was rare, but by second semester Barbara Hershey was on the shameful list. And the unspeakable failure for a girl was pregnancy before marriage. By the end of her freshman year, she was pregnant by the only man with whom she had ever slept, Michael. The precaution of birth control had not been a consideration. Forbidden acts performed in the dark earned her the punishment of pregnancy for her horrid sin. Miraculously, Michael agreed to marriage and even spared her the confrontation of confession. While she shivered outside a phone booth, he called her parents to explain their marriage, to confess their reason. The marriage was a sentence. The only way for her to gain Mom's love and a token of her respect was to be a success as a mother and wife.

Barbara stubs out her cigarette and lights another. There's no denying her failure as a homemaker, and she tried: God, she tried. But there's no fresh-baked bread in her house. There hadn't really been a home until two years ago. For ten years, they lived with her in-laws in the upstairs they'd converted to an apartment. It was as if they were never alone, fighting in whispers, keeping the babies' mouths plugged with pacifiers and bottles to silence their cries. For a week, she'd followed Big Mike's suggestions on how to care for a baby, until she was corrected by Etta O'Connor. They never considered what Barbara might want or need. She wanted to please, was desperate for approval, so Michael would be happy, so her marriage would work.

Her babies were a means to gain approval and happiness. But they were tiny tyrants, unable to survive without constant devotion. Crying and soiling themselves, demanding and demanding, they left her shaking with fatigue. Yet if she could've persuaded Michael or deceived him without his discovery, she would've had three or four babies; it would have made his commitment stronger. But two babies were all he'd allow: "Two mistakes are enough." The birth control pills that she took at Michael's insistence were hidden. Her mother-in-law would expect her daughter-in-law to practice the rhythm method. Etta believed abstaining from sex was decent.

Barbara hadn't put her babies in rubber pants because Mom said they'd get a rash. As soon as the babies were wet, they were changed, and the crib sheets had to be stripped. Her father-in-law said bare-chested babies got chilled; Etta O'Connor said girls looked cute in dresses, so they were dressed in smocks. If a stain appeared on an outer garment, off it came along with the undergarments. From early morning until afternoon, laundry churned in the tiny portable washing machine in the kitchen sink. The machine did a fifth of what Etta's washer could handle, but Etta never offered to lend hers. The senior O'Connors were outraged by the electricity bills, telling Mike his wife was a spendthrift. So she laundered by hand.

When Amy began to crawl, Barbara vacuumed daily, washed the throw rugs until they were threadbare and stripped, washed and waxed the hardwood floors and linoleum regularly. Gram O. said the slickness of the floors and the daily sweeping overhead "could drive a person crazy." But there were plenty of silent chores: the dresses to iron, bottles to boil, windows to wash, furniture to dust, drawers to straighten, kitchen shelves to arrange by a classification system to rival the Dewey Decimal System. Weekdays, after Etta O'Connor pulled out of the drive in her old Pontiac to go to her job at the Post Office, there was time for the noisier jobs, time to let the babies cry. Mom believed instant gratification created undisciplined adults. Barbara's life was a penance for having gratified her sexual desires as an irresponsible girl. So when her babies' crying called to her, she went as far from the sound as she could and washed a wall, or scrubbed on her hands and knees, between the bathroom tiles, with a Brillo pad. If she could only get everything perfectly clean, then everything would be perfectly right. But Etta complained to Michael that his wife was "nasty neat." Big Mike told his son, "A woman who loves her babies don't let 'em cry like that."

And although she'd invited her parents to visit, the trip from Oneonta was too long for Pop since his colitis had become so severe. When Mom planned a weekend visit alone, Barbara slaved in preparation, even rehearsing possible conversations. The perfect babies and immaculate apartment won Mom's approval, but the family dinner was so silent, they heard one another chewing; conversation fizzled and died with one word answers, so Big Mike became the host. His tasteless jokes and horrid grammar were embarrassing, accentuating everyone else's silence. Later Barbara overheard Etta O'Connor tell Big Mike, "That Mrs. Hershey thinks she's real smart. But teachers are a dime a dozen. Cops make more money." The remark made Barbara feel a fierce affection: Mom was no ordinary person. At the end of their visit, Mom and she hugged one another, a rare gesture in their relationship, and she felt closer to her mother than she could ever remember. Fear of a repetition of the disastrous visit kept her from offering another invitation. Their letters were superficial, the phone calls stilted, visits to Oneonta delayed. Mom became more distant and more ideal.

Their relationship was another sacrifice to Barbara's failing marriage.

Michael was the man who slept beside her. He rarely sang snatches of ribald songs as he had in college, or tickled her and nibbled her ear. Occasionally she was his audience for jokes he'd perform to win a sale. In the mornings, she saw him in his white shirt and tie, poured his first cup of coffee that he didn't acknowledge with the smile he'd flash for a waitress. She'd ask how many miles he'd travel, how many stores he'd visit. He'd give brief answers that she hoped were true. He rarely asked what she'd be doing. He knew the antiseptic prison she kept occupied her time. He never mentioned his stops at the Royal Sports Tavern, but remarks of Big Mike's meant he was a regular. His defense for visiting the bars would relate to business: "Have to know what the other peddlers are trading." But he went to the bar to remain in the days and ways of his high school buddies, to let the beery haze take the edge off Etta O'Connor's shrill voice and the hard sheen of their sparkling apartment. Drinking insulated him from the stacks of unpaid bills, the children scrambling up his knees, and the thin wife with bright anxious eyes whom she'd become.

After she got her job, she grew to dread weekends, when the housework she used to complete during the week had to be finished in two days. She only saw Michael for a few hours. He slept late on Saturdays and went to the bar at noon to catch whatever sports event was on TV. She never suggested he stay at home to watch TV. The dark barroom, where he sat with his cronies at his elbows, sustained him. Lost in sports statistics, he forgot the miles between him and his next paycheck, a check that would never buy an exit from the endless traffic jam of his life. She was afraid to ask him for more. He punished her with silence. She let him go his way. For nine years, the numbness spread. Her pleasures were small and fleeting: a letter from her mother, her children at play, silent lovemaking at midnight, Michael's slender, naked body lying beside her or walking through the bedroom. These were the secret pleasures that she never shared.

Her job at the children's branch of the library was an escape. The paycheck was next to nothing, but the chore of reshelving books satisfied her. For seven hours a day, five days a week, she was out of the O'Connors' house, away from her frenzied role as the perfect homemaker. She grew comfortable with her job, so when Big Mike died, it hadn't caused a great ripple in her life, and she assumed the same was true for Michael. But three months after his father's death, Michael disappeared, leaving a five-word note, "I have to get away." She'd crumpled the paper until the letters blurred, but she couldn't erase the image of him driving alone on the Pennsylvania Turnpike into the rising sun with no map and no luggage. The layers of sedation she was wound in were torn away, exposing bloody flesh and a pain she didn't know she could feel. Nothing she had done since their marriage had ever begun without the thought of what Michael needed, what he wanted. Without him, she was a dark and endless tunnel. The terror of the meaninglessness of her life obsessed her so she couldn't sleep or eat or talk.

She explained the desertion to Mrs. O'Connor by handing her his note. The girls were frightened of her puffy eyes. But when they asked, "Mommy, what's wrong?" she covered her face with her hands and cried. So they went downstairs for dinner with Gram O., then for breakfast, then lunch. Living alone like a semi-invalid, never dressing or leaving the room, Barbara sat in front of the TV with her eyes focused beyond the screen and only ate bites of the food Mrs. O'Connor sent upstairs three times a day. The old woman became afraid of her and didn't try to make her speak. As Barbara began to heal, she feigned insanity to keep Etta from her. The energy spent trying to please the in-laws had chased Michael away. Her desperation to be accepted by them turned into hatred.

During the weeks and months with no word from him, she believed he had disappeared forever. She began to rehearse how she would reject him if he ever returned. He would never, never be her life again. When he called six months later from Arizona, long distance wires hummed as he muttered, "I need you," and she had instantly agreed to meet him. She had failed, but they would begin again. The howling inside her stopped. They'd escape to Glendale, Arizona, a bedroom community for Phoenix; she prayed they'd be reborn like the bird in the legend.

The girls are unusually quiet in the kitchen. They ought to be checked, given a hand. The kitchen light is out. Barbara switches it on. They're gone, their job finished with a touching lack of perfection. They're so young, so inexperienced, so dependent, and yet she's unaware of them so often. Tonight is a perfect example. They finished their chores and tiptoed by her as she sat in a cloud of smoke and self-centered thought. Such cute children, so intelligent, so loving. They must be taught to be self-sufficient. God knows, they'll probably have to be—Prince Charming had not whisked *her* away on a white horse. Today, it's shameful to admit how incredibly young and impetuous she'd been when she met Michael. Her girls must not make her mistakes. She hears them fussing about what to watch on TV. As she calls, "Stop it," her tone is angry, her throat so tight she might burst into tears.

She slips off her waitress oxfords, flexes her swollen ankles, and begins to enjoy the cool linoleum beneath her feet. The front door opens and closes. Michael. God, thirteen years she's been with him and still the sight of him makes the pit of her belly twist. The girls are galloping and whooping from the living room. He holds out his hands in a pretense of fending them off, the lovable drunk. She rises from her chair and pushes it into the table, sensing the stench of whiskey he breathes on them, her mind a jumble with rehearsed approaches to the confrontation. And now he stands in the living room, and she's terrified to approach him, afraid she'll send him away. She goes to the kitchen and leans against the sink. She tries to reconstruct his drinking patterns. He never eats breakfast. Probably never eats lunch. But his business deals must be completed at lunch. He must eat sometime; he can't just drink and maintain his illusion he isn't a drunkard. She picks at the garbage the girls left in the drain, sick with the awareness of his downward spiral. Occasionally at work she is clutched by flashes of disasters that might visit him, but usually she forgets him. Images of his exhaustion and continual illness are blocked as she rushes to serve her customers, to keep the cooks and the manager happy, to avoid the humiliation of public failure. If there's time to spare to worry about her family, her thoughts drift to the girls.

Careful to remain out of his sight, she watches the trio in the living room—Michael in the middle with a girl on either side. They watch his face with the attentiveness of loving puppies. She hates their uncritical love for him; she loves it. She hates being the bitch who keeps the family together; she loves it. Retreating to the sink, she swallows slowly, testing the rawness of her throat. She should stop smoking, but even the thought of it sets her craving. She wants to curl up in the corner and breathe her lungs full of smoke, to walk out the back door and walk further and further into the night. What do they want from her? She is tired. Too tired to stage a drama with Michael. Total silence will be seen as hostility. Any word she'd utter would have the tone of a snarl. She stands at the counter, thankful for the mess before her that will keep her in the kitchen a long while. She has to make a plan for Michael, for all of them; it must be original. Her mother can't serve as a model. *Woman's Day* has no how-to-cope plans in the recent issue. Numb with indecision, she begins her mindless chores.

Chapter **6** |

Michael sits at the stoplight. As he squints then opens his eyes slowly, the tiny ruby grows to a giant one set against the black velvet jewel box of the night. Christ, this is a good glow. He feels like a fuckin' poet. No traffic in front and the old rearview shows none behind. Just to be sure, swivel the head and peek over the shoulder, a momentary visual blur. This car is silent as a tomb. Better make some conversation to liven it up. "Can't always trust a mirror." And his right hand slips from the steering wheel and slides across the seat to the woman's knee. His palm cups its curve and travels up her thigh until her hand touches his. He squeezes the warm denim covering her leg. Like to pinch the soft flesh until she yelps, but best relax the old grip and slide the hand back to her knee. Look at the little rascal just sliding along innocent as can be. No fair looking at her face, got to keep this impersonal as possible, just something warm between the bod and the mattress. The kid set it up: sitting at a neighboring barstool, sharing an ashtray, not picking up the tab for her drink. She made her message clear. She wanted a little—a little sex without conversation or guilt. Jesus, she's muttering something. Christ, she better not be making up rules now. Ah, the light changed.

He drives slowly to compensate for any impairment of his reflexes. An absolute bastard wouldn't take such excessive care at the wheel. Fifteen years of drinking and driving and never been arrested. Proof there's an ace at the wheel. Booze is a fine tranquilizer—just use it, don't abuse it. Sober, these reflexes would be lightning fast; bombed, they're probably normal. And the motel scene was sobering, lying beside this skinny kid, the hard-on gone. Watching the neon flash behind the ventian blinds, he felt so lonely he might as well have jerked off. Shit, hadn't had to fake it with her, wasn't like he barged into her house, hadn't snowed her. But a woman like her makes a man feel real guilty. Ding-y dames are better, just wanting a couple of compliments, a laugh or two, satisfied with the oldest routine in the world. But these kids, raised on the pill, handled sex like a guy—just a step above whacking off. Sharing a cigarette after coming their separate ways, he couldn't manage to say thank you. He might as well be a cabbie driving her to some dumpy duplex as payment for her favor.

Alone on the road going home, he's suddenly flooded with guilt. He makes a resolution: No more fuckin' around: feeling this shitty is sick. Tomorrow, it's back to a steady diet of beer. No big step. Done it before, can do it again. Hell, Glendale's a drying-out town, perfect place to taper off. The Royal Sports with all the grammar school buddies, staying stewed to the gills, is two thousand miles away. And Phoenix is just a bunch of crummy bedroom towns with bars filled with drifters: clubs with no dues. Phoenix is a city without a heart. Geez, give credit where credit's due—not a single rule of the O'Connor Cure has been broken: no drinking at home, no bar that's home base, drink with strangers or alone. The invisible drinker: nobody knows your name, nobody to keep a daily tally. Meant to keep one, but the fuzzies set in and counting doesn't matter. Hell, doing okay, fuckin' a-okay.

Even Barbara wouldn't buy this crock. He's been shit-faced every day. There's a flask full of booze in the glove compartment—and no recollection of when drinking in the car got to be a daily routine. Christ, buying the little fucker seemed like such a simple solution: whiskey's highly concentrated medication, more convenient than beer, faster than beer—quicker route into the haze; no time wasted in a bar—taking the medication is a solo number. Only planned to keep the flask in the car for a week. Geez, if whiskey's medication, beer's mother's-milk. A family tradition. Big Mike drank at least half a gallon a day 'til the day he died, had since he was a kid. Hard to remember the old guy without a beer in his hand. Big Mike wasn't a broken-down drunk, just an Irishman with a gut full of beer. Beer's harmless. The way to go. Start playing it smart, playing the angles. Yeah, the flask has definitely got to go.

Regularly, he's been pulling into the alley behind the house for one last swig before going inside. The whiskey's getting outa hand: hung-over every day, fighting the sucker 'til noon, taking the edge off at lunch, parking behind some grocery to get greased to make a sales pitch. Always the same: one long swallow, then another and the counting stops. The rest of the day slides along like a fast ball. But when the fog of the afternoon blahs rolls in, the symptoms can't be denied: his hand lighting the cigarette shakes, his sandpaper throat and aching head. But it takes one hell of a boost to open the door and manage a smile and get through a couple of hours of the kids pawing and Barbara giving her silent dirty looks with her moony eyes. Got to get home and get some sleep. With a rumbling, he accelerates to pass. Christ, the goons in Phoenix drive like old ladies.

Sleep's so crazy lately, Michael dreads getting in bed. Once he hits the mattress, sleep is instant, but not for long. Hell, he hasn't slept through a night for a year or a year and a half, and there's never a night without waking cold and sweaty in the middle of a dream. Waking at two, old bod covered with sweat turning cold; too hot for the sheet and blanket, too warm under just a sheet, too cold with nothing: skin begging to be scratched so bad he has to keep his fists clenched to keep from clawing himself. And the limbs that ache, moaning to be shifted, promising to fall asleep at just the right angle: first the stomach, the right side, then the left, then the back. But even behind closed eyes, the ceiling's the lid of a coffin. Somewhere around two, sleep drags him under until a nightmare yanks him upright and the tossing and turning start over. The will to lie still and rest gets lost when the old bod pulls its tricks taking the mind into a web of nightmares. Sick of the battle, the pacing begins, smoking nonstop, debating what to do from five until eight when it's time for work.

Christ, it'd be great to go to work at five and speed from store to store, filling out the frigging forms so they'd get their fuckin' toilet paper. What wears him down is waiting for the manager, winking at the checkout girls, thinking up new jokes, remembering the ones he's told. Every place needs the fuckin' merchandise. They all buy the merchandise. The world's got to wipe its ass. But fuckin' Tristram uses its salesmen as their samples. Ah, sure, you get a cut of the action as long as you seem essential. Got to spend your days building castles of paper. But the truth is what's done in an eight or ten hour day could be done in two or three if you'd get your own little honey for a secretary. Any fool could figure that out. It's only a matter of time till the assholes runnin' Tristram do. And the truth is, this is one shitty job, but it's the only way to make a buck in this jerkwater town. Could get another job tomorrow, but any job'd turn out to be the same, maybe even worse.

Michael parks the car in the carport and sits for a moment. The house is dark—he hopes they're in bed. He checks his watch and is surprised by his naked wrist. Shit, the watch is in some burg in northern Arizona—Wickenberg to be exact. He left it at a filling station as payment. Maybe one little goodbye drink from the flask will mean instant sleep.

He tightens the cap on the flask and slips it under the papers in the glove compartment. Tomorrow, it's good riddance. He locks up with the tiny key; the twin was thrown away, no need for Barb to have one. After digging in his pocket for breath mints, he turns on the overhead light, runs his fingers through his hair, then checks his face in the rearview mirror. Not as rotten-looking as he'd imagined: thin, tired, skin the color of a fading Chink, but not the face of a Bowery bum. Could be identified as human. He forces a smile. Put on the happy face. Jesus, that smile looks like shit. The old double dimple could be a scar—the face of a psycho, or something abnormal. Ma always said his smile could charm the angels. The old doll ought to see it now. Jesus, Mary, and Joseph: Ma—hadn't thought of her in months. He picks at the dried blood of a razor nick—not thought of her in months: what a laugh. Thirty years with her crazy explosions could shoot a life to hell and gone. Thirty-two years old before he left home—the smile in the mirror goes sour, a look even an Irish angel wouldn't love. Well, getting in shape is on the agenda; flogged by crappy feelings, he'll stay in line.

As the key in the lock gets frisky, he curses, trying to see in the dark, imagining Barbara lying on her side of the bed, pretending she doesn't hear, turning away when he crawls in beside her.

Chapter 7 |

After their special dinner, when Daddy hadn't appeared, Amy had waited until he finally came home and he'd swung her so her feet lifted from the floor, and she'd squealed and gulped air tasting of whiskey and smoke and Daddy. And when he let her down, dizzy with happiness and fear, it was Flossie's turn. While she shrieked with laughter, Mom stood in the shadows of the kitchen, her face frozen in the mask for fighting. Mom was waiting to be alone with him, to say what she didn't want Amy and Flossie to hear, so Amy'd crept off to bed. From the bedroom, she planned to force herself to listen to their fighting so she'd know if he'd run away again, but there were only sounds of the television.

She wakes in the morning, ashamed to have fallen asleep. She will sneak down the hall and check their bed. If he's still there, she'll pretend to be too sick to go to school, so she can be alone with him for a while after Mom goes to work. The front door closes. He's the only one who uses the front. Leaving this early, he must be going to work. He isn't running away. There is still a chance to help him get better. A day alone in the quiet house plotting how to make him love her enough to stay would be wonderful, but ditching is too risky with the silent anger in this house. School will provide time to make plans. As she sadly rummages through the closet, she feels someone watching. Mom stands in the doorway with a look of pity on her face. Amy barely manages to say hi to the woman who can never make things right.

Mr. Crandall is returning the spelling tests. Duane turns to poke her with the pencil he's turned into a weapon by sticking a straight pin in the eraser. He flaps his paper in her face. An "F" is circled on the top: she hadn't let him cheat since the day he made Mr. Crandall mad. His face is twisted into a hideous Halloween mask. Her heart races, but she can't move her eyes as his big pink tongue slowly inches out of his mouth. Leaning back as far as she can, she is victimized until he turns around. As she stares at his hunched shoulders, she searches for a word to describe his gesture: obscene; yes, obscene. A vocabulary word, which had made her laugh when Mr. Crandall defined it but made her feel queasy as Duane acted it out.

For the rest of the morning she tries to pay a minimum of attention to his unintelligible whispers. If she ignores him, he might leave her alone. And she can't tell Mr. Crandall. He might make fun of Duane in front of the class. And although Duane can't do schoolwork, he's performed masterful tortures, like catching a little boy in the middle of the crowded playground and twisting his wrist with an Indian burn until he blubbered loudly. Once he'd tickled a girl until she wet her pants and pee ran down her legs. So Amy busies herself with her assignments and watches the clock move toward the time to escape to the lunchroom and the playground.

She gulps down the school lunch of tacos so she'll be one of the first on the playground. She doesn't sit under the ramada with the girls who like to play jacks and tell secrets. Girls bore her with their giggling and talk about silly things. And it's Marcy who is the center of attraction under the ramada. With her cute little dresses and her hair tied in ribbons, girls who want to be like her gather around. Amy rarely wears dresses, and only on special occasions puts yarn in her hair; usually a rubber band will do.

With a group consisting primarily of boys, she plays dodgeball. Running about, they bump into one another, calling encouragement to their favorites, insulting the opposition. She's in the midst of a wild scuffle in the center of the circle when the bell rings. She enjoys the sound of her trouser cuffs rubbing together as she trots toward the entrance closest to class, one kids rarely use because it is frequently used by teachers.

As she charges around the corner, a long, muscular arm blocks her face. Her eyes smart from the impact. She cups her palm over her nose and looks through tears into Duane's squinting, excited eyes. Rivulets of sweat trickle from his scalp through the dust at his temples. He smells like old movie popcorn and rancid butter. She steps backward, and he grasps her shoulders with his powerful hands. She whispers, "Duane," but her plea does not stop him. His obscene tongue is darting from his lips, snaking toward her face. Bracing her shoulders, she thrusts her chin in the air. The tongue is fat, wet, and warm on her jawbone as it slowly laps, moving toward her lips. Sinking to her knees and curling into a ball, she sobs, "No, no."

He stands above her, his bony arms limp at his sides, his knobby hands empty, his face flushed. Total humility might make him leave. His staring makes her quiver. He sniffs loudly, and scuffs the toe of his worn boot. He is considering kicking her. He shifts his weight from foot to foot and turns and ambles toward class.

She begins crying softly but doesn't dare to move until he's out of sight. Her crying turns to hiccups. Trying to control her breathing, she listens, sniffs, then swallows. She must wait, for someone might see her. When the last bell rings, stragglers might round the corner. When the second shift for lunch is dismissed, kids carrying brown bags come tearing down the steps to dash to the ramada. She sits up and rubs the dirt from her palms and swipes at her wet, dusty eyes. Someone's approaching. She stiffens. The woman who patrols the playground walks toward her. Scrambling to her feet, Amy begins to run. The woman calls "Stop!" Not looking back, Amy sprints toward the gate leading to the street.

In the afternoon heat, she sits on the slab of cement Mom calls the back porch. For over an hour, Amy sits, holding an open book, turning pages, squinting at print swimming before her. The story of Nancy Drew makes no sense, but a book is the only place to run, the only color escape she can afford. The snowy picture of their TV will not stop Duane's tongue from coming closer. She'll never eat again, because the monstrous thing touched her lips. Her face is raw, scoured by the hottest water she could stand with a rough washcloth and soap. If she sits on the step and reads the whole book, the afternoon might go away like a bad dream or an awful movie, or something happening to someone else.

Chapter 8

Standing at a crossroad beside his Mustang, he stares at its flat tire, knowing he doesn't have a spare. The wind whips about him. He wants to sear his insides with whiskey, so he can crawl in the back seat and go to sleep, but he has to be in Tucson by noon. Digging his cold hands into his pockets, he walks around to the trunk. He turns the key in the lock. The lid springs open. Hundreds of crumpled, yellow order sheets float about him. He tries to catch them, but they flutter through his fingers. Phoenix, Tucson, Flagstaff—wasted, all wasted. A rifle shot explodes. He turns from the sound, shaking his head to rid his ears of the ringing. The living room . . . home . . . morning. Christ, he never made it to bed. The noise from the kitchen is Barbara taking out her anger slamming cupboard doors, working up steam for one of her nagging sessions. Last night, she was ice. Today, she'll be fire.

Tired as he is, it would give him a lift to piss her off. He grins as he hustles toward the shower. Nothing gets to Barb like being ignored. He forgets his aching head as he imagines Barbara's clenched fist of a face going slack when she races to the bathroom to start her whining and finds the door locked. He undresses and turns on the shower full blast to wash away the fog wrapped around his head. Lathering his chest, he manages a ready whistle, just in case she's listening at the door. He finishes showering and dressing, gets out of the bathroom and out of the house without a confrontation, which gives him a little boost; he's a damned good sneak.

Out on the road there is no need for pretense. Jesus, he feels like shit. Today is not the day to start any fuckin' cure. Getting by's tough enough. A Bloody Mary would be fine, but filling up the flask at the Circle K will have to do.

Giving the old broad behind the counter his last ten, he

buys a styrofoam cup of coffee and two pints of bourbon: one for the road and a little for emergencies. Outside the store, he pours out half the coffee and fills it to the top with bourbon. The old broad's probably watching, so he crumples the bag from the bourbon and tosses it in the gutter. Before he backs out, he takes three long swallows so nothing will spill. Waiting to enter traffic, he pounds the steering wheel. Shit, these fuckers wouldn't give a break to a cripple. He chugs from the bottle and finishes off the coffee, flattens the cup, tosses it on the street, and hurls the pint with so much force it smashes. Damned efficient solution to his problem. Already the old head feels clearer. Pushing the shitty product will be a game: getting that Wop manager to laugh at a joke about the Pope is hitting a homer.

Out in traffic, he flips on the radio, dialing to find a station with something besides country western or acid rock—some Sinatra or Peggy Lee, something decent—but the only station without tons of static is right out of shit-kicker country.

By the turnoff to Paradise Valley, he's feeling mellow, a sweet spot where he'd like to stay. The singer is wailing, "One night of love don't make up for six nights alone." Man, he's right. A good woman all the time is a hell of a lot better than scoring with a chick every other night or every sixth. Michael loosens his tie and stretches his arm across the top of the empty passenger seat. Barbara's sleeping a heartbeat away, her mouth slightly open, the tiny blue vein in her forehead pulsating. When his fingers trace her breast, it's as soft and warm as his insides. That smile of hers could charm an angel, could be an angel's. She's moving against him. Man. When she rests against him, he can lower the straps of her nightgown and kiss the curve where her neck meets her shoulder; she'll moan, and he'll let his hand follow the curve of her ribcage til it dips to her waist. His fingers will knead the soft flesh of her buttocks. His arm stretched across the seat begins to fall asleep. He shakes his hand.

The glare of the morning sun cuts through the bourbon. Making love to Barbara was never that good. She could be Helen Keller screwin' in the dark. The rustling of the sheets is the loudest sound she makes. Feel like a fuckin' bull, grunting over her pale, silent body—so shy, too shy. He flexes the fingers on his numb hand. Hell, screwin' a stranger is more intimate than Barbara after thirteen years. Her fuckin' nightgown—calling it her overcoat hadn't lightened her up. He took it off her once, turned on the lights and she was sitting on the edge of the bed, crossing her arms over her breasts, begging to get it back. She could make you feel like a pervert. To her, making it during the day is a sin—always worrying about the kids, how they might hear, might walk in. Jesus, those girls—

He grasps the steering wheel with both hands, his jaw clenched with concentration. Got to keep the front left tire skimming along parallel to the white line. This could be the same road as yesterday or last week or last year—life's a fuckin' squirrel cage—going nowhere fast because of Barbara, because of the kids. If she hadn't got knocked up, he wouldn't be here today. He'd be playing with the Red Sox or in the minors for sure. Jesus, she hadn't been so fuckin' cold when she was nineteen and they were going at it in the back seat of the Ford. She'd giggled and kissed him so he burned. She'd begged him to stop in a voice that said go on. Well, Jesus. With the back of his hand, he brushes the tears misting his eyes. Christ. No sense doing this now. The knot's tied. Got married, had the kid, and as if one wasn't enough, had another. Every day it gets harder to remember why they'd done it. The last years of high school, the summer before college, that semester in college, are lost in a cloud. Mighta been a Bob Feller, a Sandy Koufax, a Vida Blue—a kid who could hold a world record. Shit, those guys played on local ballfields once. Somebody thought Michael O'Connor was good, good enough for a free ride if he played ball. Oneonta—what a screwball place: all those scrubs thought they were ballplayers and didn't know their ass from a hole in the ground, all those bushleague professors who thought they had a corner on truth, and dopey Barbara, a virgin with hot pants, the original prick-tease. The ache at the back of his eyes is beginning again. Hell, thirty minutes to go before it's sales pitch time. A pit stop for fueling up to be in tip-top shape is in order.

At a roadside park, he doesn't get out to sit at the table under the ramada. Sitting outside drinking from a bottle is a little obvious. He finishes off the second pint, paying meticulous attention to the ritual of drinking: each sip has to be equal, and the same amount of time must elapse between each swallow. When the last swig is gone, he gets out of the car and stands for a moment, leaning against the fender. Hey, that trashcan couldn't be more than thirty feet away. Put the heel in front of the toe and measure the distance. Thirty-five steps. Hell, still got a terrific eye. The double-check count on the way back to the car proves he's right. He's up for the trip to Food Town in Paradise Valley. Lay some Dago jokes on Nick Vitale. No problem selling to that Wop.

Chapter **9**

Barbara's day at the restaurant goes quickly with the usual frenzied activity at lunch and the slow spell in the early afternoon. She must concentrate on Michael. Someone has to analyze their life and take charge. For thirteen years she's waited—quietly, angrily, tearfully—for him to take care of her. Being pretty and passive hasn't worked, and her mirror shows her every day her prettiness is buffed and worn. As she hurries from the kitchen to the customers, balancing trays loaded with hamburgers and Swiss on rye, she remembers when her babies wailed in the night, commanding her to drag herself out of bed where Michael lay in a drunken sleep. Between orders for Cokes and french fries, she tries to recall when he had actually been her protector: his explanation of their marriage to her parents, his face above hers as she woke after giving birth. But those are the only scenes she can recall, and they were so long ago.

After the lunch crowd disappears, she tries to make the tacky stainless-steel "silver" look as perfect as possible. But like the "slightly soiled merchandise" her mother warned no man would marry, the flatware has lost its appeal. Sleeping with Michael before marriage had been a mistake. But she'd had no defenses against him. He wasn't like her high school boyfriend who'd been content to neck. She'd lost her virginity to Michael on their second date. But it was after they'd been sleeping together for three months that he asked her to meet his family: the brothers, the mother, the Irish father—all the characters of his hilarious stories. She believed his invitation was the first step to marriage, in spite of her "slightly soiled" condition.

In the beginning, the drive from Oneonta to Mt. Kisco had been lively. With a cooler of beer in the back seat and a lap robe over her legs, they might have been going to a football game. She snuggled beside Michael as he drove with one hand and crooked his arm about her neck so he could hoist a beer to his lips. Then it began to rain. He needed both hands on the wheel, so she held the bottle to his lips when he demanded, and patted his chin dry if any beer dribbled. They had laughed about her "cleaning up baby." But the closer they got to Mt. Kisco, the more somber he became. They hadn't spoken for thirty minutes when they pulled into the drive of the white clapboard at the end of a block of identical houses.

Westchester had sounded so glamorous, yet this house, where she would live for over ten years, was simpler than her father's. Outside it was very quiet. No rosy-faced Irish father bounded down the steps to greet them as they bypassed the front door and went to the kitchen entrance. When Michael picked up the key from under the doormat, she felt sorry for him. Her family didn't have to lock their doors.

In the kitchen, dirty dishes filled the sink and adjoining counters. To mask her dismay, she stared beyond the room to the next, but the pattern was repeated. The dining room table was covered with a dusty lace cloth, yet plastic place-mats were set in front of each chair. Dirty plastic flowers and two candles with long black wicks formed the center piece, surrounded by three full grocery sacks. Michael steered her through the passage from the kitchen to the dining room, avoiding a bag overflowing with garbage.

They sat in the living room on a couch draped with sheets. Because he was embarrassed, she'd been furtive as she appraised the contents of the room. She'd tried to be charitable. His mother must've spent money and time to create this decor. Across from them, a pair of antique French chairs, upholstered in soiled rose brocade, was separated by a battered gate-leg table, topped by an ivory Chinese lamp without a shade. Behind the shadeless lamp, a gilt-edged mirror hazily reflected their faces against a backdrop of sheers veiling a wallpaper mural of Venice in dull green. At the end of the room, opposite from the dark tunnel of the entryway, a staircase led to what she guessed must be the bedrooms. The banister was partially buried in winter clothing; some hangers were tossed about as if the process of cleaning closets had been interrupted.

Her awed silence was broken when Michael touched her knee and muttered, "I told you Ma was different." She glanced from his pained eyes to an ashtray overflowing with lipstick-stained cigarette butts, a crushed pack, and a half-eaten cookie. If she smiled, he might think she was laughing at him, and she wanted so desperately to protect him from the shame in his eyes. This was the house where he'd lived as a child, a teenager. "Different," he'd said. "Different."

The first member of the family Barbara met was his brother Jim. Although he was eighteen, slight and delicate as a girl, his direct gaze and soft manner drew her to him. Moments after meeting him, the kitchen door slammed and heavy footsteps approached. Etta O'Connor fumbled with her purse apparently unaware she was not alone. Beneath a frazzle of dull black curls, her thickly powdered and heavily rouged face still had the transparent glow of the tissue-thin skin of the Irish. She snapped the purse closed and lifted her watery eyes. Her face in repose with its sagging jowls looked like a green-eyed beagle. As she stared at Michael, she raised her penciled eyebrows, and her fuchsia lips puckered and emitted a long, nasal "Oh," as if someone had stepped on her toe. Michael sank further into the cushions where Barbara sat frozen. Her palms turned clammy. She hoped the mother and son would rush to one another's arms. But Michael didn't move and his mother rocked back and forth in place, watching him. Barbara wanted to vaporize and float over their heads out the door. The sore loser of the staring contest, Mrs. O'Connor shifted her gaze to Barbara. When Michael leaned forward as if he might divert her attention, she averted her eyes, chirping, "Oh, hi, hi," and turned to the kitchen.

"Mother," his voice stopped her as if he'd suddenly jerked a choke chain, "this is Barbara."

Clutching her purse, as if Barbara might steal it, she repeated the pained "oh," then scuttled from the room like a giant squirrel. Michael let his hand rest on Barbara's knee, making her chill subside as Mrs. O'Connor shouted from the kitchen in a voice too loud for the short distance between them. "Did ya have a good trip?" she said. "How long did it take ya?"

Michael called to her that they were going for a walk, but she continued talking. They left through the front entrance, which appeared not to have been used in years. For what seemed like an hour, they wandered the narrow streets. She was lost. Everything was the same: everything was foreign. As the sun set, lights began to come on in the rows of doll-sized houses. In some of those homes people must be happy. From the house at the end of the block, a chandelier much too large for its setting threw light on an overgrown hedge bordering the window. She didn't recognize the house as Michael's until he tightened his arm linking hers and said, "Well, are you ready?" Entering the heavy silence of his house, she was touched by his ability to sense her tension.

The family was seated at the table, except for Etta, who was violently stirring the contents of a large, dented pot at the stove. She called, "Hi, hi," over her shoulder. Standing behind Michael, Barbara didn't know whether to parrot the greeting or advance to the table to be seated with a group clearly excluding her. Michael grabbed her hand. "Pop," he called to a bulbous-nosed man, "Pop, I'd like you to meet Barbara, my friend."

As the man hoisted his heavy body by leaning on the table, Barbara murmured, "Oh, don't get up," but he moved toward her, smiling, holding his arms open, his pink face twisted with a half-crazed smile. This beardless Santa with his thatch of strawberry blonde hair was what her mother called "shanty Irish." Fear that he might hug her must've shown, for he clapped loudly then clasped her hands in his. "Ah, my whata pleasure," he sang, bobbing his head.

"Thank you," she whispered. Hopeful this alliance was admission to the clan, she stared in his eyes that were as vague and impenetrable as his wife's.

His head cocked toward his son, he repeated, "A pleasure, a pleasure. . . ." Then he grabbed her hand and stroked its back, purring, "Barbara, of course, Barbara."

His intimacy repulsed her: she wanted to fall into Michael's arms and whisper for him to take her away, but she nodded yes to verify her name. Mrs. O'Connor walked toward them, carrying a platter. "Ah, go on now." she snapped at Big Mike. "Go on and sit at the table."

But Big Mike just raised his hand to silence her and said, "Ah, come along, children. Let's eat."

Six people filled the tiny dining room. The only family member left to meet was the eldest brother, Walter, who was as large as Big Mike but red-faced, unlike the childlike coloring of his father. Walter nodded grimly at their introduction, making her wonder why Michael had identified him as his favorite, "the best of the lot." Elbow to elbow at the cramped table, she passed him the steaming platter of roast beef and boiled carrots and potatoes. Her tiny family with its familiar plot seemed infinitely more simple than this mysterious group. The roast was dry and the vegetables scorched, but above the sounds of eating she addressed her hostess, "This is very good, Mrs. O'Connor, very good." And to prove her sincerity, she took another mouthful, praying she could swallow.

The woman looked at her in disbelief, flicked her wrist, so her hand fell forward, and made the strange "oh" sound, followed by an elongated "nah," and returned to sawing at a chunk of beef with the side of her fork.

Michael smiled his most dazzling smile. "This is Ma's specialty."

She chuckled, shoulders trembling, "Ah, go on," and smiled at him, tilting her head coquettishly.

After the meal, Barbara tried to offer her assistance to Mrs. O'Connor, who discounted the idea with a flick of her limp wrist. Frantic her offer had been interpreted as insincere, Barbara offered again. The urgency in her voice caught Mrs. O'Connor's attention, who looked at her as if she were very strange, then said, "Really, there's nothin' much to do." The rules of this house were incomprehensible. The place was a hopeless mess, yet this woman assumed everything was under control: to argue the point was insulting.

In the living room, Michael read the newspaper, sprawled in the identical pose as his father and brothers, who read other sections. She sat beside him. Without lowering the newspaper, he spoke to her in a whisper. His question was as confusing as his mother's reply: he wanted to know if they could leave soon. Although he probably only plotted a brief escape, it would be a blessed relief. She needed to go to the bathroom, to comb her hair, to know where she'd spend the night. Finally she asked, "Where's the bathroom?" He put down the paper and led her to the door.

Inside she felt as if she were at Scout camp visiting the latrine with her counselor waiting outside. Her involuntary response was to breathe through her mouth. She must leave quickly to prevent contamination. As she rinsed her fingers in the steady leak of the hot water, she curbed her desire to scour away the toothpaste blobs and whiskers spotting the bowl. The knotted towels emitted a sour odor. She nudged the half-open door to the linen closet with her elbow. Sheets, cosmetics, and towels were stuffed on the shelves. She blotted her fingers on a towel and stared at the floor of the closet. The objects littered there held her attention with sick fascination. Canned goods were stacked in uneven pyramids about to topple among the dust kittens on the floor. A family-sized bottle of catsup was shoved in a back corner. She didn't bother to comb her hair.

Michael waited outside the door. He knew she showered twice daily, did more laundry than anyone in her dorm, and ironed her no-iron blouses. Shamefaced, he touched her shoulder. "Ready to leave?"

With relief, she followed him. The car would be a haven after the tension of the dining room table, the stinking shambles of the house. She hoped they'd drive back to Oneonta tonight. "You'll need a jacket," he warned as they stepped over the clutter on the stairway. At the top of the stairs, he pushed open a door and flipped on the light. On the wall before her, a mounted head of a buck hung above the single bed, its shining eye staring at her. Michael nudged her, "Get your jacket," and she stepped toward the bed where her suitcase was lying. As she worked at the clasps, she shuddered at the thought of sleeping beneath a decapitated animal. "This is Walter's room," he said, moving her aside to open her suitcase.

Beneath the carefully folded garments, she found her jacket and the gift she'd brought Mrs. O'Connor. The bow she'd taken so long to tie symmetrically had been crushed. But the color was the perfect shade of mauve to highlight the lilac flecks in the wrapping paper. Lilac was her mother's favorite color. Taking the package from the suitcase, she turned to Michael. "I brought this for your mother." His expression was bewildered but pleased.

Perhaps the gift for Mrs. O'Connor would erase the disastrous introduction. Her jacket over her arm, Barbara brushed by Michael, the gift held before her, a charm to break a spell.

Mrs. O'Connor was at a sink billowing with soapsuds. If Barbara dropped the package, she could help wash all the dishes and scrub the kitchen. Instead, she stood for a moment, hoping the woman would sense her presence. Smoke wreathed Mrs. O'Connor's head like a cartoon dialogue balloon. Caught in a private moment, smoking at the sink, she was almost lovable. She must feel trapped by this horrid house; cleanliness was not a measure of her worth the way it was for Mom. Mrs. O'Connor's smoking made Mom seem hopelessly unsophisticated; at forty-eight, she'd never had a cigarette and only accepted a drink when it was forced upon her. Yet Mrs. O'Connor was enjoying an intimate moment alone with her cigarette. Her world was so different: maybe she yearned to share it with a daughter-in-law. Barbara stepped closer and spoke. "Mrs. O'Connor."

She jumped as if she'd heard an explosion. "Ya scared me," she accused, stubbing out the cigarette.

Barbara held the gift toward her, an apology: "I thought maybe, you . . ."

Mrs. O'Connor cooed, "Oh."

Nodding stupidly, Barbara pushed the gift into the pale hands with the chipped red nails. "It's just a little gift," she murmured.

Mrs. O'Connor yanked the band of ribbon over the edge and tore the paper using her thumbnail like a letter-opener. Mom, who saved used giftwrap to recycle, would've loosened the strips so the paper wouldn't be destroyed. Now Mrs. O'Connor had reached the original box and was jerking at the lid.

"I taped it," Barbara confessed.

Splitting the cellophane with her thumbnail, Michael's mother lifted out the fluted vial filled with dried petals and muttered to herself, "Pot-poor-ee. Yardley's pot-poor-ee."

With the eagerness of a saleslady, Barbara said, "Scents for sachets, for your linens and your—" The image of the closet with the catsup bottle interrupted her explanation. She added lamely, "They really smell nice." But Mrs. O'Connor had replaced the lid on the box. She wouldn't be interested is making hand-stitched sachets for Christmas gifts like Mom.

Michael was beside her, resting his arm on her shoulder. "Barbara and I are going out."

"Oh." Mrs. O'Connor held up the box as if its small size revealed its lack of worth. "Nice, huh?" she muttered. Later Barbara learned Etta O'Connor returned every gift she could for cash refunds. The most experienced saleswomen in Westchester were intimidated by her, making exceptions for the bizarre customer who claimed she'd misplaced her sales-slip.

Barbara wished Michael wouldn't touch her in his casual yet intimate way in front of his mother, for the woman's eyes were fixed on them disapprovingly. But Michael tightened his grip as he said, "We're headin' over to Rye. Ronnie Shotes, the kid I graduated high school with, got married. Got a place in the new apartments on the edge of Rye."

His mother's eyes sparkled. "Rye? That Ronnie Shotes is

livin' in Rye? Whoda' believed it!''

"Yep. That's what he says, Ma." He turned Barbara toward the door behind them and they walked out.

In the driveway by the car, he took her jacket, and as he helped her put it on, she asked if they shouldn't have stayed to talk to his mother. He spoke with infinite patience. "She was gonna talk about money. I've heard it a million times."

"Oh." She let him button her coat, feeling as if she were six and he was her father preparing her to face the cold. His harsh judgment of his mother seemed confusing, but it could be remedied by love and understanding; she'd dedicate herself to changing him.

They drove in silence. Discussing his family might anger him. Ronnie Shotes was a safe topic. Her voice was childlike as she asked, "Who's Ronnie?" Stopped at the light, Michael stared at the curb littered with papers from the newsstand and the candy store. She spoke to his profile, "Ronnie, the newlywed in Rye." The word "newlywed" appealed to her. She spoke a little louder so he would understand. "Ronnie, who's Ronnie?"

As he shifted gears and screeched away from the light, she decided he'd been too preoccupied to hear her. He growled, "Ah, Ronnie's nobody." His gruff manner, his ruffled hair: he might have been a young Marlon Brando, or James Dean. She was filled with a need to mother him. He squeezed her knee. "Nah, forget about Ronnie." He winked. "I got other plans, Charley, a little surprise."

Warmth moved up her thigh. She traced a distended vein in the back of his hand. Being called Charley was so inappropriate, but the touch of toughness, the big-city sound of his strange humor, made her love him, in spite of her fear of a man who lied to his mother. She was disappointed not to be visiting the married couple, but curious about his surprise. She sighed, "Okay."

He pulled up in front of a building with a red neon sign. Afraid this was the surprise, she whispered, "What is it?"

He looked at her in mock disbelief. "You don't know? My dear, this is the Royal Sports Tavern, the watering hole for the future greats of America's ball parks."

She followed him into a dark barroom, noting with amused affection the character he became. His shoulders slightly hunched, his hands stuffed in his pants pockets, he swaggered by booths with tables lit by minature juke boxes mounted along the wall. He greeted the shadowy figures slouched behind their beers with a tilt of the chin or a wag of the head. The loudness of the series of grunts must determine the status of the person he addressed. All eyes were upon them by the time he stood at the bar. Not knowing her role in this ritual, Barbara felt nervous. She sensed her presence in this setting was an unusual event. If she misbehaved, his powerful position in this group might be damaged. All eyes watched Michael as he waited while the scrawny barmaid, with her back to them, filled a tray with glasses at the beer tap. When she turned with her loaded tray, he called, "Hiya, Eileen," just loud enough to break her concentration.

The tray shifted at a dangerous angle as she set it on the counter. "Jesus, Mary, and Joseph, it's Michael O'Connor." He let her fall over herself to reach him and kiss him on the cheek to hoots of "Hey, Michael."

When the hubbub subsided, Michael caught Barbara's hand, pulling her to his side to tell Eileen and his audience, "This is my girl from college." Eileen rubbed her hand across her apron before offering it for introductions. Her awed expression and the respectful hush in the room made Barbara feel foolish. Once Eileen, the housemother of the ragged fraternity, had overcome her shock at seeing Michael and his friend, she made introductions down the bar and commanded the couple to sit directly across from the tap, so she could call out snatches of conversation while she worked. As she set glasses onto a tray, she asked questions, then insisted on serving them a boilermaker on the house. Barbara didn't like beer and had never drunk straight whiskey, but she couldn't refuse this gesture of hospitality. Michael would be her guide: each time he drank, she'd drink. Pretending it was medicine, she swallowed. He finished his whiskey in a gulp and swallowed the beer in three. Shuddering as the whiskey flowed down her throat, she managed the entire process in six gulps.

The stool beside him was the spot where the informal receiving line ended. At ten-minute intervals, Mike's buddies sat on the stool, eyeing Barbara, waiting for their introduction. A sentence or two from Michael, a punch in the arm, a laugh followed by a slug of beer, and the stranger would drift back to the darkness. She met Bugsy and two other Mikes and a Jim and twin brothers named Fred and Fritz, and lost count of the number of drinks she and Michael had consumed.

If her bladder hadn't been bursting, she would have obediently sat beside him smiling and nodding at faces she could barely see. After Al Pichanini bowed his farewell, she tugged Michael's sleeve, whispering her problem in his ear. The question stumped him. A ladies' room: ladies didn't visit the Sport. He called to Eileen, who answered from the end of the bar loud enough to get several laughs, and Barbara got several more as she moved slowly across the floor, which had tripled in length since her arrival, until she reached the door marked "Queens."

She was glad the room was tiny, so she could propel herself from one spot to the next. Hunkered above the stool, afraid to let her flesh touch the chipped wooden seat, she felt as if a giant beer tap had been turned on inside her and a bottomless glass was being filled by her. Her arms cramped as she braced herself so her buttocks would not be contaminated. The floor undulated. To hold her head, she would have to sit on the stool. Life was too complex. She teetered in indecision, then surrendered herself to syphilis and sat, holding her head in her hands. She wished she could crawl to the darkest corner of the room, curl up against the wall and sleep. But Michael couldn't rescue her here. If she could lift herself and navigate the journey to the sink, she could splash water on her face to gather enough strength to get her back to Michael. Twisting her torso to reach the handle behind her, she saw a whirling kaleidoscope. Her mouth filled with bitterness. More easily than the liquid had flowed down her throat, it began to rise. Confused by the sudden watering in her mouth, she managed to scramble from the toilet seat and fall to her knees before the bowl. With a retch, the gush of waters left her. She knelt on the floor afraid to swallow again, afraid to move. After a few moments, a tiny, involuntary swallow moved through her throat into her breast. She was better. She'd be all right.

Her hair parted severely and combed with deliberation, her gray lips brightened by a slash of lipstick, she walked back to the bar with the care of a hospital patient taking the first walk after surgery. With each step, she muttered, "You'll be all right." As she sat at his side, Michael patted her knee. His sobriety mystified her. Eileen whirled by on a trip to the booths, leaving a cup of coffee and an order, "Drink this." Michael hung one arm about Barbara's shoulder and held the cup to her lips. The steam warmed her face, the odor filled the top of her head. He kissed her on the temple and murmured, "Ready for the road, Charley?"

He drove slowly through the old neighborhood, pointing out where the shortstop from his high school used to live, stopping for a moment before the house of Fritz and Freddy, acting out a role of their father the baker, who weighed at least three hundred and had rotten teeth. The fifteen-minute journey home took thirty-five with his commentary. His enthusiastic energy was contagious, and she had begun to feel almost normal when he eased the car to a stop beneath a tree in front of his house. As the tires squealed along the curb, he scolded, "Whoa, Nelly" and patted the dash as if it were the neck of a horse. Then he turned

to Barbara. "If you'll come here, my dear," he stroked the
seat beside him, "I'll tell you the story of the great pitcher,
Michael O'Connor, who once lived in this very neighborhood." He traced her chin with one finger. "Who once
lived," his voice cracked with tenderness, "in this humble,
little house."

She let herself be pulled toward him, drawn by the
warmth of his breath on her face, the odor of beer and whiskey and shaving lotion. Dizzy, she nestled her cheek on the
wool of his coat and murmured into the curve of his shoulder, "Oh, Michael."

He shrugged so she had to lift her face and look at him.
He pinched her chin with his thumb and index finger and
looked into her surprised eyes. "But my dear, it's true." He
touched his lips to her nose, her chin, her lips, then groaned
softly. She trembled when his tongue brushed her lips but
didn't attempt to escape his hands holding her face. She
moaned, "Michael," feeling his tongue touch hers, hearing
his breathing quicken, knowing he wanted her in this cold,
cramped car.

"Um," was his muffled acknowledgment. Without releasing her, he managed to scoot himself from beneath the steering wheel and push her across the seat. His fingers burrowing into her bra were cold. Her heart ricocheted against his
palm. Kneeling above her, he touched her breast and kissed
her neck. She arched her back, wanting him to tear away her
blouse and kiss the valley between her breasts to her navel.
His fingers might slide where her vagina was growing warm
and wet. The word excited her. She wanted him inside her.
Shamed by her thoughts, she turned her face with a whimper. His fingers worked at her buttons. Her arm pressed
against the seat was growing numb. She clenched her free
hand into a fist to keep from helping him. He pulled away.
She closed her eyes, her dry throat constricting. They must
stop. She heard the release of a buckle, the whine of zipper
teeth unlocking. Covering her face, she said what she didn't

mean and knew wouldn't be heeded, "No, Michael, no." He held his hand over hers, guiding it to his penis. As they jerked the stiff, trembling cock, she prayed he wouldn't come on her. He bent over her, kissing her mouth, her breast. Behind her closed eyes, she saw gold.

The car shook with pounding on the window above her head. Michael fell over her to hide their nakedness. "Oh, God," she whispered, cold and stiff with fear. Releasing his penis, which had shrunk to a soft warmth, she wormed her hand between their bodies, pressing her back into the seat as if she might disappear. Sandwiched between the unyielding seat and Michael's hammering chest, she watched the fogged window beyond his profile. Her tension began to release: he would fight to protect her. She turned her face to the dash where the faint light of the radio glowed.

He whispered harshly, "It's okay" and abruptly rose, leaving her naked and shivering as he yanked his coat about himself and threw hers over her. "Button up," he commanded, oblivious to her inability to locate the armholes as he fumbled with his zipper and swiped at his face and hair. "Come on," he pulled at her, "sit." He jerked her coat across her breasts, "It's Pop."

Through the steamy window, Pop's hulking form was silhouetted by the porch light. She stared at her hands as Michael reached by her to roll down the window. She prayed Mr. O'Connor would turn away, but he stood his ground, less than an arm's length away. Her chin trembled as she attempted an innocent pose. She could not force herself to look at him. "Evening," he said, his gruff voice filled with accusation.

"Evening, sir." Michael fumbled with the keys in the ignition. "Just talking, sir," he muttered, shoving the keys in his pocket and buttoning his coat.

"Good," growled Mr. O'Connor, not moving.

"We'll be in in a minute, sir." Michael said slowly, angrily. Hugging her coat about her, she dared to look toward the window. Mr. O'Connor was walking toward the house. He was wearing his nightclothes. Hearing their car, he must have thrown on a robe and come to the street. Michael touched her hand. "It's okay," he watched his dad's broad back, "really."

In the morning, she woke early but was afraid to leave the bed. Occasionally, she heard a deep voice. Mr. O'Connor must be telling his wife about the scene last night. He was probably still wearing his pajamas and a bathrobe. To face those angry blue eyes would be too humiliating. She scrunched beneath the covers to be closer to the foot of the bed away from the mounted head, so if it fell, it wouldn't hit her. She'd listen for Michael and not get up until she heard him.

It was noon when footsteps on the hollow wooden stairs woke her from the fitful sleep of a flu victim. Her body ached and her mind was weary of the flashing images of scenes in the car. The memory of the urgency of Michael's need seared through her. Oh, Michael, Michael, Michael: the name made her warm, his voice made her pulse quicken—seeing him walk across campus, or enter a room, she felt a rush; touching her hand to her heart, its palpitations were like those of the tiny Easter bunny she'd had when she was a child. This was a strange disease. Without him, she was a hollow rubber doll; with him, all of her senses magnified. She threw back the covers and sat shivering in the cool dusty room, anticipating his knock at the door. His quiet rapping set her skipping across the worn carpet. Trembling in her long flannel nightie, she peered around the door into Michael's face. His tan had faded to a yellowish hue, and his eyes were the gray of a foggy sea. "Michael," she said slowly, enjoying the sound of her favorite name of all, one she'd written on her notebooks during lectures in every imaginable style. Recently, she'd been experimenting with "Mrs. Michael O'Connor."

Although it was Saturday, Etta O'Connor was gone.
Saturdays were Mom's marathon cleaning days, yet the
house her mother attacked as dirty was infinitely cleaner
than Mrs. O'Connor's had ever been. The woman's disregard
for her hopelessly filthy house was so baffling that Barbara
couldn't mask her amazement when Michael said his mother
was shopping.

Staring into a kitchen cupboard, he searched for clean
cups for their coffee. "Mom's a big-league shopper," he said,
rejecting a cracked cup and turning to the sink to see what
was there. "She shops on Saturdays, and Sundays—if she
can find a place open—lunch hours, after work, at night.
She'll window-shop if nothing's open."

Barbara wished she could press a wrinkle in her jumper,
but she didn't want to burden Michael with the chore of
finding an iron in this house. She wondered why Mrs. O'Connor, who had such disregard for possessions, would be interested in acquiring them. She stared at the bag that had been
on the table since her arrival.

"Loves shopping." He poured coffee, consisting of thirty
percent grounds, into the cups he'd found, took a sip, swallowed, and shuddered. "Wow, that's real crap." He held up
his hand as a warning. "Forget it, Barbara, unless you
wanna get sick."

She nibbled at her fingernail, studying his face to see if
this pained him. But he was reaching across the table to
check the bag for a roll. He sniffed, then curled his lip,
tossed the roll back in the bag with a thunk, and shook his
head sadly. "Jesus, they musta been two days old when she
bought 'em." He crumpled the sack and tossed it on the
table. "If she'd been around, she'da bought Manhattan.
We'd be millionaires today if she'd had wind of that bar-
gain." He wiped his finger under his eye as if maybe . . .
"Christ, she'da loved it. A get-rich scheme with no work is
Ma's dream." He looked away from her to ask, "Well, kid.
Wanna split?"

She shrugged then nodded. Her silence caught his attention. He stood beside her, his face concerned. "What's wrong? Worried about the old man? Forget it. He's gone. Working overtime. Won't be home till Sunday morning by the time he logs his drinking time."

She smiled at his ability to read her mind. Perhaps he'd stoop to kiss her. She looked into his eyes and thought, kiss me, kiss me, and he bent his head toward her so she closed her eyes.

Michael decided to drive to Manhattan. He managed to find a place to park on the West Side not far from Central Park. Preparing to leave the car, he buttoned her coat and turned up her collar. He rubbed her hands between his and asked, "What's on the agenda, kid? The Statue of Liberty? The Empire State? Central Park Zoo?" He kissed her nose. "Or will it be the Guggenheim? Lincoln Center?" She smiled, speechless in the face of all of these options.

The day was so cold the bones in her face ached. Even through their linked arms, she felt him shiver when gusts of wind hit them. As they almost ran along the street parallel to the park, he sang snatches of old lyrics, repeating his favorite, "The Sunny Side of the Street." This was more exciting than her last trip to Manhattan. When she was ten, her father had been the family's guide. He had been so intimidated by the hostile drivers, the push and shove of the pedestrians, and the disdain of the shopkeepers that they had spent most of the day wandering aimlessly. Mom had not even tried to hide her contempt for Dad's failure.

At the stoplight at 59th and Fifth Avenue, she stared at the park to their left, then a white wedding cake of a hotel called the Plaza to their right, and towering buildings in the distance for as far as she could see. This city would be their playground after they married. She must show him how she belonged here. He leaned toward her, speaking loud enough for the pedestrians to hear, "Should we skip the tour and check into the Plaza?"

She blushed at his outrageous suggestion, but she let him put his arm around her and snuggled into his shoulder in what Mom would have described as a "cheap public display of affection." The Plaza could be the setting for a rendez-vous where she might lie beside Micheal in a sumptuous suite on satin sheets. At her request, they walked through the lobby, where Michael dared to sit in a giant wing-backed chair and suggested they explore the hotel. They passed a haughty porter to get on the elevator to ride to the seventh floor. Alone in the ornate decor of the halls, silent with the serenity of money, they pretended they were going to their suite. In the lobby they passed the Palm Court; she glanced inside. Each table was set with white linen and a crystal bud vase with a single yellow rose. Not wanting to risk rejection by the waiter, she refused Michael's offer to buy her a cup of coffee. She murmured that their time was too, too precious to waste.

On the street, they stood within arm's reach of a dappled-gray horse harnessed to a hansom cab. She wanted to stroke the horse's nose. Instead she glanced at Michael, who looked longingly toward the park and asked what she wanted to do. She was sorry to be so indecisive. Defining her desires was as difficult as writing a composition for her English class; each sentence she formed was so flawed she couldn't bear to complete it.

Michael petted the horse's nose, calling him "big fella," and unaware of the coachman's cross look, asked, "Wanna pet 'im, baby?" The coachman waved his quirt at the in-truder. Realizing his blunder, Michael linked arms with Barbara to lead her to safety. "How about a tour of Central Park?"

For more than hour, he led her through the winding lanes of the park. Then F.A.O. Schwartz provided them with a side trip. Lionel trains with miniature villages and plaster of Paris hills delighted Michael. He must have been a charming child. He said they ought to hop a freight to go out West. In the basement of the store, they picked out the log cabin where they'd live together. At Tiffany's he guided her by the disapproving personnel to evaluate which tiara and ring would be bestowed upon her at her coronation.

Michael decided she had to see Greenwich Village, and a ride on a subway had to be part of the New York tour. The dank air and darkness of the tunnel and the clatter of the train on the track frightened her. As they boarded the crowded train, he ordered her to take the one vacant seat near the door, so she sat a quarter of a car away from him. The faces of the passengers were uniform in their detachment. Realizing she was staring, she read the ads above the windows, studied shoes, and then, because he was as aloof as his fellow travelers, she analyzed Michael. She pretended she did not know him and tried to guess who he might be. He must be from a wealthy family. Her mother always said people with old money weren't concerned with clothing. His khaki windbreaker might have come from Abercrombie and Fitch, yet it was faded with wear and the turned-up cuffs of the sleeves were slightly soiled. In spite of his shabby clothes, Michael might be the only son of a senator from New York.

He must have felt the intensity of her gaze, for he turned to her and smiled, lifting his eyebrows as if to say, "What goes?" She loved his face: the curiosity in his eyes, the lines about his mouth from his frequent smiles, the sensitivity of his lips, the slight flaw where his angular nose had been broken. He winked at her, a gesture of such intimacy she blushed although she knew no one watched them. She couldn't lift her eyes to look at him again—this boy, the only man with whom she'd slept, the one who made love to her on a deserted beach in her recurring erotic dream.

It was dusk when they reached Greenwich Village, and Michael said he needed a drink. In a basement café with sawdust on the floor, they sat in a dim corner where he quickly downed three beers. He asked the waiter, "When you gonna clean the hamster cage?" and ordered a boilermaker. Michael finished the whiskey in one gulp and chugged the beer, and when an effeminate folk singer began to wail, "Blowin' in the Wind," stood abruptly, saying, "Bleedin'-heart liberal fags need punchin' out." He grabbed her hand to pull her to her feet.

They hurried by craft shops, bookstores, and florists until they reached a liquor store, where he bought a fifth of whiskey, dropped the bottle top in the gutter, and twisted the paper bag about the neck to drink "Prohibition-style." As he drank, he grew more talkative. Walking by a branch of N.Y.U., he said, "My mother's baby brother, Sean Murphy, teaches here." He pointed with the whiskey bottle toward the iron gates. "Dr. Murphy, professor of Irish Literature, could put those goons at Oneonta to shame." He glared at her. "Got a Ph.D. from Columbia, a Fulbright at Dublin, taught at Harvard, has a chair at N.Y.U."

Michael sounded so defensive Barbara was puzzled. Educators were usually ridiculed by him. She said lamely, "He must be very special."

"Nah, he's a bastard, an arrogant asshole, but smart, smart as hell." He took a sip, wiping his sleeve across his mouth, and then he took a long swallow and shuddered. They walked without speaking and his silence became so intense that she didn't dare to look at him, as he paused to sip from the bottle. She was wondering how she might break this frightening silence when Michael pitched the bottle so it smashed in the gutter. A bottle thrown with such force could have damaged a car, a plate glass window, a pedestrian. She didn't scold. His unleashed wildness might turn on her. He might shake her, or hug her. She must persuade him to drink some coffee, or eat, so he'd sober up. Tentatively, she slipped her hand beneath his upper arm. He looked down at her with bright, fierce eyes.

"You think I'm a shit, dontcha?"

She was as stunned as if he'd slapped her across her face.

She'd never had such a thought. Michael was the love of her life. Pained by his anger, she wanted to lead him from the filthy street to some place warm and clean, some place where she could make him feel her overwhelming love for him. But as she reached up to touch his cheek, he dodged her hand. Tears glistened in his eyes. But he let her touch his sleeve. She wanted to say, "I love you," but she could never speak the phrase unless they were in bed in the dark, where she might manage to whisper it.

He stared at the sky, closed his eyes, swallowed hard, and said, "Ah, shit." He violently shook his head, brushed his eyes with the back of his hand, and held the hand toward her. The gesture saddened her. A stranger might judge it as insignificant, but to take Michael's hand was acceptance, to ignore it rejection. She clasped his hand and they embraced, rocking silently as she asked, "Can we go somewhere?" He nodded.

In the sleazy hotel, the elevator rose with a palsied shudder. Alone together in the small, stuffy room, Barbara escaped to the bathroom. She turned on the reluctant taps to disguise her activity and sat on the closed stool. Repeating to herself how she loved Michael did not cleanse her of debauchery. The passion she'd felt for him on the street was a knot of nausea resting in the back of her throat. She should turn off the water and go to him. Covering her eyes, she pressed her fingers into her brows as if the pressure might make her see clearly. She spoke to God. When Michael knocked on the door, she felt a release. God was telling her to give her life and will to Michael.

She let him undress her, then lay down beside him. She wanted to pull the heavily starched top sheet over their bodies, which were washed with the harsh neon of city lights. His lips were dry and feverish kissing her forehead, her eyelids, her cheeks, her mouth. She'd permit him to do whatever he wanted, but she wouldn't respond. The whiskey on his breath set off a tremor within her that he might mistake as passion. Her interior monologue held her immobile as he touched her. This was a rendezvous; this was sophistication: Manhattan, a lover, stolen hours in a hotel—all the elements of fantasy. But she didn't feel like a woman whose lover was going to war. She couldn't improvise a scene of great passion. The hotel was dingy. Michael was drunk. Her body was bony. Behind her tightly closed eyes, she tried to remember how she'd felt last night. In the dark, cramped car, she'd been on fire, wanting him. They'd always made love in cars or on the sagging divan in his apartment before his roommates came home. Now no one would bother them, yet she might have been a doll stuffed with sawdust as he turned her about, arranging her for his pleasure. His silence enraged her. She hated him for sneaking, for lying, for using her. He could be a pervert, raping a store dummy. She silently wept, forgetting she was the one who had asked to come here, forgetting she'd stroked his trousers until she'd felt his penis stiffen. He was fondling her clitoris, touching her too hard, but she said nothing. Anyone would know the movement was wrong, and this hotel was where men brought whores. She sniffed loudly and covered her eyes with her forearm.

As he stared down at her, she cried convulsively. At his touch, she curled away, jackknifing her knees, burrowing into a tighter ball at each of his questions. Finally she let him cover her and rock her until she drowsed. When she woke, he was sitting on the foot of the bed, fully dressed, smoking and watching her. For a moment, she didn't know where they were. He touched her ankle. "Let's get outa here."

On the deserted subway, he told her autocide was a foolproof way to commit suicide and leave insurance for the surviving family—a swerve of the wheel and death would be instantaneous. He would drive his car into a concrete pillar if she left him. His eyes were solemn. He must love her more than anyone ever had. As he slouched beside her, holding her hand, her mind raced with plans for their life together.

The drive back to Mt. Kisco was silent as dawn was breaking. She wanted to ask if his parents would be waiting. Rounding the corner of his block, she expected to see Pop in the yard in his bathrobe, glowering at them, and Ma peering out the dining room window, clutching a cup of her bitter coffee. But their yard could have been any one in the neighborhood. Michael stooped to pick up the newspaper, skimmed the headlines, and tossed it back on the ground, covering their tracks so his parents wouldn't know of the all-night adventure.

It was noon when she crept down the stairs. Wearing a skirt and sweater and penny loafers, she hoped she looked like a girl from *Seventeen,* not a harlot who slept in fleabag hotels. Michael was alone at the cluttered table, drinking coffee. The overcast day was a day for staying inside. They could read the Sunday paper with Jim and wait for the folks to come home from mass. Ma would have dinner at two. Or they could drive to a lake where Michael had gone as a kid. A long drive to a lake was far more inviting than an afternoon at the table with his crazed parents. She eagerly found her coat and followed him to the car.

The sand was deeper, the water darker and colder than she had imagined. Michael walked beside her, his hair ruffled by the brisk wind, his sallow coloring almost healthy in the damp air. Hanging onto his hand, she trudged through the sand trying to keep up with him. His silence was as brittle as the cracked ice that bordered the lake. As he stared at the jagged edge of frozen water, he began to talk in a low voice, his words lost except for "sorry." He must mean her failure in bed last night. She crouched in the sand, emptying her shoes, a clumsy diversion.

Kneeling beside her as she fumbled with her shoes, he was within arm's reach. "I'm sorry, Barbara. Sorry about—"

"It's all right." She emptied her shoe in spite of the futility of the action.

"It's not all right. I made you think," his voice quaked, "things here are different from what they are." He began to pick at the sand and flip grains back on the beach. "Jesus, I made up a lot of stories at Oneonta. Made everybody think that I'm from somewhere special." He looked past her into the murky water. "But those rubes, Christ, it was so easy—"

"I'm from Oneonta."

He dropped a fist of sand. "Christ, I've done it again." She hugged herself, wondering, Rube, what does he mean by rube? He dusted his palms. "I mean, I lied." As the powerful word sank in, he dug sand that fell back in place as quickly as he scooped it. "Yeah, I made it sound like my folks had money. My old man was somebody. My old lady— well, that she wasn't like my old lady." He squinted as if it were hard for him to see her. "Like, you didn't think my family would be like they are, right?"

"Well . . ." She couldn't say how appalled she'd been by their crudeness.

"I made them seem like something they aren't."

"It's all right," she whispered. Resting her chin on her knee, she felt as serene as the still waters. No need to question the purpose for her life. Her reason for being was Michael: to love him in a way he'd never been loved, heal him, mother him, protect him.

The voice of Mildred, the swing-shift waitress, cuts through the reverie. "Hey, Barb, why the hell are you still here?"

Barbara sets down the saltshaker she's been filling. Mildred stands in the kitchen doorway, a quizzical grin on her face. Apologetically, Barbara asks, "It's after five?"

"Oo-ee, wish I loved my work the way you do." Barbara smiles shyly. She's rarely included in the jokes of the restaurant workers. Hurrying to the kitchen to punch out, she's eager for the busride home for time to scheme. She's been lost in the details of their lives for thirteen years. Mom says people can't see the forest for the trees. Barbara needs to see the trunks, the strong arms holding the leaves. As she places her card in the time clock, she feels happy, a feeling she hasn't felt in a long time. Hope: there's hope. She'll change him, change their lives.

Amy isn't home and Flossie doesn't know why. The familiar grayness starts to spread through Barbara. She must not let it overtake her. Amy will show up and there is dinner to prepare. As she stands before the interior of the cluttered refrigerator, the phone rings. A man announces himself as Mr. Crandall; the name is unfamiliar. He pauses as if he expects her to know him, then identifies himself as Amy's teacher. There must've been an accident; her pulse quickens. But his voice is calm. "There seems to be a problem. Amy left school this afternoon without permission. Ran from the supervisor when she called. She seemed very distraught." As he enumerates each of the irregularities, Barbara twists the phone cord. This is the teacher who thinks Amy is bright, cooperative. He's asking a question. Something about a conference, wanting to see them before school in the morning, wanting to know if it's convenient . . .

"No. It's not convenient." The sound of her anger is surprising. "But if it's necessary, we'll be there."

He's trying to calm her, explaining the logic, but she cuts him off. "We'll be there," and she slams the receiver on the hook.

Huddled on the porch, Amy seems so small, so defenseless —a model good girl, not the problem child described by that incompetent teacher. Barbara kneels beside Amy, brushing the fall of hair along her cheek. She feels feverish but flinches at the touch of the examining fingers on her forehead.

"Oh, Mommy." Her face crumples.

Such emotion must be staged to cover guilt. Barbara

catches her by the shoulders and holds her at arm's length; this is the child of Michael, the granddaughter of Etta O'Connor, this child who rocks and moans like a widow at an Irish wake. Amy could have done what the teacher accused her of doing. Barbara says, "Amy," as if the word were a slap to jar an hysteric into the rational world.

"It was awful."

Barbara waits, willing to discover what has been so dreadful, and learns of Duane, of the terror of being touched by him, of the fear of someone seeing them, of how Amy had to run, propelled by shame. It is fear and shame that force Barbara through exhaustion day after day. Her children will not be shamed. She turns Amy's face to the light. "A boy forced you to kiss him? He attacked you?" Her baby was violated and no one cared, and she's to be brought to trial before she can go back to the classroom. Well, they will just see about that. First thing in the morning, Michael and she will set that teacher straight.

Chapter **10**

During silent reading, Mr. Crandall slips a folded paper on Amy's desk. She's still in trouble. His talk with Mom this morning wasn't punishment enough. There will be more. He must know about the absences. As she gathers her courage to open the note, she feels a burning in her bladder so intense she's afraid the urine will boil up inside and ooze on the desk seat, then run down her legs making a dark lake for everyone to see. She bites the insides of her lips for control. Mom finally figured out what Mr. Crandall meant when he said, "Amy's been absent once a week for the past few weeks." She knows about the ditching. He hadn't left class to call up Mom to talk about it, but adults are mysterious and powerful—like God—and trying to fool God was terribly, terribly wrong. She opens the note and reads in an instant, "Please wait in class during recess." She slides the note under her book. Be brave and honest: accept whatever punishment he gives without crying.

When the bell rings, he calls after the kids as they roar from the room, telling them he'll be along soon. He should be angry when the class ignores him, but maybe he'll be as gentle with her as he was with them. Crouching by her locker, she pretends to be looking for her sweater, an explanation for not rushing from the room. She must protect herself against the savagery of her classmates.

Mr. Crandall hitches up his pants and tucks in his shirt, and looks as if he'd love to be seated instead of standing. He points to the chair beside his desk and says, "Sit, we'll talk." He shuffles the spelling papers. "You did well on your test."

Amy plucks at the button on her sweater, wondering why he chooses to compliment her now, and manages to say, "Thank you." She got her spelling words right. But now that he knows about the ditching, being a good student doesn't matter: all the good papers will be forgotten. Now he knows she's a liar. On the days she ditched, she never imagined that Mom would know, that he would know—oh, Daddy, not Daddy too.

"You do nice work, Amy. Very nice work." The skin puckers at his neck as he clears his throat, getting ready to be cruel. "Would you like to move away from Duane? Switch seats so you're behind Marcy?"

She swings her foot violently. "I don't want to sit by Duane." The smell of Duane so near meant she'd never look up from the top of her desk.

"You don't like Duane any more?"

"No." She sneaks a glance at Mr. Crandall's face to see if he believes her; his jowls tremble like a hamster's as he bobs his head in serious concentration. It's safe now. "I don't like Duane."

"And why's that?"

She ducks her head. He must think she liked kissing Duane. She can't ever look at either of them again.

"You used to seem to like him. You helped him a lot. I appreciated how you helped him," his voice becomes very secretive, "because, as we know, Duane has some problems. But sometimes I saw you smile at him, you laughed together. I thought, Amy likes Duane—as a friend."

She can't speak because she might cry, but nods yes. Yes, she's helped him, liked helping him. She even liked him. But as she nods, Duane looms over her, looking down at her face, still wet where he licked it.

"He chased you, on the playground. Is that right?" He wants her to say yes. She draws her arms tighter. "And he teased you?" Her chin brushes her chest. "And he kissed you?" A curtain of hair falls about her face. "That wasn't your fault, Amy."

Fault: the word she chanted at mass until it hummed in her breast. Fault means wrong. He says she wasn't wrong. He doesn't know about the ditching. He's too good; he can't see evil.

Her tears make him look away. To give her time to stop crying, he's studying his chubby fingers. "I'm sure you were a friend to Duane."

No one should lie to such a kind, good man.

His voice is tense and quick. "Duane's older than you, Amy. And I'm sure he thinks you're pretty, very pretty. He may like you as a friend, probably does like you, but he is very attracted to you." He stops and his eyes flick across her face.

She pretends to understand in order to escape. "Oh." Attracted: he said it so carefully; it must be a nice word for doing "it." "You mean, he likes me, like that?" She wrinkles her nose with distaste. This is silly.

"Yes, that's what I mean—but I don't think Duane can be your friend, right now. He wants you too much as a girlfriend."

She shrugs. "Oh, well." How sad. The Duane she liked is gone. This is what she owes for being bad. She looks at the toe of her shoe. Afraid Mr. Crandall's soft body will disappear, she looks at his face. His little dark eyes are good. It will be all right. Even if Daddy never comes home until the middle of the night, drunk and stumbling and crazy, she can come here. It's all right here. Mr. Crandall thinks she's a smart girl. He likes her. Someday, the class might even believe she's good.

He smiles so his jagged, cream-colored teeth show. "This means you're okay, Amy?" She looks down and he brushes her soft curls at the side of her face, and she hopes she is pretty, so pretty he won't see how bad she really is.

On the run home, she decides it will make things better if she writes a confession to Mom about ditching. In catechism class, the nuns said it's necessary to confess sin. With a tablet and eraser, she will write a record of all of her bad behavior. "Bad three days." Maybe, she should add another half day to each of those for the time spent scheming. She never stole any money. Never got in Mom's purse. Never kept the change when she bought Dad's cigarettes at the Circle K. She'd kept the money that fell out of his pockets when he slept in his chair. Sold bottles from Mom's Pepsies, the quarts she bought because she had to carry them from the store and never took them back because she didn't drive the car. The money wasn't too bad. But calling school and writing notes with Mom's signature was forgery—that was evil. Sister Katherine said planning to be bad is far more serious than carelessness or acting on impulse. This confession she's writing should be organized. Mr. Crandall says organization is essential. She should start each sentence with "I."

The list of crimes gets longer, too long for the original two-paragraph plan. She ends the whole confusing paper with, "I love you, Mom. I'm sorry I was bad. Amy."

Amy hears the kitchen door open and Mom hurries through the room, leaving her purse on the counter. She's so fiercely energetic she'll never listen. She walks through the archway. Her face is startled, angry, but she accepts the envelope addressed to her. Watching her read, Amy prays to win her total approval so she won't tell Daddy. He must never know about his evil daughter.

Chapter **11**

Unlocking the kitchen door, Barbara is grateful the pain in her head hasn't traveled throughout her body. She has survived this day, a day when she might have been a yo-yo in some masterful expert's hand. She'd zipped from the restaurant kitchen, where the heat and stench from the dishwashers and stoves made her head swim, to the dining room, where her skin prickled in the air conditioning and her head throbbed from forcing her smile as she served customers at the dozen tables of her station. And all the while, her mind had been spinning, analyzing the events of the day. Late to work—of course, she'd called to explain she might be a little late, but still she'd trembled punching her card in the time clock. She decided her boss hadn't scolded her because he planned to fire her. She was queasy with tension, but there'd been no time for illness with every booth filled and a line of men waiting to be seated. By mid-morning, thoughts of Michael contracted her stomach into a hard fist. She barely made it to the restroom before she vomited.

It was after twelve before she'd been able to have a cigarette and coffee and examine the astonishing news that Amy was cutting school, more astonishing than Michael's benders. His fall had been coming, advancing as slowly and surely as the cold of winter. Staying out later and later, last night he'd come in too late to tell him about Amy. They hadn't spoken except in passing for days. The silence between them was full of her accusations of him. But Amy had seemed above the slightest suspicion. Still, there was that morning about a month ago when she wouldn't get out of bed until the covers were yanked from her and she was ordered to sit up. After a quick check of her eyes and her forehead, throat, and tongue, Barbara commanded Amy to dress and hurry to school. Oh, God, maybe she should have stayed home. At least they might have talked. That must have been the first truancy. The memory of the day is lost in the monotony of their routine. There must be a pattern to this wayward behavior. Amy's current helpfulness around the house was not a sign of maturity. Forcing Flossie to help her to clean the house and fix dinner was a plot to cover her tracks. Perhaps she does have a conscience, recognizes right from wrong, feels guilty enough to want to pay for misbehaving by being helpful. This afternoon, they'll have to have a long, calm talk, with no lecturing, so Amy won't be afraid. Amy mustn't fall in love with escape, love it better than reality.

As Barbara pushes open the flimsy kitchen door, she is oppressed by a stab of pain. All she wants to do is lie down in her darkened bedroom with a cloth on her forehead and her feet up. But she braces herself to be patient and insightful for the encounter with Amy.

Controlling her urge to clear off the kitchen counters and sweep up the crumbs and dust scattered on the floor, she sets her purse on the edge of the counter. The poverty of this house can't be be cleaned. The pits in the vinyl tile are filled with dirty wax, a pathetic testament to her attempts to make it better. She's never been able to resign herself to this shabbiness, to not care; because, after all, she doesn't own the place but is only one of the endless procession of renters. Yet she hates the cracked porcelain sink and the peeling paint. Living in this shoddiness makes her feel dirty.

She continues on into the heart of the house. Its stillness makes her feel uneasy. She unbuttons her sweater, the saggy yellow one her mother knit ten years ago, the one Michael calls "the shroud." Her stomach contracts, but she's purged. She has to keep moving. Nausea clutches her belly. Michael isn't home. She'd desperately hoped he'd be here—sober and easy—so they could talk, so they could mend their marriage. But he's not in the house—not tonight, maybe never.

She moves through the dining area in a few brisk steps, planning to get through the evening without hysteria, without letting the girls feel her terror. There is someone in this house. Someone in this room. A rapist. A thief. She stops, deciding whether to hide in the kitchen, to call out, or to advance with determination and face the intruder. God, let it be Michael. That sliver of hope is a hook pulling her forward. But his chair is empty, the indentations of his body in the sagging upholstery. She stops. One of the girls is seated on the couch. It's Amy, silhouetted in the dim room. What foolishness. Sitting in the dark. Playing a foolish prank. There's no time for nonsense. Amy. Flossie would never be so calculating. Touching the wall behind her, Barbara finds the light switch and traps Amy in a flood of harsh light.

She blinks her big eyes. The transparent glow of her skin belongs in a painting of an artist whose name Barbara can't remember, although she stared at his paintings, awed by their beauty. That angelic smile is Michael's. Michael's soft-sell is being rehearsed behind those eyes. Listen, be patient, dig your fingers into the loopy stitches of the old sweater, and hold on to be the audience for this performance. The Persian-cat face with those innocent eyes. Oh, God, Michael: this child could be no one else's daughter. Thirteen years with Michael, thirteen years a victim of the deceits of Ma's "blue-eyed-angel." And now his daughter—Barbara bites her knuckles to keep from slapping the sweet, calculating smile from Amy's face, to make her cry and tell the truth. Oh, God, she's my baby, only a baby.

Amy is offering an envelope, one of the messages from school about the P.T.A., from those women with time for worrying about whether or not the teachers are doing their job. Something to throw away. But Amy has written "Mom" on the envelope. The contents are written by Amy, not the act of a naughty child. The diligently formed letters are symmetrical; the words are arranged in sentences. This list of activities is shameful: lying, sneaking—things no good child does, nothing Barbara had ever done. But Mom and Dad were good examples. Amy lives with cheats. Through all of the silence of this family, Amy has felt how wrong their lives are. A spanking and tears, a hot bath and restriction to her room, will not return Amy's innocence. She is frightening. Smarter than any of them, more special, she'll outgrow everyone in this family.

Reading the note a third time, she says, "I see." The bright eyes are evaluating her response. My God, how much does she know about Michael? Replacing the note in the envelope, Barbara says, "I see" and doesn't see at all. She'd like to shred this note, but Amy is watching. Michael should see this. Oh, God, when will she accept he's a shadow who hides from them? Turning from Amy, she hurries to her purse for a cigarette. Disgust for her surroundings overcomes her, concern for Michael, for Amy. This place has got to be cleaned. She calls over her shoulder for Amy. They have to clean this house.

Barbara whisks through the bedroom. For thirty minutes, she and Amy silently work side by side, replacing possessions to their rightful places, preparing the evening meal. Even Flossie joins them, too frightened by their intensity to rebel. As Barbara stoops to pick up a sock, she sees stars. Sitting at the foot of the bed, she hears her short, choppy breathing. Her hands and feet are cold, her head swims. She breathes through her mouth to ease her panic. Amy is only one disaster. Michael is disappearing. He isn't coming home. His drinking, his damned drinking—she will have to make him stop or their lives can't continue. When they were reunited after his desertion, she'd promised herself never to be totally dependent again. But she's failed. Oh, God, she needs him more than she ever has. His loss is as frightening as death, beyond consideration. She's sat on this bed far longer than she intended to: she must breathe, breathe, and not think beyond each tiny task to perform. Confront him tonight. Force him to see what he's doing to them.

She is trying to light a cigarette as he pulls into the driveway. Her hands tremble so the flame of the match misses the mark. Since midnight, she's waited in this chair: she won't run. The children must be protected. He's deceiving himself and her, and by being silent, she's part of the deception, part of the betrayal of the children. The key rattles in the lock. She runs behind the chair, terrified as if a thief were entering her home. She can open the door or hide in the bedroom as she always has. Her heart seems to beat within her throat. The door opens.

He's cursing at the key, probably cursing her, saying how stupid she is for locking doors when he's told her a million times, "No way in hell you can lock out a fuckin' thief." He walks in the room, stuffing his keys in his pocket, looks at the light by his chair, and squints at the ring of brightness. His eyes look blind, frightened—afraid of news of a death in New York, an injury to one of the girls. In a cloud of whiskey, he backs toward the door. Then he sees her and pats his shirt pocket for cigarettes. The match flares. His pale irises, even in this shadow light, show hatred. He jams the cigarette pack in his pocket. "Christ, what is it?"

Her voice is scraped from her throat. "Your drinking." All the things she's thought to tell him, and this is what she says. He does just what she knew he'd do: turns, refusing to look at her. He won't hear anything. She moves from behind the chair. She'll grab him, hold his arms to his sides, force his eyes to look into hers: force him to state what he is. But the door behind him stops her. In a second, he'll be out that door. Dizzy with conflict, she can't hold back her harsh whisper, "Your drinking, your drinking."

"Shit." He holds the burnt-out match before him and looks hard at her. He seems too weak to run, so sick he might vomit. Dropping the match on the floor, he smears the charcoal tip across the worn carpet with his toe. "Shit."

He looks up from the smear. "Yeah, I been drinking." He snarls it with the tone he uses in traffic. He might as well have said, "Up your ass, buddy," or "What's it to ya."

He turns his face. "Yeah, well—" but his voice quakes. He won't speak again. He's telling his secret. He studies the floor, his temple pulsing as he tightens his jaw. He's going to go to the bedroom. There'll be no more confessions.

Her hands are fists, opening and closing. "Michael, you can get help."

He closes his eyes. "Jesus, God. Gimme a break."

"But Michael,"—she regrets the whine in her voice—"you need help." She rests her hand on her breast. "We need help. The girls. Me."

He shakes his head as if he'll shake her off and holds up a hand: his stop signal. No. He's preparing to make an oath, but he keeps his eyes closed as he carefully states, "I'll do it. I promise, I'll do it." She doesn't dare say, "I don't believe you can." But he rushes on to keep her from speaking. "Tomorrow, I'm quitting. I'm going cold turkey, tomorrow."

She whispers to his closed eyes, "Michael, it's already tomorrow."

He covers his eyes with his hands. "I promise. I promise. That's all I can do."

She watches Michael sleep. She almost strokes the skin across his shoulders, but waking this way would be too abrupt. The boyish Michael might come back, the lines of tension gone, the circles under his eyes erased, the spark of his teasing eyes returned. Those eyes. The first time she'd seen him at the Campus Bar and Grill, she'd glanced at them so often he'd finally noticed her and gotten up to cross the room, buying a Red Delicious apple from the basket by the register on his way, a gift for introductions. His manner had been so gentle the memory still makes her feel tender.

She'll brew the coffee and set it on his nightstand so the aroma will pull him out of sleep, out of his exhaustion. If he were well, and the girls were gone, and they didn't have to drag themselves outside for money, they could lie together all day, touching one another, kissing, finally making love. She turns from him and reaches for her robe. The dream is too painful, too remote.

As she places the coffee on the nightstand, she kneels beside the bed and watches him. The smell of the coffee does not penetrate his sleep. She speaks his name, louder and louder, feeling uglier as her volume rises. His eyelids flutter; his stare is hostile then resigned. He turns from her, lying on his side, watching the wall. "Okay," he says, hunching his shoulders as a response when she explains there's coffee. She waits for him to accept but realizes he won't turn until she leaves the room. In the silence of the kitchen, she's sorry she has nothing to offer him but coffee.

Chapter **12**

Seated on the edge of the bed, he sips the mug of coffee Barbara brought him, its heat radiating to his brain. Steam cuts the congestion in his nose, lungs, and chest, loosening up the phlegm. He stares at his feet. The nails need cutting. Christ, the skin is so white it's blue, dead white as the underside of a toad. A couple of swallows of Barb's coffee will get him going. Hold the coffee in your mouth as long as you can, a burning tongue means you're still alive.

The dream that flashed through his head during the three hours in the sack coulda been S-and-M stag movies with one violent scene right after the other. First the motel room and the faceless, voiceless girl, humping her dog-style, hating it, being really turned on—better sex in the dream than awake, weird but electric. Then the diesel—driving tear-ass through rock canyons, blasting the whistle, leaving a trail of black fumes. And another Big Mike dream; this one in Saint Cyril's, where they had Pop's funeral. The dream had to be on a Saturday afternoon, with the neighborhood women waiting in line for confession and a few old geezers in the pews, some of them kneeling, but most of them looking like they're waiting for a bus to Philly. In the front of the sanctuary, there's a big pine box. Three kids in short pants run right by the altar, yelling and laughing so loud the ceiling could crack. And a voice that could have been God bellows, "Silence!" The second time it yells, it's clear the voice from the casket is Big Mike's. Even death can't put the old guy away. For once, old Barb did a good turn. Waking up, even if it was to her face, was a relief. He sets the empty cup on the bedstand and sighs loudly. To get from this bed to the can has got to be the toughest thing he'll do today. After a cold shower, he makes his way to the kitchen.

Geez, she's still in there, making a big deal out of pouring coffee. She can sure make you feel like shit, and so goddamned lonely. Last night, ah, Christ, he should've fallen out that door into the long empty night before she made her moves, grabbing his balls and wringing them with her "drinking's a problem" scene. She wants a weeping martyr, a regular bleeding Jesus, creeping along with no balls. Christ, nobody knows about drinking—no righteous jerk-off who calls himself a doctor and never, never Barbara with her scared-shitless, dopey eyes.

He sits down at the table, but he's invisible. She's not getting the satisfaction of one word, not even a glance her way. Drink the second cup of coffee, crawl to the living room and get in the chair for a couple of hours.

She's moving around, looking real determined: a cat with a bird in her mouth. Last night wasn't one of the nightmares; it was for real. The little furrows between her eyes and at the edge of her mouth mean business. Jesus, she thinks she's making progress. There'll be no denying the conversation. He stares at the last half of the coffee and swallows around a lump of phlegm. Christ, she's got it all: a confession and a sentence. Sitting down, she squares her narrow shoulders, like she's ready to take on a load. Hard to believe two babies came out of that body, babies getting to be something he can't even imagine. At another time or another place, being with Barbara might've been better than good, but it's been so fucked for so long, one good moment and then there are weeks, maybe months, when the only way to take it is in the haze. The last of the coffee is cool and bitter. Shit. Running a fuckin' treadmill for her, all for her. Up and showered and dressed for her, going out on the goddamned highway selling paper for people to wipe their asses. It's a hell of enough for today, Barbara, just one hell of enough. First stop is Bloody Mary time. The thought's a lift. He looks across at her and manages a half-smile. Oh, Jesus, she's gonna cry. He looks at his empty cup. If she didn't think quitting just meant you stopped—no problem, Barbara, terrific plan, try it some time. Just not today. Better get up and out of here before she gets started. Just get some smokes. "Cigarettes." It's a voice from the grave, Michael O'Connor's died and gone to hell.

She's up, all in a swirl, to be a great waitress. Stretching to reach the top shelf, the soft skin of her inner arm tightens as she grabs a pack—that long white neck, that fragile jaw. Jesus, she's really pure sweet—all the others coulda been a drunken gang-bang. Married twelve years and still hasn't figured it out. Ah, anyway you slice it, she's easy to con. Now Pop and even Ma were a whole different story. They figured it out when he was sixteen and went to Jersey with a carload of guys to see the strippers and hit some bars. He ended up passing out—his first black-out. The guys got drunk but he got passing-out drunk. Fuckers just drove by the house and shoved his body out of the car into the gutter. Pop came out of that house screaming, "Leave the bum in the gutter," and Ma was hot on his heels yelling, "Yeah, that's where drunks belong." And after that there was no way they didn't know. Geez, Big Mike's claim to fame was spending a lifetime drinking but not being a drunk, but he sure as hell could tell one when he saw one.

Accepting the cigarettes, he brushes her cheek with a dry kiss. It's worth a thousand words. Get the hell outa this house before the kids get up. Those voices would be exquisite pain. And Amy's old lie-detector eyes would be the end.

In a Paradise Valley shopping mall, he holes up in an imitation English pub, congratulating himself on holding out so long: hell, it's eleven, he's set a record. One Bloody Mary will be a medicinal lunch—and this place is such a turnoff, you couldn't get loaded if you tried. Some fag decorator who thought he was Queen Elizabeth covered the walls with pictures of royalty. But the upholstered booth is okay across the shoulders and those milkmaid costumes on the waitresses show about half their jugs. The TV is right past the booth and there's a baseball game showing. Shitty luck, it's the skinny one's station. Her long, slim thighs are too much like Barbara's. Dammit, a Bloody Mary just won't cut it. Got to have beer with baseball. He tells her to just keep 'em comin'; he's going to watch this game.

By two, he knows if he doesn't get on the road he never will. And because the waitress is probably married to a bastard like him, he leaves her a pretty big tip. He feels better about only visiting two accounts today, but by all rights he should've called in sick. Damned responsible, considering his condition. By the time he reaches the entrance to Bashau's, he's looking for his breath mints, wishing he'd stopped at a filling-station john to spruce up a little. But Christ, it's probably three by now. And while he's debating what to do, he notices some weirdo pushing carts to the front of the store really staring, so he gives him the old "buzz-off-you-creep" look.

"Mike? Michael O'Connor?"

Jesus, it's the manager. What the hell's his name? No time to check the forms to get the spiel. A little cough into the fist to check for the smell of booze. What the hell, what's wrong with having a beer or two in the middle of the day? "Hi-ya!" Use the killer grip, confidence is the name of this game.

As Michael guns the car out of the grocery parking lot, he checks the clock on the dash. Jesus, thirty minutes felt like three hours. Lucked out with the "how-do-you-spell-your-name" trick with the manager, Marvin Behueler. But ol' Behueler's probably shaking his head after what he saw.

Really caught his eye with the old trembling hands pawing through the attaché case to find the fuckin' order forms. Christ, if the prick decides to call the distributor, they'll put his ass in a sling. But it's been pretty good with this store, up till now. Tomorrow just drop by, looking sharp. Do some fast talking.

Fat's looks like a working stiff's bar, a spot to get a drink for the road. He opens the door and pushes through a pair of swinging doors: nice touch, private. The place is a decent shade of dark, and it only takes three steps to get to the first stool in a line of stools so close you can rub thighs. Sounds like pool in the other room, some booths, even dancing. Three stools down from the door is even darker, except for the neon Miller High Life flashing with a rhythm to put you to sleep.

The woman sitting two stools away isn't the kind to look at twice—kinda bony, too many teeth. But her eyes are showstoppers: long, straight lashes like a pony's, and even in bar light her irises are such dark chocolate the whites look blue. "Wow, lady, you got a strange pair a eyes."

She laughs, shaking her golden, frizzed hair as if she's

just climbed out of a swimming pool. "Hey, that's nice." She strokes her long throat with a tanned hand with a ring on her middle finger.

The way she says "nice," that hair, that ring on the middle finger—this one's on the make. And on second glance, her body isn't skinny, it's slender. And the blouse that looked like a beat-up white one is really ivory silk. It shifts so the world can see the tan on her hands goes all the way to her belly and her small breasts are a lighter shade. The way she's leaning on the bar, a full breast shot flashes off and on. For a short space her skirt blocks the view, but the buttons down the front are undone midway up her thigh. One lovely naked leg is crossed over the other so when she swings her high-heeled sandal in a crazy circle, light dances on the glossy paint on her toenails. One stool closer and he could slip his hand under her skirt and very possibly discover she's wearing nothing else but warm flesh. He spins on his stool so he can face her. "Come here often?" Wow, what a line. She can't believe it either, but she laughs so lots of teeth show, then purses her lips to say dramatically, "I don't come here often. I live here."

"Oh, yeah?" He lights a cigarette and glances toward the john to see if some gorilla is coming their way to sit on the stool between them. Drunk or sober, this woman's too good to be alone. Hell, he's already sounded like a clod, might as well stay in character. "You alone here?"

She holds up her left hand and studies it. "That's a debatable question." There are four rings on the hand and the one on the ring finger looks a hell of a lot like a wedding band. "Right now, I'd say I'm alone, except for you, and I don't know if you meant for me to count you or not. But three hours ago, I walked through that door with three men: my friend, my husband, and his friend." She slaps her hand on the counter so the rings clang. "And do you see anybody?"

Her crazy eyes look so close to crying, he hasn't the heart to confess he has no idea what she's talking about. Leaning forward, he tries to sound reassuring. "I don't see anybody right now, except you. And I certainly notice you."

"Well, then I'm alone."

He could assure her she's somebody and therefore not alone, but getting closer so she'll have a shoulder to cry on is a real smooth move. "Mind if I move over?"

She shrugs and the flap of her shirt gapes for the full shot. So he makes his move before she makes up her mind. With their elbows on the bar, and their thighs inches apart, he decides to table the personal information quiz. He's calculating how to invite her for a ride when she turns, her chin on her knuckles, and rolls her incredible eyes. "Wanna dance?"

"Sure." Haven't danced in ten years, but this is progress. "Sure." And as he finishes off the beer, she spins her stool so her back is to him, then she stands. From the back, her sensuous costume is the girl next door dressed like a hooker. She teeters on her heels like Amy and Flossie playing in Barbara's shoes.

In the back of the room, behind the pool tables, five or six couples hug each other and slide across the slick floor. Following her into the room, it's a pleasure to watch her hips shift as she navigates the dangerously high heels. At the edge of the floor, she stops so abruptly to turn, they almost collide. She steadies herself against him so they stand nose to nose and she asks, "You dance, don't you?" as if it's just occurred to her that somebody might turn her down.

"Yeah," he lies, resting his hand on the small of her back, wondering what she'd do if he let it glide down to cup the apricot curve of her ass. By pulling her hand down to his side, she's forced to move closer—the old bear hug, specialty of the swingers at Mt. Kisco High.

She turns her chin so she's wedged into his shoulder. "Well?" She whispers, her breath warm on his neck, and her long leg slides between his. Drinking has turned their bodies into the music. A little hesitation, then a swirl, her body just rides along, smelling like lemon blossoms, with a little smoke thrown in, and her little breasts burn against his chest. Ah, she follows with no stumbling, no hesitation. This is screwin' with your clothes on, except you can do this all night.

By the second dance, he gets around the floor twice without opening his eyes. But now she's bored as hell, won't talk, sneaks looks at other people. He can't grip her any tighter, but he starts to hum along with the jukebox, hoping the extra involvement will get her back where she was. She laughs, like it's all been a joke, and says, "Um, a music man," and then the record is ending and he has to release her.

She backs out of his arms, stroking her hair, looking away awkwardly. The kid is not a pro. Somebody ought to grab her by the scruff of her neck and make her button up and get outa here. She's the original prick-tease. He catches her wrist. "Hey," he punches at her with the word, but she still doesn't stop staring across the room at a dark-haired man who glances her way once and looks away. "Hey, I'm talkin' to you, what's happenin'?"

She sighs loudly and with her hands on her hips looks at him. "Would you like to come home with me?" She's got a real dazzler smile. "My friend wouldn't mind. Our place can accommodate two, an extra bedroom—things like that."

"Um." This is something kinky. She's a strange one all right—exotic, with that kidlike face and the great body. But a nasty little mind. A really good girl gone bad can be the worst. Oh, shit, she'd want to get into some long, involved game. Got a husband, a boyfriend—"What'd you mean, your friend won't mind?"

She reaches out and holds onto the shoulder, like she's not going to let this one get away. "Ah, come on. I'd like to be with you." There's an edge of fear. She takes a step closer so she can whisper, "And really, they don't care, really."

"Don't care?" He's embarrassed at how husky his voice sounds. "Sure they care."

She shakes her head sadly. "Oh, you don't understand, but," she reaches out and plucks at his sleeve, "could you trust me?"

"Sure, yeah."

He follows her out of the bar and doesn't dare to take his eyes from her. Trust her, yeah, sure, God. Get rolled, punched out. Walk into a setup 'cause she's got a great body, 'cause she's a weird kinda turn-on. Geez, the parking lot is darker than the bar. Might get clobbered by some bozo, dragged into an alley. Phoenix is the unsolved-murder capital in the U.S. Kid's making pretty good time in those crazy shoes, getting pretty far ahead, could be good news, could be bad—What the hell time is it, anyway? Feels like midnight. But it's the top of the morning to the old bod—full a energy: nothing like being scared shitless to clear out the cobwebs. God, if that sappy crusader Barbara could see this. Hot on the trail of a hussy at midnight in Phoenix. She's stopping by an MG with a bashed-in tail. Fits. She's fiddling with her keys. Geez, where the fuck's the Mustang? Could use it as a getaway car. Follow the kid and if things get hairy, gun it, lose her.

He leans against the dented fender, enjoying the view as she bends forward to turn the key in the lock. Shit, go with her, come back tomorrow, next week, never. She straightens a sarape thrown over the seat to hide the torn upholstery and asks for some help to fasten the top back, says they need fresh air. She's a regular know-it-all, but that has style. Even her crappy car has a certain style. After she backs out of the parking place, she flips on the radio and carefully finds a station with some strange West Coast jazz. A woman who likes to make things pretty: that's heavy. Likes to drive like a bat outa hell too. He leans back in the seat, breathing deep, his eyes tearing in the cold wind.

The apartment house where she pulls up could be any one of a thousand milk crates in Phoenix—gray cinderblock, a two-story job, probably thirty units built around a pool. A little disappointing. Her class mighta come from money. The place doesn't even have garages. She parks her car in a spot with a number. On the ride over, he managed to get her name: Gwen Beckett, she says. Could be lyin', supposedly lived here three years, has a "friend," who splits the rent and whatever else she dishes out. Where's the fuckin' friend? He could be a lover, could be a fag, but for sure he's got some claim on her.

Weariness hits Michael in his knees as he climbs the concrete stairs behind her. His back and shoulders and neck are knotted by the time they reach her apartment. Staring down at the collection of cacti she's got around the door, he waits while she screws around with the key. Turning it, she says, "See, there's nobody here."

Sounds like one hell of a setup, fighting off two guys, who'd go for the groin; poor old Charger flattened by some goon's knee. She flips on the lights. It's a little apartment and as odd as she is. A six-foot square painting that looks like an explosion in a paint store covers the west wall, and the place is a jungle with plants hanging from the ceiling, stuck in every corner. The furniture's a strange combination: antiques and chrome and glass. Baskets cover one wall. The place oughta look like a mess, but it all fits—a page right out of an interior decorator's magazine.

He sits in a white, overstuffed chair she points to before she disappears into what must be the kitchen. This place is immaculate—quiet, too. Maybe she lives with rich hippies. They like weird shit. She's real quiet in the kitchen. Hey, you're not gonna get killed or get your face smashed. Old Charger might even get charged instead of stomped.

She comes in carrying a tray with a couple of glasses, a couple of beers, and a box. Taking a bottle, he says, "Well, Gwen Beckett," trying it out to see if the name's a phony.

She sits on the floor by a rosewood table. "Sounds fictitious, doesn't it?"

He holds the bottle, not wanting to mar the perfectly

waxed surface of the table. "Yeah, you're right." He glances furtively toward the bedroom. Where's the fuckin' friend? What the hell is this?

She laughs and starts to light a cigarette. "My friend's not here. He's not coming home tonight. I told him I had plans."

Michael takes a long drink. She's probably twenty-three, twenty-five tops, and really into screwin' around a lot. Sure doesn't look like she oughta be. "Do your plans include me?" She looks kinda spunky thinking that one over. Well, Jesus, she's got him here in Phoenix without a paddle. "Got somethin' on your mind?"

After one drag, she stubs out her cigarette. "Well, sure." She lifts the lid of the box on the tray and holds it up so he can see it's filled with joints rolled in orange and blue papers. "Want one?"

"Nah. You smoke that shit?" He straightens from his slouch, repulsed by the idea of the crap touching her lips. Potheads are creeps. Sitting in a circle and passing a joint is in there with being a fag.

She shrugs. "Makes me feel good, so why not?"

He slouches back in the chair. Feeling good is a powerful argument. She holds a blue one toward him, but he holds up a hand. "No way." She lights it and inhales with a hiss, holding the smoke inside for a long time. With her eyes closed and her head thrown back, she could be screwin'. After the third toke, she sets the joint on the edge of the ashtray and takes off her shoes very slowly. Then she begins to giggle about wasting her "poison." She holds the joint in her lips and points to the hi-fi. He can barely understand her as she repeats, "Record." She points at him and then at the record. She expects him to put it on to play. She's back to her smoking before he gets a chance to tell her they're getting off on the wrong foot. Housework and chores are for women.

Her record collection says a lot. The record jackets have

names like words on a Scrabble board. At least the Buffalo Springfield has a decent country scene on the jacket instead of some degenerate strutting around with a microphone jammed into his teeth. The On and Off switches and the tuner buttons are confusing, but the queen is so into her marijuana she can't be bothered. After fiddling with it for a while, the sound comes through, violins and guitars and a mournful cowboy wailing. He turns to see if she approves. She's lying on the floor on her back with her ankles crossed and her hands folded on her belly. Her blouse has fallen open so her breasts are framed by the ivory silk. She stares at the ceiling, then turns. "See. You figured it out."

He has to laugh. She's some weird kinda psychic. This is the third time she's told him what he's thinking as he's thinking. Being read so easily is sorta scary, kind of a turn-on. She lifts her arm to shield her eyes from the light and her small breasts rise. "The light," she says, and he gets up and walks toward the switch. In the dimness, he looks down at her. There's a naked V from her throat to her waist where the shirt bunches into her waistband, and there are three big buttons holding the skirt closed before it flares open over her thighs. She looks as if she might be asleep with her head turned to the side, her face pale in this light. He steps carefully around her so he won't disturb her and almost trips when her hand catches his ankle. She giggles, "Whoa, big fella."

He looks down at her teeth and crinkled nose. Her eyes are pinched shut, convulsed with laughter. What's the joke? He sighs and kneels beside her. In a couple of moments, she stops laughing and manages to open her eyes. She pats him on the thigh. "That's a good fella."

He touches her hand, hoping it will sober her some. He sure picks the winners. "Hey, do you do this often?" Being somebody's joke isn't funny.

She turns her face away. "Would you believe me if I told you the truth?"

Jesus, what a line. He settles onto his haunches and pats his pocket for a cigarette. "Lay it on me." A beer might go good with this.

She lifts herself on the elbows, rakes her finger through her hair, and now her face doesn't look like a kid's. "You're pissed aren't you?" She sounds real surprised. She fingers the top button on her skirt. "Sorry."

Her little pose with her head hung and her lower lip pouting makes it easy to forgive her—a sexy, cute kid, a bit of a bitch, all sorts of things, but it's good, sitting here now. He reaches out to touch the hand fiddling with the button. She gives him a sidewise glance and a smile that asks, "You're not mad?" He traces the delicate bones fanning from her wrist. "Forget it."

She throws back her frizzy hair and is laughing again, but this time it seems like she's laughing for herself. Then she's humming and then, just out of the blue, she says clearly, "Let's fuck."

He almost says "What?" "Fuck" is not a word she oughta be saying. Decent women talk about "making love" or "going to bed," nobody talks about "fucking" but whores. But she's flopping onto her side, moving closer so her little tits bounce a few times. She plants her elbow on the floor, props her face on her hands, and she speaks like a Motown star. "Wanna get it on?" She taps her fingers provocatively on the carpet and races them toward him.

He's getting the hell outa here. This flashing in and out of character is too much. Now her face is a vixen's, narrow, pale, bright-eyed. She's scooting toward her prey, her hand scurrying in front of her like some kinda spider. Her forefinger's tracing the balls. Her palm's on old Charger, giving him a nice little squeeze. Oh, God, have mercy: she's got her a hard-on.

She's on her knees, moving right in between the knees, unbuckling the belt, unzipping the fly. Jesus, he could be a baby, the way she's pushing him around. But old Charger isn't losing interest while she pulls off the shoes, the pants, unbuttons the shirt. Man, she's after that cock like no good girl he's ever known. Women do cocks as a favor, to get in good. Jesus, Barbara has to be begged, such a martyr it's no good. But this Gwen is some kinda wild woman. She's pinned him, fondling, stroking. God, she's—Oh, Jesus, old Charger is driving into the dark cave ready to explode into light. Christ, she's pulling away.

He opens his eyes. What the hell's happening? She's climbing aboard Charger, hitching up her skirt where there is, in fact, nothing on underneath. She's wet and warm and slides right on. God, he's got the whole shaft right into gear. He's dopey with sex. She's wearing her half-on-half-off clothes, rocking back and forth, burning inside. She's working at the buttons of her skirt, taking it off, and then the blouse, and as she undresses, she's laughing, saying, "Hey, big horsey," her nose crinkles, "wanna gallop?" She slows her rocking to a rhythmic gyration of catch and leap: "Or do you wanta trot?" She shifts quickly up and down, teasingly close to leaving. As she swings her blouse above her head as if it's a lariat, she's laughing, they're laughing, something he rarely does during sex. Up till now, it wasn't a laughing matter. Then she lets her blouse fly, and she falls on him, warm and exhausted, her little heart racing. "I feel like a frog fucking," she whispers and they laugh as her knees and calves pull tightly to his side as if she were doing a frog kick. "I'm a sex jock." She shifts so she's a long line on top and lifts herself so her tiny breasts are just a kiss away. "If you'll touch me, if you'll kiss me, I'll come. But you have to promise you won't come. Not yet. Wait, do it my way." And then she comes, and Jesus, it almost makes him cry, she likes it so much. Never had a woman who liked it so much.

Holding her buttocks with one hand and the small of her back with the other, he thrusts hard three times and comes. He holds her tightly, feeling their heartbeats, hearing his breathing slowing. But she turns when he tries to kiss her. Jesus, she's mad. He lets her go, but she makes a big production of not looking at him as she scoops up her skirt from the floor, saying, "Thanks a lot."

He feels very naked with his clothes thrown out of reach and no smokes around. He sits up, encircling his knees with his arms, covering up as much as he can. "You enjoyed yourself. How come you're pissed?"

Searching for her blouse, she acts as if she hasn't heard, letting an extraordinary amount of time pass before she answers. "Well, I thought we were going to do something else." She picks up the blouse and turns it right side out.

He watches her dress. Her tan's so dark that nude, she looks clothed in an off-white bikini. She's going to sulk 'cause she didn't get her little sex fantasy fulfilled. Musta wanted old Charger a lot. A little faggy, kinda kinky for a nice kid like her to want it that way. He speaks clearly, hoping she'll listen. "Sorry, I didn't think you were serious."

This seems to be apology enough. She crouches beside him. "Sure, I'm serious." She bites her lower lip as she scans his face. "You look tired. Want to stay?"

"Unless you're planning on getting dressed and taking me somewhere, that's the plan."

Her bedroom could be an attic in a farmhouse. Massive antiques fill the small room, but the bed is deep and soft, and the patchwork quilt is light yet warm. She's not a cuddler. Staying on her side of the bed and pulling the starched sheets over her tawny shoulder, she says, "Night," and then all he hears are the long, even breaths of sleep. Ought to wake her in the morning to let her do what she wanted to do, but now it all seems forgotten. She's unbelievable. Taking command of her would be a trip. But he's tired now and falls into a leaden, dreamless sleep.

He wakes in the morning with her calling his name, shaking his shoulder. Dreamily, he watches her. He could be in an institution. The bright-eyed woman in the navy blazer is a clerk sent from accounting to have him fill out insurance forms. The second time she says his name, he recognizes Gwen. Wearing a denim suit and a red gingham shirt, she's the flip side of the woman last night. Her voice is brisk, ordering him to get up if he wants a ride because she'll be leaving for work soon.

When she leaves the room, he turns back the covers and dashes through the cool apartment to the bathroom. A glance at the mirror shows how shitty he looks. He thinks about using her toothbrush and finding a razor, but first he'll hit the shower. In a pool of water at the edge of the sink there's a man's razor. Christ, "the friend" came home. Now she wants her Thursday night mishap outa the house. He'll just spend a hell of a long time in the shower. The least he can do is use up her hot water. As he's adjusting the showerhead, the door opens, and she thrusts a stack of his neatly folded clothes onto the counter beside the sink. Before he can speak, the door clicks shut. In spite of his plan, he hurries. The way she shut that door meant she's not waiting, and the Mustang's a hell of a long way from here.

His face is gray and smarts from the close shave of the stranger's razor. Michael waits in the living room for her to appear from the kitchen. The drapes are open, the ashtrays emptied, last night erased. The tall, dark-haired man at Fat's last night strolls into the living room, gives a quick check with his hard, gray eyes, nods, picks up the newspaper, slumps in the white overstuffed chair, scowls at the front page, and begins to read. Gwen flies into the room, her shoulder bag flapping behind her, buzzes by the chair and brushes her lips to his temple. He doesn't flinch. She stands, seemingly unconcerned about being ignored and looks toward Michael. She asks pertly, "Ready?"

She tosses her purse and a stack of books and papers in the MG. Her purse only covers half a red book called *Animal Friends.* She lifts the canvas top and gets in the car. Then she snaps the top in place as if it's easy for little Miss Priss. Wonder if the sucker had happened to slip, what Queenie would've done? What a ballbuster.

He climbs in and slams the door, feeling like he's in an anchovy can. Jesus, it would be curtains in a rearender. But she loves being in the driver's seat, setting her purse and crap in the back real fast, putting on her shades, sticking the key in. A real little nun ready to whip those brats in line. "You a teacher?"

"Um." She's really biting her lip now as if she misses her smokes, probably drying out for school. "First grade," she says like it's a confession.

"No shit?" Little Miss One-Night Stand coulda taught Amy, Old Floss.

She's really watching the rearview, like driving this heap faster than anybody else is a hot time for her. "First grade teachers wear Enna Jetticks and raise cats, right?" She slips her specs down her nose, so she can see without the dark glass fuckin' up the show, but gets pissed by the poker-faced routine and shoves the glasses back in place to get back with her race driver bit.

Who the hell's Enna Jetticks? "I never coulda guessed you taught little kids."

She gets a good hard nip at her lower lip. "Fuckin' around isn't your idea of what a teacher should do for enter-tainment."

Jesus, what is it with her? She thinks she's Sophie Tucker. Somebody oughta wash out her filthy mouth. He stares out the window at the landscape flashing by and pats his shirt pocket for a cigarette. He asks her reflection, "Gotta smoke?"

"Probably not. I don't smoke at school." She nods toward the back. "You could check my purse. See if any fell inside. Might be some stale ones in the glove box." She's really yanking the wheel around, passing a slow car. "And how do you earn your keep that makes you so special?"

He is shuffling through maps and charge car receipts. "I'm a salesman."

"Oh, my God, who'd buy a car from you?"

He finds the Camels. Must be the friend's. What the hell. He rips open the pack. Fuckin' lighter looks broken. "I don't sell cars."

"Well, just let me guess."

He raises his hands in surrender. Confession will be merciful with this nun; she could go on for hours with a list of insulting occupations. "I work for Tristram."

Oh, Geez, she looks like even she can't be mean enough to go with this one. She giggles, "Toilet paper?"

He gets the match lit. "Yeah, that's how I make my living." He bashes the glove compartment so it falls open and throws the Camels inside. "You wanna let me out here?"

She slows the car, yanks the glasses down so the peepers are showing pure sincerity. "Hey, sorry. Just playing tit for tat."

"Yeah, well, I guess I had it coming." He feels like an ass for hitting the glove compartment so hard. "But, you, do, ah, mess around a lot?"

"Tell me what 'mess around' is and I can tell you if I do it."

"Ah," he stops before he says Shit, "Ah, you know what I mean. Last night."

"Well, of course, there's a story." Miss Priss feels just a little sorry for herself. Give her some room and she'll tell all about it. "And this is a short drive. And I'll probably never see you again. Wanna hear it? Make you feel better? Okay."

Pushing her buttons feels too easy. She takes a deep breath like this will be swimming under water. "You know I'm not living with my husband. He lives with another woman."

She acts like she's dealing with a fuckin' retard. "Yeah, yeah."

"His friend Paul was my friend too. After Sutton left,

Paul and I got to be friends. And now I guess we're lovers and . . . "

Jesus, get the ashes to the ashtray, Michael. "Yeah?" What the fuck's she talking about?

" . . . I just had my thirtieth birthday. And Paul's been teasing me about, well, never making it except with three men. Sutton, that's my husband, and a kid when I was in high school, and now Paul. So he set up this little dare."

He jams the Camel in the ashtray. "A dare?"

"Well, actually, he never said it in so many words, but I thought I'd show him. I mean, pull off a one-night stand." She tacks this last part on as she's flying through a yellow light.

"Oh, yeah." Jesus, he coulda been Charley MacArthur, Mortimer Snerd. He's a fuckin' dildo.

She whips right into the back entrance to Fat's. "Your car?"

"Here's fine."

She picks up on that one, sliding to a stop so the gravel crunches. She doesn't pull her glasses off but says to the street, "I—I'm sorry. It's nothing personal. I didn't think . . ."

"Nothing personal?" He's out of the bucket seat and slams the door. Little bitch thinks she can fuck around with him when she wants to, where she wants to. He works on getting the pause just right then leans down to look at her through the open window. "I'll give ya my address so ya can mail my stud fee."

Her mouth drops. He turns his face before she gets a word in. She rips out scattering gravel. He controls the urge to kick her fender as his parting shot. But walking away, hands jammed into the pockets, pulling the pants tight across the ass, is a good enough shot—like who the fuck cares about that queen.

The clock on the Mustang dash has stopped. He smashes his fist in its face. How the hell is he supposed to keep on going? With a couple of bucks, same shirt for two days, and a sixteen-year hangover. He slumps on his side in the front seat, massaging his aching fist, holding his hands between his knees. Never getting outa this fuckin' car. It'll be your fuckin' casket. Let the city haul it away and crush the sucker, a cana Irish stew. He huddles on the seat. Jesus, did she or did she not shove her leg against the Charger? Screwin' standing up for two fuckin' hours. Did she or did she not get pissed because she didn't blow him? How the hell do you know if you're awake or asleep? The old knuckles are a reminder. Skin's only split on the forefinger. Could be the hand of a normal person. Flex the old fingers. Ah, Jesus. Make a fist and see if you can shove yourself up. Ah, God. The sun in this fuckin' town is hell-fire. It's Phoenix, all right. You could fry eggs on the streets in December. Old intestines don't like sitting up when they've been fueled on beer and whiskey and beer for three, five—ah shit, who the hell keeps track? Find the fuckin' keys.

He slips the key in the ignition. Home's the only place left to go. Just cruise till you pass a bank sign flashing the time and temperature. Make sure Barb's at work. If the kids were dying, she'd go to her fuckin' job. Never misses a beat. He turns the key, wishing he could just turn off Barbara. Jesus, her face won't go away. Just cut your losses, baby. You could do better. He rolls into traffic to the blast of a horn. He leans out the window and yells, "Up yours, buddy!"

Barb left something taped on the fridge. Oh, Jesus, she had to put something in writing. He rips the note off the door, crumples it with his injured hand and paces the room cursing. He clenches his fist for as long as he can stand the pain, then winces as he straightens out the paper. Jesus, her writing is so tiny, so mushed together.

> Michael, I don't know if you'll ever read these words. I don't know if you've left for good this time. I know you are not

happy with me but I don't know what to do. If you could tell
me what you want, I would try to help you find it. I love you.
I love the girls. I know our life is bad now. I would change if
you would tell me how.

They called from school and work. There are problems. I
went to the school. But you have to call your boss at his office
before you go to do a job. Please call him.

I pray I will see you tonight and we will be able to talk.
Remember we love you.

Barbara

He moans, "Oh, Jesus," and folds the wrinkled paper in
half, then in fourths and eighths, and slips it in his breast
pocket behind his cigarettes, a little lump of paper like a
religious card above his heart. Jesus, she makes it sound so
easy. Call work. Come home. Change your life. Can't be that
simple. Be great to believe it even enough to try. Looks like
there aren't too many choices today. Got to go to work. Got
to try.

Jesus, it's ten-thirty. Took an hour to get through traffic
to this armpit of Phoenix. Shoulda phoned, but personal appearance has always been the ace. The little receptionist does
a doubletake when he walks in. "Mr. O'Connor." She's all
excited. "Wait a minute." Ah, Christ, this is gonna be the
pits. "Mr. Lanier would like to speak with you. Let me tell
him you're here." She holds up her finger, a warning not to
run away, and starts dialing, looking like she just reeled in a
big one. Yeah, the shit hit the fan. She hangs up. "He'll see
you in a few minutes."

He'd met Bert Lanier, the big gun in personnel, two years
ago. Acted like it was a favor to hire somebody for this
shitty job. Creepy little guy. Got his diplomas framed and
hanging on the wall. Got a picture of his wife, a real porker,
and the kids who look just like her. Probably got a "Have
you hugged your kid today" bumper sticker on his station
wagon. A cigarette would sure go good now. Look at those

hands, doing hand jive. Keep the suckers in your pocket.

The creep doesn't even get up. Doesn't offer his hand, just shoots from the hip. "Nick Vitale at Food Town and Behueler at Bashau's have filed complaints. Say their needs are not being met by their salesman. Claim you drink on the job."

Michael pushes the base of his thumb into his palm and realizes the old hands are shaking up a storm, Jesus . . . He glances at Lanier. The guy doesn't even need to breathe. "Ah, not exactly." Creep's holding out for more. "I had a beer, maybe two, at lunch." Still not enough. "I ran outa order forms."

Now he's going for the laser look. "And what they said is true?"

Son of a bitch. Vitale always laughed his ass off at ethnic jokes, even asked for 'em, but got pissed and complained. Old Lanier's waiting for an answer. Forgive me, father, for I have sinned, my fault my most grievous fault . . . "Well, sir"—get your hands in your fuckin' pockets—"I guess it wasn't one of my better days." The guy's a wolverine going for the jugular. Musta sounded too phony.

"Mr. O'Connor, any more days like yesterday and you won't work for this company." He sits back on his fat ass. "Do I make myself clear?"

The old noose is being pulled tight. This could be the last rites. "I understand."

Lanier is rocking his chair. "If there's a problem with drinking, face it." He swivels and watches the wall. "Get help. And I don't mean your neighbor. I mean a psychiatrist, a psychologist, A.A."

Michael studies his chubby profile. God, if he'd only lighten up. They could talk about how the Irish like their suds. They could laugh this off. Now old Lanier spins around to deliver his clincher. "I'm an alcoholic, you know. Been in A.A. for years. Been sober since."

Geez, this guy's been sober his whole goddamned life.

A.A., my ass. Big Mike said an alcoholic's just a drunk who goes to meetings. A.A.'s a fuckin' joke.

Lanier leans back again. "We can talk about your drinking, talk about A.A." He's crossed his arms behind his head. The old armpit shot means he's really into it. "I can take you to a meeting, get you started."

"Well, ah, thanks, but I really don't think I've got a big problem." A.A. meetings. Jesus. Hanging out with fuckin' degenerates. "I mean it's not a big deal in my life." The old chair just keeps creaking back and forth.

"Well, I'm asking you as your employer and as an alcoholic, look at it. Really, look at it." He sighs. "Ask yourself how long you can go without a drink. Figure it out—drinking can ruin you, lose you your job, your family."

Michael studies the glue holding the vinyl in place, waiting until it's safe to leave. "Well, I guess it can be a problem, all right." For a second, Lanier looks real sad, but now he's getting all businesslike, grabbing a portfolio about new products, finding some order forms. But his last little smile warns: strike two.

He sits behind the steering wheel for a moment getting up the energy to start the engine. Jesus, he's sweating like summer and it's almost winter. It takes two tries to get the Palsy Twins to light a cigarette. Cool it. Cool it. A temporary condition. They'll be settling down soon, five minutes, twenty, an hour. He inhales past the rawness of his throat, chokes, coughs up phlegm, spits out the window, waits, and inhales again. He stares at a chuckhole in the asphalt. Make it through today, Michael. Try the A.A. motto "One day at a time." You're not some fuckin' pansy who can't control yourself. You were one hell of a ballplayer. Get hold of yourself. Fuckin' heroin addicts go cold turkey. How hard can it be? He holds the cigarette between his teeth as he puts in the key, muttering, "Get to first."

Michael takes the two sixpacks of beer out of the grocery bag and sets them on the kitchen counter. Acting out his new plan, with his daughter by his side, he almost feels righteous. At the sound of Barbara's footsteps behind him, he turns, brushing Amy aside. He speaks slowly, softly, as if he were dealing with a deranged person. "I'm having a beer, Barbara, a beer." She's doing her moony stare. Christ, it's a way to live with it. Can't just quit cold. Proved it today. By eleven felt like an onion skin ready to tear. Another hour without a drink and a double Scotch woulda been the first of a downhill slide. Worked out a compromise: beer. Cruising from shopping mall to corner grocery sipping beer, it all fell in place. Like father, like son. Drink beer at home like Big Mike. But Barbara's got to get with this program: starting now, starting here, it's beer. Oh, Jesus, old moony-eyes is gonna make it tough. But little Amy, who ran across the lawn to meet you, to hug you, is leaning against you now, her head almost reaching the center of your chest; she could turn you into a Lanier family man. Christ, it's already hard to remember that little tramp last night who turned into Mary Poppins this morning. Living at home and drinking beer is the cure. Not too late to get back your health, to get back balance. In a month or so, just cut out the beer. Hell, might even get back to baseball—just local stuff, but clean. Geez, next year is the big three-three. Never planned to get that old. Barbara's face is a fist, waiting for the answer to her problem. Well, here it is, honey. "I'll be drinking some beer. Drinking here at home."

Chapter **13**

Standing in front of Daddy, his hands on her shoulders, makes Amy almost a part of him, able to see Mom as he does. Mom is so angry when he says "beer" that she turns her face, treating him as if he were Flossie asking for a cookie. Mom's going to ruin it all.

He had come home so happy, carrying a big bag from the car, tossing his jacket on the chair, breaking Mom's rules— such silly rules, only girls and women or men like Mr. Crandall obey them. Dad's jacket smells of tobacco and whiskey and aftershave. Its nubby fabric under her fingertips is the nap at the edge of the blanket she rubs while she touches her secret place. She had been about to touch his jacket when he called to her to come to the kitchen.

He'd winked at her as he set the bag on the counter, and the dangling ash of his cigarette fluttered through the air as he said, "How's it going, kid?" and hadn't waited for her to answer as he dug in the sack and pulled out a six-pack of bottled beer. He didn't seem to think she knew he hadn't come home last night. He still thought she was little, going to bed at nine or nine-thirty, having Mom drag her out of bed in the morning with threats. Amy was still his baby doll, his pal, who ran his errands, who waited at the edge of the lawn for him to come home, so he could swing her by her hands, carry her on his shoulders, then bounce her on his knee. Pulling a bottle of beer out of the pack, he'd asked her to get him an opener, and she'd dug in the drawer to get him one. He seemed so excited about drinking beer, it must be very good. She couldn't remember ever seeing a beer in this house. The little bottles were cute, like old-fashioned bottles of Coke. This was something different: "Let this be good, God," she repeated to herself as she pawed through the drawer where Mom kept the opener.

Beer couldn't be as bad as whiskey, an evil potion to transform him into a sick man. His symptoms are mysterious, for he never comes home until late at night when she's in bed. At Gram O.'s, she'd dreamed of his heavy steps on the stairway and waked to a storm with the wind rhythmically beating the shutters against the side of the house. In this house at night, she listens for the sounds of his stumbling and falling. And then Mom's silence.

Amy had turned over utensil after utensil in the drawer, muttering, "Opener, opener." He'd rested his hand on her shoulder, and she flinched and he said, "Take it easy, Queenie, we'll find the little rascal," and he kept his hand on her and leaned against her to find it himself. His breathing moved his belly, so she'd tried to match her breathing to his, chanting to the rising and falling of their bodies, "Oh, Daddy, stay home, Daddy."

As they had rummaged through the drawer, she'd heard Mom come in. Her face was as serious as when Mr. Crandall had mentioned the absences. To warn Daddy, Amy tensed against him. He looked up from the drawer and froze, confused as the dog they'd run over that night as it stared blindly into the headlights. "Barbara." Mom turned her head and the little blue vein in her temple jumped.

And now, he continues about his business. But her eyes are hateful. He stops, and Mom's eyes are holding him: his breathing quickens. And then he's a rattlesnake, tightly coiled muscles ready to strike. Mom's lips silently form "No." Then she sees where his hand rests and her eyes move to the beer bottle hanging from his hand. Her face is sick. She speaks so it's hard to hear, "No. Not that. Not here." Then she says it louder and pounds her clenched fists against her thighs, screaming so it must tear her throat. Her face is white and splotched with red, her enormous eyes ferocious. Her voice, the shriek of a monster.

Mom's face pulls at Amy, inching her from Daddy. Mom is furious with them for touching, for playing at finding a bottle opener, for being happy. Another tiny vein throbs in the middle of her forehead. With Daddy behind, and Mom in front, it might be safer to crouch and crawl beneath the table to watch. Daddy's breathing harder. Mom's eyes move to his face. And he's moving away, sand shifting beneath her feet in the ocean.

She turns. He's shoving the unopened bottle in the drawer. She's invisible to him too. He watches Mom, side-stepping her, an attacking dog. He must want to go to the dark living room. Mom is saying, "You will not drink in my house, in front of my children." He moves toward the door-way. She shouts, "I will not have it. Not after the promises you made." Mom reaches for his shirtsleeve. Without look-ing at her face, he pushes her hand away. She screams, "You can't do this," then cries, "you can't . . ." as she stum-bles after him, trying to grab his shirt.

He scoops up his jacket from the chair, but Mom catches him, grabs a fistful of his shirt, and yanks. He turns and there's a tearing sound. In a single graceful backhand stroke, he slaps her chin, her mouth, her cheek, her nose. She makes no sound, backing from him, falling, her face in her hands, blood at the opening between her fingers. The door clicks closed.

Mom huddles and whimpers on the floor. She's like the dog twitching in the road, dying as Big Mike drove away. Amy had wanted to wrap the dog in a sheet and bury it. Staring at the trembling form, Amy backs along the walls to the hallway, then turns to run to her room, almost tripping over Flossie, who crouches, staring, big-eyed, at Mom. They kneel together, hugging and crying. Flossie is Carolyn, the princess doll. Her flighty hair can be smoothed again and again behind her ears, away from her forehead. Her tears can be wiped from her cheeks, her hiccupping shoulders pat-ted. Mom's animal sounds become an occasional whimper. Amy hums to cover the sound, louder and more melodious, and Mom grows silent. Flossie sniffs. It is safe to stand. She touches Flossie lightly, a signal to stay, as Amy stares into the dark living room.

Amy goes to the bedroom to get a blanket for Mom. Flossie catches her hand. She is frightened. "It's all right. It's all right. We can take care of everything." Things will be right, the way home has never been.

But he doesn't return on Saturday, or Sunday. All weekend, he doesn't call or drive in the drive. He doesn't circle the block. He isn't coming home right away. But if she is very, very good, he'll return. Everything has to be perfect for that day.

Mom is the silent, sick person she was at Gram O'Connor's house when he'd gone away before. She lies on the couch with her back to them. She isn't the mother any more. They will play nurse. Mom is the patient and they have to tiptoe around her and bring coffee and chicken noodle soup. They will undress her, put on her robe, and walk her to the bathroom. They do not talk about Daddy as they comb her hair, then wash her puffy, bruised face. Flossie must help. He might return at any time. They will do his laundry, his ironing, hang his clothing in the closet. The house and the meals will be prepared with more care than Mom ever used. She was always too tired. Only once, during the weekend, does Amy feel close to tears. Flossie forgot Daddy was gone and set the table for four instead of three.

On Monday, Amy practices her Girl Scout skills to prepare a breakfast of oatmeal, orange juice, coffee, and cocoa. She brings coffee to Mom and kneels by the couch. The steam and scent from the coffee will wake her. She opens her eyes. It seems safe to ask, "Mommy, are you going to work today? Can you go to work today?"

"Yes, baby." She rises on an elbow to take the cup and whispers over the brim, "Could you bring my clothes?"

Mom doesn't want to go to the bedroom. She is as sad as Duane. How simple it would have been for her to keep

Daddy home. It was only beer. It was making him happy. If only Mom had been prettier. If only she hadn't nagged . . .

Amy goes to school early to see Mr. Crandall. He looks up from the papers on his desk to see her and smiles. He has so much to do before the bell, she'll be careful not to take long. But she needs to see his face, to be in this room where happiness occasionally happens. His eyes in his jowly face are small and sad. He must work at being happy. But his voice is lively. "What can I do for you, my dear?"

"Oh, nothing." She flashes the smile Daddy calls her "dimple puss." "Everything's fine," she giggles, and adds a line of Daddy's that she's always admired, "Just stopped by to say hello."

winter | 1971

Chapter **14**

As the classroom calendar monitor, Amy keeps the class aware of the date by marking off the days with giant x's; she also keeps a secret tally of the days Daddy's been gone—fifteen. Halloween is coming and she and Flossie must have costumes or be disgraced. Using Mom's makeup and an old sheet, Amy transforms Flossie into Caspar the Ghost. Cinderella before her transformation by the fairy goodmother is an easy costume for Amy to create. When they model for Mom, she smiles and makes a strange whimper. Daddy would love how grown-up and pretty Amy is in Mom's old blue dress and apron, wearing a touch of rouge.

The kitchen cupboards are bare, and there are no pop bottles in the shed, and Mom says garage sales are for poor people. But each day she gives less money to buy the groceries on the way home from school, and Daddy's checkbook, the one that appeared when they bought clothes or a carful of groceries, has disappeared. To ask Mom about it means mentioning his name. When Amy searched the cupboards for it, she found a stack of unopened envelopes. The little plastic windows meant they were bills. Mom hides the bills that she doesn't pay. They are poor people.

Mr. Crandall and the nurse at school must know about the poor; they collect old clothes and canned food for the banks to help them. But Mr. Crandall must not learn that Daddy has gone, that they need money. The poor people in the *Weekly Reader* get food stamps and welfare. People at the store with baskets full of groceries pay the clerk with something like Monopoly money and call it food stamps. But Mom wouldn't know about the stamps; she never knows anything.

Amy will have to do research. Mr. Crandall said intelligent people solve their problems by getting information. He said the public library in Scottsdale, the scene of her stolen days, is a source of "useful information for survival." So she saves her her milk money for a week to have the bus fare to go there on Saturday. When the grouchy librarian tells her to phone Information and Referral Service, she almost cries. There is a phonebook in their kitchen. After school on Monday, while Mom is still at work, Amy begins dialing. Every agency answers a question with another phone number. On Tuesday, she finishes her research. Mom's salary plus tips has to be figured. Mom will have to sign papers. She must understand: she must agree.

Twenty-five days since he left: almost four weeks. The house is cleaner, quieter. There are more hours in their day than there have ever been before. Amy watches traffic for the Mustang, listens for the phone, checks the hall. She plans the meals and cooks and tells Mom and Flossie what to do. They are doing well. Mom goes to work, eats dinner at the table with them, has gone back to her room, but sleeps on her side of the bed. And she likes to watch TV with Flossie, who has become an obedient helper.

This Wednesday evening, Amy carries the paper with the

figures about food stamps, waiting for the right time to talk to Mom. But her face is always dazed. To talk about money and Daddy will make her cry. He hasn't been spoken of since that day. Thursday comes and goes and still there is never a time that is right. Leaving for school on Friday, she promises herself she'll find a moment this weekend to sit with Mom and explain the plan as carefully as explaining fractions to Duane. Mr. Crandall said a persuasive speech needs props and facts to be convincing. Perhaps Mom needs to see the stack of unopened bills she's been secretly shoving in the cabinet, or to be reminded that for three and a half weeks they've eaten macaroni and cheese, noodle soup, peanut butter, or Spam. Mr. Crandall says a speaker has to capture the attention of the audience. But Mom is so strange. It won't be easy to get her to listen, but having the stamps would help until Daddy comes home. Amy runs and skips toward school, unsympathetic toward the wails of Flossie, whose chubby legs rub together as she tries to keep up. There is too much to do to wait for her. There is a weekend to plan on the run to school. Amy must keep being the best she can be to bring him home.

Mom has news on Saturday. She has a second job. She'll be selling tickets in the evenings at a movie theater. "Two jobs will help make ends meet."

Amy nods yes, she'll be glad to keep "helping out," taking care to see "Flossie does her share." No need to ask about the food stamps; there will be more money, but Mom will always be away.

Mom is almost well, talking to them as she changes to go to her second job. Sometimes she almost sounds happy. And it's understood without discussion that Amy will continue to shop and cook and clean, and now she'll haul clothes to the laundromat, but the most important of all, she'll be the decision-maker. This is playing grownup all the time. To control Flossie, Amy controls the television. It's turned off during supper and cannot be turned on until after the dishes are done, so Flossie will race about the table, her jeans swishing, gathering dirty dishes, hustling them into the kitchen to get her tasks finished for the reward of watching her favorites. "The Newlyweds" delights her. She laughs out loud at the silly couples. It is sad to see how happy she is, how easily she's forgotten Daddy. But she's easy to order about, never asking why she must obey, more obedient than Duane. And as they complete the daily drudgery, Amy imagines when Daddy comes home how pleased he'll be to see how good she's been. He'll surely want to stay with such a good girl.

Trotting to school or coming home or going to the grocery, she always looks for him. A yellow Mustang chugging down the road sets her heart to hammering. Today she sees a man slouched behind the wheel who might be Daddy. She races after the car calling, but the driver doesn't slow down.

He could be traced scientifically. Nancy Drew would use logic. She would find the company where he works. The Phoenix directory will list his business address, his office phone. By disguising her voice, she could make a phone call that might be very informative, but a call might get him into trouble and send him away permanently, or she might learn he has disappeared. If he has left Phoenix, she might never find him. For days she plots the best approach. But the time is never right to make her call.

Each day she collects the mail from the box on the porch for Mom. Shuffling the few pieces, she sighs. There is never an envelope with Daddy's wild scrawl—just the envelopes with little windows. So she leaves the neat stack for Mom, who will shove them unopened into the cupboard now bulging with envelopes.

School is just another chore—a place to run from the minute the dismissal bell rings. Each day she races through the kitchen door to check the clock, pleased if she saves a couple of minutes on travel time. Today Mr. Crandall is introducing units for Thanksgiving: in art, they draw turkeys; in math, they convert recipes, using fractions; in history, they read about the pilgrims; in English, they write about the dinner their mothers might prepare for the holidays; and in home room, tomorrow, they'll began to collect canned goods and money to provide a happy Thanksgiving for needy families.

Like the other kids, she obediently writes her essay. The following day, Mr. Crandall tells the class he will read "an excellent essay, an anonymous piece because the identity of the writer will not be revealed." At first she hadn't recognized the writing as hers. It describes a family having both turkey and ham. The mother, the father, and the grandparents too, participate in the preparations. The father loves to cook and help around the kitchen. He is eager to carve the turkey and will probably make his famous pecan, pull-apart sweet rolls for Thanksgiving breakfast, so the family won't become too hungry as they wait for the late afternoon feast. As Mr. Crandall reads, she blushes and the kids around her whisper loudly, "It's hers. It's Amy's."

To help the class support the poor, she scrapes around and brings some canned goods and a quarter for her donation. But she wonders if the nurse will come to her house and discover that she and Mom and Flossie could qualify. Having a dinner for Thanksgiving will have to be managed. Families always had Thanksgiving. Maybe a chicken would do.

On Tuesday she corners Mom to present the rehearsed plan. "Mom, about Thanksgiving . . ."

"Honey, I'm sorry, but I won't be home. The restaurant's open. It's a chance for big tips."

She manages to keep the tremble out of her voice. "Sure." Mom is so blank and stupid and empty. "You won't be home at all?"

"Well of course, I'll be home. But not at noon. But go ahead with your plan."

Amy ducks her head. Her plans hadn't been for a rush meal. One o'clock in the afternoon is the time for Thanksgiving dinner. Gram Hershey did it that way. The cooking starts the night before. The turkey has to be stuffed, then the pies baked, the cranberry relish prepared. Her "imitation" Thanksgiving dinner has been plotted to be served at one. She'll have to throw out those plans to start again. She feels like crying. Now there's no hope at all for happiness. She swings her leg violently to keep from crying—all she can see is a dark, empty day in the cold house. If she doesn't cook, it will be a day with nothing to do, a day when everyone else in the world is busily preparing a feast, toasty and warm in a house smelling of spices and baking bread. What will fill their home? The humming of the TV, the dripping of a faucet. She hates Mom. Her pale hand is reaching toward Amy's knee. She swings her leg harder, as a warning for the hand not to touch her.

Mom's hand withdraws; her voice is soft as she murmurs, "Honey, I'm sorry. Couldn't you change your plans around a little? Make dinner a little later?"

As school dismisses on Wednesday for the holiday break, Amy goes to her locker to get her sweater. Mr. Crandall loudly opens and closes drawers. "Have a nice Thanksgiving," she says so only he can hear. She imagines a woman who looks like him will carry an enormous turkey to their dining room table surrounded by grandmothers, grandfathers, uncles, aunts, and children: all with identical puffy faces.

He's walking toward her in his worn Hush Puppies. "Amy, would you like to have some of the Thanksgiving decorations we made in class? We've got so many, and you worked so hard."

"Well," she pretends to be concerned with the contents of her locker; she should not accept, "well, I guess we could use them," and even as she says it she has to control the excitement in her voice as she visualizes the decorations as a centerpiece on their table. Maybe he'll give her the crepe paper tablecloth made by Hallmark. Oh, she hopes he will. It would make up for having to prepare a chicken. Dinner at seven-thirty wouldn't be so bad. She could even stick some candles on a plate and put them in the center of the table. "Yes," she says as she pulls on her sweater. She looks up at him as she scrambles to her feet. "I think it'd be nice."

He loads a cardboard box for her. The shellacked gourds pouring from the cornucopia are her favorites. To ask why he doesn't want these beautiful objects would be rude. Handing her the box, he says, "We're going to my mother's this year, so we won't need these." As Amy thanks him, she tries to imagine what sort of a wife would not cook for her husband.

By noontime, she manages to pry Flossie away from the telecast of Macy's Thanksgiving Day parade. Setting the table, they argue about how to fold the napkins. The phone rings. It so rarely rings in their house; they look at one another. Flossie's pout wins her the privilege of answering.

She says "Hello" breathlessly, totally ignoring Amy's repeated whisper, "Who is it?" It can't be Daddy or Flossie wouldn't be giggling. It could be one of the grandmothers. It must be Grammy H. because Gram O. would've asked for Daddy right away. It's Grammy H. because Flossie is saying, "Mommy isn't home." And she's adding, "Daddy isn't home," but "Yes, Amy is" and "Yes, Amy can talk."

Suddenly the receiver is in Amy's hand and she's saying, "Hi, Grammy, hi Grammy," in a crazy-sounding baby voice. And she bites her lower lip hard, so she won't cry.

Gram's voice is rolling along like a fat ball of yarn unwinding. She talks about snow and baking and a new stitchery project. She is snug inside her little trailer banked by drifts of snow, the wind howling outside, the aroma from the kitchen everywhere. Her gnarled fingers must hold the receiver, her "project" beside her: a canvas covered with a rainbow of silk threads. Her voice as soothing as when she read them to sleep, she keeps on talking if Amy makes an occasional "um." But now she asks,

"When's your mother getting home?"

Amy is yanked from the warm bath of Grammy's words. "Oh, Mom will be home at seven," she says quickly, hoping Gram will think it's perfectly fine for Mom to be gone. Shivering in the stillness of the pause, she clenches the receiver. Gram wants to know why Mom's so late. Amy mutters, "She gets paid for overtime."

Gram sounds farther away, as if she decided to sit down, and speaks away from the receiver. But then her voice is clear again with its usual happy, take-charge tone. "Well, I'll just call back around seven and catch your mother then. I haven't talked to her or heard from her in what seems like months—and you haven't been a letter-writer either, young lady." And then she laughs, so it isn't a scolding, and adds in a rush, "And school is fine." Amy nods, forgetting how Gram can't see her until she prompts, "School's all right."

"Yes, yes," and Gram is off on another topic. Amy keeps her propelled, grunting happily. Grammy tells one of her stories where she is a silly old lady. Amy laughs. Daddy will not be discussed. She won't have to protect him with a lie. She hopes she'll never have to lie to Gram.

It's Flossie's turn to talk now. Amy hands her the receiver, wanting to say, "Don't mention Daddy," but knows Flossie would protest loudly. All Amy can do is sit in Daddy's chair, staring at her while she talks, and chant to herself, "Please, God, please, God." If she visualizes God as she speaks, He might hear her. She remembers the calendar pictures in Catholic school of Jesus seated on a rock, wearing a white robe, looking peaceful, with a halo over his head. Sister Mary Agnus said God and Jesus and the Holy Spirit were one. So calling Jesus "God" isn't incorrect. Religion is so hopelessly confusing she only turns to it in emergencies. And she enjoys imagining conversations with Jesus—a handsome, blue-eyed blonde, like Daddy with a beard. But today she has nothing to offer for a favor from Jesus. She wants this day to pass with none of the dark grayness it promises. She knows it can never be like the story she wrote: the one the class believed was about her. But there is hope for a moderately cozy day, if Flossie will cooperate. She has to be filled with cheery warmth to make her bubbly and lovable. It is Flossie who has the power to make Mom almost laugh. "Oh, Jesus, Son of God, don't let Flossie tell Grammy about us. Don't let Flossie remember the sadness of Daddy going away. Let talking to Grammy be good for Flossie and make her happy. Please, God. Please, God."

Jesus performs a minor miracle. Flossie is nodding, saying the words that reveal Gram is asking her usual grandmotherly long-distance questions. When Flossie hangs up, she is practically purring. Grammy has stroked her fur and tickled her ears, so she hums with love. She even submits to folding napkins as instructed. She likes Mr. Crandall's gifts so much that she doesn't complain about washing cranberries until her stubby fingers turn into albino prunes beneath the cold water tap.

Prayer has brought relief. Perhaps the Baltimore Catechism should be reviewed. Not that she wants to be a bride of Christ like the nuns who were so strange. But maybe if she had knowledge of Catholicism, life could be as smooth and as pleasant as today. There must be useful secrets within the faith. She hasn't been inside a church since they left New York. She misses mandatory chapel: the candles, the incense, the cushioned walk on the worn carpet leading down the nave into the cruciform where light poured through the stained-glass clerestory. She often tried to follow each step of the mass. But the old priest spoke rapidly in a monotone and her attention would slip away from his words, and soon she would study the statuary at the end of her aisle, or the lint on the shoulders of the uniform on someone in front of her, or the ceiling of the church which was the inside of a beautiful Easter egg. In her four years in parochial school, she liked the stories of the saints, loved collecting their cards, watched with fascination as the costumes of the clergy and the decor of the church changed, but she'd hated her uniform, the craziness of the nuns, and the tension in the classroom. Her family wasn't as Catholic as some of the families. Mom didn't even belong. And Daddy only went on Christmas or Easter, "just in case." Gram O. had sent Amy to Catholic school. But Mom had never visited the classroom, nor had Daddy. Amy was an outsider. No matter how well she did her work, the nuns never noticed. They liked the Italian kids whose fathers supported the church. She hadn't known how much she disliked the school until she left. In Mr. Crandall's class, school wasn't filled with fear and boredom and endless frustration.

Watching Flossie slicing cranberries, her angelic curls bobbing as she hums, Amy forgets about Sister Mary Katherine's moustache twitching as she slapped the fresh boys' hands with a metal-edged ruler. If a chorus of the boys singing "Ave Maria" a cappella filled the kitchen with their heavenly sound, she wouldn't be surprised. She's seen *The Song of Bernadette* on television. She knows about miracles. Perhaps she should buy a religious medal, a St. Christopher to hang on a gold chain about her neck as a sign of unquestioning faith in God's love. Today God, in the form of Jesus, helped her, maybe He might even bring Daddy back.

There is a quiet knocking, but Flossie continues humming. Amy touches Flossie's wrist to stop her red-stained fingers from mutilating the cranberries and whispers, "Listen." She tilts her head toward the knocking which is growing stronger. It must be a thief.

Flossie's eyes are not frightened until she looks at Amy's, then she covers her mouth with her hand, streaking her face with berry juice. She shakes her head as if she's denying guilt. As they listen, Amy squeezes Flossie's wrist and turns. She tiptoes to the bedroom, intrigued by the erratic rhythm of her heartbeat. Who could be at their house? No one ever knocks on their door. No one comes here unless it's the Jehovah's Witnesses. Mom always tells those people to go away. And they always ring the doorbell loudly. This is a soft sound as if someone is testing how strong the door might be. Mom said, "Never, never let anyone in the house when you're alone."

Gram O. told a story about a crazy man who dressed like an Avon lady and came into women's houses and raped them. That was the first time Amy heard of rape. She waited for the right time to ask Mom about it, but she just said, "It's when a man attacks a woman—sexually." For a long time, Amy imagined a man who raped a woman wore a uniform and carried a gun. The sexual part was very strange. A man must make the woman take off her pants and stick the gun into her. Maybe he took off his pants and stuck in the crazy, floppy-looking thing hanging on men and boy dogs —the thing that was pink on men instead of furry.

Amy crouches next to the bed. The penis of the rapist must be like pictures of naked men. The only live naked man she's ever seen is Daddy. Once she walked into the bathroom when he was toweling himself dry. He looked up and his face was as surprised as if he'd been caught in a searchlight. He held the towel to his chest. Between his legs he had gold wiry hair and a thing like raw parts of a chicken. He couldn't attack with that dangling thing that looked as if it would bleed if it touched anything. She had stared at the bruised cabbage rose with its tarnished gold setting, then forced herself to look back to his face. He'd closed his mouth and not taken his eyes from her as he dipped his chin, wrapped the towel around himself, and closed the door. Once she'd seen him sleeping naked on his bed. She'd tiptoed in the room to look. He wasn't hard and cold like statues of naked men at the art museum. His skin was the color of doeskin gloves, and his belly rose and fell with his breath. His eyes were covered with the back of his forearm, and the skin on the underside was a pale shade, almost like the marble of statues, and in the hollow beneath his arm there was tarnished golden hair, all soft, not spiky like below. From the doorway, poised, ready to run if she heard someone coming, she'd looked closely at his penis—a rosy mushroom on a long stem in a field of golden clover with two baby mushrooms at the base of the stem that had grown up crooked because of the wind. It could never attack unless the sun were so bright and warm the penis grew. It wasn't like a weapon, not a gun or a knife or a hatchet. Her confusion about rape magnified so, she made it a practice to examine men's flies, but they all seemed as harmless as Daddy's.

There is another knocking at the door. She falls to her knees and begins to crawl toward the sound, imagining what might assault her. In fourth grade, in the giant dictionary in the back of the class, girls stared at the open pages, giggling. As they returned to their desks, they ordered her to look too. "Penis" was underlined, and four children's drawings were in the margin: first a side view of a floppy-looking thing, like a melting candle doubled over; then the thing was beginning to unbend, with little lines around indicating jerky motions; a third drawing showed a crowbar sticking out, with a wedged-shaped end with a hole shooting raindrops; in the last drawing, it was doubled over again like the first picture. She wanted to study the series but the girls were watching her, so she made a face to show her disgust and looked at the definition circled in red. She needed to read it slowly so she'd understand, but she heard them giggling, commenting about her as she read, so her eyes jerked along over the lengthy entry. Snagging on incomprehensible words, she quickly memorized one: "copulative." At home she'd looked up "penis" in Mom's old dictionary. But it wasn't there. But "copulative" meant joining together words. And just above it on the page was "copulate," meaning "to engage in sexual intercourse." Then she understood. The penis had to get hard, like in the picture, so it could join with the inside of the lady. That was it. It didn't stay floppy all the time. And those little drops must be the stuff to make the eggs grow in the lady to turn into babies.

Her heart beats so loudly she can't hear anything else. Daddy's penis growing hard and going inside Mom to shoot little stars is repulsive. But still Mom had two babies, so they must've done it a couple of times. Late one Saturday morning, Amy had opened their bedroom door and seen Daddy's back bouncing beneath the sheet. When Mom squealed, "Michael," he rolled off her. They were so embarrassed that they must've been "doing it." But did they still do it? And what was the difference between sexual intercourse and rape? How often did Daddy rape Mom? Even watching them closely, it was hard to tell. They didn't talk often. They didn't even look at each other. Amy's legs cramp. It doesn't seem possible for her parents to copulate. She tries to stand on shaking knees.

Flattened against the wall by the window, she pulls back the edge of the curtain and peeks out. No cars are parked on the street. She presses her cheek against the cold glass but still can't see much of the driveway. If she goes to the living room window, the man will see her. The knocking begins again, more insistently now. She could stand here and wait, but the pulse hammering in her ears and her dry throat is more painful if she's still. She must move before the person has time to figure out how to get inside. She races to the doorway of the bedroom and stops to listen for a moment.

The doorbell has been ringing so long that it's begun to sound like a dentist's drill. The man wants in. She darts through the hall, past the dining room, and shoots Flossie a glance so she'll remain in her chair. Approaching the door, Amy moves as slowly as a stalking animal. She crouches by the keyhole, even leans toward it as if she might be able to see through the tiny opening, but then she rocks back on her heels. Holding a hand to her heart, she whispers, "Who is it?" As she waits, she realizes she's spoken too softly. She stands, aligning her cheek against the rough wood. She presses so hard the words reverberate as she asks, "Who is it?"

"Dad, it's your Daddy."

She goes limp and would have fallen if it hadn't been for the door. When this barrier is gone, he will kneel and scoop her into his arms. And the month of praying for his return, watching for his car, listening for his call, imagining how he'll return, will be over. Only this flimsy hollow door keeps him away. She gnaws at her thumbnail, her crotch burning as if she might pee, and she wants to be in her dark, warm bed at the edge of sleep with her hands between her thighs. Compelled to rip at a jagged nail on her right hand, she fumbles with the night chain with her left. Two hands are needed to release the chain. She backs from the lock, crouching, doubled over, to alleviate her distress, and presses her left hand between her thighs to stop her bladder from disgracing her.

"Amy? Flossie?" His voice is louder and closer.

On the other side of the door, his face must be quizzical. He's saying "Amy." She swallows hard, fastening her teeth on the last shred of her thumbnail. But he repeats "Flossie" too as if he doesn't know who is inside. In spite of her bladder, she stands straight and forces herself to take the thumb from her mouth. She makes a fist to hide the bloody cuticle. "It's Amy," she says, her voice loud and clear enough to be heard through the door.

He's wearing a white shirt with the cuffs rolled up, just as she'd imagined. And he doesn't have on a jacket, although he should because it's cold. He should hug her, at least reach down and put his hands on her shoulders, or look into her face. But he stands on the edge of the concrete porch. He must've backed away when she opened the door. He's too far away to have rung the doorbell or have knocked so softly, so repeatedly. She looks at the open throat of his shirt and the line of his jaw turned slightly away as he looks intently at the dying hedge bordering the house. "Hi," she says, interlacing her fingers, pressing them hard so her thumb can't return to her mouth.

"Hi, kid," he says softly, only glancing at her once. "How ya doing?" And now he looks past her inside the house.

She squares her shoulders, a signal for Flossie to stay in her place. Even staring hard at his face doesn't draw him to her. She sounds insincere when she says, "I'm all right," and she wants to say "Daddy," but the word won't come out.

And now his eyes are on her face, on her throat, at her feet—on her face again. "That's good. That's good." And then his eyes are gone, darting back and forth above her head. "And your Mom? How's she?" Now he has his hands in his pockets, where they make fists while he stares at her.

She looks at the hedge, swallowing. He's come to see Mom, his wife: the one with the teary eyes, the sad face, and the gray life. He's come to see his wife. Amy lifts her chin, praying her face isn't flushed. "Mom's working." And immediately she regrets the snippiness of her tone. Now he won't be asking to come inside. It would be useless to step aside and offer an invitation. He prefers the strange sulkiness of Mom.

"Is that Floss?" he asks as he stares through the living room. And he moves a step closer.

Her heart is beating so wildly that he might hear it. "Yes." She steps halfway behind the door to make a path directly for him. He has a right to go to Flossie if he wants her. Amy will let him pass. Flossie is stumbling over her feet in her eagerness to get to the door, calling, "Hi, Daddy, hi, Daddy." And the skin about his eyes crinkles as if he might cry. And he crouches, holding open his arms for her. He hugs her and pats and rocks her, and they laugh.

Amy holds the edge of the door, unable to watch. Flossie is not his favorite. She's never served him, anticipated his needs, wheedling him into mood changes to play-act together. Flossie has always been the outsider, unless a plan has been made to include her in their games. Look at her now—fat little arms waving, illustrating a story—a poor imitation of Daddy, of Amy. But his face has the gentle half-smile, the readiness to laugh, the total attention he has always saved for Amy.

She waits for them to finish, needing to disappear into the bathroom but remaining in her spot, her pose, to show it doesn't matter. They're whispering: his fingers fluff Flossie's curls, his lips brush her brow. They must be finished, but still they don't part. Flossie turns and leans against his inner thigh, bracing her elbows against his knee, lolling her head against his shoulder.

Flossie's wide blue eyes fasten upon Amy, who looks once at their steady gaze, filled with a confident glow of ownership. Daddy's bland smile is easier to bear. He's played Flossie's game, pretending he adores her. He is tired. There are fans of lines about his eyes, indentations beside his mouth; they are deeper than when he lived here. She looks over Flossie's head into his eyes, but they don't look back with love. She lowers her eyes. All these years, she thought she was the favorite.

She knows she'll cry if she opens her mouth, so she keeps a tightlipped half-smile. A curt nod, a smile, a signal to Flossie to get back into the house, and then Amy might speak to him with some dignity. The edges of her mouth begin to tremble. Still Flossie stands her ground. Amy looks away, deciding whether to go or to stay, and she hears their movements—Flossie is being kissed and kissing in return. Then she dashes into the house, tramps down the hall, and slams the bathroom door. The cold, brass knob twists beneath Amy's sweaty palm. He stands, takes a step closer, waits. She gives the knob a hard snap and lets her hand fall at her side. She looks full in his eyes, ready to let him do what he wants. He looks away and touches his hand to his shirt pocket. And it's strange because the usual pack of cigarettes isn't there. Maybe his heart hurts, the way her insides do, but he's taking a paper out of the pocket, an envelope, and he's handing it to her. "This," he says, "is for your mother, and Flossie and you."

She holds out her hand to take it, and she has to stretch to reach him, but one step closer might offend him. He said her name last, which means she's the least important. Mom was first, then Flossie, and then, at the last, Amy. She's the last one. That's for sure. And he's not going to touch her, not even their fingertips brush. "Thank you," she says. And this time she knows he's going away. He's left her. She'll be living alone. And she feels so ashamed for all the times she felt so special, so totally, crazily happy being herself for him. It hadn't been enough to hold him. She hasn't been good enough, and she hasn't even known it. She looks at him so her eyes might say the words she can't, "Daddy, I'm sorry I wasn't good enough," but there aren't going to be any second chances. He's looking toward his car, pulled under the carport as if he'd planned to stay. He must've made up his mind not to stay when he saw her. Maybe if she'd hugged him, kissed him, if she'd at least looked at his eyes when he first came in the house, but she hadn't. And now he's turning, shading his eyes against the afternoon sun. She tries to say, "Wait, Daddy, wait. If you'll come back this time, I'll try. I won't laugh so loud and be so rowdy and . . ." but no words come. She holds the envelope and waits for him to leave. She will watch everything he does, so she can remember it so well, she'll see it again and again.

He turns halfway, the hand at his forehead, shading his eyes against the sun, forms a fist at his brow, grimaces into the light. "I, ah . . ." and then he stops as if he doesn't really know what he wants to say and finishes quickly. "Please give it to your Mom. Tell her I'll be in touch." And in the second before he turns, he might stop and come back inside, and it will be over, and he will come home. But he turns into the sun blinding them both, lowers his head, and walks quickly to the car.

She could've left Flossie alone in front of the TV, singing herself into an ecstatic state, and gone to her room, crawled into bed, and willed herself to die. But she isn't ready to accept defeat. She confesses her failure. She has tried, but not to the limits of effort. She only thinks she's tried. She must learn diligence and excellence far, far better than she's known before. Flossie's joy is a penance. Smiling and moving woodenly through the afternoon's activities, Amy doesn't interrupt Flossie's inane monologue about Daddy. Caring for Flossie will be good training. At least now Flossie won't have to be nagged into working. Her smug little smile means she believes Daddy will return soon, and she'll be his consuming love. She'll be a slave to make the perfect setting. Each time Amy is tempted to slap the silly face babbling on about what isn't real, she will turn away. This vow of silence is a small sacrifice compared to the others she is willing to make.

Amy will recall the golden image of this afternoon as it should have been. He is standing outside the open door. Fists in his pockets, the sad half-smile on his face, he turns the afternoon into laughter. She will be good and beautiful, standing in the doorway of the house that is filled with the warm aromas from the kitchen. Like God and Jesus and the Holy Ghost, Daddy will be with her. She will conjure his spirit to be present with her not only at home, but everywhere she is lonely: she will prove to him how she can be worthy of his love. She must be perfect. Nothing short of perfection will win him.

Chapter 15

Barbara had never been struck in the face by another human until Michael's assault. Even weeks after the incident, with no warning during the day, the scene flashed in her mind: his unblinking eyes the moment before the blow,

and the lightning bolt of his slap. At night the image re-
played so uncontrollably her throat, her chest, and her bow-
els were seared, burning her into exhaustion.

Since his disappearance, over a month ago, her energy has
been spent in a way she has never known. Going to bed by
nine or even eight, exhausted by thoughts of Michael, she
falls into a deep sleep and doesn't wake until the alarm pulls
her from a great depth. When she wakes, she is as tired as
when she went to bed. She gets through each day, each one
the same. She puts one foot in front of the other and she's
crossed a room, filled an order, done a job. Her mind and
body are numb. To be attentive to the commands of her customers requires great concentration: the rest is a haze. To
respond to the obvious efforts of Amy, who cares for her and
Flossie, requires an energy far beyond her strength. On the
rare occasions when Barbara speaks, her voice is as muted
as if she were wrapped in gauze. She doesn't dare to pick at
the edges of the insulation muffling her feelings. If she tears
away the protection, she might be paralyzed by the pain.
Perhaps tomorrow, or the following day, the shock will wear
away. But the days flutter by like the calendar days of the
1940s movies Etta O'Connor watched. Barbara's face shows
symptoms of distress: the skin around her eyes is puffier, her
complexion a little more sallow. But it's not the face of the
madwoman she'd expected it to be. No one at work knows
she's lost her husband. Except in her role as a waitress, they
ignore her, and their indifference is a balm.

On every other Friday, she cashes her paycheck and puts
the money in envelopes: one for the current week's food, one
for next, and one for rent; whatever is left she'll use to pay
bills. This method is one she learned in Mt. Kisco when she
became the coordinator of family finance. She'd tried to con-
sult with Michael about their phone being disconnected for
payment two months in arrears, and he'd screamed, "I'll
pay the fuckers when I'm good and goddamned ready." He
called her system "budgeting for bird-brains"—a comment

typical of a man who could add figures as quickly as his cal-
culator and as accurately, who could cite baseball statistics
since 1950, but who didn't want to be "hassled" with recording a check, or opening a bill, or keeping track of what and
whom he owed. Michael—always so critical of how others
coped—had left their life in a shambles. Men are obligated to
manage money for their families. Dad always had. Well, it
doesn't take a math whiz to see there is no need to return to
the bank to deposit money. And she has no idea where the
checkbook is; there's only one, and Michael never bothered to
tell her when he took it or where he left it. She could find the
checkbook and attempt to pay their bills, or she could let
them accumulate, to wait for his return. The stack of unopened bills stuffed in the cupboard shows how little she
owes others compared to what Michael owes her.

Today Amy waits at the front door. Her anxious eyes
foretell the latest disaster. She says, "The water won't turn
on." A phone call explains the dilemma. The bill hasn't been
paid for two months. Barbara cries and thumps her fists on
the counter and curses Michael. A fee to turn on the water
has to be paid, and soon the electricity will go and the gas
and the phone and . . .

Frightened, she begins to open the mail. The bank state-
ment is a hopeless jumble. The low balance is probably lower
by now. She'll have to open a new account and start all over,
a solution she's used before, vowing she'd keep her figures
straight with the new bank. She'll figure in pencil in the
checkbook, so she can erase her numerous errors and check
and recheck her math so an error won't send her to jail, so
her children won't be cast out on the street hungry. Society
would probably be cruel to a woman and her dependent children who couldn't cope. Michael always said, "The world
loves a winner; when you lose, you lose alone." There has to
be more money before she can pay these bills.

She volunteers for overtime until it's an embarrassment

to ask the manager for something he can't offer. She looks for a second job, so days she works as a waitress; nights, she sells tickets at a movie theater. She's giddy, smiling constantly, muttering and giggling, reminding herself about what she's supposed to do. And people respond as if she were a lighthearted scatterbrain. She disciplines herself not to think about Michael, for thoughts about him are so convoluted they twist her until she can't function. She promises herself he'll be back. He will return because life can't go on without him. She focuses her energy on each task to be accomplished. Every action is counted in a series of three. First, she gets out of bed, then she showers, next she puts on clothes. Each day she strings beads to make a necklace. At night the string breaks and the beads scatter about her. The next morning she begins again: stringing beads in groups of three. Weeks pass this way.

By Thanksgiving, her tiny family has a routine. She works two jobs, almost sixty hours a week, and manages to hold both. Waitressing is second nature. Three years at the same job with the same demands and she can perform her duties half-asleep. She shifts into a gear where no energy is wasted, and her earning power has increased. The second job is easy. She sits in a booth in front of the theater, winding out tickets from a dispenser, making change, and asking and answering the same questions over and over. At home, Amy takes charge. For the hour when Barbara comes home to shower, change, and eat, she doesn't have to work. She asks a few routine questions as she flies in the door and listens to the answers with half her attention as she heads toward the bathroom. The shower gives her a lift, to propel her through dinner and on to the evening of work. Amy will keep the household routine of domesticity clicking along on track. And someday soon, Michael will return.

It's late by the time Barbara gets home on Thanksgiving Day. With all her ideas about holidays that they can't afford, Amy has managed one of her Girl Scout adventures. Barbara whisks her scarf from about her neck, pretending to concentrate on folding the wrinkled nylon as she hurries through the room, to allow the girls time and secrecy to finish their little project. She doesn't say a word about the dining room festooned with crepe paper, for they've turned out the light in the room and are whispering in the kitchen.

She sits on the bed to warm up for a while before she takes off her coat and changes her shoes. Her girls are painfully dear. She'll try to be happy to please them, to play their little game just the way they want. This must be Amy's doing. What a peculiar, yet lovely, child she's becoming. School must be going better now. At least her strange teacher hasn't been phoning. Amy does a good job keeping everything going, but a child shouldn't have to take on so much responsibility. It's abnormal the way she does everything so well without any prompting. Her motives are probably questionable. But someone has to take charge.

As Barbara bends to remove her waitress shoes, she feels guilty because she has failed in her job as a parent, guilty because her husband has left her, guilty because she is too unskilled to earn a decent living to support her children, guilty because she doesn't get off the treadmill of earning nickels and dimes to support them and ask for help. Michael has to come home. That is all there is to it. She ought to find him and demand his financial aid, make him pull them out of this limbo—or at least his children. She must make him protect his children. She pulls the oxford off her swollen foot. As she sets her right shoe on the floor and begins to untie her left, she notices the veins on her inner wrist are distended. How easily a razor blade would press into them. Aligning her shoes on the rug, she sits back on the bed and steals a few moments of idleness in the dim bedroom.

Her hands fall to her knees backside down, fingers curling limply toward the ceiling. She glances at her exposed inner arms and covers her right wrist with her left hand. She closes her eyes and becomes aware of her breathing, aware of the rawness of her throat, the ache in her chest: all the reasons why she must smoke less. The front of her head has gathered itself into a fist. It will be a headache soon if she doesn't make it let go and shake itself loose. She presses her fingers firmly between her eyes and furrows her brow, pushing her fingers upward, surprised by the thin layer of flesh separating her fingertips from the bone. She has endured eight hours at the restaurant; three hours at the theater; at least an hour for the bus, waiting at the stop or riding—hanging on by the strap in the back or huddled on her side of the seat, holding herself carefully still so she won't brush against strangers. Her exhaustion should anaesthetize her, but home is a searing pain—filled with Michael. His possessions watch her; she feels them at the corner of her eye. Each day these rooms become smaller, the contents shabbier. One day someone might open the door and find three strange creatures, their hair grown long and tangled, their faces pale and drawn from lack of sunlight, their speech a strange dialect comprehensible only to one another. She opens her eyes to the sound of the door being opened and Flossie murmuring, "Mom."

Barbara says, "Hi, baby," to the innocent face in the halo of hair and is sorry she's sounded so close to tears, for she's frightened her child, who is turning to leave. Barbara calls, "Floss . . ." and she's back carrying a plate with a glass of juice in the center, saying happily. "I made a cocktail for you."

Stuffed by the main course and nursing a reheated cup of coffee, Barbara decides this dinner has been Amy's greatest cooking success to date. She shared the credit with Flossie to be polite, but the credit belongs to her. Let her bask in the glory, knowing a second round of applause will occur when the dessert is presented. But the phone is ringing. Oh, Christ, it must be Michael. "I'll get it," murmurs Amy, passing behind Flossie, who sits open-mouthed, confused by the family drama.

Barbara closes her eyes as Amy walks toward the phone. Oh, God, he would choose now to call. A month and nothing. But Thanksgiving Day. Of course. Drunk and alone, Thanksgiving Day. Then the ringing stops. Amy's greeting is light, her voice happy. It isn't Michael. It's Mom. Oh, God, Mom must not learn about them. Amy is saying, "Yes, Mommy's home. Yes, we ate dinner." There must be some conspiracy between these two, but Flossie, the one who can reveal intrigues, has turned her face toward Amy, who stares at Barbara, a signal that she's on the phone next. She folds her napkin and lays it across her plate. On her way to the phone, she tries to catch Amy's eye, but she's elusive: such a schemer, another Michael.

Pressing the receiver to her ear, Barbara speaks. But Mom speaks simultaneously. They laugh like two pedestrians narrowly avoiding a collision, waiting for one to take the right-of-way.

Mom begins again. "Honey, how are you?"

"Honey" isn't one of Mom's words—too phony. Oh, God, they've conversed for thirty seconds and she's weighing words, searching for subtle messages. She snaps, "I'm all right," and her nasty tone shames her.

Mom's voice is almost a whisper. "I talked with Amy."

Barbara wants to shout, "Say what you mean, Mother." But she holds the receiver as if it were her throat and says, "Oh." This time she'll hold out, let Mom explain her remark. Amy is clearing the table, managing to stay within hearing range. Barbara wishes she could grab her wrist to make her confess if there has been an earlier conversation. A long stare will melt her thin, icy mask. Her grandmother and she grow closer as she matures. At first it had seemed good, a sign of Mom's approval. But the two might talk about Barbara, blaming her for the crumbling marriage. She closes her eyes, holding her bitterness and jealousy inside.

Mom sounds old and far away. "Michael's not home on Thanksgiving."

Barbara says slowly, carefully, "He's not home now," and congratulates herself on the line in the face of Mom's uncharacteristic frankness.

"And when was he home last?" The voice is coiled steel.

Barbara swallows hard, a naughty child confessing. "I don't know." Mom is silenced by the dilemma; a situation beyond any experience she's endured or even witnessed. When Michael had first deserted them, Gertrude had not been told until the truth couldn't be hidden. Their phone conversations could've been scripts for television advertising for the phone company. Their reason for the move was vague. Now Mom must sit in her immaculate trailer, facing the reality of her daughter's failed marriage.

Mom sounds detached as she says, "Well, it's been very cold here."

Barbara's spine sinks, her chest curves in, she breathes through her mouth to keep from wheezing. The weather, they're going to discuss the weather. And she is so concerned with her breathing, so sure Mom's through with her now, she almost doesn't hear the old woman's rambling.

"You know, I'd like to see some sunshine. To see the girls. Never have been to Arizona."

Barbara nods, wordlessly, her mind short-circuited: Mom at the airport, Mom in their shoddy kitchen, Mom on their lumpy couch. This cannot be. This nightmare is worse than her daily life.

When Barbara hangs up, her right hand is stiff from gripping the receiver. She shakes her hand to ease the aching. Mom is coming to this house. To absorb the shock, Barbara sits. Mom didn't say when, but this is not just a wish to visit. Mom never proposes what she doesn't do. She'll be coming, coming soon. Michael can't be retrieved, his health restored, transformed to the responsible family man he ought to be. My God, Mom will see what's become of their lives. Barbara reaches for a cigarette. This can't be happening. Once Mom witnesses her life, she will confirm it is real.

Chapter 16 |

Amy watches Mom. The hateful expression when she spoke on the phone with Grammy is gone. Mom's too sick and pitiful to fear, with her lifeless eyes staring across the room. "Mom, Mommy, is Grammy coming?"

Mom nods once, a definite, unhappy yes.

Amy says "Oh" with no shade of happiness or regret so Mom won't be offended. Then Amy looks hard at Flossie to keep her quiet. There must be time and silence. This is all so confusing. Grammy is coming because of Daddy, because he's gone. And being with Grammy will be good, like being a baby again; but this must mean Daddy's lost forever.

The image of Daddy holding out the envelope plunges her into sickness. She hasn't given Mom his mysterious message. Amy hasn't kept it to be mean or to steal; she just hasn't known how to give it to Mom. If only the paper would disappear, so she wouldn't have to hand it to her, so they wouldn't have to change. And now it is clear why he visited in the middle of the day; he isn't coming back, or he would've come when Mom was home. The envelope's so thin it could be empty; it's sealed with no address. She could have torn it open, or let the wind carry it away, or shredded it and flushed it down the toilet. But he'd said, "This is for your mother and you girls." So it wasn't hers to destroy; it's more theirs than hers. He trusted her so completely; he expected her to obey. She'd folded the envelope, feeling guilty about creasing it, and slipped it in the back pocket of her jeans. Now there's no time to rehearse her lines. She works the envelope out of the tight pocket and holds the wrinkled square toward Mom, who watches it unfold to a rectangle and holds out her hand. Amy murmurs, "It's from Daddy. He came today."

Mom doesn't speak, but her face is total attention. She tears at the flap that doesn't give, so she eases a table knife beneath it and saws, then tosses the envelope and a check to the table, holds up a slip of paper, and stares at his careless scrawl. Her eyes snap across the paper, then she crumples it and lets her fist fall full force upon her breast. She slashes the envelope and check onto the floor. She seems blind, pushing herself from the table and rushing to her bedroom as if she might be sick.

Amy gnaws at her finger. There's a piece of cuticle to tear away. She sucks blood and rubs her finger against her jeans. This room is dim, too dim with only the Thanksgiving candle light. She blows out the candle and rolls the ball of hot wax between her fingers, pressing the soft wax against her wound. The table is cluttered. The kitchen is worse. Mom hasn't closed the door to her bedroom, where she makes strange noises.

Crouched in the hallway, Amy sees Mom on her knees at the side of her bed. She pounds the mattress, its flabby softness absorbing her blows. Now she rocks on her heels and beats her thighs with repeated, bruising blows. She's growling like an angry dog, "Bastard, bastard." It is shameful to spy on a grieving animal. Mom's so angry with Daddy she's forgotten everyone else. He's gone and will always be away. Be good, be very, very good, and maybe Mom won't go away.

A rough edge on her thumbnail demands attention. She files at the ragged edge with her incisor. If Gram H. comes, and Mom says she is, there's a chance. Gram H. has never hated her, run away from her, wanted to erase her from her life. Amy takes one last savage nip at her nail and turns to the light switch. Flossie has slumped in her chair like a puppet without a puppeteer. She's an orphan too. "Come on, Floss," she calls to the disheveled figure. "Let's leave Mom alone. Let's clean the house to help her."

When the dishes are done, they tiptoe into the dark living room and turn on the TV to low volume. Lying on the floor in front of the gray haze of the screen, they sprawl on pillows from the couch. Amy shifts her weight on the aching arms, propping her head. In the commercial a team of horses pulls a sleigh through deep, falling snow. She tries to think of nothing but the sleighbells, the horses' hooves rising and falling into the soft snow, but the lighted houses at the end of the road are all filled with loving relatives, celebrating the holidays. And the father is who Daddy should be, his hands on the shoulders of his beloved daughter.

She is drifting into a dream when she hears Mom's houseslippers slap-slapping through the dining room into the kitchen. The lights in the kitchen flash and a cupboard door bangs so loudly it might have shattered. Flossie jumps, her sleepy eyes widening. Amy touches her hand to silence her. They huddle on their pillows, afraid to move. Mom drags a chair across the kitchen. Again she bangs the cupboard door. There's a whoosh then soft slaps as the envelopes flutter to the floor. And then there is a shuffling and tearing and a voice that doesn't sound like Mom's, shouting, "You and your goddamned money!" And there is ripping and slapping as she shrieks the words again and again.

Her bunched shirt exposes her skin to cold gritty linoleum as Amy crawls on her elbows toward the ring of light from the kitchen. Staying close to the wall and the protection of the shadows, she shakes her hand sharply to stop Flossie's pursuit. Her fist over her lips to silence her breathing, her chin on the floor, she stares through the legs of the table across the pitted linoleum. Envelopes are strewn in a single layer, fanning out from between Mom's legs. Her face is hidden by a tangle of hair. Her trembling hands tear at the envelopes, pulling out the contents, hurling them across the room. She shreds some. Some she stuffs in the pockets of her robe. Now her sobbing ceases. She is starting to stand.

Amy dashes to the TV and turns it up, then flops on the pillow. Mom is sweeping, closing cupboard doors, turning off lights. The slippers are slapping their way through the dining room; they stop at the edge of the living room. She stands in the doorway, her ghostly blue robe flapping about her thin legs. She rakes her hair with one hand and shakes a fistful of envelopes. Staring at the front door, she speaks to the nightlock: "This is what he left us." She tucks the envelopes under her arm, whirls about, and disappears into the bedroom.

Amy crawls to Flossie's side, but there is nothing to say. She doesn't turn from her television, her face haloed by the glow from the set. Amy strokes the curve from shoulder to shoulder until Flossie lets her eyelids close and drifts into sleep. At least she doesn't seem to know what Daddy has done, how Daddy doesn't love them, how they aren't good enough for him to love.

The house feels empty when she wakes. Mom's gone—maybe to work, maybe forever. Amy tries to go back to sleep. The Friday of Thanksgiving break means no school. The house is cold and dark. There's no school to go to and no money to go away. She burrows deeper into her bed. It is mid-morning before her bladder forces her to get up and go to the bathroom. Flossie is a small lump at the foot of her bed. She might stay buried under the covers for another hour. Amy moves silently, wondering how they will live as orphans, wondering what she'll do about Grammy's visit, what they will say to one another.

On the table, she sees the note from Mom. This must be a farewell note. She skips to the middle of the page. "Grammy will probably come tomorrow or the day after for sure." Relief. It's a note of instructions: "Tie up the laundry in sheets. Leave it in the living room. Grammy will sleep in

Amy's bed, so we'll sleep together." For two pages, Mom lists chores, her writing becoming more cramped as the list grows, and she ends, as if she ran out of time, with a warning to be ready by 5:30 to go shopping and take the laundry to the coin-op place.

Mom is frighteningly excited when she comes home. She phones the theater and says she won't come in to work, then adds, with a laugh, she'll never be working again, and to mail her last check. She hangs up and is off to her room, muttering, "I'll change and we'll get going." Speechless, Amy and Flossie sit on the giant bundles of laundry, waiting to see what she'll do next. There hasn't been time to even ask about dinner. She'll probably scream about lack of responsibility when she learns nothing has been started. But she comes into the room, slipping on her sweater, commanding them to grab the laundry and follow her to the bus stop. She doesn't look back as they struggle up the steps of the bus with their arms filled with laundry. She is setting her box of Tide on the floor so she can deposit the proper coins.

They travel across town on the bus for what seems like an hour. When they get off, the sky has turned dark and Amy's glad to carry the bundle, sinking her cold fingers into it, bunching it against her like an enormous muff. Before them is the biggest shopping center she's ever seen. They stand beneath the three-story entrance, where a roof extends beyond them like a concrete sled. They huddle next to Mom, who has brought them to this fairyland. She laughs at Flossie's open mouth and touches Amy on the cheek when she whispers, "Thanks, Mom." Then she hustles them through the entrance and takes a stroller provided for customers. They stuff their bundles into it and argue about which girl should have the right to wheel the giant snowman through the mall.

Mom is the lady she was long ago when she used to laugh. At a snack shop, she orders foot-long hot dogs, foaming orange drinks, and even french fries. She pulls a twenty dollar bill from her battered wallet and has to stuff the change around a wad of money. It must be from Daddy. She hadn't thrown it away.

Out on the mall, they dash from store to store. They buy bedspreads for Amy and Flossie, a tablecloth to replace the one with the cigarette burns, a throw to hide the holes in the living room couch, and glasses to replace the jelly jar collection. As they find another stroller to carry their packages, Mom goes to a pay phone. She's counting quarters, and as she deposits them, her face is serious with concentration. She hangs up and says, "She's coming tomorrow." They follow her through the stores, suggesting purchases, but she seems to be finished with disguising their house; now she's buying clothes for them. There are shoes for Amy and Flossie, new socks and undies, shirts and nighties. A voice over the intercom warns the store is closing, ending their spree. As the saleslady tallies their purchases, she asks if they'd like the packages delivered. Such generosity from an enormous store is impressive. The woman must not know they are poor and live in a little house set right on the ground, surrounded by weeds—a sad house they don't own and the owners care nothing about. Mom smiles at the clerk and says, "Yes, deliver the packages in the morning." She acts as if she's a wealthy woman on television, one who isn't ashamed to have others serve her. And as the clerk asks their address, Mom says almost rudely, "Oh, forget it. I need the bedspreads right away." Dazed by Mom's sudden wealth and this unexpected luxury, Amy doesn't complain about carrying the laundry home, laundry they had never found time to do. With the bundles of dirty clothes and a shopping bag hanging from each arm, the twine handle cutting into her inner elbow, Amy moves as quickly as she can.

Numb from walking two blocks from the bus stop to their door, they beg, "Please hurry" as Mom fumbles at the lock. Once inside, Amy and Flossie stagger to the couch to drop their bundles and huddle beside them, their teeth chattering, while Mom surveys the room, muttering to herself. She nods yes when Amy offers to make hot chocolate. As they sit at the kitchen table sipping, Mom says, "Thanks for helping," but she pulls forth each word as if she owes it, and there's a long silence ended by Flossie's noisy slurping. Mom's happiness is over; the silent stranger has returned. Bed is an escape.

Trying to sleep, Amy listens to Mom moving about the house, replacing old possessions with the new. It's a tiny bit like Christmas used to be, listening for Santa, waiting to fall asleep, to wake in the morning and go out to the living room to discover what's new and beautiful. Mom had said, "Grammy's coming, sometime tomorrow." Mom doesn't want to talk about Grammy. But perhaps she'll arrive during the night and stand by the bed like a fairy godmother, smiling at her granddaughter until she wakes.

She is shaken awake by Mom and her smoky breath hissing, "Get up. Get up. I need you." And before she can rub her eyes, Mom is rocking the lump under Flossie's covers, commanding, "Get up. We've got a lot to do."

During the night, like a magician, Mom tried to transform their house. She put new bedspreads over their beds while they were still in them, draped the throws over the ragged furniture, and picked up everything. She even put a bouquet in the center of what she calls the dining room table, the one that belongs in a kitchen with its chrome legs and red plastic top. But the new tablecloth almost brushes the floor and the flowers are plastic. It looks so terrible it's sad to see. It will have to be changed before Grammy arrives. It ought to be changed immediately, but Mom wants to strip the beds, to add the sheets to the laundry. Amy obeys. How silly they'd been dragging the laundry through the shopping mall. Now she and Flossie have to go to the laundromat while Mom finishes the house. And when they get home, they'll just have time to put away the laundry, get dressed, and get the bus downtown to connect with the limousine to take them to the airport.

At the laundromat, watching the clothes go round and round in the suds, Amy tries to think of how she might change the house. Before, it was so beat up it had what Mr. Crandall called "character." But the new possessions make the old ones look worse. Flossie thinks it's beautiful, which means it's very sad.

On the journey to the airport, buses connect on time at the transfer points, so they're the first passengers in the limousine. It's a magical vehicle, like a doubledecker bus in London. She might be a member of the diplomatic corps, or perhaps the First Lady, or the first woman president. But these fantasies do not calm her fluttering feelings. She hasn't seen Grammy since they moved to Arizona. Grammy can make stories real, can make beauty out of nothing. Even though Mom frowns, Amy invents a song as she sings, "Grammy's coming."

In the waiting room, they watch the old woman emerge from the coach section of the plane, and Amy jumps up and down, waving wildly, although she knows that the sun glaring on Gram's glasses blinds her. And Amy keeps on jumping even when Mom squeezes her shoulder with the "settle down" grip and frowns with the tightly-closed lips of the "behave yourself" look.

Galloping recklessly, disregarding everyone else in the world, Amy throws her arms around her Grammy's waist and presses her head against her bosom, so she feels her heartbeat. The pulse is faster and crazier than she'd expected, but she doesn't let go until Grammy hugs her hard in return. And even when her hug is over, Amy doesn't let go of Grammy's hand when she stretches to kiss Mom, who turns her cheek so Gram can barely touch her.

Chapter **17**

Lying on his back on his side of Gwen's bed, Michael stares at the ceiling and tries to figure out how he just moved into her apartment, right into her life without any discussion. The night when he split from Barbara, the night when he tried to drink himself to death at Fat's, Gwen was there and just poured him into her car. She's all right. Doesn't think drinking beer all day Saturday and Sunday is a fuckin' crime. No bitching from her. And she's cut down on the dope. The shit's addictive. He told her she'd be an addict the way she was going at it, and she cut down, but it was obvious she thought that line was a crock by her "you're-nuts-but-I'll-go-along-with-you" smile. Now she has an occasional beer with him, nursing it for hours. Without so much dope, her sexual workouts are pretty tame. One orgasm's enough and she's pretty straight. But the kid's got potential. To show her he's a sport, he's even taken to joining her pot-smoking sessions sometimes. A regular weekend is sleeping late, reading the paper for half a day, watching a football game. She can even talk football. But what's really great about Gwen is that beer's no problem with her—she doesn't bitch about it. She sets him up, gets him happy, and disappears for hours into her spare room, where she shuffles stacks and stacks of papers covered with kids' sloppy writing. Yet she keeps her eyes open and makes surprise visits. If she thinks he's lonely or bored, she always comes back to play.

Saturday drifts into Sunday, Monday rolls around, and work's a breeze to get to and get through. But to get to a phone and get to Barb is something else. Remembering hitting her is not the greatest—like thinking about a hit-and-run accident. What to say, and how to say it. Maybe he should just leave her alone. Who the hell knows what to do?

The phonebooth scene would be a killer. To go into a booth and start sweating like a bandit. Just to dial would be a bitch, with the old finger trembling, then listening for the ring, waiting to hear her dopey voice. Jesus, Barb is never there anyway. How the hell can a man be guilty without a chance to plead his case? Take them some money. Walking back in that house will be walking into hell, but you got a wife, you got kids, you got responsibilities.

Sending a check is chickenshit. Not that it wasn't a plan to try out. Ah, Christ, the things you'll do in desperation. Lori at work wouldn't mind typing up the envelope for Old Blue-Eyes. She's always been turned on by the slightly raunchy look, just a little mother who wants to take care of a man when he's down and out. But an envelope looks so fuckin' impersonal. He'll have to make a housecall, to explain a few details.

God, the scene at the house on Thanksgiving was the worst. The baby, Floss, was all love and kisses, a real sweet kid who can rip your heart out. But Amy. Shit, the kid's got a case against her old man that's turned her heart to pure hate. She's got every right—eyewitness to the Barbara scene. The kid could turn him in for assault and battery. Christ, she hates his guts! Thinks her old man's a wife-beater. Seeing those kids made sending a check make a lot more sense. Seeing Barbara is another obligation. And getting her fuckin' checkbook straightened out. Just got to time it right. Everything's a matter of timing.

Living with Gwen's the greatest. Winter in Phoenix is spring in New York. Mornings, with a belly fulla coffee after a night with Gwen, even the toilet paper biz looks good. Could wipe the ass of the nation, get a gold star on the sales board in Phoenix, hell maybe even New York. He feels like he's twenty-one again, up since five fuckin' with Gwen. Sex by morning light is a hell of a workout. Now she's gone for the day, leaving a fresh pot of coffee, a little kiss on the earlobe and a couple of obscene promises before she flew out the door, saying she'd be home around five-thirty. This is what life's meant to be. Gwen's therapy: the perfect partner for the O'Connor cure. She stepped right out of *Playboy.*

He opens his eyes wide to shake the groggy feeling he's had this morning. Mondays are always bad. He'll reheat his coffee, get another slug of caffeine. Kid loves her dope, not bad stuff either. God, the sports at the old Royal would shit to see Michael toking a roach. It leaves him with a sore throat and feeling hit over the head with a two-by-four the next day, but it can't compare with an A-number-one hangover. Just a toke or two of the shit gives a good buzz if he does it regular enough. He reaches for a cigarette before he pours his coffee. Regular, a habit. Shit, yeah, some folks might describe this as a regular habit—a toke or two every night before bedtime, blasted on the weekends. But it's fuckin' healthy compared to booze. "Fuckin's" a funny way to describe it. Screwing and dope go together like ham and eggs. And with Gwen it's always something crazy. Gwen's a doll. He pours the coffee, takes a sip, and burns his tongue, but cuts through the groggy feeling. As he shakes his head and curses, he glances at the kitchen clock. Shit, time to fly out of here. Cut off the burner, hit the lights, even make the fuckin' bed. Give the kid a break. A guy would have to be an absolute bastard to rip off a great kid like Gwen.

Chapter 18

Yesterday, waiting at the airport for Mom's arrival, Barbara had actually been desperate enough to pray for an honest confrontation. To tell Mom instantly about their lives would be preferable to slow discovery. Their home would tell a lot. All the last-minute attempts to cover their poverty had only emphasized it. This was the time to throw herself in Mom's arms and confess to the hell on earth of life with Michael. To be cared for would be such a blessed relief. God— or whatever force made things happen in this crazy world— was creating this meeting to resolve her unnamed anguish. But as the plane taxied to a halt, she felt cold with apprehension. Scolding herself, she forced a smile, but her face twitched. Everyone thought Mom was wonderful: intelligent, kind, energetic. Watching her mother's bowed gray head as she descended the stairs of the plane, Barbara was struck by how she'd aged. She would never accept the total failure of her daughter's life, shouldn't be expected to accept it. This visit would be an undetermined sentence, filled with the stress of Mom's subtle warfare, and Barbara hadn't trained in years. She craved a cigarette so much her palms itched, but she hadn't lit one. Her hands had to be free to fumble through the obligatory embrace.

This afternoon in the living room with Mom and the girls, Barbara has smoked a pack of cigarettes. From one-thirty until five-thirty, Mom has coordinated family activities, filling the hours with her version of gracious living. Past weekends were filled with shopping and laundry, tiptoeing around the house to avoid an outburst from Michael, who sat nursing a hangover in front of the TV, keeping the girls outside so they wouldn't disturb him. During this long afternoon, she fills the room with smoke as she watches Mom question one child, then the other. Art Linkletter's dialogues with children were as graceful as Mom's. Her interviews confirm how charming the girls are, how little Barbara has enjoyed them. She stubs out her cigarette. The number in the ashtray amazes her. She can't remember smoking them all.

Mom claps, a gradeschool classroom technique to gain everyone's attention, to add excitement. She's suggesting possible activities: games, stories, cooking. Barbara smiles. Perhaps the conversation hadn't been as spontaneously happy as it seemed. Mom sounds a little frantic. But the kids look happy. Her change of pace was well-timed. She lives as if she has a lesson-plan book filled with activities. Time is not punishment to be endured. She weaves it into functional yet lovely little doilies. Of the possible games to play, Amy chooses Old Maid. Gertrude turns to Barbara and says softly, "Unless, of course, dear, you had some other plan."

Flossie is dealing the cards. Barbara can't believe she actually agreed to play—thirty-two years old and playing Old Maid, the game that taught her to judge unmarried women as losers. Gertrude is becoming childish as she ages. Men are said to become fathers to their fathers, but she hadn't thought about becoming a mother to Mom. Daughter Ann ought to take care of Mom. Mom always favored her, the successful child. But she's off in Washington, writing articles for scientific journals, earning a salary tripling Barbara's, spending it all on herself—probably sleeping around, totally guilt-free. She's what Mom calls "a survivor"; she'd never sit at this table, her eyes downcast, taking orders as if she were a child.

Barbara envies her daughters' and Mom's pleasure in such simple conversation. Pleasure is the luxury of children or the clever like Ann and Mom. And what about Dad—if he were alive today, sitting here in this room, would he gaze out the window or join in his grandchildren's conversation? What a strange man he'd been. As a child, she believed he was dull and spineless. She had disregarded Dad's total dependability, a dependability Michael has not practiced with his girls. The distance of years, geography, and death reveals a gentle man who permitted Mom's criticism, even in front of his girls, because he wouldn't be cruel to another, not even to protect himself. How sad to have never spoken with him about his feelings or hers. He died so unexpectedly, and she hadn't gone home for his funeral. She'd argued with herself: New York was so far away; the girls would have to have someone to watch them; she didn't have any money; funerals were only for the living. Now those reasons seem wrong: she hadn't gone to his funeral because she was afraid if she left Michael alone he'd have disappeared.

At five Gertrude suggests it's time to plan dinner. Barbara almost says, "Whatever you like, Mother," but decides it sounds too hostile. She shrugs. Then Mom asks about the possibilities of what to prepare. Each item Barbara mentions sets Mom to bubbling enthusiastically about how delicious it will taste.

Her tiny dark eyes are sparkling behind her bifocals and the girls are practically purring. Mom has won their total devotion. So Barbara wearily plays her role in the domestic drama. It's cold and dark outside and her problems seem insurmountable. If Mom can manage a bit of lightness in this dark setting, it shouldn't be destroyed; no matter how brief it might be, they should embrace this illusive joy.

"Now, Barb, could you help me locate ingredients and utensils?"

Barbara fetches the necessary tools and does not apologize for their battered condition. She can't afford new ones. When they moved to Glendale, she stopped scouring and polishing. There wasn't time or money for perfection. Her home and its contents shame her, another proof of her failure, which even the aging eyes of Mom must see very clearly. The dull knives don't impede Mom as she flutters between her granddaughters to praise their progress.

Beneath Mom's thin disguise of gaiety there is a ritual. They are seated according to plan; food is passed in a certain direction; no one eats until everyone is served; each food must be evaluated—first it's tasted, then savored, then judged. She sets the pace and the girls follow. Amy is to the right of Grammy. What a wonderful parrot she is, mimicking each gesture perfectly. Barbara muddles through her turn. Flossie is next. She giggles but manages to capture the tone, and then Gertrude is on. By round two, Barbara has lost her appetite. She lowers her eyes and pokes at the applesauce but wants to toss the tired linen napkin, used at Mom's insistence, onto the plate, shove back her chair, and light a cigarette. She manages a little *um* as her participation.

She could be six, sitting in Mom's kitchen from noon until three until she cleaned her plate. Mom, a frighteningly intense enforcer of rules, had done her best to force her girls to eat what they should. The toilet bowl had become a garbage disposal for lukewarm milk and napkins stuffed with vegetables. For unless the plates were clean, dessert was denied. And while they'd been at school, Mom had baked pies or cakes or cookies worthy of a color spread in *Good Housekeeping.* If they hurried home from school, they'd get something warm from the oven, or better yet, they might lick the frosting from a bowl. At dinner, if they balked at a Brussels sprout, she prompted, "If you don't clean your plate, you won't have dessert." Somehow they passed inspection and won the treats. Today Mom's face glows with pleasure as she savors each bite, and all Barbara wants is a cigarette and coffee. And Ann, who had eaten everything and been roly-poly and miserable, is a pencil-thin woman, a fanatic dieter since college.

Mom sets her fork on the edge of the plate and delicately pats her lips with the napkin. "My, it was delicious, ladies," she confides. The gentle smile on the old lady's face might be post-orgasmic. Michael had said, "Gerty gets off on food like some people get off on sex." Mom's plump body does reveal a passion for food. Barbara drops her napkin over her plate to hide the little mounds of uneaten food. She will carry her plate to the kitchen and scrape it before anyone sees how little she's eaten. She looks at her daughters and murmurs, "Dishes."

Gertrude organizes an assembly line. Barbara stands at the end, mindlessly putting away whatever she's handed, regardless of whether it's properly dried or not. If she were a good mother like Mom, their carelessness would be criticized and supervised until it was corrected. If she really played her role well, she would spout some words of advice like Mom's favorite, "Any job worth doing is worth doing well." Instead she listens silently and halfheartedly to the conversation.

Tonight, "Little House on the Prairie" is on TV, a show Flossie never misses, one even Amy might be persuaded to watch. Gertrude settles in front of the set. She wants to know if the girls have read the book. In her estimation, TV is unquestionably second-best to reading. Amy mutters something about reading the series. But Mom is staring at Flossie, who is a nonreader like Michael. Barbara speaks in a voice made harsh by cigarettes and her lengthy silence. "Amy has read every book in the series." Mom doesn't seem to hear.

Thank God for television to fill the three hours until bed time. For twenty minutes at a time, she can flow in and out of the story, making a few comments during commercials to prove she's paying attention. In the story, the gigantic size of the fat man shames his wife and daughter. People laugh at him: children tease behind his back and make jokes for his daughter to overhear. New in the community, she denies he is her father. Maybe Michael's disappearance makes the girls lie. Certainly Amy has changed her behavior since he left. According to her teacher, she's a leader, but now she does so much at home she must run home from school to get everything done. She probably wants to avoid telling about what's happening to her family. Mom had criticized Barbara's not participating in afterschool activities. Mom hadn't understood her daughter's love of walking alone, kicking heaps of red and yellow leaves by the side of the road in the fall, stomping heavy snowboots through fresh-fallen snow in the winter, narrowly skirting the puddles in the spring. Mom approved of joiners, of people who got "involved." Dad was a solitary man whose concern was his business. So Barbara became a Brownie, a singer in the chorus, a ukulele player in the school talent show—anything to keep from being compared to Dad, who was so silent he was a shadow. On the TV program, the fat man is hiding in an attic so his family won't be shamed. How sad. Barbara wants to cry for him. Perhaps Michael is hiding from them because she's made it impossible for him to drink at home. Maybe the girls will see the similarity of the fat man on TV to their father. They stare impassively at the television. They have learned to cover their feelings; they certainly have learned the lesson well.

By ten, they are mesmerized. Flossie has to be pulled to her feet. Hugging her, Barbara suddenly feels embarrassed by this physical intimacy. She turns the child from her and propels her toward Gram, who will be challenged with all the potential for shaping within Flossie. The pair leave the room with their arms draped about one another.

Barbara turns off the TV to erase the weatherman's enthusiastic forecast for tomorrow's weather and glances down at Amy, who stares wide-eyed at the TV. Barbara doesn't stoop to touch her but nudges her little elbow with her shoe; her voice sounds sharper than she'd meant it to be, "Amy, let's go. It's time for bed."

Amy looks up, her face in shadows. "Mom, is Daddy coming home?"

There is courage, probably rehearsal, behind this question. But marriages should not be discussed with children. Memories of Mom's looks of disdain when Dad dared to voice an opinion still remain. Mom's ridicule of Dad behind his back is painful to recall. Barbara picks up an overflowing ashtray and says softly, "Amy, I don't know about Daddy," and as she walks toward the kitchen, she hopes Amy hasn't heard. If the wife and mother is frightened of the loss, it must terrify a child. Shaking the stinking ashes into the trash, she calls, "Go to bed, Amy. Please go to bed."

Amy rolls back on her belly on the hard floor and scrunches her cheek against the throw pillow, a numbing look of hatred on her face, then slings the pillow toward its home on the couch and pulls herself off the floor. She goes directly to bed without brushing her teeth or washing her face.

Barbara turns away, knowing no way to salvage the happiness of the child. Amy needs some time alone. Barbara will let her fall asleep lying on Michael's side of the bed before entering the room.

Turning off the lights in the living room, she walks toward the hall. But the light shines from the crack beneath the bathroom door. Mom is still performing her nighttime ritual. Gertrude methodically washes her face, rubbing in night cream, putting her partial plate in its soaking solution.

Barbara sits on the couch and reaches in her pocket for her cigarettes. Inhaling, she imagines Mom leaning toward the mirror, meticulously applying a film of cream to her withered skin. Her years as a science teacher should have made her more practical. She must know the hopelessness of lavishing such care on her appearance. Surely she's not trying to rescue her vanished youth to attract a man. Gertrude is always so sure, always so righteous; her decisions are beyond question. Barbara drops a warm ash in her hand and is struck by how ludicrous she is in contrast to Mom. In the solitude of the kitchen, she'll finish her cigarette and watch the moon through the window above the sink as she taps her ashes in the drain.

The warmth of her breath mists the window as she exhales. The moon moves behind a cloud. Perhaps the cloud moves and not the moon. She isn't sure. She scolds herself for not knowing. She knows so little about nature's phenomena. During adolescence, she'd never wondered about the world, never paid much attention in school or in life, never read a book for information. She'd been obsessed with herself. Her overwhelming insecurities had consumed all her time.

Fingertips flutter across her shoulders; she catches her breath and turns. Mom's face glows with cream, her white hair held in place with clippies. It might be a mask of a creature from an ancient Indian ritual. "Mother," she gasps and whisks the cigarette from her lips to hide her smoking.

Gertrude withdraws the hand. "Thinking?" Her voice is filled with compassion, the voice of one who might become a confidante.

Even in the moonlight, Barbara doesn't want to look at her. They aren't ready for this. Gertrude should be in the bedroom chatting with Flossie as they snuggle into bed for the night. Barbara should be in the bathroom vigorously brushing her teeth. Instead, they stand just a foot from one another, waiting to begin the confrontation.

Barbara lifts her cigarette away from her side. She's probably burning her robe. Thirty-two years old and afraid to smoke in front of her own mother. She inhales as if she were sucking anaesthesia, then attempts to exhale so the smoke will rise to the ceiling, but eventually it will drift into Gertrude's face.

Mom silently averts her face as though she's been slapped. She speaks in a rush as if she's very uncomfortable. "Barbara, can we talk—about your . . . situation?"

Barbara runs water over the cigarette. "Situation": how quaint. Mom might be suggesting pregnancy out of wedlock. Barbara turns to throw the cigarette into the trash. "Sure," she says sadly and adds, "Mom," as a salve. She gestures toward the living room where she can sit. Situation. Situation. When Barbara had been in a "situation," pregnant at nineteen and married to a boy with no prospects, they hadn't talked about her "situation." Poor Michael, who had assumed Dad was the head of the family, had explained their marriage, shivering in a phonebooth, rubbing coins together, saying, "Well, sir, we . . . sir . . . I . . . sir . . . married your daughter. Yes, that's right, sir." And there had been no discussion of why.

Barbara turns on the lamp beside Michael's chair and sits on the couch, hugging her robe about her. Gertrude seats herself on the only remaining spot, his chair. Dear Mom, if she only knew, she'd never permit her body to touch it. Beneath the light of the lamp streaming onto her, Gertrude's face is a deathmask, her dark eyes burnt holes. To fear this tiny woman, who looks so close to death, is pathetic. But a steely voice comes from the mask. "Michael has left you and your children."

Barbara's too tired to fight, too unsure, too frightened. Mom is right. She's always been right, and there is no way to defend Michael. Each instruction Barbara accepts is followed by another. She won't need to see Michael; there's no need to attempt a reconciliation. A lawyer will be necessary, but Gertrude can find a capable one and pay the fees. The children must be considered.

As Gertrude leaves the room to go to bed, she touches Barbara on the knee and leans toward her. Her eyes, which had seemed destroyed in the direct lamplight, have mysterious depths as she leans closer. "We will resolve this situation." And she's off to the bedroom, her apple-dumpling bottom soft despite her determined stride.

Barbara turns out the light. She feels like a woman who has learned she has cancer. What had been assumed to be small lumps, slight disfigurements, have been diagnosed as malignant. Coming out of the anaesthesia, she expected to find small incisions on her body. But she's lost her breasts. She might have lost her life. Tears well in her eyes, streaming down her face. She is diseased, her body filled with malignant growths. She can't reach within herself to cut out the evil spreading through her. Total submission to Mom's will is the only choice. The righteousness of Mom cannot be denied.

Chapter 19

Now that Grammy is here, no more orders come from Mom, who moves around doing what she has to do without any talking. And even though Grammy is a stranger in Phoenix and getting old, her plans are more fun than Mom's ever were. Gram's always asking, "Now, Amy, what's the name of this street?" or "Which bus route goes downtown?"

This morning Gram looks very official, wearing her reading glasses, sitting at the table with the newspaper, sipping coffee. She doesn't seem to miss a word as she drinks. But when Amy murmurs, "Hi, Grammy," she sets down her cup with a clatter and throws open her arms. Her fierce hug and noisy kiss are embarrassing even though she treats them like a joke. Nobody hugs in this family and laughing about it is hard. But Amy manages a smile and a breathy giggle.

Fixing breakfast, Grammy asks, "Honey, I've been meaning to ask you, just where does your father work?"

She says, "your father" as if she's saying "your problem," as if she doesn't know him. And this is not a question to be ignored. "Tristram Paper Products in Phoenix."

Gram brings the phonebook to the table and busily flips through the yellow pages. Focusing through her bifocals, her eyes look little and hard, and Amy is sorry she told on Daddy. She begins to hum loudly. If Grammy asks anything else about him, pretend not to hear. Like the person in the beautiful music Mr. Crandall played, Daddy is lost in the snow and some day may miraculously return, but no old lady, not even Grammy, can bring him back.

In the middle of the night, Amy wakes trembling. She dreamed she stood on the shore, drenched by the waves. She pinches the sheets. The smell of her fingers is unmistakable. The dark figure lying beside her is Mom, whose skin might be touched by this filth. Amy cautiously traces the dimensions of the puddle. God has been good to her. The urine is on her side of the bed and it's not daylight yet. Before dawn there might be time for the puddle to dry or at least the part closest to Mom. The flannel gown might dry it. She rubs her gown back and forth around the edges of the soaked sheet. When her arm begins to ache, she'll let herself rest. This is her punishment for being a disgusting person. She must continue using the greatest concentration as she works, for if she begins to forget her task, she'll rub too hard and wake Mom. Tomorrow is Sunday, so Mom will let her sleep in. After Mom gets up, Amy can change the sheets and hide the soiled ones. Later she'll sneak them to the laundromat. To hide her crime will take special care. Her arm aches, so she begins to alternate her rubbing action from hand to hand. It's beginning to be difficult to find a dry fistful of gown. Her eyes burn, but she's afraid to close them for fear of falling asleep. She must be fully awake when Mom gets up, so the plan won't fail.

Eleven years old and she wet the bed—she's still a helpless baby, whose body can shame her by peeing while she's asleep. It's almost December and the last time this happened it'd been late August. When it happens, she always wakes from a dream. Often she wades in a warm ocean near the boardwalk in Atlantic City, a place she only went once with Gram O. But there is no doubt, this is the place. The dream is always the same. Up to her knees in the surf, she is ecstatic as the waves approach, but fearful they'll rise and dampen the edge of her clothing. As they lap dangerously close, she clutches her clothes, then the waves roar away, pulling the sand with them, making her fall. And as they recede, she wakes to find herself disgraced.

But last night's dream wasn't at Atlantic City. The ocean was in a place where she was a stranger. The beginning of the dream is lost in her memory. If she starts at the end, she can piece together the scenes and watch them as if they were a movie run backwards. The dream ended with the familiar feeling of her body being beyond her control. But instead of a warmth seeping from between her legs, the warmth rose through the top of her head. Something left her body. The something must have been her spirit. It spiraled through her, like a pale blue genie, and emerged from the top of her skull. It looked down at her hollowed out body and smiled at her dying eyes. Her body's last vision was her spirit rising from the trap of her body into the sky. And before she closed her eyes in death, there had been one last message the spirit shared with her brain, "I am glad. I am glad to escape." And immediately after the spirit spoke, there was pain. A knife, dark and wet and slippery with her blood, plunged again and again into her midriff. Through her tears, she could see the knife was held in the hand of a smiling man, who plunged it again and again and never stopped smiling. And the face was familiar—the trusted face of Mr. Crandall. Now the beginning of the dream is clear. She'd been in the ocean, up to her ankles in warm surf, but had stepped out of the water to come to him, had turned her back on the approaching tide to walk to him, holding her arms open for him. He carried a long, narrow, white box, a gift for her. But before she reached him, he opened the box and pulled out a long, narrow knife with an ivory handle. He held the knife with both hands and plunged it, again and again, into her. And when she cried, no sounds came from her mouth, and he smiled continuously, the same smile she'd always thought was kind. She'd been glad when the genie had risen from head, glad it was over, and she was safe because, at last, her spirit had left her. And she became the genie, soaring above the ocean, peaceful and happy, until she discovered the puddle in her bed. Well, at least today is Sunday. She won't have to be in a room with Mr. Crandall today, or even see him, except when the dream flashes in her mind. She'll never go close to him again and never, never take a white box from his hands.

The first part of the plan about the bed went easily

enough. Mom got up early. She'd be gone for a while, drinking her coffee and smoking her cigarettes. Puffing with excitement and exertion, Amy takes the sheets from the bed,
only to be stunned. The mattress pad is soaked. The pad and
sheet changed, the bed made as neatly as her short arms can
reach, she stands shivering in her wet gown, ready to roll the
mess into the tightest ball she can, to hide it somewhere until
she can get to the laundromat. She must complete this criminal activity and get dressed and walk into the kitchen appearing as innocent and childish as Flossie.

Slipping into the kitchen, she hopes no one will study her
guilty face. Grammy is folding up the newspaper, clapping
her hands as if she were a playground supervisor. She announces she'll have to rout out the "sleepyhead Flossie," so
they can have a special breakfast, which she intends to prepare. Amy slides onto the chair, watching Mom's back.
Those tired, sloping shoulders are not going to take charge
It's no use trying to explain to Mom. No use at all. She can't
make Grammy go away or Daddy come back. She can't help
with Mr. Crandall.

Grammy makes eating breakfast, cleaning the kitchen,
and reading the newspaper into half of Sunday. They might
have sat around in their robes and slippers until the sun set
if Mom hadn't suddenly stood up, let the newspaper slide to
the floor, and announced, "I've got to get dressed."

The sun is shining, so they set off on a walk. Flossie runs
ahead as if she were an undisciplined bird dog. Amy walks
halfway between her and the older women, wanting to know
what they are discussing but not wanting them to know she
is listening. The yelps of Flossie make eavesdropping impossible, but pretending she wants to hold Grammy's hand and
to dawdle along between the two women so she might overhear them is too hypocritical. She trudges along between the
adults and the child, watching the sidewalk, avoiding stepping on the crack because she wouldn't want Mom to see she
wishes her a broken back. A green, fuzzy, slug-like thing

crawls before her. She stoops so it might crawl on her finger.
It's so strange it's pretty. The tickly feet are cool on her
skin. Inside of it there might be a butterfly waiting to fly, or
it might be a moth. It's a dustkitten now, but mysterious in
its promises. How beautiful it might be—this lonely little
orphan with its dozens of legs dancing across the concrete.
She could write a poem for Mr. Crandall pretending she was
this lumpy thing. She's just as unformed and squishy as
this caterpillar. Her waist doesn't dip in the way that it
should. Her breasts are tiny stars instead of peaches. Her
legs are hot dogs instead of rose stems. She sets her finger
close to the sidewalk so the caterpillar can step down and
return to wherever it is destined to go. She dreamily watches
it roll away on its escape from her giant hand, then scuttles
to her feet before Grammy reaches her. But it's too late.
Her sharp old eyes see the caterpillar, and she launches into
a lecture on larvae. Amy falls in step with her eager lecturer
and listens as Grammy's bony fingers massage her shoulder.
It's nice to be noticed each day, even if she has to listen to
caterpillars classified as they might be in a fourth-grade science book. She wonders if Grammy ever considered making
shoes for a caterpillar, knitting socks to cover all those toes,
lacing up shoes to fit each foot, finding a pair of trousers to
decently cover the multiple thighs. But Grammy is more of
an explorer. Like Vasco da Gama, she is a discoverer who
has sailed around the Cape of Good Hope. Instead of India,
she has found a park. In their part of Glendale, parks are as
rare a discovery as India. And this is a charming park:
small, probably only a square block in size, green with a
well-watered lawn, dotted with shrubs and flowers, and well
furnished with wrought-iron benches painted white and a
strange little house in the center of the grounds. Amy begins
to skip toward it; pointing, she cries, "What's that?"

"A gazebo," Grammy says, "a belvedere."

Amy skips through the maze of oleander hedges surrounding the structure singing, "Gazebo, gazebo." A wonderful

word, and if it grows tiresome, there is "belvedere," which
lends itself to singing too. She stops when she reaches the
steps of the structure. Up close, it is old and battered. Paint
peels from the wood, and it leans slightly to the left as if the
wind has beaten it. She could run to the center and explore
or wait until the others catch up to guide them. It would be
fun to show Flossie and to impress Mom with this discovery
of hidden beauty. But Grammy would begin her loud lecture
and ruin the possibility for fantasy with dull explanations.

Amy tests the first step to see if it will splinter to tooth-
picks beneath her weight. "Little lady," an old man's voice
to her left makes her withdraw her foot. "Little lady, you'd
better slow down."

On a bench almost hidden by the last stand of oleander,
sits a hunched, withered person, who could be a man or a
woman, but the clothing and voice belong to a man. She
takes a step backward, her fear replaced by anger. "Why?"
she asks with a touch of threat.

He taps his walking stick twice and points toward the
warped floor. "That ain't too strong. You go stompin' up
there, you might go stompin' through." He swirls the cane
in a half-circle as if it were one of his gnarled fingers.

She studies the structure and decides yes, indeed, she is
too fat for it to hold. It was built for fairies and nymphs, or
skinny little girls with straight blonde hair. She turns to the
old man to assure him she won't destroy the gazebo by
stomping on it, but now he ignores her. She hears Flossie
heavily slogging her way through the maze. Blocking Flossie
with restraining hands on her shoulders, Amy starts to explain, but the old man interrupts. "Ah, let 'er go," he says,
slashing his cane violently. Amy drops her hands and Flossie
bounds past her. The man averts his face with a slightly arrogant tilt to his chin, excluding Amy from his invitation to
explore the gazebo.

He must sense that she's not been good. Her body isn't
much heavier than Flossie's, but Flossie is obviously a good

girl who hasn't earned the suspicion of her mother and the desertion of her father. Wicked witches and good witches can see through to the heart. The man might give her a second chance. If he'd let her talk for a while, he could see a good soul hidden within her: a little, caged, yellow canary singing a pure song with heartbreaking trills. But he sniffs so his nose twitches, and he hacks hideously, then clears his throat. She turns from the gazebo and any hope of exploring it.

The guardian of the gazebo might live in the park. She could come here daily until slowly he began to trust her as a friend, telling her of his beloved wife, who must've died years ago, and his ungrateful daughters. Perhaps he has two who never come to see him in his room in the boarding-house, or maybe there's a sullen son. He coughs a rib-cracking hack, then spits. She walks slowly toward Mom and Grammy.

On the way back home, they stop at a delicatessen, where Grammy insists on buying things to take home for lunch. Amy wants a dill pickle, but Mom says not to ask an old person on a fixed income to waste money. All the way home, Amy feels like Cinderella, carrying the groceries so the adults can hold hands with Flossie. She swings between them, letting them lift her onto curbs as she giggles. Even by two in the afternoon, they cast short shadows which change shape from fat to thin and back again. Flossie is a wonderful child, someone Amy longs to be—beautiful and happy, who everyone cares for because she is naturally good.

By four in the afternoon, Amy can no longer pretend to enjoy TV, small talk, and Old Maid. She goes to the bedroom and closes the door halfway. She doesn't have the right to close it all the way since it's Mom's room. Lying on her side of the bed, she presses her cheek on the harsh texture of the new spread. It makes her nose itch. She worms her hand beneath her cheek and feels the flutter of her eyelashes against her palm and attempts to count how many times she blinks as she stares at the white wall. It could be a movie screen showing the story of someone's life: the old man's, Mom's, Grammy's, hers. But Grammy's life will not be played out in a park, or even in her trailer; she is moving in with them, just as surely as the stinking, urine-soaked sheets have to be sneaked off to a laundromat. And if Grammy has moved in, Daddy has moved out.

She didn't mean to cry, but tears slide onto her palms as much out of her control as her dream of the ocean. She cries quietly until she chokes on her secret tears. She wipes her wrist beneath her nose and pulls herself to the edge of the bed. Daddy should know. He might be sitting alone in some park on this Sunday afternoon, not knowing his wife has given his part of the bed to Amy, has given his chair to Grammy, his place at the table. The comic-book cloud for dialogue above Daddy's head, which he fills with jokes and snatches of songs or his heavy, blue silence, has vanished. Grammy fills the spaces where he's supposed to live. She's an art gum eraser swooped into their house to rub out everything. Daddy's face still focuses sharply—his smell, his pattern of breathing—but Grammy has only been here two days. What will happen in a week or . . . but to think beyond a week isn't possible.

Grammy found Daddy's office address in the phonebook: useful information. Amy could ride the crosstown bus until she found Tristram Paper Products. It had sounded so impressive when Mom told them about Daddy's "good job." In the grocery, Flossie and she used to find every product made by his company and race to tell Mom. Then Marcy Briggs told the class that Tristram made toilet paper, and everybody laughed so no one heard Amy explain toilet tissue was only one of their products. And she resented kids like Marcy, who said: "My father is a ——" and then they'd proudly filled in the occupation. Well, at least Daddy's not a mechanic like Duane's father, and she has a father, as far as the rest of them know. But he has got to come back to his bed, his chair, the kitchen table. He has got to move through their lives even if he won't smile and laugh and talk with them. If they can at least have him around, then slowly he'll come back to live with them the way it's supposed to be.

She turns on her side to consider a plan and the faint odor of stale urine reminds her of her unsolved problem. It will have to wait until tomorrow. She'll have to get home very early and sneak off without Grammy seeing her. The bus stop is along the way. She'll check the schedule posted by the bench. Daddy cares. He came here only three days ago to give them money. To find him by taking the bus would not be easy. A letter might be faster. When he learns he's being replaced by Grammy, he'll come back immediately.

She climbs off the bed and gets on her knees to check her bundle of sheets. Her eyes smart from the ammonia. Yes, he'll come back immediately when he gets her letter. Money. She'll have to find money for the laundry, for the stamps. She breathes shallowly through her mouth. But as Mr. Crandall says, "Where there's a will, there's a way."

Chapter 20 |

Gray rainy Sundays are the best times with Gwen: the morning paper spread out on the bed, coffee on the night-stand, the radio softly playing FM. Michael could be nine-teen and playing ball, working out: the graceful loop of a well-thrown ball spinning out of the sky into his glove with a smack, the pause for a breath before throwing the sucker with a whoosh, watching it sail and then waiting to catch it, getting ready to do it all over again. So smooth, so many times, he never knew how many and he never knew he was tired until he jogged into the dugout, until he showered, until he sat on the bench to put on his shoes. Sundays with Gwen, being pampered the way he was when he was the hot-shot kid on the field.

Skimming through the sports section, he stretches on the bed beside her and feels as warm and relaxed as if he were submerged in the swirling waters of a Jacuzzi. She hops out of bed, her naked feet toeing through the shag rug, her little bottom pale where the bikini had shielded it from the sun, the skin dark as caramels all the way from the dip of her waist to the sweep of her shoulders, with narrow, pale stripes where the top was.

When she's gone, a fist of anxiety grips his chest, so he reaches for a cigarette. She sure doesn't look thirty. Just a coed, dead-ringer for a California girl. A kid raised on orange juice, hanging out at beaches called Balboa, and driving a foreign sportscar with the top down. What the fuck she's doing with a broken-down drunk who's run off from his wife and two kids is some mystery. It's hard to believe she hasn't noticed she's part of a screwball couple. But if she's too out of it to notice, there's no need to bring it up. Just ride this lucky streak, keep it rolling. This kid's better than a lucky necktie. Keeping her means toeing the line. Drink anything stronger than beer and she'll vanish faster than Cinderella—disappearing as fast as she appeared. She's got rules for her little games, and they work. A "J" every afternoon, and no more than three beers. If she doesn't have double tokes, she won't want to screw.

He busies himself with the paper when she comes back in the room. Jesus, she's a beauty: a nymph on a seltzer bottle. She'd better never know how hit over the head and helpless she makes him. That kind of power's dangerous in any woman's hands. Keep it cool, Mike, keep it cool. Like stepping up to the pitcher's mound and giving your cap a casual little tug, like spitting on the ball. Keeping this kid requires style, pace, and cool. Just keep afloat on this fine cloud vapor because when you look down, right in your shadow you're gonna see her face with her big eyes.

He snaps the paper as if he were slightly irritated as she traces his collarbone. Oh, Jesus, she feels like tickling, and she's flapping those ridiculously long lashes like some flapper on the late show. She snuggles and purrs, "I fixed us a special brew, my friend," and then she giggles as she slips beneath the sheets and slides her hand along the old belly. And the smell of marijuana cuts right through the cigarette smoke. She's been taking a hit or three or four waiting for the tea to brew. Ah, Christ, old Charger's up for grabs.

An hour later, and all she's done is laugh and laugh and laugh. She's doubled over in bed, pressing her knees to her chest, biting her kneecaps to stop from laughing so hard she cries. He sits on the edge of the bed, watching his toes and smoking. A good slap can sober up hysteria, or she could just laugh it off alone. She's having a blast. All this time she's known he's an ass. Now she's having her laugh. Yeah, having the last laugh. Yeah, yuck it up, Gwen, let the rest of the folks in the apartments know all about it.

He stubs out the cigarette and leans forward so his elbows are on his knees, his face in his hands, his ears open to her crazy snorting sounds. She was kinda cute at first, all cuddly, but then she got weird, like her little joke, "Wanna wear my padded bras?" Then she messed with the chest hair, twisting it into ringlets, blowing on it, acting like it was the most hilarious thing she'd ever done. And right in the middle of a very serious kiss, she started to giggle. And she treated a command to "get serious" like a fuckin' parrot, saying it over and over till it could drive a man nuts. Ah, Jesus, what's she up to now?

As she blows in his neck, playing the piano on his vertebrae, singing with each note she plays, he shrugs hard to give her the message, then scoots a little closer to the edge of the bed. Wait her out. The silliness of kids turns calm if you ignore them long enough. Oh, wow, this kid can't take a hint. She's scooting up, getting so she'll be center stage, so close her breath bounces off the bod as she sings, "It was just one of those things." And now she's whistling, directing a fine stream of air at the back of the ears. Jesus, she's stubborn. This choice of song must be one of her not-too-subtle messages.

He reaches for his cigarettes. Another fit of giggling seizes her. She's moving in, her fingertips grabbing his elbow, talking in a stupid, baby voice, "Don't go away mad." Michael ignores her, acting like he's stone deaf. Her hand is making a move to the inner thigh, one finger tracing the long line of the thigh muscle. Now she's a sympathetic mother talking to a kid: "Oh, did you go away?" She's staring at the Charger, clucking like an old hen, patting the thigh.

He grabs her hand to keep it from getting any more personal and lets his forearm shield his crotch. "Ah, Christ." He manages to get the cigarette to his lips, hunches his shoulders, and sucks hard on the corktip, holding the smoke at the back of his throat before he lets it drift slowly into his lungs. As he exhales, the smoke streams slowly down the curve of his sunken chest and belly and disperses into a haze over his pubic hair and flaccid penis. The fella might never rise again, poor Charger. Been already to gallop, almost bouncing against the bod in eagerness to get out and run, and now it's a cripple, soggy as an old lady's water bottle. There are at least three good drags left on the cigarette before a decision has to be made. Not having a hard-on hasn't been a problem before. Always got to call the shots in sex with Barbara and any of the faceless one-night stands. Shit, didn't even bring a robe to bed—no disguises: no baseball uniform or salesman suit or alcoholic haze, not even a hit of the tea making her so nutty. There's nothing left of the cigarette but filter, and she probably gulped the last of the tea. Walking away might be a mighty big problem since there will be jeers from the bleachers after striking out.

He glances over his shoulder to see if this is the place for a fast exit. She's curled around, head on the pillow, shoulders curved so the blades are like wings trying to sprout. Her knees are drawn up to her breasts; she's covered by her upper arm and her hands are hidden between her thighs. The giggles are just little spasms now. Stand up real slow and she won't even know you're leaving.

He turns from her. Well, whatever the hell she thought was so funny about the bod, about kissing, about the whole fuckin' relationship, will have to be a memory when she's looking for entertainment in the future. Goddamn. Even though the old bod has taken a hell of a lot of abuse, it still looks good. Got a great ass and shoulders, and the old gut hasn't gone flabby, yet. Don't have to sneak outa nobody's bed, whether she's a fuckin' gorgeous college graduate or a tramp.

Before he has even taken a step away, she calls, "Michael," and there's no laughter in her tone. "Michael, are you leaving?"

Let her look at your ass, the way women do, get a load of the spread of these shoulders. Listen up, honey, strain your little ears. "That's what you wanted, right?" God, she'll think he's just following her orders.

She speaks in a low wail, ending up as a cry, "I don't know."

Jesus, she knows how to sink a hook. Get outa here while you can still breathe. Don't look back. But she's turned on the bed so her arms are thrown wide open, her hair fanning across the pillow, framing her face. There's nowhere to go but back to bed. "What'd you mean, you don't know? For an hour, you been laughin' your ass off." She's sitting up. Oh, Christ, the Charger's a saggy pecker for her inquiring eyes. Give her the old look-me-in-the-eye technique the nuns used.

She's a good little student, her eyes don't stray, not even a glance at Charger's disgrace. She's as close to groveling as any person or animal could get. She's guarding her breasts with her crossed arms, pulling her knees up, whispering, "I'm sorry."

He leans toward her, pushing her nose into her regret. "You oughta be." And it makes him feel as rotten and powerful as when he'd yanked the hair of the nuns' little favorite, Katy Callahan, until she cried. Gwen's knockout eyes are misting; she's wiping the corners with a forefinger. Ah, pretty girls in tears.

"Well, I'm sor-ry," she breaks the word into two parts, and her shoulders rock with sobs not laughter. He's on his knees, stroking her hair, parting the strands, pushing it from her forehead, kissing her brow. "Tell me." Confessing her nastiness will get her clear—like the beating Big Mike gave him when he learned about Katy. Being bad is how you learn. Uncle Charley heard about Katy and brought over a picture of St. George, the dragon-slayer, and a lecture with the gift: men protect women, they don't attack them.

She whimpers a catalogue of rejections: her husband's betrayal, the desertion of her friend. And each chorus concludes with the verse, "It's me: I make it so men don't want to stay."

"Yeah, well." Women do bitch and moan. Women push men away. So the kid's no different. She needs a little help. Confessing cleanses the soul. A good screw tames a bitch. Got to protect them from themselves. Be gentle, forgive her, come back. "I want to stay."

He eases himself into the bed beside her, and pulls her the length of his body, so they can rock together in a single, long curve. They make love slowly, for he pins her to the mattress by her wrists. The kid's all gratitude. She knows a good man when she finds him.

Chapter 21

Three days ago, she mailed the letter to Daddy, and every day she prays all the way home from school that his answer will wait for her in the mailbox. Today she's made particularly good time getting home. She's panting when she dashes through the kitchen, and as she slams down her books on the table to hurry out the front to check the mailbox, she sees Grammy seated at the end of the table and murmurs, "Oh, hi, Gram," to the startled eyes staring over the tops of bifocals. She acts as if she's been doing something secret. Amy walks slowly by her, trying to sneakily investigate her activities. Her age-spotted forearms rest across the yellow pages of the phonebook, and there's a pad and pencil under one hand. On her way to the living room, Amy realizes Gram's probably brought in the mail. Having to ask her about it is irritating. On the porch, Amy squints into the late afternoon sun to check the box. Empty. She calls to Grammy. No answer. She sighs angrily. Gram doesn't even know she's a bother.

There's no letter on Thursday or Friday. Saturday will be a day of torture. All day they'll clean house and take directions from Gram while Amy listens for the mailman. She wants to follow him down the block and ask him in private if he can remember delivering a letter to Tristram Paper Products with her return address. She knows Daddy has answered her: he wouldn't ignore her questions about when he's returning. The letter must be lost, or she forgot to put a stamp on it, or the most horrible thought of all, one which sounds more possible each day: Grammy has taken it.

On Saturday morning, Amy doesn't want to leave the cocoon of her mother's bed when she hears Grammy shuffling in her houseslippers into their room. She calls in a chirping voice, "Rise and shine," and Amy slides deeper into the warm darkness of the bed that Mom left an hour ago. Grammy's continual good cheer has begun to be wearing. For days Amy has practiced how she will ask: "How long are you going to stay? When is my father coming back?" And the more she secretly practices, the more difficult it becomes to look at Gram's face. A cooing sound means Flossie has trailed Gram and is having her hair stroked. Amy rolls over, pulling the sheets with her so she's bound like a mummy. She'll have to get up soon, but she'll wait until they've left the room. The cooing voice is being directed at her now. Amy grunts to warn she's not in the best spirits. But the bed sags as Grammy sits on it, barely missing Amy's feet. Gram rests her arm against Amy's hip. "Got to get up, lazybones," she teasingly commands. Unable to openly defy the order, Amy begins to move slowly out of the covers. Gram's foot in a fuzzy slipper swings in circles. Her dark eyes in her wrinkled face are staring into the covers. Without glasses, her eyes are frighteningly large. Amy sits up, folding back the sheets as Grammy says, "Your Mommy and I are counting on you to do a good job of taking care of Flossie today and doing the housework. We have to go to town to attend to some business." The firmness in her tone means she'll answer no questions.

All through dinner, Mom hasn't said a word, letting Grammy buzz on like she always does. But during the pause after everyone has finished eating, before time to clear, Mom suddenly stands, looking so pale she might be ready to vomit, and she says, "Divorce. I'm getting a divorce," and then turns away. Amy stares at her back framed in the kitchen doorway as she disappears into the room without another word.

Mom is a thin, pale woman, a stupid woman, and still she can change their lives. There is no use following her, pleading. It is done. "Well," Amy says out loud to herself. "Well." She stands with her hands on the top of the back of the chair. The table swims before her. She is paralyzed with frustration as Gram approaches on her crepesoled old lady's shoes. At the touch of the arthritic fingers, Amy flinches and looks into the eyes distorted by bifocals. She slaps the hand from her shoulder and then is so frightened by her action she runs to her bedroom to hide deep beneath the covers.

She'll write another letter. The other one got lost. Perhaps she copied the wrong address, or left off the zip code and confused the postman. But she remembers clearly how carefully she'd written, even proofread, before she licked the edge of the triangle flap and sealed it. The post office hadn't been mistaken; she had. What she'd written to Daddy had been wrong. She must've sounded self-pitying, and Daddy always said, "Nobody wants to spend time with a sourpuss." She tries to remember every word she wrote. She sits at the cardtable and tries to rewrite the contents precisely, so they will be exactly as they'd been. Mr. Crandall says writers can create a mood by the words they choose, so she'd tried to be a newspaper reporter, giving facts and information about what was happening in their home. She'd signed the letter "Love" and started it with "Dear Daddy." But he is my father. She moans softly. Because she had not allowed herself to write "I love you" endlessly across the page, followed by "come home," it had taken a long time to complete the letter. It had reached its destination but had angered Daddy. She studies her duplicate of the letter, searching for clues, and decides she should never, never have told him about Grammy being in this house, about how Mom is always busy, about how lonely it is without him. He would've come home of his own accord if he hadn't learned about Gram. And now she has taken over their lives. She's the one who got Mom the divorce. Gram is hateful. No one in this house sees her for what she is. Mom just mopes around and does what she's told to do, and Flossie is as stupid as a puppy, doing anything for a pat on the head and a bite to eat. The only one who understands what Grammy's really like is Daddy. And now it's clear why he never smiles when she visits. He knows she wants to take over everything, to squeeze him out of their lives. In the stupid letter, she told him Grammy was here and had not even complained about her moving in, nor begged for him to come home.

Amy hugs herself and rocks. It's her fault. Her foolish misunderstanding means he'll never come home again. He's left his women and disappeared. She squeezes her eyes closed against tears. She will not permit herself to cry, not when she's the one who's been wrong. She hadn't known how to show Daddy her love. And as she bounces forward and backward in anguish, her mind races with a multitude of plans to undo what she's done. But none of them will change what has happened.

She'll have to learn to live without a father. There are kids in her class who don't have fathers; she can learn who they are by being observant on the playground. Divorce is always a favorite topic of conversation of the girls who play jacks under the ramada. Marcy Briggs, their organizer, keeps up a nonstop conversation, with the girls taking turns contributing information. "They're getting divorced, you know," might be whispered, or "Her mother ran away," or "My mother read in the paper this morning, they're separating," or "Oh, they've been divorced for years."

Daddy says, "Make somebody think they're important, and you've got a friend for life." So instead of playing with the boys, Amy plays endless jacks games, asking the kind of questions the girls love to answer and volunteering very little about herself. If she just keeps wearing her "dimple puss," they keep talking. No one seems to have discovered her disgrace. And she learns which of her classmates come from what the nuns called broken homes. Kristy Sutton, Elizabeth Perry, and Brad Patchen have lost their fathers to divorce, so she will get them to talk to her about it.

Following Kristy Sutton out to the school swings, Amy

remembers that during a class discussion of Mexico, Kristy mentioned her mother works at La Casa. When Marcy forced the issue, Kristy admitted her mother is a waitress. Catching up to Kristy, Amy begins to talk quickly about how her Mom's a waitress too. Kristy looks as if she doesn't believe her and interrupts to say, "My parents are divorced. They were when I was three." And before Amy can offer her sympathy, Kristy says without flinching, "My dad's a drunk." Then she breaks into a run and climbs on the swing: her total concentration seems to be to gain height, pumping her legs wildly, lifting herself higher and higher into the air. Climbing onto the next swing, Amy tries to match her rhythms so they can talk. But she doesn't know how to begin, how to get to the question, "How did you feel when your father went away?" Looking at Kristy's tranquil moon face, Amy decides the girl won't be helpful. After all, she'd only been three when her parents divorced, and everyone in class knows Kristy isn't smart. She's in the lowest reading group and is always the first sent to her seat during a spelling bee. The first choice for a subject is beneath consideration. But the rest of recess, Amy plans how she might approach Elizabeth Perry.

Amy's major competition in class, prim, perfect Elizabeth, never wears jeans to school and carries a book satchel that might have belonged to her mother. Elizabeth never slouches, giggles, gossips, or teases the other kids. On the playground, she is a solitary figure. Jumping rope by herself and keeping count of each little hop she takes, or reading a book while she munches on a carrot, are her usual activities. In the classroom, the only person Elizabeth speaks to is Mr. Crandall. She volunteers to help him with bulletin boards after school, or any other chore he'll give her. Three months ago, waiting to see Mr. Crandall after school, Amy overheard Elizabeth shakily explaining, "And after the divorce, I'll only see him on weekends." Amy considered leaving: this was a serious discussion; but if she left, her eavesdropping would have been apparent; if she stayed, she might witness an embarrassingly emotional scene. As she walked toward her locker, trying to decide what to do, Mr. Crandall called, "What can I do for you, friend?" Elizabeth's mouth was a thin line, her face composed, intent upon some project Mr. C. had given her. Amy murmured, "Oh, nothing." But she'd learned that beneath Elizabeth's calm exterior there were explosive secrets.

Because of Duane and then because of Daddy, Amy hadn't been staying after school. But now, Elizabeth's friendship seems necessary to understand the complexities of living with divorce. After the last bell, Amy watches Elizabeth, who is smiling at Mr. Crandall in a unique way. She is positively in love with him: her face flushed, her eyes shining, she giggles at something he says. Amy sighs. This is going to be very difficult. She is considering giving up the plan when Mr. Crandall asks if he can do something for her. In a rush, she asks if she can help and is pleased and surprised when he says, "Yes, of course."

When Amy drags a chair up to the table, Elizabeth withdraws even further into checking papers, acting as if she doesn't hear Amy asking for some. When Mr. Crandall calls, "It's all right, Elizabeth," she shoots a withering look at Amy, separates five papers from the bottom, slides them across the table, and returns to grading. For an hour, they sit beside one another, silent except for Amy's requests for work, to which Elizabeth responds by grudgingly doling out papers. Mr. C. digs through the file cabinet, stacking papers on the table, pausing to give directions to Elizabeth, who relays them to Amy by pointing to the answer key. Elizabeth wants to confuse her, to make her fail so she'll be rejected as a helper, as a favored one. Determined not to make an error, she stares hard at the sloppy scrawl of Mr. C. By watching and listening, she is soon able to work without asking for help. Racing against Elizabeth becomes the game. At four-fifteen, Mr. Crandall glances at the clock, sighs loudly, and rolls the file cabinet drawer closed. "Well, ladies," he booms, "It's quitting time." He rubs his hands as if he were washing up, "And it looks like you've finished a mountain of papers for me. Thank you a lot." Amy watches Elizabeth for the proper response. She bobs her head shyly, puts on her sweater, and dashes for the door. Amy lingers, wanting to ask if she can come back tomorrow, but she realizes she'll have to hurry to catch Elizabeth, who will be even angrier if Amy stays. She grabs her jacket and races to the door, calling goodbye over her shoulder to Mr. Crandall.

Elizabeth is by the bike rack, crouched beside her old Schwinn, which she's painted yellow and decorated with flower decals. Amy catches her breath and considers how very much like Elizabeth the bike looks: out of style, yet well tended. Staring at Elizabeth's part and the sleek, black hair held taut across her skull by a pair of blue plastic barrettes, Amy tries to force the narrow face, masked by glasses, to look up at her. "Elizabeth," she says loudly and breathily, "Elizabeth," and feels a panicked loss of words.

"What?" Elizabeth snaps, not bothering to look up from the combination lock, spinning it to the left and then to the right. She jerks it quickly twice. It doesn't open. She looks suspiciously over the tops of her harlequin frames sliding down her nose and rocks back on her haunches, her skirt bunched around her thighs, the crotch of her blue underpants totally visible. "What do you want?"

Not wanting to lie to Elizabeth's face, Amy looks toward the traffic. "To be friends."

The bicycle chain clanks. Now Elizabeth stands, winding the chain around the bar supporting the seat, inserting the lock. "Friend" spoken in reference to her seems to strike her as "incredible": a word she uses, one Amy looked up to defuse of its power.

Amy laughs nervously and looks away, embarrassed. Of course, Elizabeth wouldn't be easily charmed like foolish people. She has won every reading contest at school. The number of books she reads often doubles the number read by the runner-up. And she doesn't read easy, skinny books. She reads constantly: before school, between assignments, and after school. Weekends she must read off and on all day. In class, she announced to Mr. Crandall, "Lousia May Alcott is my favorite, and analysis of character is my specialty," and all the kids looked at one another and rolled their eyes. Frequently, Amy has felt Elizabeth gaze across the classroom and turned to look back at her, but Elizabeth always quickly turned away. The line about friendship has been judged by Elizabeth as an obvious lie; they have nothing in common except their competition to be the smartest one in class.

Elizabeth asks in a low, hostile tone, "You want to be friends with me?"

The silence between them will crack, plunging them in deep water. Trusting to her acting ability, Amy leans forward, "My parents," she states firmly, "my parents are getting a divorce." She might as well have hung a banner across the school entrance announcing the fact, one she's never spoken out loud.

"Hm." Elizabeth spins her lock and studies Amy with narrowed eyes, more curious than angry. To avoid their scrutiny, Amy glances at Elizabeth's knee, which twitches with tension. Elizabeth speaks softly, "Do your parents fight, or what?"

Moved by her compassion, Amy plunges on, "My father left two months ago."

Elizabeth states knowledgably, "Desertion."

Offended by the authoritative manner, Amy explains, "I don't think it's desertion." The dun-colored eyes frankly appraise Amy. "He's given us money."

"Hm." Elizabeth returns to the lock. During her silence, Amy panics. Elizabeth doesn't believe her. But Elizabeth begins to speak as patiently as she might with a reluctant pupil. "But he has been out of the house for—" she pauses for emphasis, "two months."

Amy stiffens, speaking in a rush to correct the accusation. "He hasn't been living with us, but he's come to the house." Her voice should draw a line not to be stepped over.

Elizabeth is relentless. "How many times?"

"Well, once, but he wrote to my mother." She pauses, embarrassed by how irresponsible Daddy sounds. "Oh, I . . . really, I don't know how many times because of course it's her mail." Amy stops, afraid she'll reveal her letter, which he ignored. As Elizabeth ponders the topic, Amy remembers the class assignment on letter-writing when Elizabeth said her father wrote her weekly "long letters filled with information" and she'd hurried to add, "He's an English professor at Phoenix College." Because the class began to snicker, Mr. Crandall had called on someone else. But throughout the year, she'd announced when her father took her to the ballet or symphony.

Irritated by Amy's silence, Elizabeth prompts, "Your mother doesn't read you the letters?"

Amy looks at the toe of her sneaker. Until now she hadn't considered it an insult that Mom hadn't read the letters to her. Defensively she says, "She doesn't read them herself. She sticks them in the cupboard." This sounds very strange. Elizabeth will think Mom is very peculiar. And she is, but . . .

"Doesn't let you read them." Elizabeth emphasizes "doesn't" as if this revelation is truly shocking. "That sounds very strange to me."

Kicking the toe of her sneaker viciously, Amy looks up at the righteous figure before her and says angrily, "She is such a weird person," and she could be describing Mom, or Elizabeth, or the strange-looking woman who drops Elizabeth off at school, who must be her mother. And the ridiculousness of them all explodes: "I hate my mother. Do you know what she did?" The rush of words is such a relief she doesn't care what Elizabeth thinks. "She got my grandmother, her mother, to come out here and get my parents a divorce. She didn't even ask my father."

Elizabeth mutters, "Is that right?" She speaks slowly to
educate. "You mean your mother is the plaintiff?"

Amy shakes her head as if a fly were buzzing around her
eyes. Oh, Elizabeth, Elizabeth who chooses words to put
walls between them. There is no way to continue the conversation without asking for a definition. "A what?" She won't
give Elizabeth the pleasure of hearing her stumble over the
word.

"A plaintiff is the complaining party in a litigation . . ."

Amy interrupts the lecture. "Yes, my mother complained."

"What were the grounds?"

Amy holds up her hands in surrender. "Oh, I don't
know." Talking to Elizabeth is as useless as talking to Flossie, but it's worse than talking to Flossie, who is dumb and
knows it. Elizabeth thinks she's brilliant.

Cocking her head to one side like an alert wren, Elizabeth
asks, "Which way do you live from here?"

Amy points to the left.

"So do I. Let's walk."

And so Amy guesses what they have is friendship. But
what they do together doesn't seem like friendship. It's like
playing church or school. Elizabeth is the priest or teacher
and Amy is the parishioner or student. Amy confesses and
Elizabeth defines and judges. But at least Elizabeth saves
their interviews until they walk home. She seems to understand that recess is Amy's time to play jacks with the "popular girls." And when Elizabeth chides Amy, saying, "How
can you bear that vulgar Marcy Briggs and her silly
friends? I'd much prefer the company of a good book." Amy
laughs, muttering embarrassedly, "They're not so bad,"
knowing how unwelcome Elizabeth would be in the group of
gossipy girls.

Each afternoon as they walk together, Elizabeth in-
troduces a topic for conversation. And she reveals her belief
that they have become dear friends, for she confesses to de-

scribing their friendship in a letter to her father, "We're like Meg and Jo in *Little Women:* we have sisterly love." But one afternoon as they trudge along, Amy is particularly silent, so Elizabeth strays to the topic of her mother. At first it appears that her mother might be entertaining, another of the fictional characters Elizabeth discusses. Elizabeth laughs and says, "Oh, my mother drinks too much. Sometimes she wanders naked through the house, drinking wine and crying because her roses have died or she can't find her shower shoes, or . . ." and her voice begins to tremble, and Amy turns to discover Elizabeth is silently crying. So they walk along side by side until she can compose herself. Neither visits the other's home. Amy knows her shabby home and dull mother will shock Elizabeth and are best kept secret, and if Elizabeth's mother drinks alone at home it might be disastrous to visit. They limit their conversations to the books they exchange. And Elizabeth is willing to loan all of her books with the lovely illustrations and Newbery and Caldecott awards emblazoned upon them, and inscriptions inside in Professor Perry's feathery script, which Amy reads feeling as guilty as if she's spying on lovers.

Amy no longer rushes home from school to pretend she's a housewife. Now she stays in Mr. Crandall's room to share chores with Elizabeth or dawdle along through alleyways with her companion on the way home. Elizabeth pushes her bike along, leaving a scalloped trail as she speaks. At the fork where they part, they chat minutes longer each day. This is the time when Elizabeth opens her bag to give Amy a book to read for the evening, and Amy returns the one from the previous day with a remark to prove she's read it. After Elizabeth turns from her, Amy begins to run, anticipating dashing into her room, closing the door behind her, throwing herself across the bed, and reading until Gram makes her come for a quick, silent dinner, followed by cleanup, which she sullenly completes in a slapdash manner bordering on hostility: then it's back to bed with the book to race to the conclusion before she's ordered to turn out the lights. And she lies awake in the darkness composing the story over and over, and Daddy is the main character, who comes home after a long and heroic adventure to find his daughter has become a beautiful princess.

Chapter **22**

For seconds after waking, Michael is unable to guess what time it is, but he couldn't be anyplace else but Gwen's bedroom, with its Chinese dragon kites hanging from the ceiling and its nasty-looking masks staring from the walls. The place makes him feel like a kid ditching school and sneaking into a porno flick with his buddies. But Jesus, the time's a mystery—could be early morning or late afternoon, has to be the weekend or he wouldn't be this loaded. Dope really knocks him out. That and screwing Gwen. It always turns into a sporting event when she gets stoned. This mighta been a tripleheader. The shower's running. God, that kid's got energy.

She's got style, making it in the weirdest ways. First she wanted to play hide-and-seek. And she can look like such a sweet, tearful little girl he just had to cuddle her like she's three. Felt like a jerk at first, but she made him feel like such a big daddy he agreed to staying in bed to the count of fifteen, giving her a chance to hide. Tiptoeing through the apartment looking in closets and behind curtains—wow, that dope was strange shit. Looking behind the curtain was a trip, watching the pleats fall back in place. It took five minutes to open a door. Started chatting, saying, "Hey, where are ya?" And she started giggling. Seemed real natural to crouch on the floor like detectives do in apartment building shootouts and talk like the goons in gangland movies, "Come

out with your hands up and there won't be any shootin'—
stay inside and I'll empty this mother into your gut. We'll
use teargas, tommy guns—we'll blast you." Her giggles gave
her away. She was behind the couch. "I got you in the sight
of my gun. You know I can crush you." And she tried to
crawl across the room real fast but got nailed with "Up on
your feet and against that wall." She had a lot of spunk,
looking tough, giving hard looks, but the Nazi pistol of the
index finger and the thumb cocked got her. "On your feet.
Now. Move it." She shook her hair and sat back on her
haunches. Christ, when she moved her breasts looked beautiful. First they were soft, moving freely and almost flat when
she stretched, but all perky and alert as she shifted her
shoulders, and then she rose to her knees, only six feet away,
so she looked at the imaginary gun aimed right at her.
"Turn around and get up against the wall." He gave a little
nudge in the ribs with his forefinger and she walked toward
the curtain. "Not there. A flat place." She raised her hands,
palms up, the hostage. Every wall in the little living room
had furniture along the open spaces and the drapes covered
glass. The only flat place in the joint was in the dining room.
But she might get away. "I'm backin' up ten steps and so
are you. Then we're turnin' around. Got it? No foolin' round
—for now." Seen from the rear, the half-moons of her ass
dipped and rose with every step, so it was damned hard not
to cup them, but the old pistol was aimed at a spot beneath
her shoulderblade. On the tenth step, he got her hands behind her back and grabbed her wrists to cuff her. "Try to
make a break for it, lady, and you're dead." She got real
serious when the barrel of the pistol pressed against her
temple. She managed to brush those moons against old
Charger so he rose like the flag at dawn. But he kept her
moving by giving her the old Indian burn, twisting her
thumb and forefinger real slow, the kind of motion that
made the girls at St. Cyril's cry. He got her up against the
wall. "Put those hands against the wall, spread those legs."

With a long-suffering smile she obeyed, laughing and complaining about "cops who cop a feel." She really got into her role, so it didn't seem crazy to act out fantasies. She was such a sport, laughing and whispering, "Oh, inspector, you can probe all you like, but you won't find hidden drugs there." And after fuckin' like crazy, she just slipped into the kitchen and got a glass of wine and what was left of a joint.

Her wine break turned out to be more than a seventh-inning stretch. She wanted to play doctor, Dr. Feelgood, gynecologist, exploring with "the detector," then she got into a moving-man fantasy. Some crap about the masks and how she had to have costumes. She got into an Oriental robe. Damnedest thing, looked sexier dressed than naked. It was rough to walk with the Charger the size of a ball bat. Then Gwen got a little too bossy, saying, "If you lie down and put your feet up, you'll find the effect very soothing," like a little geisha or something, and then she got after old Charger, down on her knees taking him into her mouth. But it was too much, like she got too greedy. Like a little ballbuster. Somehow it felt a lot better doing the old missionary style— and she took it okay when she had to be on the bottom and old Charger got to be on top. He had to keep that kid under control. She's wild. She can beat a man down.

After naptime, late Sunday afternoon, Gwen does a stripper number. Jesus, she'd better not want to screw again. It might be damned embarrassing. Thank God, she's putting on the panties. Probably going to get dressed, but she's a hard one to figure, putting on her drawers as if she's anxious to get 'em ripped off. Well, old Charger has risen the last time today. Maybe once more . . . nah. Shit, let the stallion rest. The kid'll calm down if you rub her smooth brown belly and sing her a little of "Yummy, Yummy," the song the girls used to like. Gwen seems to think it's okay not to screw for a fourth or fifth time for the day.

He sits in her kitchen and watches her sauté green pep-

pers for an omelet. She's got the world's most beautiful ass
and legs. And there she stands over a hot stove with nothing
on but a pair of pants a stripper might wear. Christ, the
Royal Sports would kill for this. It's not exactly a scene
from home. Ma and Big Mike would croak. And, Jesus,
Barb—in Gwen's outfit, she'd be as appealing as a plucked
chicken, with her goosebumpy white flesh and blood-red lipstick that looks like a wound.

He covers his eyes, presses hard on his brow, then looks
beneath the awning of his fingers. Yes, Gwen's naked, laughing and jumping back from the stove where the pan of bubbling butter sputters. But naked for Gwen isn't nasty or
repulsive. In no way is she a whore. And he's sure known
enough to know. She's something special: strange, pretty,
smart. A real take-charge woman—maybe a little too pushy
at times, but generally a woman who knows how to take care
of a man.

He leans back in his chair to admire her some more, not
feeling at all exposed although he's wearing the fuschia "fag
shorts" she bought him that are almost as skimpy as hers.
She keeps up a line of chatter as she prepares the eggs, and
then she eases them onto the plate, leaves the pan in the
sink, and sits down across from him so he can admire her
breasts as he eats his eggs. The scene will return again and
again on lonely drives across the country, a reason to come
back to her each night, mindless as a homing pigeon. Every
evening, the first thing Gwen asks when she comes through
the door is, "How'd you do today, Tiger?" She likes to
growl it, then give one of her sloppy kisses, then she wants
to see the receipts and to squeal about success. She flops in
the chair with a fistful of papers and reads each one out
loud like an announcer at the Academy Awards. She knows
as much about the shitty details of the job as it's possible to
know without doing the work. She can drop names and talk
details like a hardcore sports addict. It's a pleasure to tell
her stories about the day. She's the best damned audience,

laughing like crazy, always saying, "Nobody tells a story like you, Michael."

Even though it's Monday and the slow-motion feeling of the-morning-after-of-a-weekend-of-being-blasted-and-screwin' is mighty powerful, it's not too bad to go into the office. The cute little receptionist likes to make arrivals into a main event. Michael stands at the mailbox for a minute, and she wheels her chair back and strokes her hair. Give her a wink and she'll scoot her chair up to the desk and lean forward so her boobs rest on the phony oak veneer. Likes to flutter her fake eyelashes and when she finally says something, she whispers although there's nobody else around, unless of course she's got someone hiding under the desk doing a job on her. From the stories around the men's room, it's not too far-out for her. She gets real disappointed if you don't stare at her knockers resting nicely on the desk. She says, "Mr. O., if you'll wait a sec," whistling when she says sec, "I'll get your mail. You haven't been by in ages." She's too much, this broad. When she hands over the mail, she gives a direct shot to the eyes, and the hands, but her eyes really get frozen on the fly, checking out what's under the tight fit of the continental slacks old Gwen bought. Better never let this body go to fat, it's your ace. She's muttering, all in a flap, as she hands over the stack. "You really ought to come by more often."

In the slow stroll toward the coffee machine, the third envelope in the stack stops him. It's light blue with a happy face on the back. The address is written very carefully by a kid. Jesus, a letter from Amy. Just shove it in the slacks, but the suckers are too tight. Leave it till later: this one's for reading in private.

En route to the coffee machine, he has to walk by the typing pool. The ten girls at their keyboards aren't strangers to him. Four he has screwed on more than one occasion, two were one-nighters, and the others have potential. He delivers a series of individual greetings, each one a shade different from the other, each one tailored to suit the relationship. As he stands at the machine pressing the button while coffee drips into his cup, he decides it wouldn't be a waste of time to poke his head into Bert Lanier's office. Since the little peptalk about A.A., Bert's been a shadow. But the old employment folder's probably been shifted to the drawer where it can be pulled in case there are complaints. A dismissal letter is probably typed out just waiting to be dated. One more fuckup and you can kiss this job goodbye.

When Michael knocks on the door, Lanier calls, which isn't unusual, but his "Oh, hi there, Mike" is cool. And Lanier doesn't offer a chair. Jeez, this would be the day Gwen suggested wearing the fag slacks. But old Lanier is saying, "Sales are good." Hey, maybe there'll be a little promotion coming up. Nah, he's looking grim, saying, "We've had some complaints." And the bozo's not gonna let you get in your two cents. "Not about sales—about your private life." Oh, Christ, when and where or who . . . Old Lanier is tapping his pencil, looking at Old Blue-Eyes like he's got x-ray vision. "A couple of businesses have given us a call about some unpaid bills. They've sent you bills, got no payments. Called your home, got no answers. They traced you to Tristram." He lets his pencil fall when he says the company name, like it's some fuckin' big deal. "We don't want deadbeats associated with Tristram. Pay those bills. Get 'em off your back." Jesus, "deadbeat": that's a kick in the nuts. Better look real serious, let the fucker finish. Old chrome-dome is nodding like he's said it all. "That's it."

Leaving the building, Michael tries to act cool. It's good to be on the street, get some space, some air. Damn, the prissy old prick is right. Been negligent about the "private life," ignored some goddamned important responsibilities. But this warning's good. Got some time to do something fast. Get behind the wheel and do some serious thinking. If this fuckin' traffic would clear, you could get out on the road into some real space . . . damn Barbara, what the fuck's she doing? Gave her money; she ought to pay those bills. Always took care of it before, acted like J.C. Penney was her god-damned uncle, who'd tell the world if she didn't pay up the day she got the bill. A truck rumbles by. Suckers won't give you a break. Christ, maybe she's gone crazy, charging up a storm on all the credit cards, whatever the hell they are. That domestic crap's her responsibility. Probably owes Pen-ney's, maybe Sears. Shit. Today when you buzz by the malls, drop in. They must have hotlines to the credit departments all over the valley. They'd love to see cash, take care of it right away. But get this Mustang on the road. What the hell's the ceiling on those suckers? Never paid attention to detail. That's dopey Barbara's department. Never thought of her becoming the enemy. Wonder if they'll close the ac-count without her consent . . .

Roaring along on I-10, even the radio can't cover the sounds of the sick Mustang. Christ. If it goes, you're up the creek. Every sucker in the world can pass this mother—it's the worst clunker on the highway. What the fuck did those other guys do to get ahead? How the hell do they have new cars? Big Mike would've said, "Not a one of them paid for it." But owning this heap isn't much. Jesus, what in hell did Barbara do with that money? He gave the girls and her plenty of dough. Took it over there himself. That bitch—all she had to do to be decent was cash the check and pay the bills. She knows this marriage's gone rotten. He could drink himself to death and she'd never let go. No, sir.

He begins to cough, tearing his chest and throat with ex-pulsions of phlegm. When the spasm is over, he settles back in the seat and pounds his fist on his wheezing chest. For moments, he shifts his attention from the rattling of his clunker to the rumblings of his breathing. Shit—might even cut down on the smoking. Already done the impossible, switched overnight from being a drunk to being a moderate drinker. Moved out of a burning building. He pounds the steering wheel. The goddamned marriage was a killer. Knocked him out, so he hadn't known he couldn't breathe. It was a real slow death. Shit, he'd been just a kid following his hard-on right into a trap—life with Barb. Can't even remember what the fuck she was like at nineteen. But whatever she'd had sent him out to bust his ass for thirteen years. Goddamn.

He gnaws the inside of his cheek and stops for a red light because there are cops in this part of the city. Otherwise he would have sped right through. He drives sixty all the way to Picacho Peak when it's time for coffee. As he's locking the car, he sees the stack of mail he'd tossed on the back seat, and there's Amy's letter laying on the seat like a piece of the sky. He pushes down the button to lock the door. He can pretend he hasn't seen it. Who the hell will tell? But damn, she fills up his mind, her face so clear, right down to the last freckle. Not looking at the letter will mean not looking in the mirror.

Although he only wants coffee, he sits in a booth. Probably piss off the waitress, probably break some house rule, but she doesn't look too tough to get around. He'll be needing a lot of space to read the letter, didn't need some nosy fucker looking over his shoulder. Yeah, this waitress is a piece of cake. Amazing what they'll do for the O'Connor charm. Now it's time to face the music. Ah, shit. The kid could be a nun. Writes like a penmanship manual, all the right angles. Sister Frances would've sent Amy to write on the board every day. Just a baby and the kid can fill a page with sentences and words all spelled right. She's sure not like her old man. Well, she signed it "love," all careful and perfect like she means it, and starts out, "Dear Daddy." Jesus, where's the fuckin' waitress?

He orders another cup of coffee, even though heartburn is traveling fast up his chest into his throat. Then holding his breath, he plunges into reading the letter. So Gram Hershey has come to town. Damn. Should've figured on the old doll movin' in on them. From day one, she thought Barb got a loser. Not that the old broad ever said a word. All she had to do was lift her eyebrow or clear her throat. She got her messages across without any screaming. Well, well, well. Better get hold of the waitress—offset this pain with some Rolaids. A tip ought to send her hopping. But Jesus—out of cigarettes too. Well, kid, this is facing-up time: you can never go home again. Getting out of this marriage is going to be a hassle. Money's a bitch, but whatever it costs, it'll be worth it. Ah, Christ, seeing Barb, seeing that face you tried to smash, would be worse than having Big Mike come back from the dead. And the old broad, Gram Hershey, is still alive. But hateful as she is, she'll take care of Barb, take care of the kids. Old doll never hurt for money or common sense. She's so straight she invented the word. Hey, she'll be the husband yours truly could never be. But divorce—it's something to think about.

Shit. Getting up and getting to work's enough of a hassle. Going back to that marriage, no matter how lonely the kid is, just isn't possible. The letter makes him feel worse than Oneonta and the old sinking feeling when the notices came from the dean. Life's supposed to be sunny, but it keeps on raining till there's nothing but puddles, and shaking your fist at the sky doesn't stop the rain. Swallow the coffee. Get some fuel in your gut. Get a way out. Hey, you got it with Gwen. She'll know what to do. Spill the beans and that little teacher will do the homework, the legwork. She has saved your life: she can keep on pushing on your chest: in, out, in, out, till you're not so fucked up you can't even breathe.

He slouches in a chair in front of the TV sipping a can of beer and staring at a basketball game. Gwen appears in the doorway, one hand in a fist on her hip, the other dangling a pair of his slacks. In a glance, he lets her know how he admires her legs in her cutoffs, her braless breasts revealed by her flimsy T-shirt, but she looks very businesslike, no nonsense now. The little homemaker's got a question. She walks right in front of the TV, holding the slacks. She leans forward so he can see the tops of her naked breasts, framed by the gaping neckline. This kid loves to be stroked, the right look and she purrs, but today she's wired, got something on her mind. She exhales with an angry puff. "Hey," Michael says. "What's up?"

Her chin bobs; she's taking a big breath. "That's what I'd like to know." And she's waving a crumpled paper and her eyes are waiting for a response to her discovery. The lump in her fist is blue; it's Amy's letter: the one stuffed in the pocket, shaped by the body, tossed around in the head, the one that won't go away. Ah, shit.

"Yeah, well."

Christ, Gwen, you'll just never know how bad I wanted them to have never been. If I never told you, it meant they didn't exist. I just wanted it to be us, and nobody else ever.

She turns on "yeah," the old turning-the-other-cheek, but her voice is more pissed than it's ever been. "Yeah, well what?" And she's watching from the corner of her eye.

There aren't any words. What the fuck's on her mind? Does she think Amy's a girlfriend? Shrug, smile, let her take the lead. Be the poor little boy in her class, the one she tries to teach to read, the one who loses his lunch money, the one she stays after school for, the one she worries about driving home from work. Ah, Gwen, she's a sweetheart, a pure good heart, she's softening all ready, holding up the letter, willing to listen. But Christ, there's Amy and Flossie and Barbara and the old broad—you're a freak with four arms. There's no way in hell to ever explain, and old Gwen knows how to get little boys to confess, backing 'em up against the wall where there's no escape, stripping 'em of their defenses. Hey, get calm, stay cool, keep your cards against your chest, be the boy who's sorry, and you might get out of here with your balls. And Jesus, you're sorry. Just go limp when she kicks you. "Who's Amy?" she whispers in a voice that could coax a cat out of a tree. "Who's Amy?"

He holds the arms of the chair as if it might rise from the ground: the words from his past can send him reeling from this room, caught up again in a whirlwind. The old hands on the chair look like claws, with the fingers splayed on the armrest, nails digging into the fabric. Well, Gwen's a beauty all right, someone to hang onto, but right from the start it's been a lie. The only way a fuck-up like you could have something so good was to lie. Been a real Alice in Wonderland adventure. Drunk and disorderly as usual, you stepped into a hole, but this time you fell into a land where the whole game of living has a style you never knew except in the movies. Well, your number's up, punk. Gwen wants to know what's real. She's asking again, "Who's Amy?" The same question, the same pitch, the same pace: it could be a Peggy Lee record stuck on a ballad, "Who's Amy?" You struck out, buddy, right here in Yankee Stadium. Just lose with some style. Don't curse, or spit in the dust so the fans can see, just yank the bill of your cap over your eyes and stroll back to the dugout. But Jesus, Gwen's still stuck, a regular broken record, "Amy . . . Amy . . ." Just lay it on the line. "My daughter. Amy's my daughter."

Gwen's "Ah" sounds like she got hit in the throat with a neat little karate chop. She's adding it up: daughter means wife, wife means marriage. She must have laundered most of the writing off the letter except for "love, Amy." Old Gwen has lowered the letter she'd been waving like a flag. She sighs, her spine wilts, all her pert starchiness gone, washed right out of her. She hugs herself as if it keeps her from falling over. "You're married." She bites her knuckles. "I knew it—I knew there was somebody, someone . . ."

He gnaws his lower lip then mutters, "Well," drumming his fingers on the arm of the chair. Better be going—time to split. She'll think everything you ever say's a lie, like you love her more than you ever thought you could love anybody, like you didn't know what it was till you knew her. Get out of her life, creep. She's swallowing like she might be crying. The edge of the envelope's sticking out of the pocket above her left thigh. Got to have that letter. Make a clean fast break, but the letter's going too, the one that says "love, Amy," the letter from that crazy, stupid kid, who doesn't have enough sense but to love you. That letter's going into the pocket right over the heart. Christ, you don't have to steal it; just ask her, nicely, softly. "Gwen—"

"What the hell do you want from me?" She's a cat in the corner, her spine stiff, her eyes narrowed for attack. Those eyes of hers cut straight to the heart.

"I—ah—want the letter, and then—"

"Take your fuckin' letter."

He catches it before it hits his eyes. "And I figured you'd want me to get outa here—"

"Yeah, you figured right. I want you to get the hell outa here." Eyes furious, voice shrieking so loudly it must hurt her throat, "I want you out, out, out!"

He curls into the chair away from her, unable to get by her, to get out the door. Let her beat you with words, let her pound you all she wants, then go away. You owe her this. She can spit and cry and curse. Don't walk out the door until she's ready to let you go.

Her hands are in fists, balanced on her hip bones, but they might just escape her control and attack at any moment. Her voice is hoarse, "Just get the hell outa my life. Walk out that door. I don't need you. I don't want you." Jesus, she's got a needle into a nerve and she's jabbing it in again, "I don't . . ." but she's covering her face with her hands, sinking to her knees.

She must be finished, her head and shoulders bowed. Your heart's in your mouth, swallow it and you'll never breathe again. Just slip the old envelope behind those cigarettes, the old breast pocket where your heart used to be. Ah, Jesus, Jesus, everywhere you go, you fuck up. Just get out of this chair, get around Gwen, get your shit from her bedroom, and get out of her life.

As he sidesteps her, a hand reaches out and grabs his ankle. The voice speaking from beneath the tangle of hair is muffled; it could be the voice of a child. The fingers tighten on his ankle. "Please." And because the face she lifts up to his is streaming with tears, he stops and stoops to kiss her. She reaches up to him, and he feels how her anger has washed from her. Ah, Jesus, he's forgiven. He can stay.

Gwen comes home every day, windblown but still smelling faintly of perfume, veiled in cigarette smoke. Likes to give him her hugs and crazy kisses and ask if she can get him a beer, as she kicks off her shoes and starts shedding clothes, hanging them over furniture so she walks half-naked into the kitchen. Back in the living room, she serves the beer—always the little waitress—then she sprawls in the over-stuffed chair, swinging her leg so her crotch keeps flashing as she reports her progress on the divorce. Took that right over when she figured Barbara and the family shit was strangling him. Between sips of beer, she summarizes how the lawyer's moving along nicely. Then she wants a detailed report of what's happening with Tristram, rolling her eyes to show how she agrees the guys at Tristram are idiots. Her favorite line is, "Any asshole can see this job's beneath your contempt." He has to laugh when she screams, "Michael, they're fuckin' you over!" At first she seemed out of line, but it was nice to hear so he let her talk, and lately, lately, by God, it seems the kid's pretty goddamned perceptive. Sharper than he gave her credit for being. She's fond of yelping, "Tristram Paper Products can take it and shove it!" This Gwen's a tonic. He's feeling good these days, never better.

But sleep hasn't come easy for a couple of years. Dope can knock out Gwen like a sledgehammer at the temple. She likes to smoke a J, mouse around, and screw until she yawns, then asks if it's okay for her to take a little nap. She always invites him to wake her up, "in some sexy, surprising way," but she digs into the covers making comfortable noises as if she plans to enjoy herself. Waking her up would be cruel. Tonight the ceiling looks like the lid of a coffin. He gets up to smoke and watch TV.

By now Carson is over and old movies are on. Leaning back in the chair, he pulls his robe around him, trying to get warm and comfortable, trying to figure out why the Indians are getting massacred by the Confederacy. Shit. Movie's a bummer; feet are cold; another cigarette might help. With his feet on the table, the ashtray in his lap, and the newspaper draped over his bare skin, he must look right out of skid row, but it beats searching for a blanket or jacking up the heat. She pays too damned much for the utilities now. Yeah, this is the ticket. This chair's okay, comfort at last, just close your eyes while the moron selling cars gives his spiel.

"Daddy, Daddy." Amy, a fat toddler, races as quickly toward you as her stubby legs will carry her, moving across Barb's waxed hardwood floors in the old apartment. You stand, leaning against the doorway at the top of the stairwell, having a smoke, feeling happy to see the fat little tyke, feeling tired: the day has been a bitch. You have a smoke in one hand and want a beer in the other. Big Mike is stomping up the bare wooden stairs, coming to visit. His heavy clomping is coming up behind you. The old fucker ought to stay away, ought to keep his nose in his own business. The last thing you want is to sit in the dinky living room and hoist beers with the old man. But the apartment is in Big Mike's house. According to Big Mike's rules: You owe a man money, you're his "nigger." When you hear the old man whistling, puffing at the strain of climbing the stairs, you want to turn around and scream at the old fucker, Go home, stay home, but you don't, you can't, you stand in the doorway, pretending you don't hear the old guy, and watch Amy stumbling toward you, laughing, holding her arms out, wanting you to bend down and scoop her up. You cluck and coo, teasing her on, making her run

faster, knowing the old man is getting pissed at being ignored.
You call, "Come on, sweetie, come on," and hold one hand to-
ward her, snapping your fingers as if you were coaxing a puppy to
come nuzzle your hand, when the old man bellows, "Michael, my
boy!" You glance over your shoulder to warn the old guy to shut
up, but the second you turn to look down the staircase, the bow-
legged baby steps on her shoestring and sprawls, face first on the
floor. You turn back at the sound of the fall. For a moment, she's
a silent heap, but she lifts her face from the floor, howling as
blood gushes from her mouth. You want to stoop to lift her from
the floor, to comfort her, to silence the wailing, to stop the flow of
mucus and tears and blood, but your hand has become a part of
the wall, your knees don't bend, and the hand you hold toward
your baby is waiting for the bottle the old man will be putting
there in a matter of moments. Just a matter of moments, and the
old fucker squeezes by you, booming bullshit in a voice whistling
at the end of words. You take the bottle as if it were a baton. It
fits right in your hand, and you're ripped out of the wall by the
old man's burly shoulder and stuck like a shadow on the old
fart's sleeve, and you walk right by the baby, slipping in her
blood and tears and piss, and walk into the dining room and sit
and finish your beer and belch and have another. And you can see
the baby melt into a pool.

The smoke of a cigarette burning another wafts about his
head. Jesus, just a dream. But you did it once. You'd do it
again, you son of a bitch. Crush out the smoke. Start a fresh
one. This is not a night to risk a another nightmare. Daughter—a hell of a word; got two and still don't know the meaning. Two strange little creatures who came bellowing into the
world, demanding to be fed and clothed and cared for. Hey,
buddy, you busted your ass to earn them a buck. They've
waited out on the lawn for you, bathed and dressed, all excited, waiting for Daddy. The nightmare was a lie. He never
deliberately ignored their pain to spend time hoisting a bottle. That's a fuckin' lie. Someday soon, you'll take Amy,
maybe even Floss, out to lunch. Wearing frilly dresses,

those little girls will turn people's heads. You'll hold their hands, and they'll look up at you, and folks will think: what a handsome family.

Chapter 23

Amy might be getting the flu. Her lower back aches slightly, and her stomach is strangely puffy. But she doesn't feel nauseated, see stars, or feel feverish. And even though she concentrates intensely on her symptoms, her illness doesn't get worse, so she doesn't get to stay home from school, where Christmas projects fill each moment of class and spill into homework assignments. Even if she vomited continuously and had diarrhea, it would be worth staying home from school. Such a violent illness would win special privileges: drinking Seven-Up poured over crushed ice and having a clean, cold washcloth held across her forehead by Mom. Or Grammy, who'd be even more concerned, would exclaim, "You look peaked, so pale you're almost a ghost." And after a bout of vomiting, Amy could study her pale reflection, which would be frighteningly fascinating.

But after two days of ignoring schoolwork to concentrate on her flu symptoms, they haven't developed and are unlikely to do so, for her appetite is enormous. At school, she eats her lunch quickly and accepts all the samples offered by the other girls. After dinner, clearing the table, she sneaks leftovers. To satisfy a craving for salt, she buys a bag of potato chips and secretly eats them in her room while she reads. Her breasts feel strange. All this year they've grown. But Mom won't buy a training bra like the popular girls wear: "It's too extravagant." Yet the swelling pushing the front of Amy's shirts makes her look bigger than most of the girls who wear bras. Playing kickball is a problem. She doesn't want Duane Fenton and his nasty friends staring and talking. Once she'd seen him doing it, and instead of being ashamed because she caught him, he grinned dopily and moved his lips silently, "Boobs, you've got boobs."

This week, the sides of her breasts are sore. Sometimes in the midst of class, they'll tingle, demanding all of her attention. When no one is looking, she presses her fingers testily at the puffy contours. It can't be denied: they're growing. At night, getting ready for bed, she sits in the bathtub longer than usual, staring at her chubby thighs, then slides down into the water until it comes to her collarbone. Beneath the inches of soapy water, her breasts seem much larger. She pinches the right nipple; it turns rosy. She pinches the left; it does the same. They almost look like women's breasts. As she stands, drying with the soft old towel, she decides, happily, she'll probably be a woman with big, round bosoms. She turns to see her profile and leans forward to analyze the size of her breasts hanging from her body. They are single scoops of strawberry ice cream. She'll never have the lush curves of women she's seen unfold from the center of Daddy's *Playboy*.

She doesn't want to go to school, because her paper about her family Christmas is due. This year, Christmas should never come. When she'd written the paragraph about her family at Thanksgiving, the words had flowed as she visualized Daddy behaving the way she wished he would. It was only when Mr. Crandall said out loud, "An anonymous paper, one of the best in the class," that she recognized her lie. The class whispered, "It's Amy's." She'd smiled so everyone would believe what she'd written. To write such a tale about a happy Christmas would be a premeditated lie. Mom hadn't even gotten a tree last year. And the year before they'd shared the tree downstairs in Gram O.'s part of the house. She had bought an ugly, dried-up tree on sale on Christmas Eve and had started opening presents as soon as the tree was in place, instead of waiting until Christmas morning the way Mom liked to do. And Daddy had gone to the Royal Sports for some "Christmas cheer" and come home so late they'd had to be quiet all Christmas Day until he got up in time to go to Gram O.'s dinner, where she yelled, "Michael, you're drinkin' your life away!" And the memory of the Christmas before was sad. Mom had bought a teeny-tiny tree and Gram O. had scolded, "You're wastin' Michael's money, gettin' a big tree and a standin' rib roast." Mom had cried as she sliced the bloody beef. And the Christmas before was when Gram Hershey had planned to visit, but Gramps had always been too sick. So they never spent a Christmas with Gramps and Gram Hershey. It would be perfect if Daddy stayed around the house the entire day and everyone opened presents together, and ate at a table laden with carefully prepared food, and laughed as if they were the families barely visible behind snow-framed windows on TV beer commercials. But Gram and Daddy hate each other, so there will never be a Christmas like that, yet it's the only story she wants to write. She'll just pretend she forgot to write the paper.

She'll finish Elizabeth's current reading assignment even if it is more difficult than the others have been: "the noble, lonely, Jane Eyre." Amy's eyes grow heavy and the words swim before her as she attempts to follow her adventures. Setting the book on the nightstand, she wonders if the reading is too difficult for her or she's just too tired to concentrate. She'll have to catch up later or risk losing Elizabeth's respect. Lying in the dark, she tries to think of what to say to prove she understands the book. But before she can decide on a good illustration, she drifts into sleep.

The creature seated in the metal folding chair might be a hideously deformed human. The head is like an enlargement of the one in the Anatomy of Man kit in the science corner at school. White swirls of snowy shaving cream smelling like antiseptic ooze from the split in the top of the skull. The creature is bald, the face dull gray and slack-jawed. The head lolls forward as if

*the monster is almost dead; the eye sockets seem hollow. The
arms are a skeleton's with skin stretched over them, and the bony
wrists cross in the lap over the thighs. But one long foot swings
slowly. Tiptoe closer to examine this repulsive being, see if it
lives or is a mechanical monster. The pace of the swinging foot is
as precise as a machine. Step closer, closer. Stroke the gun-metal
gray shoulder, see if it is as cold as it looks. Let your index finger
touch the shoulder and feel the movement, rising and falling, less
than an inch, with the rhythm of breathing. Pull back your
hand. The great head lolls forward and the eyes rolling in the
sockets are the bloodshot brown eyes of Gram. Her yellowed teeth
moving within her withered lips say words that can't be heard.
The shaving cream moves white and sluggish, a giant, skinned
worm.*

Amy wakes with the light in her face and the pillow
crushed to her chest, smothering her scream. She closes her
eyes against the glare of the light bulb. Mom has risen on
her elbow to stare down at the person who woke her. Gram is
scurrying into the room, knotting her bathrobe. "Honey,"
she murmurs, kneeling by the bed. "Were you having a
nightmare?" Her voice is deceivingly kind. Amy can't look
at the face from the nightmare. She hugs the pillow, frightened she's soiled herself. She lets one hand slide between her
thighs. The crotch of her panties is moist, but not with a
river of warm urine. She pats the sheets surrounding her
body; it's hard to tell wet from warm. The sheets are dry,
but there's something heavy and wet in her crotch. She wants
to throw back the covers and examine herself. But Mom
is staring and Gram leans forward cooing, "Amy, Amy—"

She opens her eyes to the light, squinting against the painful brightness. "Yes," she says, her voice small and far
away.

"Are you okay?" Gram makes soft whistling sounds when
her partial plate is removed.

Mom snaps, "Oh, Mother, she just had a dream. Go back
to bed."

Amy nods, watching the naked places on Grammy's gums. Even though her eyes are the ones in the dream, and the hair stretching over the row of rollers on her head could be the segments of a worm's body, and her skin is silvery under the cold cream, her big eyes look loving, a love to erase fear. But the stuff in Amy's pants has soiled her hand, so she's too dirty to touch Grammy, to dare to accept her hug. "I'm okay," she murmurs, hoping Gram will go away quickly and not discover the filthy panties.

"Can you go back to sleep?"

Amy murmurs, "I'm okay," to ease the doubt in Gram's face.

"Should you go to the bathroom? Do you want a drink? Do you want to get in bed with me?"

Amy shakes her head at each idea. "Oh, I'll be okay. I promise. Really."

She feels the desperation she used to feel apologizing to the nuns. "Honest, I'm okay." Something warm and heavy gushes from between her thighs.

"You're sure?"

"Um hm."

It seems like hours before Mom begins her soft snoring. Amy pulls her knees to her chest to ease the ache in her back, to stop the seeping between her thighs. Maybe she's ruined her body, and she'll pee just a little all the time. Maybe she's sick because she touched her secret place too many times. The moist warmth, and fishy smell, the glow, had been too much to resist. Being so nasty has destroyed her body. No one she knows has been so awful: not Elizabeth or Marcy or Mom or Flossie, and never, never Gram. Nobody else is as filthy. And now because of her secret activities, she's in trouble. When Mom has snored one hundred times, Amy crawls out of bed and tiptoes to the bathroom. As she moves, the wetness trails down her left thigh. She rushes down the hallway touching the walls to keep from stumbling.

Once in the bathroom, she locks the door, turns on the light, and lifts her nightie to stare at her panties. The crotch is dotted with dark blood. She's injured. Holding her pants half on, half off, she hobbles to the toilet. The only discomfort is a tiny pain in her back, and she can't remember doing anything to injure it. She sits on the stool and mops herself. Except for one dark streak like the seat of her pants, the tissue is crimson. She drops it into the toilet bowl and gathers fresh paper to repeat the process. This time the paper is almost clean. The sore, or whatever it is, has burst and now it's all right. She flushes the toilet and sits, promising God to never touch herself again, praying if she reforms this disease will never return. As the toilet gurgles, she stands, checks the seat for cleanliness, carefully closes the lid and goes to the sink to wash her hands.

She glances at her pale face in the mirror. Her cheek is streaked where she wiped her fingers, so she looks like a savage Indian in warpaint. Running scalding water in the sink, she dips in the washrag and almost burns her fingers trying to wring it. Pressing the dripping rag on her cheek, she winces as she scours. Flushed and clean, she tries to squeeze the stain from the rag, but it stays like a magenta scar. This is menstruation: her menstruation. She is a woman. She can have babies; not like the Virgin Mary, but the dirty way.

About a year ago, in this bathroom, Mom explained how blood had to be removed in cold water, as she held a pair of underpants under the faucet, rubbing the crotch together with a bar of soap. When Amy had caught her at the task, Mom seemed flustered, so she quickly finished washing and hung the panties over the shower rod. Later Amy found a little book called *Becoming a Woman* on her pillow, the same one the nurse at school showed the girls when they saw the Walt Disney movie about menstruation. Mom must've put it on her bed. The illustrations showed the insides of a woman, drawn with fine blue lines. The part where the menstruation came from looked like an upside-down pear, or a cow's head with curvy horns coming out of the top. But it was hollow inside, and a lining built up and dropped out once a month, unless the lady was having a baby, then it stayed inside and helped to make the baby. Amy read the little booklet several times, thinking Mom would ask questions about it, but she never had.

Wringing out the stained washcloth, Amy feels confused about why it's happening to her now. The book said girls start when they are twelve or thirteen or even older, and she won't be twelve until July. She sadly decides that she's one of those girls who get sexy early, one of the girls she's watched contemptuously, the girls with "boobs" who boys tease. She leans against the sink and begins to peel off her panties. She'd better wash out the stain or it will stay forever. Periods are supposed to last for at least three days or maybe even a week. She'll never leave the bathroom with this mess coming out of her. She'll certainly never go back to school. From touching the stain, her fingers smell like meat left out to thaw on a hot day. Maybe everyone will smell her when she enters a room. Dogs will sniff at her in an embarrassing way. But right now she had better get something to keep this dripping from getting on everything. In the back of the booklet there is a picture of a little belt that women wear, and some big bandages to hook onto the belt that are called "sanitary napkins." There are white metal machines in ladies' bathrooms labeled "Sanitary Napkins, ten cents." Mom used to keep a big blue box with "Modess" printed across it. Once last year when Mom was at work, Amy and Flossie had taken the box out of the closet and taken one of the napkins out. They unfolded the gauzy stuff around it and found layers and layers more of the gauze, so they folded it back. Flossie had dared Amy to put the thing between her legs, so she had, and it had felt like a little saddle or lumpy underpants. It felt yucky. And because they had messed up the napkin, they tore it into pieces and flushed it down the toilet.

She runs cold water over the stained pants, but they don't seem to get any lighter. She starts to shiver in the cold bathroom and sniffs back tears as she wonders how she will get to the box of Modess hidden in Mom's closet, and how she can find one of those little belts in Mom's dresser without turning on the lights. The panties aren't coming clean, so she leaves them to soak and tries to wash the stain from her gown, drenching it before the dark spot fades.

She wads up the washcloth to stuff between her thighs until dawn when she'll sneak into Mom's bed. A knocking at the door startles her, so she drops the gown, and leans against the sink, and stares in the mirror at her frightened face. If she stands perfectly still, perhaps the knocking will cease, perhaps it is only her imagination. The rapping becomes insistent. Gram says "Amy!" so sharply she might wake Mom. Moving to the door, she whispers, "Yes."

"Amy." Gram's getting irritated.

Even if Amy sinks to her knees to peek beneath the door, she'll only see Gram's fuzzy slippers; her face will be too far away to read. "Yes," she says with resignation. Knowing Gram will not go away, Amy opens the door.

There's no way to hide the streaks of water splashed down the front of her nightgown. And her panties float in the soapy, bloody water. Gram's eyes burn into her. This is worse than wetting the bed. Gram clears her throat, so Amy hangs her head to accept the blow of words or a slap. The sink gurgles. Gram's wringing out the panties, the ones with "Wednesday" embroidered on them, part of the gift set she gave last Christmas, panties Amy wears on the days of the week they name. Now the crotch is ruined, ugly and brown. She wants to tear the pants out of Gram's hand but is paralyzed by shame. Gram speaks so softly it's hard to hear her ask, "Is this the first time?"

Amy mumbles, "Yes." "The first time" sounds innocent: she hasn't intentionally been bad. As Gram runs water to rinse the panties, another gush journeys down Amy's thigh.

She presses her legs together, feeling helpless and irredeemably soiled.

Gram's done with the panties. Now she's ready to clean up her dirty granddaughter. Gram's voice is breathy: "Now, young lady, we'll get you fixed up." Amy feels limp. Total submission is the only choice.

Bathed and in a fresh gown, with Mom's frayed rubber belt adjusted to stay about her hips, the lump of a sanitary napkin squeezed between her thighs, Amy curls in the bed, as far from Mom as she can without falling off the edge, and pretends she's sleeping. Gram's so excited about the whole mess, calling it "a normal, healthy, human process." This means staying home from school won't be permitted. Gram promises that tomorrow she'll buy a book on the reproductive system, an explanation of menstruation "for girls your age." And Amy nods to be cooperative. It will probably be the same book she'd seen at school, the one Mom showed her. And walking back to Mom's bedroom, Gram lets her spidery fingers run across Amy's shoulders and pats her back. It's just like Gram to touch her even though she is dirty. Gram picked up her cat when he was run over by a car and wrapped him in a towel and buried him.

Mom is still sleeping, leaving Amy alone to imagine how she'll manage to walk around for days with a lump between her thighs, smelling nasty. And she'll have to stand for hours while the class practices for the Christmas pageant, singing songs like "There's no Place Like Home for the Holidays" and "Deck the Halls." She'll wear a double pad, so nothing can drip down, and press her legs together, so no one can smell her. And she'll act as if she'll be seeing Daddy this Christmas. To be sure no one in class guesses about the divorce, she'll print, "For Daddy and Mom" on the card for the candle she's made as a gift for them. On her way home, she'll tear up the card and scatter the pieces in the desert. Gram and Mom will get the candle, now that Amy's one of the "weird kids," the kids who are going to have "problems," because they come from "broken homes." Her head is beginning to ache from squeezing her eyes too tighly shut. She wishes she could enter the blackness of sleep, to block out tomorrow's arrival. Daddy never answered her letter, and since she's menstruating, she isn't his little girl any more. He must've known it was coming last time he saw her. Something in her eyes must've told him when he stood on the porch and left the envelope of money for Mom.

There is no way to stop Christmas from coming. There is no way to stop the flow oozing from her body. Christmas will come without Daddy. Christmas will be with Gram, gushing about love for everybody, touching them, wringing out bloodstained panties, pretending not to smell the stench, making believe it's a happy holiday. And Amy will have to be more careful than she's ever been, keeping her disgrace secret.

Chapter **24**

To continue to function, Barbara must remedy her bone-weariness of body and spirit. The pending divorce must cause these symptoms, but examining the source of her ills seems as impossible as examining the end of her nose. The day at the attorney's office is a blur. She and Mom had avoided each other's eyes as they sat in Ms. Lawry's office. Barbara had shifted the wad of Kleenex on the bleeding cuticle to shake the woman's cool hand. At least dealing with her hadn't been difficult; the woman was as cold and smooth as a metal file cabinet. But Mom, my God, Mom. She had advised divorce, initiated the plan, but she was not prepared, and would never be, to learn about the marriage.

What Michael had wanted had determined their lives. His disappearance scooped Barbara's insides out, and Mom had provided a structure to fill the void he'd left. But she hadn't known lives like his existed until the thirty-minute session with the lawyer. Reciting answers to her questions, Barbara had felt Mom's shock. "Yes, he deserted us. No, he has not provided consistent financial support. Yes, he was physically abusive. Yes, he struck me; he knocked me off my feet." Mom's face turned as ashen as if massive volts of electricity had passed through her. When they moved out of the building into the sunlight, Barbara stared at the pavement, the clatter of heels seeming to echo, "It's over, it's over." Being alive must mean looking forward. Move forward; in spite of the amputation of thirteen years of your life, step forward.

The very same day of the appointment at the lawyer, Barbara announced the divorce at the dinner table. Gripping a salt shaker to steady herself, she said "divorce" out loud and stated for the girls and herself, "I'm getting a divorce." Rushing to the kitchen to avoid the accusation in their eyes, she was numb. But leaning against the sink, she'd been swept by a soothing objectivity. How simple to make changes: just pretend your life belongs to somebody else; live as you'd advise someone else with a similar problem. Reduce all the tiny, horrid details to the lowest common denominator. Print the simple facts on a page and let logic be the guide. Treat life like a scientific formula. The system served Mom well for sixty-eight years, while Michael moulded Barbara's life. And for thirty-two years everything she touched has failed. Women like Mom and Ann and Ms. Lawry know how to survive. No man determines their lives. Mom is one of the women in the tribes where women rule that the sociology class studied. These women aren't soiled by male sperm. How Mom and her kind arrive at truths is beyond Barbara. But she can follow their lead. She'll be like a nun, following the commands of the Mother Superior. Total submission to Mom is the answer.

But day-to-day living with Mom fluttering about, chatting endlessly about boring topics, is sandpaper rubbing raw flesh. Solitude might be a blessed relief, or exquisite pain. The possible experiences of life alone are too great a risk. Just to get through this evening without showing irritation toward Mom will be a victory of will. At least the second job allowed an escape from the house in the evenings, but when Barbara suggested returning to the theater job Mom said, "It's foolish to exhaust yourself for such a paltry wage. I've got money and I can't take it with me. Besides, the girls need to see you in the evenings." And Mom's money is theirs. It stopped the floodwaters of debt washing them under, kept them from drowning, provided mouth-to-mouth resuscitation. She is so good—so unquestionably good. This awful feeling of irritation with her could only be the reaction of a miserable person.

Mom leaves the kitchen, chirping to Flossie, "Let's drill on those multiplication facts. No granddaughter of mine will fail math." Barbara swipes a Brillo pad across the greasy broiler rack, which she's vowed to scour before returning to the oven. What a disappointment she's been to Mom—failing algebra in high school, failing everything in college. Yes, scouring baked-on grease has been her major accomplishment, and look what it earned her. It's strange how Mom dotes on Flossie—the one who'll probably marry before she gets to her senior year in high school. She'll be the Barbara of the family, yet she receives Gertrude's unconditional love.

Amy's another Ann, so bright, so frighteningly intense. As an infant, Amy bellowed until she turned purple to get what she wanted. Now she's more subtle, withdrawing into her books and her mysterious friendships at school. She's become so moody since the news about the divorce, since the menstruation business, followed by her little scene when she insisted on moving back to her room, where she'll probably read until all hours. The energy she wastes on reading could be used around the house. Oh, God, maybe reading will free her from living in such a mess. Barbara flips over the broiler pan. The hard-crusted stains have been baked again and again until they are beyond hope. She turns on the faucet and watches the scummy residue swirl down the drain.

Amy's menstruation starting at such an early age is sad. But she'll be all right. The family can weather her coldness until she decides to come back to them; Gertrude has assumed her responsibilities. It's rather amusing to see how irriating Mom has become to Amy, rather heartening to see a woman the rest of the world seems to think is flawless become so flawed in the eyes of a child who had once held her in such esteem. "Heartening" is the wrong word; "shameful" would be more appropriate. It's childish to resent Mom —understandable behavior for an eleven-year-old, but shameful in a woman of thirty-two; surely at thirty-two . . . She swipes at the grease congealing on the side of the sink.

Longing for the narcotic effect of mindless chores, she empties every cupboard in the kitchen. Dishes, boxes, and bottles jam the kitchen table. The sink is filled with tepid, dirty water, where she slops a sponge before she mops at dusty shelves. Nothing is coming clean. And her mind won't stop whirling. This Wednesday, or next week, but sometime soon, the newspaper, thick with Christmas ads, will announce to the world the death of her marriage. In the Public Record, wedged between the list of "Marriages and Deaths," in the middle column headed "Divorces," her name will appear: Michael's Christmas gift to his family. Michael, Michael, he's always been worst at Christmas. The time the family is supposed to be feeling the closest, the season of love, he's always gone out to "hoist a few" on Christmas Eve, never coming home till dawn, being silent and sick the next day. It was impossible to even pretend they were happy. But at least he'd been with them. Jesus, Michael, of course, you'd time the divorce for Christmas. And now the world gets to know, gets to see the failure published. Their marriage had been invisible, her life has been invisible. No one at work needs to know. It is so unfair to have the facts published. She never asked the people of Phoenix to be aware of her presence; she should not be included in their statistics.

At the end of the final visit with the lawyer, as Barbara stood to leave, she murmured stupidly, "This is it, then?" and, after the cold handshake of the woman, managed to say thank you and get to the door. But she'd narrowly avoided running into the secretary's desk guarding the inner office door as Ms. Lawry called, "Don't hesitate to call if there are any problems." She nodded dumbly as she hurried toward the exit. Blinking against the glare of the warm December afternoon sun, she'd shivered. She must wait for the bus that was never on time and consider problems. For a lawyer, problems mean money, Barbara can't afford problems. She has no money for problems.

Four quarters grew sweaty in her palm, all that was left of the ten dollars' change from the check she wrote in the grocery store. Enough for two bus fares, she'd be almost penniless on the ride home, totally powerless against the fates. The exhaust fumes of the bus were suffocating as it lumbered to a stop, almost brushing the curb with its filthy tires. The glass doors ground open and she stepped onto the bus and steadied herself against the pole to drop her coins with a clank. On the ride home she tried to imagine being in the same room with Michael again. With their lawyers as liaisons, she had not had to see him during the proceedings. The necessary compromises were easier to agree upon when they were posed in writing. Michael was reduced to a number in an equation. Two months apart and she'd begun to forget the smell of him, the minute details of his rhythm. Nausea rose in the back of her throat. She closed her eyes and shook her head to quell the watering in her mouth and looked for another place to sit, somewhere closer to the front, where she wouldn't have to sit sideways, where the shock of the stops and starts would be absorbed better. But the seats were filled, and the passengers looked as if they were riding a long way. She pressed her lips together and tried to will the sickness away. In a month, or maybe less, she'd see him. They'd agreed he could see the children on weekends. Her throat filled with a flush of fresh saliva. She covered her mouth with her hand, swallowed hard, and stood. Pressing her fingers with bruising force against her upper lip, she managed to stumble across the aisle and pull the rope for the bell. Passengers stared. Her embarrassment or her abrupt movements delayed her sickness for the half-block ride until the bus stopped, and she ran down the steps. As the bus pulled away with a heave of gears, she braced herself against the signpost and vomited twice. Wiping her mouth and blotting her tears, she swallowed the sour after-taste. There seemed no end to the humiliation she would suffer.

Shame gave her the strength to walk, weak-kneed and shaky, to the next bus stop, where she thanked God for providing a covered, empty bench. Two days, three, even four—the girls wouldn't have to be told details immediately. They knew a divorce was in progress. They knew he wouldn't be coming home. Christmas was coming; Michael had timed everything for the maximum pain—they'd miss him most on holidays. He'd always failed them on holidays, but they were always hopeful. She must have time to free her voice of hysteria when she tells them of a future that she can't even conceive of herself. And Mom. God—she prayed Mom would give her the gift of silence. As she waited for the bus, she repeated the prayer, "No questions, God, please make her leave me alone."

Barbara turns from the shelf to the table to see if all the cans have been returned to their places. She stares at the table and for a moment she can't remember what it is she is looking for in the rows of dusty boxes. Canned spices, yes, she is separating the boxes from the cans. She must keep at this. There is this to do, and then another chore. Something has to matter. Something has to be done. Fill the back of the shelf with the largest boxes, the ones not used very often. As she turns to place the box of cornmeal against the wall, she hears Mom, and flinches when she touches her shoulder. Mom's voice is a whisper, "Hon, can I help?"

"No, I—" and her voice breaks in noisy gasps that might be mistaken for laughter. Mom's tentative touch becomes an embrace. They rock silently, like the blind or retarded, to the rhythm of "I am, I am." Then Mom coos, "Oh, honey, oh, honey." The soothing sounds wash over Barbara; she is safe. She is a child who is protected; her sobbing ceases. But when the rocking stops, their embrace becomes an embarrassment. As they release one another, avoiding each other's eyes, Gertrude says, "Get some rest. I'll finish here."

Weak with the aftermath of hysteria, and wanting to obey, Barbara unties her frayed apron and turns to the door. Laying the soiled garment on the table, she murmurs, "Thanks, Mom," but Gertrude has turned to the blessed escape of the mindless dirty chore.

Chapter **25**

Hanging around the office makes Michael nervous, so he puts off coming in for as long as possible. But Mondays can be pretty rotten on the road, so every other week for a day or a day and a half, he comes to the office to fill out forms, file receipts, to con the secretaries into doing as much of his clerical work as he can. Ding-y dames are amazing. They can type up a storm, file and shovel through a load in nothing flat. Hell, no need to learn to unwind red tape with all these little honeys around. All it takes to get 'em going is a little attention; a little ingenuity gets these girls to jump through hoops.

He's sitting at a desk thinking about going for another cup of coffee when he sees a stranger come into the office: weird-looking little guy, short and dressed in what could be a janitor's uniform, except it's too grungy for one. He sure acts like a hot shit, considering how cruddy he looks. He's leaning over the receptionist's desk, acting like he's got an important message. She nods her bubble head, then wheels around her little chair and points her claw-like fingernail. Christ. She's pointing at yours truly. The little weirdo is moving in fast. Shuffle those papers and look real busy. Figure out who the fuck he is. Could be a bill collector. But Barbara paid the bills. And the guy's too creepy to be an ex of Gwen's. "Michael O'Connor." Christ, the bozo's got the attention of every dame in the place. "Michael O'Connor, I'm a process server." The fucker's shaking a folded paper open, holding it so it can be read. "You are Michael O'Connor." The message could be a tape recording. You'd have to be deaf not to hear it. Michael nods once and the man slides the paper onto the desk, turns, and walks away, and now every bugeyed dame in the place is watching.

His face burns. A vein in his throat throbs. Grabbing the petition and his jacket, he fumbles with the paper. Stuffing it into the inside pocket, he sticks an arm in a sleeve and the jacket flaps behind him, so he tries to pile papers on the desk as he dives for the other sleeve. He misses the sleeve and scatters the papers. "Christ." He bites his lip. And then, very deliberately, avoiding everyone's eyes, he finishes putting on his jacket—a good-looking tweed Gwen bought—scoops the papers into his attaché case, loudly snaps it closed, and walks with as much dignity as he can muster from the office, which he knows will erupt in chatter as soon as he's out the door.

He drives at least five miles before he sees a bar, quiet and anonymous enough for him to stop. As he heads for a back booth, he shudders at the decor: blood-red walls, black vinyl upholstery, and soiled gold shag carpets. The Phoenix version of Spanish elegance looks like the aftermath of the Spanish Inquisition. Christmas lights are flashing over the bar. Jesus, this is the perfect spot for fuckin' up Christmas. The worst fuckin' shit comes down at Christmas: drunk is the only way to take it. Well, this oughta be the right setting to check out what's coming down. Old Barb, dopey Barb, is trying to get tough, trying to tighten the thumbscrews. The brains behind this dumb-shit scheme must be Gertrude. Barbara's minding her momma. Oh, Jesus, those two: nothing ever turns out right.

By the light of the plastic candleholder mounted above the booth, he opens up the petition. And in boldface print, beneath the heading "In the Superior Court of the State of Arizona," is his name, all in capitals, underneath Barbara's. She's the plaintiff. He's the defendant, and across the page in big letters with spaces between them blazes the word "Complaint," and underneath, in case there is anyone in the world who doesn't know by now, in parenthesis: domestic relations. He tries to read the page all at once, his eyes darting over the stiff legal jargon. Three pages of shit: dates and names and lies. She's reduced their lives to three pages of shit. He turns back to page one and starts to read each word separately, but they don't hang together until he comes to the third part, and there *Amanda O'Connor, 11 years: Florence O'Connor, 8 years* stops him. He stumbles through the next sentence, which is six lines long. She wants the kids. Of course, she'd want them. That's right. Never could do shit as a father, and a kid's gotta have a mother. Jesus, better get Gwen to get the kids something for Christmas.

He's saddened by Part V, generalizing about their community debts. But the VI section yanks him out of sentimentality. The word "guilty" sinks a deep hook. He reads with shame and rage: "That the defendant has been guilty of cruel treatment, excesses and outrages toward the plaintiff; that said specific acts are known to the defendant."

He folds the papers, slips them into the inside pocket of

his jacket, and stumbles out of the bar at exactly three-fifteen, because he wants to be home the minute Gwen walks through the door. Squinting into the sun, he reminds himself to drive slowly. Got the old buzz on so bad, couldn't walk a line for some fuckin' cop. Gwen's got to see these papers. Got to read the part about being guilty of cruel treatment and the rest of the shit. Jesus, Christ, you gave 'em money. You tried till they almost killed you. You got out from under and they go for your balls. Whatever Gwen's doing to help hasn't been enough. Got to get a lawyer with balls. Gwen better get tough. As soon as the nuns made it tough, Ma always called the school. Those old broads sure backed off when old Etta got into it. A few of her threats and God himself woulda taken a back seat. She'd scream down the house, "Whadda ya mean my blue-eyed angel's been bad?"

Chapter 26

January is already here, and Amy wants to hold back the days so she won't menstruate again. After the first period, Gram had given her a Hallmark datebook to keep a record. When Amy confessed she'd disgraced herself for seven days, Gram drew a red line through each day of the period. She said it wasn't unusual for the women in their family to have "long, heavy men-stroo-a-tions," saying the word as if it were a sentence. "Now," Gram said, looking up, "what you have to do is count the days between. There will be twenty-two to twenty-eight days between a period, just depending on you. But if you're like the rest of the ladies in this family, you'll probably get that period of yours right on the button, every twenty-second day." She smiled as if it were marvelous to be so dependable.

Amy had hidden the calendar and the pencil in the bottom of her drawer. She hadn't counted the days, because her period wouldn't come again. It'd been an accident. In two more years, it was her turn to start. And her period wouldn't be seven or eight days long. According to Gram's *Book of Reproduction,* periods were shorter. Amy isn't going to be like Gram and Mom and have long, heavy men-stroo-a-tion.

But this week her breasts itch and are sore, and she cries when the can opener won't work. And she's so hungry she sneaks a jar of Gram's dry-roasted peanuts into her room and eats every one by herself. She gets out the calendar and counts the days, and yes, it's coming tomorrow or the next day. She sits on her bed and cries, wondering what she will do if an enormous red puddle oozes out of her when she's in class.

At school, Elizabeth is the only one who knows she has "the curse." On the afternoon when they drew names for the Christmas exchange, she confided in Elizabeth. Together on the pathway home, she explained how her first menstruation was occurring. Elizabeth shook her head sadly and said, "What a shame. It's painful and messy and smelly and you'll get it the rest of your life, or at least until you reach menopause." Deflated, Amy kicked a stone. She decided not to quote Gram about "passage into the special world of women." Elizabeth was just jealous, Gram said she was a girl who liked to be "center stage." And Elizabeth had begun talking about a letter from her father with his inter-pretation of *Jane Eyre.* As they walked to the end of the block, she quoted him, her voice trembling with excitement. Elizabeth probably saw herself as the "exceptional heroine," Jane Eyre, which left the classification of "conventional her-oine" for Amy. By the time she reached home, she felt dirty, smelly, and stupid, and not at all like struggling through *Jane Eyre.* Instead, she sneaked by Gram to the cookie jar and stole as many Oreos as she could hold.

But Elizabeth was a faithful friend for the five school days while Amy menstruated. On the playground, when no one was within earshot, Amy whispered, "I've got to go to the bathroom," and Elizabeth immediately pushed her jacks away and led the way to the girls' restroom, where she knelt and peered under the stalls to see if they were empty. While Amy was in the stall, fumbling with the sanitary napkin she'd hidden in her purse, Elizabeth hissed, "Hurry, hurry." As Amy managed to remove the soiled napkin and wedge the fresh one in place, Elizabeth paced from the entrance to the exit. When Amy left the booth with her used napkin rolled in toilet paper and buried it in the trash beneath the paper towels, Elizabeth murmured, "Oh, my God."

On Monday, January tenth, Amy wakes early and finds her panties stained. All week long Elizabeth will be her constant companion, the watchdog at the restroom. The last menstruation meant spending recess and lunch break with her and not joining Marcy's group. On Monday and Tuesday, Marcy ignored her absence. But by Wednesday, she stopped Amy in the lunchroom to ask, "Why aren't you playing jacks with us?" Hearing the excuse of discussing *Jane Eyre,* Marcy raised her left eyebrow in disbelief. It hadn't been a lie. They had discussed the book. But getting back into Marcy's group meant saying carefully planned flattering remarks, flirting with the right people.

Because Mom would never let her stay home, Amy goes to school, but wonders how she'll stand Elizabeth's unbearable bossiness all week long. Although she's willing to loan books and loves to talk about them, their dialogues have a pattern. Amy gets to ask the questions, and Elizabeth gives the answers. And Elizabeth won't even listen to Amy's opinions. But the January menstruation passes without the humiliation of discovery, so Elizabeth's companionship was a small price to pay.

The fun of February should not be destroyed by having to hide in the bathroom with a dirty sanitary napkin. This very Wednesday is Valentine's Day. The maps and educational displays on the bulletin boards have been replaced by red construction paper bordered with scallops of doilies. Snowflakes cut in geometric designs are stapled over pink construction paper hearts, so the bulletin boards look like a valentine bakery cake with vanilla icing. And last year's dusty valentine box has been refurbished with fresh doilies and a red crepe-paper bow. The box sits on Mr. Crandall's desk, so students can deposit cards for one another and for him until Wednesday, when a party will be held during the last hour of class. At the end of the party, the box will be opened and all the special people, the ones everybody loves, will receive the most elaborate and the greatest number of valentines.

In the past, Amy had always dreaded parent participation projects, for Mom had no time or money for extras. But this holiday, she excitedly waited for the list being circulated for Valentine's Day party contributions so she could clearly print, "Amy—cookies, three dozen, fancy." Of course, Gram will volunteer to bake her fancy cookies. And Marcy will be sure to be impressed and can be counted on to circulate information about the donor of what will surely be the grandest contribution.

But on Saturday, Amy wakes early with the black sticky feeling; the red disease of menstruation has returned. She wants to curl into a ball and claim she is sick, but Gram will be disappointed. Today is the day they plan to go shopping for the ingredients for the cookies and some valentines. After dawdling in the bathroom for a long time, she dresses for the day, wearing a long-tailed shirt dangling over her fanny to cover the lumpy outline of the sanitary napkin through her jeans. She tugs it before she enters the kitchen to have her solitary breakfast. But Gram is puttering with the coffeepot at the stove. Without looking up, she calls, "Morning, sunshine." Amy sullenly sits at the table. Sunshine isn't the right name for her today. Gram turns and asks, "Isn't it a good morning?"

"No." Gram seems shocked by this answer and will demand an explanation. Amy adds apologetically, "I started my period."

Gram brings her cup to the table and sits. "Let's see. I guess you're right on time." She blows on the coffee to cool it. "Did you mark your calendar?"

Amy shakes her head irritably.

"Well, you know, you should mark your calendar."

She jabs at the table. "Why do I have to write it down? I feel like a balloon before it happens."

Gram laughs. "You're right about that." She shakes her head in agreement. "I'd forgotten. You get a puffy feeling, don't you?"

She manages to murmur "yeah," wondering why Gram enjoys these nasty discussions. It isn't possible for the bloody, smelly stuff to come out of her.

Gram swallows coffee and stares at the refrigerator. "The reason is water retention." She checks her student's response. "Most of your body is water, you know. Salt makes you retain water. You really oughtn't to eat extra salt." She laughs and takes a quick sip of coffee. "Leaving salt alone is something I can't do. I puffed up like a balloon before every period. And when I was pregnant, whooee. I needed a wheelbarrow to cart myself around in those last few months. Both times. Oh, how I dreaded old Doc Kopp's scales." She smiles as she carefully sets her cup in the ring of its saucer.

Imagining Gram pregnant is impossible; her wrinkled face and knobby hands could never have been young. Amy speaks softly, embarrassed by the daring of her question, "Did you get fat when you were pregnant with Mommy?"

"I looked as if I might explode."

Amy laughs, enthralled by the image of the domed belly. "How fat did you get?"

"Oh, forty pounds heavier one time, forty-five the next."

"Gee, how big were the babies?"

"Just round chubby babies—seven pounds, seven and a half."

"That's all?" Amy weighs less than a hundred yet feels tiny compared to the grownups she knows. "What happened to the rest of your fat?" She giggles at the rudeness of her question. The rest of Gram's fat must be in her cushioned fanny and saggy bosom.

"Oh, the fat went away." She pats her midriff. "This is a more recent acquisition, gained during the past twenty years. I was skinny as your mother when I was her age. Grampa used to call me his slip of a girl." She picks up her cup as if embarrassed by the affection in her tone.

Amy sits back, feeling fat as a toad. "I wish I was skinny."

"You do? I don't know why you'd want to change. You're so pretty. You're going to be a beautiful woman."

Amy studies Gram's face for signs of insincerity. But she sips her coffee so it's impossible to read her face. Of course, grandmothers have to say those things. But for a moment Amy tries to imagine her childish face emerging from its pale moon, and her doughy body expanding so her bosom and hips look like the centerfold girls. And probably when she's really grown up, she'll get married and pregnant, stretching her stomach into a giant, white watermelon. But such a marvel occurring doesn't seem possible. She crosses her hands over her soft belly and asks a question she is sure about. "Gram, remember today's the day we're going to get started on the cookies?"

Gram is swept up by the idea. The efficient teacher immediately starts the project: making the list of ingredients, planning the shopping. On Tuesday night, by the time the thirty-six perfectly shaped hearts are baked, her plans for the project have expanded. She asks if she might call Mrs. Briggs and volunteer as a helper, adding with a tone of self-importance that Amy finds embarrassing, "I remember, from my years in the classroom, how those room mothers could always use another hand." Amy makes an excuse about Mrs. Briggs having other helpers. It isn't true, but no one has ever had a grandmother, instead of a mother, come to school. It's just too strange to risk. The class might laugh, making Amy and Gram feel foolish. When Amy rejects the plan, Gram seems a tiny bit hurt. It takes several compliments about the beautiful cookies to soothe her. But then she fusses about how their "creations" will make it to school in one piece. Amy assures her carrying the big box of cookies will be no problem, fearing all the while her reassurance isn't true. When Elizabeth proudly announces her mother is driving her to school on Valentine's Day, Amy timidly invites herself along. To her amazement and relief, Elizabeth agrees. And Gram is impressed when she learns Elizabeth's mother, the wife of a college professor, will be driving Amy to school.

Dressing for the day, she doesn't want to seem as if she's gone to a great deal of trouble, but wants to look her best. A new outfit is out of the question, so she settles for her faded red cords because the red and white checked blouse looks so fresh and she can wear brand-new red yarn in her hair, which Gram says looks pretty. Scrubbed and waiting for her ride, she's so excited she hums as loudly as an ecstatically purring cat.

Elizabeth's mother is late, so Amy rushes out of the door to get to the car. Elizabeth climbs out so Amy sits next to Mrs. Perry who glances at Amy during introductions. Her eyes have a cold-blue cast, and her eyelashes are so long they are tangled at the outer edges. Her voice is throaty, soft as a cat's tail swishing against your leg. She murmurs, "'lo," then turns to stare out the windshield, not even attempting conversation. Although it's a cool desert morning, the woman is practically naked, wearing a cotton shift, heavily embroidered with tiny mirrors stitched about the neckline and hem. The word "ethereal," which Elizabeth has used to describe her mother, is well illustrated by her pale, bony blondness.

After setting Amy's package of cookies in the back beside boxes overflowing with clothing and old newspapers, Mrs. Perry starts the car. As it lurches forward, she yanks her skirt into a knot in her lap, exposing her legs from the thigh to her naked toes, which flex in her shower shoes as she presses the gas. At each intersection, her right arm becomes violently active as she pushes at the gearshift. The small muscles flex beneath the skin and her five brass bracelets rattle. But when the shift doesn't slip easily into place, Mrs. Perry says, "Oh, shit." She repeats "shit" five times. Amy is stunned. She's never heard a woman utter the word before, and Mrs. Perry says it without flinching. Daddy only says it when he's terribly drunk or when something awful happens. But Mrs. Perry is just having a little problem with the gearshift. Amy stares ahead to make it appear she hasn't heard, then sneaks a look at Elizabeth. She must have heard the string of curses, yet she sits very straight, staring ahead as mysterious as the ostriches in the zoo. As they jounce along for the last few blocks to school, Amy looks at Mrs. Perry's toes: the nails are long and ringed with dirt. Her legs are covered with long blonde hair. Amy watches the radio the remainder of the ride.

When they stop by the gate, Mrs. Perry leans forward to see around Amy to Elizabeth. "I don't have to pick you up, right?" The sweet fragrance Amy had assumed was cologne is coming from Mrs. Perry's mouth. Elizabeth busies herself getting her packages from the floor. As Amy tries to say thank you, Mrs. Perry stares at her, breathing the overpowering smell, saying, "Nice meeting you, Mary. Heard a lot about you." Humiliated for both of them, Amy silently scrambles out of the car.

Kids rush into the room carrying foil-wrapped plates or grocery bags with party goodies. Everyone, even Duane, comes with envelopes for the Valentine box. The pregnant-looking box, bulging with mystery, is in the center of Mr. Crandall's desk, so no one can sneak up and dig into it to end the agony of anticipation. Finally, at one-thirty, the beginning of the party is signaled by the arrival of the room mother, Mrs. Briggs, and a woman who looks like her. Mr. Crandall turns the class over to them as if they were substitutes. The class examines the new leaders' perky faces, wreathed with short brown hair. They wear boxy pants suits in blinding colors and smile at each other more than at the children. The women organize activities pitting classmates against one another. When the excitement is a frenzy, Mrs. Briggs calls, "Refreshment time," and points to the back of the class, where a miraculous feast has been spread by a tired-looking Mr. Crandall.

Moving through the refreshment line, Amy can clearly see Gram's cookies are the best contribution. It is sad to see the lovely shapes crammed into mouths as thoughtless as Marcy's and as dirty as Duane's, but cookies are for eating. She's always kept her chocolate Easter bunnies until they whitened with age and Mom threw them away. To eat their ears or paws seemed cruel. She wraps her cookie in her napkin to carry home as memorabilia.

Mrs. Briggs calls to the class, "And who'd like to pass out valentines?" She chooses a boy who loves to show off, who drags out the process, so everyone is aware of how many valentines each person receives. Amy seems to be getting more cards than anyone else. Her anxiety begins to unwind into a slower tempo of a purr. The stack of valentines on her desk proves her classmates love her. At home in the privacy of her room, she can read each card to guess at the senders' feelings. Here in the class, she must carefully maintain a smiling disregard and not give in to the urge to openly display her delighted curiosity. Mr. Crandall finally intervenes to stop the tortuous process. Time is running out, so he divides the remaining cards among the room mothers and himself. They distribute them rapidly, ending just as the bell rings.

The unimportant kids, the ones who haven't made contributions to the party, slip out of the room quietly. But the core who control the class remain to pick up empty plates. Amy clutches her stack of envelopes, more than half unopened, and hurries to the back of the room to find her bag and plate. She wishes everyone knew about her valentines, but she is frightened: they might be jealous, they might be mean. The only other person who received a lot of valentines is Marcy, who is still at her desk, laughing loudly, repeating, "I don't know how I'll carry all of these." If Amy walks the long way around, she won't have to pass her. To catch Elizabeth, who was the first to leave, she must hurry. As she picks up her plate, covered with red sugar and crumbs, Mrs. Briggs says, "Those were certainly beautiful cookies."

Amy doesn't want to look at the red lips, and the birdlike eyes, which are like Marcy's. Mom says it's rude not to look at someone talking to you, so she watches the front of the brilliant pants suit and murmurs, "Thank you." This lady is a storybook mother, who doesn't work, who has a husband: a normal lady; but she makes Amy feel so creepy that she longs for escape.

Mrs. Briggs teases, "I'd really like to know where you bought those cookies."

Injured by the judgment that her family sent store-bought cookies, Amy shakes her head. Gram said, "It's trashy to bring goodies from the store, but some folks haven't any choice." Realizing her silence seems rude, Amy says softly, "My gramma baked them."

Mrs. Briggs croons, "Isn't that nice."

Amy dips her head, a plea to be excused. Mrs. Briggs's compliment seems like an insult. The woman is watching her, waiting for her reply. Amy nods as if she has suddenly become mute. Now Mrs. Briggs is turning away, so it's safe to hurry around the table, pick up the shopping bag, and get out of the room before Marcy catches her.

Elizabeth is half a block beyond the gate when Amy reaches the exit. Trying to run down the concrete steps, she almost trips, but she hasn't time to watch her feet. She must catch Elizabeth. Shouting her name, Amy races by the bike rack, where kids stare at her. The lumpy, heavy bags swish noisily against her body as she runs after her friend.

She's hoarse and breathless by the time Elizabeth finally stops, cocks her head, turns, and looks quizzically, hands on hips. "Well?" her voice is sharp, pricking the skin for as deeper incision. The bags have angered Elizabeth. Amy murmurs, "Um . . ." sorry it's too late to turn and run.

"You look like Santa with your stuffed brown bag." She shifts the crumpled, half-empty bag she brought in the morning behind her.

Amy apologizes, "This bag has plates in it. And this bag has—" She starts to say "valentines" and realizes why Elizabeth is angry, so she finishes lamely, "things."

"They must be really awful 'things' if they came from those people." The whiteness ringing Elizabeth's lips means she's about to cry. The round shape in her bag reveals she's bringing home her contribution of fruit punch.

As they walk side by side, Amy chats to herself, hoping to hit on a topic to lift Elizabeth's sulkiness. At the mention of Mrs. Briggs, Elizabeth is alert with anger. "Mrs. Briggs and her friend, whatever her name is, are obnoxious and vulgar." She pauses for the maximum impact of two of her vocabulary favorites. "Those women are Junior League types. My father has to deal with silly women like them when they work on his committee from the community." Elizabeth kicks at a stone. "The whole idea of exchanging valentines is silly."

Amy nods, a sign of agreement which she doesn't share. Valentines are silly only if you don't receive them. She wishes she could slip a few of hers into Elizabeth's nearly empty bag. They are silent until they part, when Amy mutters, "Good-bye."

Elizabeth speaks rapidly as if someone is twisting her arm, "Your grandmother's cookies were quaint."

Amy studies Elizabeth's harlequin frames, confused by the word and hurt by the tone. "Quaint?" This confession of ignorance is immediately regrettable.

Elizabeth flushes with excitement at this opportunity to instruct. "Quaint is pleasingly old-fashioned."

Racing home to ease the sting of Elizabeth's words, Amy finds the house is empty. Gram's probably shopping. On Wednesdays she clips coupons and takes intricate bus routes to reach her destination, so she's often gone all day. But Flossie might arrive at any moment, so Amy hurries to her bedroom and locks the door. Sprawled on the sloppily made bed, she opens envelopes while she presses the sugar crumbs on the plate with a moist finger and sucks off the sweetness. She received a valentine from every person in class, and there are a couple of special ones, not just the tiny punch-out kind, but twenty-five-cent Hallmark cards. One is from Elizabeth, a sedate, classic valentine with Cupid shooting an arrow and a carefully rhymed greeting, addressed to a "dear friend." The other is from Marcy. Now that's a suprise. The recent poor attendance at lunch time jacks games could have relegated her to the punch-out card category. The valentine is silly, featuring an overweight white dog. Maybe it is a little insulting, but it's a special card. The uniqueness of the purchase is an honor. To doublecheck, she makes a neat stack, counting again. Yes, she's done well. Marcy could not have this many. But poor Elizabeth. Maybe Elizabeth only received one card, the homemade one Gram had helped make. And there were three just alike: one for Elizabeth, one for Mr. Crandall, and one for Marcy, because of her power. Elizabeth deserved an extra special card. Already the glow of receiving the most valentines is dimming.

After school the next day, Amy is relegated to tearing down the doilies and stuffing them in the overflowing trashcan while Elizabeth marks spelling. As they begin their trek home, Elizabeth seems fascinated by the process of guiding her bike. She speaks, hesitantly. "My father and I would

like to invite you . . . to . . . to come with us to the ballet."
Amy controls herself from squealing, "He wants to meet
me!" for Elizabeth's still talking. "He'll call your mother to
tell her the details."

Saturday, the day she's waited for so long, has finally ar-
rived. She'll get to go inside the Scottsdale Center for the
Performing Arts to see a living dream, the ballet, an event
she's only seen on TV where the dancers are so tiny they
seem to belong on a music box, spinning perfectly like no
human she'd ever seen. Living dancers, living musicians, a
stage filled with color—no Walt Disney movie could ever be
so grand. She'll be escorted by Professor Perry of Phoenix
College. Mom said he sounded quite dignified when he called
to arrange to pick her up for the matinee.

Fifteen minutes before the scheduled arrival on Saturday,
she's bathed and dressed, waiting in the living room, listening for Professor Perry's car. She wears her new dress, one
Gram bought for the important occasion. To be polite, Amy
chose Gram's favorite, an old-fashioned style, which is a little embarrassing to wear. But Professor Perry will probably like buttons and lace and bows. And because Gram
thinks it's appropriate, Amy wears a pair of her white
gloves. The itching from the ferocious scrubbing of her face
is heightened by her hair being swept back from her forehead and secured in a shiny cap by a series of Gram's combs.
Amy looks like a different person with her large bright eyes
crowned by her pale forehead, which never sees the sun. She
sits on the arm of Daddy's chair, afraid wisps of hair might
spring from the combs, or her snowy tights will bag at her
ankles above her Mary Janes, or the butterfly wings of the
bow of her sash sag. She opens and closes the rhinestone
clasp on the evening bag Mom has loaned her, or swats her
purse with the white gloves. There is no clock in the living
room, but to check the time requires leaving her perch and
risking a damaged appearance on the walk to the kitchen.

Flossie stands in the arch of the dining room and sneers, "You look weird."

Professor Perry is fifteen minutes late. The Perrys must have changed their minds about their invitation. Please God keep Mom and Gram in the kitchen, talking about whatever it is they talk about on Saturday afternoons while Mom stinks up the house with her endless smoking. Hail Mary full of grace, keep them away, let me go to my room and rip off this ugly costume and scratch all over. A shower would dissolve the layers of talcum turning to paste with perspiration and the sweet, nose-itching odor would wash down the drain. Elizabeth will never be a friend again even if the only one left in class is Mr. Crandall. Elizabeth deserves to be punished for her hours and hours of boring lectures, for making promises she doesn't keep. A car is coming up the driveway. Footsteps approach the front door. Someone is knocking.

Professor Perry is the ugliest man she's ever seen. His narrow face is almost covered by hornrimmed glasses with heavy stems that disappear into the wispy hair fluffed about his ears. His scraggly black and white beard bobs when he smiles to reveal jagged, yellowed teeth. Elizabeth announces with pride, "This is my father, Professor Perry."

Amy wants to dash by them into the sunshine and get into their car, but she manages a little gesture somewhat like a curtsy and says, "Won't you come in?"

Neither Professor Perry nor Elizabeth frightens Gram. She picks up the conversation and fluffs it up as if it were a pillow needing a good shaking, while Mom stands in the background breathing smoke. Gram sounds so intelligent she might be a person who teaches at a college. Professor Perry listens, nodding as Gram presses his hand and talks about the ballet and the cultural events in New York. She's the one who checks her watch and exclaims, "If you're going to be on time for the curtain, you'd better leave now."

En route to the theater, Professor Perry drives with spastic rythms. Braking and starting are spine-jarring experiences. As he circles the parking lot, he mutters to himself as Elizabeth chatters gaily. They bustle to the theater entrance and wait while he speaks to the woman inside the ticket booth, then he turns to report they'll have to wait in the wings until intermission. Elizabeth's face is not critical: she thinks he is wonderful.

From behind the velvet cord, guarded by a snotty usher, the stage is barely visible. The dancers are as tiny as they are on TV, but the forest setting with peasants whirling about is far better than a television picture. Professor Perry reads in a hoarse whisper from a booklet with glossy photographs as they peer down the tunnel of the aisle to the kaleidoscope on the stage. To duck under the cord and run to the edge of the stage is not permissible. She must stand silently by Elizabeth's side, like a patient pony being groomed for a show, her only sign of life the shifting of weight from the right leg to the left.

At intermission the cord is unleashed and the audience surges up the aisle. Professor Perry ignores the usher and forges ahead. Mr. Crandall would not choose him as a leader; he does every thing wrong, yet they follow him as he brushes by saying, "Excuse me" and "I beg your pardon." And Elizabeth whispers over her shoulder, "These are excellent seats—expensive ones—close to the stage, the center row." Then they climb over the knees of blue-haired ladies and collapse with a whoosh in their seats. After a moment's pause, Professor Perry is up again, back down the aisle. As he passes, a flurry of white gloves adjust skirts. She's careful not to meet the eyes of the ladies who probably assume the scatterbrained man is her father.

Amy cowers in her seat as Elizabeth begins a loud lecture about the ballet. "We've just seen the Dance of the Polovtsian Maidens and the barbaric splendor of Borodin's ballet."

"Barbaric" is such a wonderful word, Amy sneaks a look

at Elizabeth and sees she's reading from Professor Perry's booklet. The men who leapt across the stage in their black tights and blousy shirts looked barbaric; they could be darts tossed into the clusters of women in their embroidered vests and flowing skirts.

Professor Perry enters the aisle; his slow progress is a comic ballet. As he apologizes to the people whose feet he steps over, he musses the hair of the people in front of him with the programs he's brought from the lobby. He reaches his seat and collapses. Breathing heavily and smelling of pipe smoke, he says loudly, "They're doing Copland's *Billy the Kid.*" And as he explains the movements, the houselights dim.

The curtains part and a rainbow of desert colors light the street of a frontier town. Mexican ladies with roses in their hair, wearing white blouses and skirts of red or green with flashing black sequin roses, sway as the violins swell. With a boom of drums, a handsome man leaps from the wings. He seems to live in flight, touching the stage for a moment and vaulting in the air again. The audience applauds, for he is the music. He flashes a knife with a long, sparkling blade above his head. The twin moons of his buttocks whirl by, as high and round as a young girl's. Back arched, his weight on one leg, he is silhouetted against the setting: framed by the spotlight, against a yellow sky, the knife above his head. Then he plunges the knife toward the earth in a swoop to kill an invisible enemy. Now he flutters like a wounded bird. He ought to shake the knife from his wrist, bury his weapon, to disguise his action before the women on the stage discover his crime. In the dim light, his face is frightening, with shadows lining the hollows of his eyes. But now he slows to a rocking, the movement following a long cry. Tearing the scarf from his neck, he slowly draws it across his body, hiding the knife, the scarf turning bloody in the shadowy light. He slowly circles the stage. But a woman dancer leans forward and the others gather behind her. They hover,

ready to cradle him if he should fall. With the rolling of the
kettledrums and the gasping of violins, the dance ends and
he stands center stage: his body still, his face lifted into the
light, the women a shadowy crowd behind him.

Before the curtains close, the audience rises, clapping
frantically, some even calling, "Bravo!" Amy rises too, clapping wildly and trying to glimpse the dancer between the
bodies of the adults before her. But a glance to her side reveals she shouldn't be on her feet. Elizabeth and Professor
Perry are seated, clapping rhythmically, staring ahead with
unsmiling faces. She's probably been rude to stand when her
hosts haven't, but she must clearly see the dancer every moment he remains on the stage. He steps forward, bowing, his
face glistening in the full light of the theater; and now he
smiles. He is magnificent: his shirt unbuttoned to his navel,
his chest rising and falling. He lifts one arm to the ceiling,
so his body is a long, sensuous line. She doesn't sit down
although Gram would probably have advised her to do so.

In the car, Professor Perry fiddles with his pipe and talks
around the stem, "Isn't it just like Phoenix to give a standing ovation for *Billy the Kid?*" Elizabeth smirks to show her
contempt for the audience, and Amy rolls her gloves into a
ball. He sucks noisily on his pipe. "A little horse opera will
always move these crowds." The pipe doesn't light. He digs
in his coat pocket for the lighter.

Elizabeth smiles at his profile with the pipe drooping from
his lips. "They aren't sophisticated, are they?"

He lights his pipe and drops the lighter in his pocket.
"It's not Philadelphia." This must be what Mr. Crandall
calls an inside joke. She isn't quite sure what Professor
Perry means, but she knows she stood to applaud, and she's
never been to Philadelphia.

They stop at an ice cream parlor which Elizabeth says is
"quaint." As they sit in their wrought-iron chairs beneath a
whirring ceiling fan, the conversation over ice cream is as
numb as Amy's tongue. She ordered first since she was the

guest, and because she loved it she had ordered a strawberry ice cream cone. And Professor Perry peered over the tops of his odd, half-moon glasses, ordering a "blueberry frappe," pronouncing the word so it was barely recognizable. Daddy always said frappe so it rhymed with trap, but Professor Perry makes it sound like two words, dragging out the last syllable *pe* so it rhymes with *lay*. Elizabeth was exotic in her choice too, ordering a dish of pistachio almond fudge with chocolate sprinkles. As they sip and mince over their delicacies, Amy licks her cone as slowly as possible so she can listen closely to their conversation. The format is familiar, but the roles have been changed. Professor Perry is the interviewing instructor and Elizabeth is the interviewee. Amy laps at a drop of ice cream rolling down the cone. "And Amy," Professor Perry stares at her as he swishes his frappe with his spoon, "what are your impressions of the ballet?"

She swallows. "Um . . ." Impression might mean idea or maybe feelings. Studying the swirls of her ice cream, she says, "I liked *Billy the Kid*."

"Ah. You prefer Copland to the Russian classics?"

She hasn't pleased her host. *Billy the Kid* isn't sophisticated.

Elizabeth leans toward her father and says confidingly, as if she were an interpreter for a person with a limited command of English, "This was Amy's first ballet."

He smiles as if Elizabeth has answered his question. And she is right, this is the first ballet. Perhaps the Perrys have seen far more than she, just as stories are more meaningful to her than to Duane, who reads too slowly for the words to hang together to make sentences. It's very apparent she's "uncouth," another of Elizabeth's words. The Perrys finish their ice cream with none of the slurping and licking of spoons that reveal her family's zest for eating. To eat her cone would make loud crunching noises, so she hides it inside her left glove.

On the ride home, Professor Perry finds a station on the radio with strange music like the ballet. Images of the dancer brandishing the knife superimpose themselves on the Phoenix landscape. Folding her hands over the cone hidden in her gloves, Amy analyzes the curve of his buttocks and focuses upon the suprisingly large mound at his groin. The dancer's penis and testicles were larger than she'd imagined they would be. He couldn't possibly be the "fag" the boys said men dancers were when Mr. Crandall explained the availability of student tickets for the ballet. The dancer might make love to the beautiful women dancers, his penis growing long and hard to slip inside them. She looks out the window to divert herself from such a deliciously nasty thought. But the landscape flashing by is filled with a billboard of a lady wearing a bikini. She is five times larger than life and toasty brown all over, even at the dimple where her belly button is. Professor Perry's eyes stray from the highway and the cloud of smoke wreathing his head to the nipples beneath her wet bra. His weak chin bobs up and down once as he sucks on his pipe, then he turns his attention to the road. It's hard to imagine that he "does it." But he must have, lying naked on top of Elizabeth's mother, bouncing up and down, pushing his "thing" in and out of her. As retribution for her nastiness, Amy slowly and methodically crushes the cone inside her glove. She won't permit herself to eat it in the secrecy of her bedroom as she'd planned.

When the Perrys stop outside her house, she thanks them repeatedly, considering all the while how she ought to invite them in, but she finds no words to offer an invitation and fears they might accept. Totally humbled, she backs away from the car, having to close the door twice because her attempts to close it softly fail. Skipping to the house, she hopes she looks happy and prays none of the crumbs from the cone fall from her glove.

Gram is sitting on the couch reading *Time* magazine, but

at the sound of the door closing, she lowers it and eagerly asks, "How was it?"

There's no escaping. She speaks quickly, hoping the dirty gloves will be overlooked. "It was really neat."

"Neat?" She chuckles. "How was it neat, honey?"

"Well, there was this dancer." Gram's glasses glitter in the afternoon sun, obscuring her eyes, and the words for his beauty are impossible to speak. She looks at the sodden mass of the gloves. "He was just neat. That's all." He soars, the black tights delineating the exclamation point at his groin.

"What dances did he perform?"

"He was Billy the Kid."

"Aha." She tilts her head so the glare of her glasses is deflected. "I've seen the ballet. Very exciting—Mexican women, the young cowboy."

"You did?" Gram saw the naked man and found him beautiful too. "What was his name?"

"Oh, honey, I saw it a long time ago, in New York City. But I remember how exciting it was." Her smile is tranquil. Amy wants to ask if there had been a standing ovation but decides it's a silly question. New York is more sophisticated than Philadelphia. And this is an easy exit; Gram's drifted off to the past, a place she seems to like more and more these days.

It's a luxury to be alone in her room. She studies herself in the mirror. Most of the hair that was pulled back by the combs has wriggled loose, so wispy curls wreathe her forehead. She sucks in her cheeks, attempting the gaunt look of the ballerinas. But her hair must be dark and sleek, her face translucent and pale: she isn't right at all. And her body is absolutely hopeless. Elizabeth says dancers have bones like birds and long legs and necks. Amy lifts her skirt to look at her chunky thighs. Most of her body is torso. Her legs are like a Shetland pony's, and her neck is a fist instead of a reed. She drops her skirt and collapses on the bed. At least she can dump the crumbs out of the gloves, wash them up, and get them back to Gram, and she can get out of this dress, which belongs on Flossie instead of someone who will be entering junior high next year. She stares at the cracked ceiling; it might be a giant movie screen where the dancer will leap. He is nameless, ageless; he has no home. Some research could make the daydream sufficiently elaborate to make it seem real.

But as she braces her elbows on the soggy mattress to hoist herself up, she realizes that she hasn't brought her program with her. She gnaws at her thumbnail. The program could be in the Perrys' car, or at the theater, or the ice cream store. Oh, she hopes it's in their car. Otherwise she can't have his picture, and she'll have to borrow Elizabeth's and have to return it, and then answer all her stupid questions. Curling back on her bed, she tries to put all his features together to make the man whole. His face had been too remote to recall, but the black profile of his tights is vivid. Stripping away the tights and the trunks, there is still another layer. He wears something like a loincloth, a thing men wear to keep from bouncing all around. Once Daddy left one with his baseball uniform in the bathroom. If the elastic straps were cut away, the cone, pressing the dancer's penis and testicles against his body, would fall away and the soft innards of the snail would swing loose. Like some snake-charmer's performer, it would writhe and dance with a life of its own. She rolls on her side and slips her hands between her thighs, her eyes close tightly on the image of the pink mushroom swaying its long stem as it lifts its single eye to the sunshine. Curls of golden hair glisten above the twin bulbs where it is rooted. The dancer's body disappears and the mushroom grows as large as the billboard lady, as large as a sahuaro, five times larger than what she imagines might grow from the limp, pink blob she'd seen when she saw Daddy toweling himself dry in the bathroom. She wants to sleep forever, curled in the warm tight ball with the mysterious plant blossoming in her brain.

Flossie comes in, banging into the room, smelling salty with sweat and breathing as if she'd run a long way. Amy sits up, shaking her head clear of the image, smoothing her skirt where she's pressed her hands between her thighs. "Can't you see I'm sleeping?" she asks, stooping to unbuckle the straps of her silly Mary Janes.

Flossie seems unimpressed. "How was the stupid thing you went to?" She picks up Amy's brush and rakes through the top layer of her disheveled hair.

Amy crosses her legs and swings her top foot viciously. "Leave my brush alone."

"Well, excuse me." She tosses the brush on the dresser and bustles from the room, her chubby thighs rubbing together with swishing sounds. She looks as if she might cry soon.

Amy hugs herself, hating the snappish older sister she's just been, knowing it's impossible to return to her vivid fantasy. What to do? She could put on her dirty bluejeans and empty the trash for Mom. But still there's Saturday night with the waiting-room anxiety of small talk with Gram and the droning of the TV. There is Sunday with cooking and dishes and a novel to read to keep up with Elizabeth. Somewhere in an airplane, flying above this little box where she lives, the ballet company flies to another city to create another wide-screen extravaganza for hundreds of applauding people; somewhere Daddy will begin another day with no thought of his family, with no thought of returning. She promises during every spare moment to create daydreams starring the dancer, whose face has begun to look amazingly like Daddy's.

Chapter **27** |

Michael rolls to the middle of Gwen's bed, plumps up her pillow, and hugs it. The kid's a real sweetie. Off to the spa early this Saturday, so she'll be back in time to go to lunch with the girls. Ought to crawl out of this bed and do some situps to fight off getting a beer-belly. Old Gwen takes better care of her body than foreign-car nuts take care of their cars. Always running, always working out, pounding on herself calling it a massage, and bitching about how flat her chest is. Well, she's no Jane Russell, but she's sure a woman in bed.

Sure got lucky with Gwen. He was scared shitless she'd say "fuck off" when he asked her to come along with the girls, but she picked up on how he needs her without being told. Her eyes all glossy like she was about ready to cry, she said, "I'd love to go. I really want to meet your girls." The kid's a hell of a lot deeper than the flash she showed at Fat's. When she got loaded and got to talking about her old man, he got a clue there was a hell of a lot going on with her. Her father was some kinda weird reformed drunk. Sounded like a real son of a bitch who made it hard on her when she was a kid. Some kinda country lawyer who was always away and when he was home was a secret drunk, the kinda guy who made her feel like nothing she ever did was enough. Said the old guy thought she was a flop because she taught grade school instead of being an English professor. Seems he liked poetry, or some kinda shit. Gwen said he thought she was dumb, or lazy, or both. If she'd just been better, he would've thought she was okay. He really did a number on her. Hard to believe that somebody as pretty and smart as Gwen could have an old man like that. But she thinks what he said is true and that's what counts.

A hell of a worker—always doing that stupid shit for her

first-graders, a regular Sister Theresa, a little saint, except when she got in the sack, whooee, then she was something else. She could sure give old Barb a lesson or two.

Street-smart too. Got that lawyer lined up, got the case rolling. Old Gertie just got the jump on her; had to get up damned early in the morning to get ahead of that old bird. And wouldn't you know, the lawyer Gertie got Barb is a bitch on wheels, probably a dyke. Gwen said all those lies on the paper were routine. Had to prove fault. She learned that shit from her old man. Funny she didn't get a divorce for herself. Must be her midwestern, tightass background. She said, "Nobody in my family has ever been divorced. They go to the grave hating each other." Kid's a regular Jekyll and Hyde: a little nun in the day, a drug crazed sex fiend at night. Don't knock it, buddy, if it weren't for the dope she'd have enough sense not to hang out with a bum like you. You need a woman's touch with the girls. And old Gwen will do a hell of a job.

Chapter **28** |

When the doorbell rings, Amy thinks she might wet her pants. In moments, she'll see Daddy for the first Saturday visit, "part of the terms of the divorce," Mom said angrily. Flossie can greet him. To battle over who will open the door would be silly, and seeing his face up so close so soon might make her cry. It will be better to have him look over Flossie's head and see his oldest daughter seated with her hands loosely clasped in her lap. She'll show him what a lady she's become in the past five months. The corners of her mouth twitch as the door swings open. Wearing worn bluejeans was a mistake. She should've worn her dress for the ballet, in spite of what Mom said. Staring at the doorway, she freezes in a pose for a photographer. He's watching Flossie, kneeling to touch her. His hands on her shoulders are as slender yet strong as they were before. Pulling Flossie's doll-like body to him, he buries his face in the crook between her shoulder and face.

Amy rocks, looking at her lap, curling tightly against the sagging couch to disappear into its overstuffed contours. Daddy and Flossie are speaking. To understand their overlapping words, she must watch their faces, but it is too painful to look. She swings her foot, banging her heel against the couch with a dull thud. How foolish to believe he'd come home to see her. A single breath could scatter her like milkweed in a million invisible pieces about the room. He's walking toward the chair, kneeling: "Amy." But even as his fingers touch her folded arms, all she can say is a tiny " 'lo."

The Mustang is a little car with bucket seats in the front. When Daddy opens the passenger's door and pushes up the front seat, Amy steps past Flossie and crawls in the back. While he walks around to the driver's side, Flossie takes a peek at herself in the rearview mirror, then settles in the seat. Leaning against Daddy's arm resting across the back of the seat as he backs out of the drive, she acts as if this were her first date.

The morning is spent wandering through the Phoenix zoo, where the animals look bored and sick and it smells. Flossie giggles continuously at everything Daddy says about the animals and permits him to buy her a pennant, popcorn, and a Coke, even though she doesn't need them and knows they're a waste of his money. Because it's getting embarrassing to say no continually, Amy lets him buy her peanuts. His face is slightly flushed, and she can never remember him talking so rapidly, performing so continuously. She doesn't dare suggest leaving. This must be how Daddy is when he's the "super salesman" that Mom says he can be. He is certainly handsome. As she squints up at him in the glaring sun, his hair is wreathed in golden light, his freshly-laundered white shirt tucked neatly beneath his belt. Eyes watering in all this brilliance, she glances at his fly, strips away the gentle curve of fabric and exposes his penis. Mortified by her nastiness, she crushes a peanut shell on the asphalt.

The strange restaurant where he takes them is called Dr. Munchies, and the entryway promises a grand interior. But a heavy velvet rope keeps them from joining the diners. Just as she decides children are not permitted in such elegant places, a haughty-looking young man approaches. Daddy nervously rubs his chin as he speaks to the bored man, who says, "Ah, yes," and loosens the rope. They pass a bar of rich, carved wood filling the length of the room. Real ferns hang from the ceiling of shining metal shaped in intricate designs. Eating out with Daddy has usually meant McDonald's or, to be fancy, Sambo's. He must be celebrating a very special day.

The man who thinks he's so smart has made a mistake, for he's leading them to a table where a woman sits. But she's smiling at Daddy and putting out her cigarette. She is as beautiful as a movie star, with skin the color of caramel apples and hair swirling with crazy curls. The closer Daddy gets, the more she smiles, so the skin around her eyes and nose crinkles. And as she crushes the cigarette, several bracelets jangle softly. She's as slender as the ballerinas. When Daddy reaches the table, he stops. Her dark eyes never seem to leave his, but they're serious now. She dips her chin, urging him to speak. He says, "These are my girls."

The woman's eyes are a very soft brown and her voice is as soft as she says, "You must be Amy." And then she turns and greets Flossie. This mysterious woman knows their names. Daddy pulls out a chair beside her, so Amy sits less than an arm's length from her and tries not to stare at the peach silk blouse hiding her bosom. The woman might turn at any moment from Flossie and be insulted by prying eyes.

When the scooting of chairs stops, the lady smiles encouragingly at Daddy, who grins at her and fidgets. Finally the woman says, "I'm Gwen," and blushes for having to remind him of his manners.

He laughs, looking at the table, murmuring a string of I'm sorry's, like a bad boy in class corrected by Mr. Crandall. His face glowing, Daddy looks at the woman and says in a low voice, "This is Gwen Beckett, a friend of mine."

Because Daddy is so fascinated by Gwen and everything she does, Amy performs for her. Gwen is as good at interviewing as Mr. Crandall. She repeats just the right words for emphasis and makes the most ordinary experience into a story with several pauses for laughter. Even though it's difficult to watch her luminous eyes unhesitatingly, their warmth is a guide to move Amy through a halting response into a slow lope, into a wild gallop, and soon she is giggling and warm with excitement as she races through detailed descriptions. Gwen is delighted, and Daddy is flushed with pride for his entertaining daughter. She feels closer to him than she has felt for a long time.

When lunch is served, they play Gram's polite conversation game. First Gwen, then Daddy, and finally Amy report on the quality of their food. Everyone turns to Flossie for her response. Her face is sulky. But Gwen continues to question in a voice loud enough for the neighbors to hear. Flossie's face puckers. Daddy firmly repeats the question.

Flossie jabs a potato slice with her fork. "It's terrible." Her mouth turns down. One more word and the wailing will begin. Furiously, she mashes the potato, so Daddy snaps, "Don't play with your food."

Tears inch down her cheeks; she blubbers, "I won't eat this garbage."

Daddy pales, his lips a tight line. Flossie snuffles loudly, so Gwen leans toward her, with a jangling of bracelets, and speaks as if they were alone, "Would you like to go to the restroom?" Flossie bobs her head so her chin brushes her breast bone, shoves her chair from the table, and half-blind with tears rushes to the exit. Gwen touches Amy lightly on the wrist, so a whiff of citrus perfume clouds the cigarette smoke. Her voice is breathy, "Would you go with her to the restroom? I think she needs you."

Staring into Gwen's chocolate eyes, Amy blinks, her throat tightens. "Oh, yes," she says. Scooting back her chair to accept the responsibility, she hurries to catch Flossie.

Amy waits outside a metal stall where Flossie has loudly locked herself against intruders. Busying herself by staring in the mirror, fluffing her hair, Amy waits to soothe the loud sniffler. Banging out of the stall, Flossie pretends she's alone. When the faucet doesn't turn for her, she pounds it, whimpers, shakes her hand, and cries. Setting her comb on the sink, Amy coaxes, "Let's see."

She violently shakes her hand. "It's all right."

"Ah, come on. Let's see." Flossie yanks her fingers from Amy, who shrugs, "Well, okay. I thought maybe I could help." The urge to shake her until she stops blubbering is so powerful, Amy puts her comb in her purse, snapping it shut, as if to say, "This is your last chance." They've been gone so long, Daddy might forget them and leave with Gwen.

As Amy turns, Flossie says, "Well, you just go on out there." The words are a slap. "Just go out there and sit with that . . . that . . . whore." She says it so "whore" rhymes with "sure," and it might've been funny if she hadn't spoken so hatefully. Now she's finished crying, proud to have used a word she doesn't understand, except that the bad boys say it and write it on walls. Gwen is not a whore. Daddy likes her because she's so pretty, because she isn't whiny, because she isn't grouchy and tired like Mom, because she isn't a boring child like they are. "She's an old whore. Taking Daddy away and . . ."

"Taking Daddy?" Flossie is so wrong. Gwen has brought Daddy back when he went away.

"Hm!" Amy's shock pleases Flossie, proof she knows

more than her sister. Flossie's tear-streaked face is set in its baby-doll mask. It's no use to try to reason with a girl who laughs when Elmer Fudd is hit on the head with a pile of bricks. In a couple of years maybe Mr. Crandall can explain to her that there is gray as well as black and white. Pulling Gram's hanky out of her purse, Amy offers it to Flossie, who sniffs loudly to ignore the ladylike remedy. Amy holds the hanky to Flossie's nose and commands, "Blow."

Gwen is smoking, her knife and fork lined up at the edge of the plate in the signal Gram says polite people use to tell waiters to remove the plate. But Gwen has only taken a few bites of her crabmeat and tomato. She's so thin, she's what Elizabeth calls "chic"; in fact, Gwen's "très chic." Elizabeth must see her to be convinced of her elegance. But unless Flossie behaves, they might never have another visit. Gwen smiles at Flossie, who settles at her place with both elbows on the table—poor etiquette, according to Gram. Embarrassed, Amy hopes to correct her with a frown. But she's scowling at Gwen, who asks if she'd like dessert. Gwen has made a big mistake. Daddy looks up in disbelief; he won't permit such an indulgence, and Flossie can't resist such a temptation. But Flossie pouts and says, "No," and adds with a pause long enough to be rude, "thanks." Amy tries to clean her plate. It's hard to swallow when she isn't hungry, but she must to make it clear whose side she's on in this war.

To fill the rest of the afternoon, Gwen said they could go to the library, or shopping, or a movie. To go to the library with the lake and the swans and the art museum next door would be wonderful, and Elizabeth would be so impressed. But Flossie kicked Amy's ankle when "movie" was mentioned and said loudly, "Yeah, let's see the movie." Gram has told them repeatedly to say yes, not yeah, but it was too risky to reprimand Flossie.

As they sit through the silly movie of talking gnome mobiles, Flossie is the only one who laughs and munches popcorn. She knows she won't be punished here, so she's trying every trick. Amy carefully keeps her arms in her lap, so Gwen can have the armrest they share. Gwen politely stares at the screen and even manages a smile or two during the chase scenes. Her face and neck illuminated by the various colors on the giant screen are so beautiful, Amy feels sick with inadequacy. Midway through the film, Daddy excuses himself and comes back ten minutes later. Smelling of smoke and sighing with boredom, he slouches in his seat for the rest of the show. He must hate having to take out his girls.

Walking out of the cave of the theater into the blinding light of the late afternoon, Amy feels so lonely she wonders if she'll ever speak again. Nothing as simple as a conversation would lead her out of this dark, tangled forest. The visit is over, and next week is a lifetime away. And she'll never learn how to make Daddy happy so everything will be all right. Shambling beside her, Flossie begins to whistle in her sharp, grating way, her face so puckered her eyes are slits. Two hours of the violent cartoon have made her happy. Amy refuses to hold her hand and skip with her, their usual behavior when the humming mood sets in. Flossie will have to change for things to get better. How to change her is a mystery. But Daddy seemed just as bored with Amy as he was with Flossie.

Sitting in the back of the Mustang, Amy wonders if Daddy will come in the house to see Mom, if Gwen will wait in the car, if Mom will watch from the window with Gram standing behind her clearing her throat and squinting through her bifocals. Surely there will be questions to answer when they return like spies who've dined with the enemy. Beside her, Flossie is picking a kernel from the bottom of the popcorn container, studying it like a monkey, then crushing it between her molars. She licks the salt from her thumb and forefinger and begins to search for another. It's so easy for Flossie to forget; it's hard to believe she had been so angry so recently. Seven days before next Saturday

—anyone who changes so quickly might be taught some manners between now and then.

The car stops and Gwen turns in the passenger's seat, saying, "I enjoyed meeting you. And I'll see you again, soon, I hope." Her face is so pretty, yet so unconcerned, like a stewardess speaking memorized information. Amy murmurs, "Oh . . ." and Flossie licks her fingers. Looking at Daddy, Gwen speaks more slowly, "See you later," then scoots across the seat to get out of the car. She looks at them through the back seat window and waves as if they're puppies. And before she can unlock the door of a sportscar that looks like a toy, Daddy drives away, whipping around a corner.

The ride home is silent. Daddy is an indifferent taxi driver with two nervous girls in the back seat, strangers in the city, unsure of how to pay a fare and tip. When he pulls into the driveway, Amy begins to talk as he speaks. He orders her to continue. She says stiffly, "Thank you very much. I had a very good time," and stops before saying, "I enjoyed meeting Gwen," afraid of the intimacy of the remark. Gwen's their secret. Beside Amy, Flossie is noticeably silent, but Daddy watches too closely for a punch to prod her to speak. There must be some way to scoop the shattered emotions of the afternoon into a presentable shape. But each comment concerns Gwen. Daddy accepts the final thanks with a sad half-smile.

He reaches across the seat and tickles Flossie's dimpled knee. "Good to see you, partner." She giggles and yanks at her dress to cover her knee. His fingers march up her thigh like the hand in the Yellow Pages ad. He pokes at her midriff and she grabs his hand with both of hers to stop the tickling. "Easy, partner." He gently shakes free of her grip, then he touches her chin with his fingertip to still her. His mouth is slack, his eyes puzzled, as if lost in the process of solving a confusing problem. Then he blurts in a husky voice, "Hey, buckaroos, I'll see you next Saturday." To get out of the car, Flossie squirms between the seat and the door, showing the seat of her underpants encasing her chubby bottom. Amy follows, carefully directing her rear away from Daddy's view.

In the living room Gram's knitting bag and pattern book are sitting on the corner of the couch where she usually sits. The faint hum of her voice drifts from the kitchen. Flossie moves toward the room, picking kernels from the popcorn box. Amy trails her, plotting how to control what she says. Mom shouldn't be told about Dr. Munchies or Daddy's girl-friend. To know about her might bring back the anger she'd felt on the afternoon when she'd fallen beneath him sobbing and he stepped over her and slammed out of the house.

Gram sits at the table dicing onions, making a little hill beside the diced pickles. "Hi, girls," her voice is raspy and loud. Mom doesn't turn from the sink. Amy manages a little smile as she moves as quickly as she can to stand beside Mom. To appear relaxed, Amy leans against the edge of the counter. From here she can see everyone and can run to any one of them when things start to fall apart.

Mom bites her lower lip as she cracks a hardboiled egg against the sink. Peeling the shell, she murmurs, "Damn," and begins to chip away the pieces. "Mom," she wails, "look at these damned eggs." She holds up an egg with a network of cracks. "What the hell's the matter with these?" She's crying.

Gram is up from the table and at her side. They murmur about the condition of the egg long enough to bore Flossie, who leaves. In moments the television begins to hum. The crisis has passed: the scenes of the afternoon will fade for Flossie after a few hours of TV. Gram is holding up the egg that she's peeled for Mom. "See, Barb, it's all right, honey."

Dinner and the evening and days pass, and there are no questions. On Wednesday Mom has a phone call, a rare event in their home. The little explosions of her single-word answers mean she's speaking to Daddy. When Mom hangs up, she angrily stares at the wall and says, "He's coming, Saturday." To ask for details is to risk Mom's rage, so the fantasy of his forthcoming visit is even more secret than the first time. Scenes are filled with talking to Daddy as they drive to meet Gwen, watching Daddy watch Gwen or talk with Flossie. All week long, Amy rehearses how to captivate Daddy. So when Saturday comes, fifteen minutes before the hour of his arrival she sits, itchy clean, listening for the roar of the Mustang coming up the drive. But Daddy's arrival is not what she'd imagined. He's not alone. Gwen sits in the front seat, right in their driveway, within full view of Mom and Gram, who'll want to know all about her.

Amy runs from the house. She knows if she stands for a moment the tears will come. Not even a moment alone with Daddy. It would be hard enough to get his attention with Flossie around, but Gwen . . . If only Gwen had met them later. Galloping toward the car, Amy prays for Flossie not to bellow, "Look at the old whore, Mom! Look at Daddy and her, Gram!" At any moment Gram and Mom might come racing out to the car, shaking their fists and screaming, sending the Mustang speeding away.

But once inside the car, Amy dares to look back to the house. It is silent as they pull away. And after the day together, they return to a quiet home. She mutters her good-byes. Inside the house no one asks about her visit. No one anywhere cares about Gwen and Daddy. And she wouldn't know how to describe them if anyone asked. It is like her dream where she speaks words no one seems to understand, and no matter how loudly she screams her name, no one recognizes her. It is like her dream of the cafeteria, walking by miles of creampuffs and pieces of chocolate layercake and dozens of kinds of pies on ice, behind a wall of thick, cold glass, each dessert oozing sweetness and none of it for her.

Chapter **29**

In the bathroom, splashing water on her face, Barbara avoids looking at her reflection, ashamed to face the woman she never intended to become—old at thirty-two, burnt out, washed up, divorced and living with her mother and two daughters who are rapidly approaching adolescence. The marriage is over—there will never be another man to build her life around. She turns on the tap. Cupping her hands beneath the water to scoop it to her lips, she gulps noisily. Drinking from a glass is too luxurious.

To see if she looks as awful as she feels, she looks at the mirror. An exhausted woman returns her stare. She tilts her head to soften the lines of aging. The stilted pose doesn't disguise her defeat. Mom's right: "peaked"—she looks and feels peaked. As if she's four years old, she'll lie down for an afternoon nap, for it's easier to mind Mom than to fight her.

As Barbara walks from the sink, her neck and her shoulders, the small of her back, her thighs, knees, and calves, ache as if they've been wrenched. She runs the heel of her hand above the hammock of her pelvic bone; its contours, which are normally concave, are slightly bloated. She presses the heel of her hand hard at the side of her breast and winces at its tenderness. She murmurs, "Oh, God, the curse"—the bloating, the bleeding, the smell, the mess. She fumbles at the button on the side of her shapeless slacks and starts to undress as she walks to the toilet.

As she sits on the seat, she examines the crotch of her panties. The red-brown smear confirms her suspicions. She wads toilet paper to mop at herself, to see if this is a slow beginning or if the near hemorrhage she endures each month is upon her. The tissue is saturated with crimson framing a dark clot the size of a raisin. At least there is an explanation for her tears over a boiled egg. She starts to stuff tissue into her crotch to protect her clothes from further soiling and remembers she no longer hides the sanitary napkins in her closet. When Amy became a woman, Gertrude made a production of bringing the box to the bathroom. The napkins are above the towels.

With her awkward bandage wedged between her thighs, she washes her hands with soap and smells her fingers before she dries them. Even over the fragrance of the pine-scented soap, she's sure she smells the animal scent. She rubs lotion on her hands. Perhaps she should take some aspirin, two or three or even four. She wants to sleep the rest of the afternoon away, into the dinner hour, to let Mom take up their lives, to become her adolescent daughter again, nursing the cramps on Saturday afternoon and evening when no boy came to call at their house. She recaps the bottle and puts it back in the medicine cabinet. She's tempted to straighten the clutter. She could empty the shelves, remove them, and hold the glass under the tap to rinse off the dust and hair. She closes the door firmly and doesn't mop at the water-spotted mirror. If she cleans the mirror, next she'll do the sink, then there'll be the floor and the walls. All the cleaning her house requires could keep her occupied for hours, then she could work in the yard, and the house would be dirty again. She can never rid their lives of the clutter and filth of living.

In the bedroom, she rummages through her dresser, distraught by the tangle of frayed gray lingerie. Everything she owns is worn or discolored. If she bleaches the garments, they'll fall apart, but buying anything new is beyond consideration. The belt for her sanitary napkin is puckered and fringed with broken elastic strands. Amy has the best belt. When she started her period, Barbara had obediently fetched the necessities for Mom and considered going to the bathroom to be with Amy, but in the glaring light of the bedroom, searching the dresser for a belt, she'd felt Mom bristling with efficiency. Shamed by the disorder of her dresser drawers and their shoddy contents, and the closet where the napkins were hidden, she handed the items to Mom and decided not to follow her to be with Amy. Barbara went back to bed, feeling as if she'd been an awkward intruder, as if she'd deserted her child, but knowing Amy was being cared for by a better mother. When she awoke the next morning, Barbara was unsure if the events occurring before dawn had been a dream or reality.

If she stretches out flat on her belly on the bed, her tender breasts are flattened on the mattress. If she turns on her side, her shoulder and arm cramp. Lying flat on her back, she feels the dull ache of menstruation settle in her lower belly, so she bends her knees and pushes the small of her back into the mattress. The contraction is a satisfying fist of pain. She holds it until her head throbs, and then she rolls on her side, bending her knees and arms, a fetus beginning to stir. She won't think of Michael, or Mom or Amy or Flossie. She'll think of the slow drip of the lining of her uterus, unfertilized eggs draining from her, staining the napkin to be thrown in the trash, then hauled away and burned.

But sleep never comes easily in the middle of the day—except, of course, to Michael, who sat in his chair, closed his eyes, and slept while the TV droned and the family stepped around him. How little time he'd actually spent with them. Her time alone with him, after the girls were born, was practically nonexistent. And since she'd been pregnant before marriage, it was as if there'd always been children. They'd had no vacations and few weekends alone. Oh, once, long ago, before Flossie was born, Etta and Big Mike had taken Amy, who was only a year and a half old, for a weekend to the Poconos. The silence of his parents' house beneath their apartment had inspired Michael to explore his old home. As Barbara washed the few dishes from lunch, he startled her by patting her fanny, saying, "Come on, babe, let's go downstairs for a change of pace." She'd laughed and urged him to go ahead and promised to meet him.

He reluctantly went downstairs alone. She was having her

period. Assuming intercourse wasn't possible, he'd sulk when she'd tell him or joke about her "being on the rag," but he'd be angry and disappear to drink with his friends. It would be her fault for making the mess she did every month just to inconvenience him. But she could try to disguise her dilemma. At the grocery, she'd overheard a woman say that she used a diaphragm when she "wanted to screw during those days." Her language was crude and the idea disgusting, yet this might be a solution. Barbara put in her diaphragm to catch the flow of menstruation, willing to risk its failure rather than explain to him. As she ran down the stairs, she wondered if he'd feel a difference: the rubbery disk would be the same, but maybe her body wouldn't respond as it usually did. In a college lecture on taboos, intercourse during menstruation was used as an example. When a prim girl in class asked if people who broke taboos were perverts, the professor had laughed and said, "Possibly."

In her mother-in-law's kitchen, Michael was at the refrigerator, taking one of his father's beers. She felt guilty yet excited, being in her in-laws' house. The pulse at Michael's neck as he tilted back his head to swallow was tempting to kiss. She laughed with the breathless hysteria of a child about to be caught as he chased her from the kitchen. At the door to his parents' bedroom, he caught her shirttail, and she heard the seam of her armhole tear. She stopped and he whirled her about, stripping her shirt and bra from her. He held her breasts so he could pinch her nipples if she didn't obey and ordered her into the bedroom. Her laughter made her words an unintelligible trill as he wrestled her onto his parent's bed, raking off her pants, tearing off his clothes. She wanted him to play with her, to touch her and kiss her, but the tension of his rising passion silenced a request.

With her wrists held to the bed by his palms, he'd pinned her on her back beneath him. And though her breath came in short gasps and she was feverish, she knew she'd be dry and tight when he entered. She turned her face from him, but he kissed the curve between her neck and shoulder. The weight of his torso bruised her tender breasts. Behind her tightly-closed eyes, she believed she'd been transformed to Sandi Chute, the "punching board" of Mt. Kisco High. Michael had to score, again and again, a locker-room legend. With short, vicious thrusts, he was riding to the climax. She vowed she'd mask her discomfort by feigning pleasure. When he began to lift from her in a slow motion pushup, she opened her eyes. He looked down with the critical eyes of a stranger and shook his head. Her pretense had obviously failed; she wondered how ugly her skin looked, rubbed raw by the stubble of his unshaven face. He looked away, flexed his lean, powerful arms, sighed, and heavily rolled from her. The depth of his sigh and her release were frightening. He had to climax or his tension might turn to fury, to smolder and burn through him. She turned to him slowly, afraid to speak, afraid to be silent. She tentatively touched his ribs. He stared at the ceiling. She had disappointed him terribly. She must make amends. It had gone wrong because making love on his parents' bed was a violation; it was sex before marriage, or heavy petting on the doorstop of her parents' house. It went wrong because she was menstruating. She inched closer to the angry face that he wouldn't turn to her. If he felt her breath upon his cheek, she could easily slide her hand across his chest and turn him to her, or touch his cheek and turn his lips to hers. She slowly approached him as if he were a wary bird, sure to escape if she didn't move with care.

She'd read in a magazine in a gynecologist's office that success in bed meant a successful marriage. There must be a way to make him happy, a way to keep him home. She'd been so dry his thrusting had seemed to tear her. Self-lubrication was a remedy. Feeling nasty, she licked her fingers and touched the moisture to her vagina. Embarrassed that he watched her, she awkwardly straddled him and closed her eyes as she brazenly touched his penis to her. His soft groan told her how right she'd been. She prayed as she lowered her tightness about him, wanting him to touch her breasts to make it right but ashamed to ask. He murmured her name, but it didn't release the tight knot made by the room and the diaphragm wedged in her. She must start taking the pill, in spite of its dangers, to make it better for him.

Finally he finished, got up, and went away. She lay on the bed feeling dirty, guilty for his disappointment. She covered her nakedness with the white quilt. She ought to go upstairs and take out the diaphragm, which must be thick with menstruation, but she didn't want to face him. She curled her knees to her chest to wait while he stole another beer and turned to his usual domestic Saturday diversion: drinking in front of the TV, anaesthetized by a sports special. Startled by his approach to the bed, she sat up and felt a warm ooze travel down her thigh. Clutching the quilt about her breasts, she swallowed hard against her panic. He sat beside her, his breath beery and warm. "Who you hidin' from?" He nipped her lower lip and began to pry her fingers from the quilt.

He threw her cover aside and pushed her back on the bed. Pressing her sticky thighs together, she tried to kiss him with ardor. But his tongue was clammy, tasting of nicotine and beer. She stiffened and turned from him. His hand resting lightly at her throat moved between her breasts, forced its way between her thighs, and plunged into her pubic hairs. She pressed her thighs against him.

He pulled away. "What's with you?" His knuckles braced against the sheet were stained with menses. "You give me the come on—I touch you, and you pull away." He reached across her for a cigarette, looked at his hand, and murmured, "Jesus," as he turned his streaked fingers over and over, "what the hell?"

She whispered, "It's my period," and gathered the quilt about her as if it were a toga, so she could scoot from the bed to the bathroom, to examine the damage she'd done.

He continued to stare at his hand. "Ah, shit." He shook

his fingers as if they were covered with feces. She wanted to explain it would wash off, but he looked too disgusted to listen. With the quilt swaddled about her, she stumbled toward the bathroom.

A smear half a foot long soaked the quilting, and a half dozen bright spots freckled the surface. Oh, God, it was such an old quilt and made of cotton. The bone-white color might never come clean. The job was too big for the sink, so she ran cold water in the tub to take immediate action before it dried. She'd have to find detergent, or maybe ammonia. Mom would know what to do, but there wasn't time to phone or a lie to disguise the circumstances. Stooping over the tub, squeezing the ancient fabric so it wouldn't tear, she felt Michael watching from the doorway. She glanced at his stern face, his hand hanging at his side flexing continuously as if his fingers were in pain. But her frenzy at the task seemed to reassure him. He didn't warn her to do a good job but turned and left her with the problems of straightening his parents' bedroom and cleaning their quilt and her bloody thighs and overflowing diaphragm.

Barbara rolls onto her back, opens her eyes, and stares at the ceiling. Ten years have passed, yet the scene is still vivid and shameful. Their daughters, living beside her, growing closer to the life she is leaving, make the past more real than the present. Just as Michael left her to remove the stain from the quilt, he left her to be mother and father, left her to make the explanation of what has become of him, of how and when and if he will manage to fit them into his life. Even sedated she could never be in a room with Michael without bursting into rage, or even worse, uncontrollable tears. He'll claim the divorce was her idea. And as usual he'll be wrong. The idea was Mom's. A flash of rage at the injustice of it all burns through Barbara. She digs her nails into the soft flesh of her upper arms. She must practice controlling her anger. She has no choice. The court says she must expose her daughters to the pain Michael gives to those who love him.

spring | 1972

Chapter 30

It's only April, but so humid Amy sweats, leaving embarrassing rings of perspiration at her armholes. This might be June, with temperatures over 100°, and the sticky air, laced with insecticide, is hard to breathe. Gram says the irrigation canals surrounding the city are breeding places for insects that the farmers try to destroy by spraying.

Amy worries that Duane's sweaty smell, an odor of moldy onions and sea salt, hovers about her. Every morning she scrubs beneath her arms, putting clouds of baby powder onto her damp skin. Funny crinkly hairs sprout in scattered patches beneath her arms, and the hair between her legs is thick enough to be what the boys call a beaver. She would like to remove the hair under her arms, but Mom would get mad if her razor were used, and it's awkward and painful to tweeze. As a compromise, she sneaks a daily roll or two from her Gram's underarm deodorant stick. Rushed one morning, she forgot to recap the container. But Gram understood, leaving deodorant and talcum from Avon on the shelf with a note "For Amy." Regretting the sneaky thefts, Amy thanked Gram repeatedly for the elegant gifts, even though Elizabeth said Avon is "tacky."

The weekly visit of Daddy and Gwen doesn't interest Elizabeth; she can't see that Gwen is far more fascinating than anyone in her beloved fiction. Their book discussions have ceased, so now they only say "hi" in the mornings and "goodbye" at the bike racks. At lunchtime, Marcy and her friends are all right for playing jacks and sharing goodies from bag lunches packed by Gram. But the girls must not learn about her secret life with Daddy and Gwen. And because Amy spent so much time with an obvious creep like Elizabeth, none of the girls phone or invite her to their homes.

It's embarrassing to be seen walking home alone, so she finds an excuse to hang around school until the others leave. Helping Mr. Crandall isn't possible any more because Elizabeth has taken over all the responsiblities and always seems to be by his side, so it isn't even possible to talk to him. The school library is a place to hide out until the other kids get started on their walk home on Friday. Looking for something to check out takes quite a while because she's read almost all the fiction and the rest doesn't interest her. But the librarian grows restless to leave, so Amy grabs an unappealing book called Rootabaga Stories, checks it out, and tries to cheer up the librarian by wishing her a good weekend, but the woman doesn't smile. Amy hurries from the library, promising herself to never impose on the woman again.

For half a block outside the school gate, she tries to read while she walks. But this silly book isn't worth the effort. The traffic game will be ideal for today. Counting yellow cars is good luck because Daddy's car is faded yellow. The old game has lost some of its charm because now she knows she'll see Daddy every Saturday, but it still can be fun, like pretending there is a tooth fairy or a Santa. Each time she sees a yellow car, she pretends it might be Daddy coming to get her. Just because the car doesn't stop doesn't mean it isn't him. He's busy. If she sees six cars, he might call. When she reaches a total of one hundred, he will return forever. She walks on the side of the street where cars come up behind her and flash by. It isn't fair to turn her head or to slow her pace. Two-toned cars and neighbors on the color spectrum count a half a point. She has walked a block and six cars have passed, and the only one she counted was half a point, but it's silly to become discouraged. No matter what the outcome, Saturday will come and Daddy will arrive with Gwen, who always makes it easy to talk.

Amy waits at the corner, obeying the box lit up with "Do Not Walk." A car is approaching behind her. Of course it will stop. But to turn her head to check out the color would break a rule. There are scrunching sounds as the car comes to a full stop. The traffic light has been red for a long time. A horn toots. She flinches and turns toward the sound. The windshield glares on a dented, dusty green car. She turns to the traffic light but glances back as the car edges in closer to the curb. Something dark inside is moving from the driver's side. The window cranks down. A man with dull brown hair, his eyes covered by reflecting sun glasses, says something she can't hear. Now that he's opened the window, he sits upright as if leaning across the seat has tired him. He breathes through his mouth and touches the leathery skin by his mouth, brushing his fingertips across his lips, his nails glossy as if polished with clear enamel, light pink in contrast to the brown tones of his face. He reaches toward the door, resting his pale fingers on the edge of the glass. And his white shirt and dark suit look rumpled and old, yet dignified, as he leans toward her, his mouth serious, speaking so softly she can barely hear, "Hey, girl, please . . ."

Mesmerized by this mysterious man and his quiet yet urgent words, Amy moves toward him. "Yes."

Light flashes on the mirrored glasses. The lips open slightly. "Girl, I got a problem." His hand caresses his cheek and falls to the wide lapel of his faded suit. "I'm lost." He's wearing a bolo tie, the kind Daddy says are ugly. "I got clothes—I can't find where . . ."

His fingers knead the nubby fabric of his lapel. He might be a salesman. A tailor. A stranger in the city. She asks sympathetically, "What's the street you're looking for?"

"I got to get to Helen Street—Helen." And his hand slips inside his jacket and produces a slip of paper. He holds it so close that his glasses reflect white as he reads haltingly, "Five-thirty-two East Helen." Then he flaps the paper toward her as if she might want to check the address, but the paper is too far away to read.

He seems so tired, as if he has no hope of finding his way, that she speaks clearly and loudly so he will understand. "That's not far from here."

But he looks away. His mouth slightly open, breathing with effort, he says to the windshield, "How far?"

"Oh, straight ahead." She sounds encouraging, pointing into the sun, wishing he'd watch her as she directs him. "A couple of blocks and then you turn left and it will be another block."

Still staring ahead, he strokes the steering wheel, the paper crushed beneath his palm. "Get in the car—show me."

"Oh, no, I couldn't."

He turns his face to hers, smiling so the crease in his cheek wrinkles so deeply that it might be painful. "Why not? It's faster." He makes it seem so simple. He would be so grateful.

"No, I can't, really. My mother . . ." This is silly. Mom would say it's okay to guide a lost salesman like Dad, a stranger in the city.

He covers his mouth, thinking hard about a solution. His glasses momentarily blind her as he says, "Just tell me how to get to five-thirty-two East Helen." His face is as sad as a hound-dog. "Walk by my car and I'll drive slow. Then I'll show you the clothes. I got some pictures too."

This request seems so important to him, so easy to do. "You just want me to walk two blocks to Helen Street?"

"What's a coupla blocks?" He watches his hands resting on the wheel, then flexes his fingers, murmuring, "Just walk it, just walk it."

If she runs away and leaves him, he might wait here forever with his clothes. She must help him. She breaks into a slow trot and the man follows. Jogging is good. Mr. Crandall wants them to get ready for the president's physical fitness test. The tired car steers away from the curb and chuffs dangerously close behind, so she must run faster. The second block is not Helen. As they pass the street sign, she looks back. He is hunched behind the wheel as if this drive takes lots of concentration. Once they turn onto Helen, maybe he'll slow down. She races to the corner, her breath slicing the back of her throat, and reads Helen, and beneath it, 520. She slows down, another block and a half. The car behind her is turning laboriously.

The house at five-thirty-two is practically a shack, with thigh-high weeds all the way to the front door. The man steers the front tires into the curb with a squeal. His car is so battered he must be very poor. The brakes groan and he turns off the engine. The vehicle shakes violently three times and stops. He's leaning toward the dash, lighting a cigarette, taking the keys from the ignition. The door is opening. She inhales deeply, trying to breathe normally again. The man is walking toward her, his body draped in a crumpled, aged suit. Beneath the mask of sunglasses, he is smiling his pained smile, wheezing. "Thanks so much." And she decides that he's not as old as she'd imagined. He has some sickness, asthma or something that makes it hard to breathe, so he seems old and tired. He's about as old as Mr. Crandall.

Amy backs away, ready to leave. "You're welcome."

He is turning from her, unaware of her plan. "And my garments are in the trunk." He jangles the keys, a sad magician, and points toward the back of the car. "Back there."

When the lock clicks open, the lid of the trunk bounces up, almost colliding with the slackjawed face puffing above it. Inside, a tangle of bright clothes has fallen from hangers and boxes have overturned, spilling sandals and high-heeled shoes about the spare tire. The man moans and thumps his chest, scattering ashes from his cigarette. The clothes must be very precious. Without being asked, Amy puts shoes back in the boxes and picks through the clothes to fit them back on the hangers. And as she works on the right side of the trunk, the man, with a cigarette dangling from his lips, rummages through the left.

Flicking his cigarette into the overgrown weeds, he drags a leather case from beneath the clothing, and dangling it by the strap hoists it onto his shoulder. He waves his hand over the clothing. "It all goes in the house." Then he leans into the trunk to pull out a photographer's tripod. Holding the tripod next to his chest, as if it were a mute dance partner, he tramples through the tall dusty grass. Amy follows wondering if the old house is empty, if he will turn it into a little store.

It takes three trips for both of them before the last load is shifted from the trunk to the house. Even inside the dim living room, Amy sees beads of sweat on his face, and his breathing is raspy as he pulls at a button on the throat of his shirt and loosens his ugly tie. He should sit and rest, but clothing and boxes are stacked on the few draped objects that might be chairs. Squeezing the flesh of his throat, he says with the urgency of a movie character having a heart attack, "Water, I need water."

Amy sets a case that feels like a slide projector beside a draped object about the size and bulk of a table. She'd planned to go home now, but the man needs water. Rushing by the furniture draped with yellowed sheets, she follows old cooking odors to the kitchen, where she finds a jelly glass left in the sink. The water is slightly rusty as if the faucet has not been used for a while.

In the living room, the man is sprawled in a chair, crushing the clothes thrown there. His head lolls back on the chair, and the sunglasses are balanced on top of his matted hair. In profile, his leathery lips hang open and his breathing is easier, but he might be dying. The skin around his eyes, which was hidden by sunglasses, is pale, and his sunken eyes stare at the ceiling as if he were dead.

Amy says, "Your water," so softly she is sure he hasn't heard. But he turns pale apple-green eyes toward her and his painful smile seems to crack the corners of his mouth, showing yellow, widely-spaced teeth. Something is terribly wrong. She begins to tremble so the water almost spills.

"Closer, closer." A hand hangs from the armrest, flapping lazily, not reaching to accept the water. Amy tries to steady the glass by holding it with both hands, but still it is shaking. "Come on, come on," the voice coos as if he were soothing a frightened kitten.

Amy takes a step nearer. The pupils in his pale irises seem to pulsate, pulling her to him. Yet the hand by the armrest doesn't reach out to help her. She is close enough to hold the glass to his lips, but this is too strange. He isn't a baby who has to be fed. His other hand is resting in his lap, cradling a wad of flesh in a nest of dark hair. His nails glisten as he strokes rippling flesh. The skin is as red as a freshly-skinned animal, striped with dark veins. It jumps as the fingers tickle it. "My friend wants to visit."

A vein at the edge of the forest of hairs contracts. It travels up a mauve stump rising to a swollen arrowhead. The dead animal is a penis growing out of the hairy mass between the man's thighs. She opens her mouth to scream. Her throat constricts. She makes a small, animal-like sound.

Shimmering with eagerness, his eyes flicker across her face. "Touch it. Kiss it."

Her mouth flushes with saliva; she is going to vomit. Whimpering softly, she clutches the glass, shaking so violently water sloshes over the rim onto her shirt. The cold spot spreads like blood from a wound across her chest. As she backs from the penis, the glass crashes to the floor. She holds her hands before her to ward off the man slowly rising from the chair. She is caught in the deep sand of the nightmare, where she runs and never moves, when she tries to scream and no sound comes. If she turns, she might race from him, but in the moments it would take to shift about, he'll be upon her, so she inches from him. Using one hand as leverage on the armrest, he stands, scooping his penis out of his sagging clothing. On his feet, he lurches forward, his trousers sliding down his pale, hairy thighs. The power of his smell and breathing are upon her as she edges backward.

He has only taken a few steps when he is hobbled by his fallen clothing. As he angrily kicks it away, Amy risks escape, but her leg collides with the slide projector and she falls. Scrambling over the case and onto the couch, she rights herself for a race to the door when his sour body dives upon hers. He pins her wrists to the seat of the couch. He is inches from her, so she turns her face into the cushions, breathing the dust from ancient sheets. She is shielded from his penis by the front of the couch, but his belly is sliding between her knees. He is panting and angry as he hisses, "Be still, be still . . ." He frees a hand to yank at her clothing and she grunts, shoving with all her strength at his shoulder.

His knuckles bash across her mouth and the side of her nose. She tastes blood. Her hand clawing his neck goes limp. He tears at her clothing, cursing her and shoving the dead animal against her, again and again. Behind her closed eyes, fireballs whirl. If she pretends she's dead, she might live. Each time he rams into her, she counts. The intervals between each thrust are shorter and shorter. Then, with a grunt, he stops.

She doesn't dare to open her eyes or move. He begins to lift from her, mumbling words she can't understand. She tries to lie so still she might disappear, as he moves farther and farther from her. The front door closes and the car pulls away before she opens her eyes. She plunges her hands between her thighs and rocks back and forth. The ache travels from her belly through her fists. Her hands are streaked with blood. She rolls on her stomach and pushes herself from the couch, yanking at her clothing and wiping the blood from her hands on the back of her jeans. She must not touch anything in this house. To remain here is dangerous. He'll be back. She moves as quickly as the throbbing between her thighs permits.

Stumbling off the porch, she reels away from this place. She must go home, cleanse herself, hide in her room. Choking on her tears and the dust rising from the grass, she reaches the street where he has been. She freezes, an animal caught in an open field. The tiny houses down the block are linked together by rickety fences. She tries to run beside them, seeking an escape. A sidestreet is lined with unclipped hedges. She follows it, then winds her way through alleys, past snarling dogs, only crossing major streets when she has to, holding her hands on either side of her face, glancing at traffic through her fingers, terrified he might recognize her through the shield of her hands.

Chapter 31 |

Amy doesn't come out of her room for dinner even though Barbara has called her three times. Knocking on the door, she listens for sounds of movement. The secretiveness of adolescence has come too early to Amy, who's become so moody, spending hours alone. There will be time enough for this behavior. Her childhood is ending too soon. The divorce has hurt her deeply. Oh, the wounds Michael inflicts, the disfiguring scars he will leave.

After repeated calls with no answers, Barbara turns the knob: there are no inside locks in this simple house. The interior of the room is silent and dim; the figure huddled in the bed pathetically small. Amy must be sleeping, ill with a fever, or perhaps menstrual cramps have sent her to bed. Walking softly toward her, Barbara savors the unguarded moments when she can study the beauty of her sleeping child, who will be flushed yet angelic in her tranquil state. The face on the pillow is swollen, splattered with blood and discolored with bruises. This can't be Amy, but the unblinking eye staring at the wall is hers.

Only Gertrude can coax Amy out of bed. The old woman kneels beside the battered child, questioning her. Barbara waits at the bedroom door to hear Amy's answer. A fight. An accident. None of these is the answer. There is one question too hideous to contemplate. Barbara backs toward the kitchen as Gertrude leads the stiff and bloody child through the passageway to the bathroom, moving at a haltingly painful pace.

The house is silent except for Barbara, who is compelled to dash about the kitchen. When Gertrude says, "We ought to call the police," the question Barbara could not bear to ask is answered. She finds the phone book and retreats, listening to Gertrude quietly report to the police, "We have an emergency. Our eleven-year-old child—our girl—has been assaulted." Gertrude turns from the phone.

"My God, Mother. My God." But Gertrude flees the kitchen, leaving Barbara to throw open cupboards in a wild pretense of efficiency. Her voice calling to Flossie has a peculiar sweetness on the edge of tears, "Help Mommy put these dishes away, honey, please help Mommy."

With her hands hidden beneath her knees, Amy's hunched shoulders contract even further at the sound of the doorbell. Gertrude, who has warned her someone is coming to help them, now adds hastily, "A man from the police." But the words don't seem to be heard by the stolid child. Afraid to touch her, afraid to leave her side, Gertrude looks imploringly to Barbara, who is speechless, powerless.

The officer who steps around Barbara into the room wears the uniform she imagined he would, but she'd expected him to exude a sense of strength, to make her feel protected, to make them safe. But the person standing before them, removing his hat, is almost a child. Barbara steps aside murmuring, "My mother, my daughter." His introduction is his plastic nametag and his well-scrubbed, blonde sincerity. He crouches before Amy but watches Gertrude, a sign for her to speak. He rolls his hat to the left and then to the right. So Amy will not hear, Gertrude leans forward, whispering, "I think she's been assaulted." He nods, as if to assure it is possible. Behind the shield of his hat, on his knee, he holds a pad and his hand is poised to write.

Flossie's eyes are enormous. To protect the child's innocence, Barbara leads her from the scene, leaving the officer with Gertrude and Amy to do his job. From the hall, Mom's voice is tremulous, "I found her in bed. Obviously injured. I didn't know how or who. I didn't ask. But in the bathroom, getting her ready for the bath, I . . . I think he raped her."

Chapter **32**

Amy must be good and sit still even if Gram's hands are cool and trembling, struggling with the socks and shoes. Her fingers feel like little mice that might nip at a moving ankle. The top of Gram's head is a river of silver and black waves. Studying how the strands blend together makes it possible to bear the creeping mice, makes the mice less wild, keeps the lifeless hands still while Gram fusses. But Gram lifts the limp hands, kisses their backs, turning them into wooden blocks. The river rolls back and Gram commands, "Stand up, honey, so I can slip on your smock."

Wherever Gram leads, Amy follows as quickly as she can, letting the officer stare at her face while Gram asks if he thinks an icebag is a good idea, if aspirin might stop the swelling. He says, "Ice might help, but we should ask the doctor about the aspirin." They are leaving this house. That is why the officer has waited in the living room. He is going to take them out of the house onto the street where the man is waiting in his dusty car. And now Gram is leaving the room to get the icebag. The policeman is watching so Amy stares at the floor, like a dog commanded to stand and stay, but her breathing is quick and shallow. When he looks away, she will fall to her knees and crawl behind the couch. She cannot leave this house. The man will find her and beat her if she leaves this house. But the shiny black shoes are only six steps away. They will flatten her if she tries to escape. She waits, listening for cars, and the officer taps his right toe, making goosebumps explode on her skin.

Gram leads her out of the house into the darkness down the long, cracked sidewalk. The officer walks behind, so she can't look back, and a third person follows, a shadow behind the man's shadow. The hedges on either side of the yard are places where the man might hide. He must be following them now. She shuffles along the walk, careful not to step directly on cracks, counting the number of times her right foot and then her left moves forward, deciding that the man will not lunge at her now, with the policeman beside her, but wondering if perhaps he has crawled into the back seat of the car. He might strangle the unsuspecting policeman, push Gram out, and steal the car, a place to rape girls.

The officer opens the car door. She will not crawl into the dim cave where the crouching man hides, yet the only protest she can make is a whimper. Gram slides onto the seat, gently pulling Amy's hand, but the shadow follows. Cringing beneath Gram's encircling arm, Amy tries to hide as the shadow gets in beside her, slamming the door. The street-light shines on Mom.

The lights in the emergency waiting room are bright and the vinyl tiles glare with smears of scuffed wax. There are ten squares leading to the dead white wall. But puffy flesh on the nose blocks the view to the left, to the right. A hall disappears into dimness. A woman's thin ankles navigate boatlike shoes closer, closer. The intercom beeps. The shoes march in time with the sound. She is the hospital's executioner. The ringing stops. The woman keeps coming. The shoes stop side by side in front of the chair. The white skirt is so close the woman could reach down. Words float from her, "We can see the doctor now." Gram's hand on the wrist is a command to stand. Obeying rips open an envelope of pain.

A wide gold ring flashes on the hand patting the end of the table. The ring could slice the skin on a face if it slapped it. The hand patting the table is impatient. It must be obeyed. The table, covered with butcher paper like they draw on in school, is so high. Maybe the steel loops set on either side should be grasped to lift up like a gymnast to slide forward, but the paper would tear. Maybe the loops are where they tie up legs. Strong hands slip beneath her armpits, so the room spins and pain explodes.

She opens her eyes to a pistachio-green shirt covering the chest of a man. A fringe of black curls clings to the base of his powerful neck. Amy's hands, covering her eyes and nose, send fiery stars to burn into tears. Words beat against the fingers that won't come apart. "Amy, I'm Doctor Felix." Doctor means help. Her fingers slide. The green chest calmly rises and falls with breath, but the hair curls nastily to the edge of the shirt and a black chord is a giant V where a silver instrument dangles.

"Can you move your fingers just a little further, so I can see your nose?"

The fingers part slightly each time he says "Good." Gram is beside him. Gram will not run away. She is weak and old but she'll help. And outside the door the policeman with shiny shoes is guarding. If the man comes, they will help.

Her hands fall into her lap, sending a flash up the belly. Cool hands smelling of soap tilt her chin, and dark eyes with no pupils scan the bridge of numbness between her eyes. His breath bounces off the peculiar pink growth at the edge of vision. Goosebumps race up her arms and her teeth chatter even in the firmness of his grip. His hand is letting go. He is angry, stepping back. He will hit her for being bad. "I'm just examining your nose." But the teeth won't stop chattering. He is talking to Gram, who holds their sweaters as if they were a baby. But the doctor moves in front of Gram's face. The hands will fly up to the face unless they hold one another. God, let us go home. He's walking Gram to the door, sending her away. Now he's coming back, leaning close. The hands make her eyes cry. The shirt moves away and a voice rolls down. "She'll be coming back. We need to talk to your mother, so we can help you." The chest isn't moving through the fence of the fingers; the hands will keep him away.

Gram is right. The needle just pricked once and now the room stretches out like the insides of a balloon and the doctor's voice is drifting from acres of clouds, the way God speaks in the movies. And all the knots inside her head and throat and belly unravel like old Raggedy Ann's yarn hair, and it's nice to lie down and be Raggedy Ann with half her stuffing gone and the doctor can put the floppy legs wherever he wants. When he stretches the legs out straight, the bubble of pain cradled above them pops, spills, and spreads paler and paler. And the nurse calls from a deep in a cave, "Amy, the doctor wants to examine you," as she lifts up the skirt and pulls down the panties. And the arms won't make elbows to sit up, to get away, and the doctor is there and the nurse is there. But Gram is here now. Her glasses glare as her old lips whisper, "The doctor will help." This is a lie. But even a strong man couldn't slip out of their grip to kick past the nurse, to run to the door where the policeman sits with his gun, guarding the long, slippery hall, and outside the man waits in his dark car wanting to do it again and again. She is too weak and small to fight them. She hasn't the energy to cry. She will be as limp as she was beneath him: the pain of her nose scoops out her eyes. She will be blind; the birds can pick out her eyes. Like the wicked sisters in Cinderella, she will be blind and bleeding. The blind hear distant sounds. She will not hear the doctor or Gram. They are pulling her from the table, putting her heels in the silver loops. But her knees will fight him. They will not open for him. His voice is lost in a barrel, "Amy, we'll put you to sleep for a while. You'll see double, then feel cold, and then you'll sleep." She'll pretend she's dead and they'll leave her alone. But the cold spot rubbing her arm opens her eyes. A needle is going into her arm. It will break if she moves. The silver needle retracts with a dull bite. Her right knee doesn't multiply. The doctor is a liar. Her veins are filling with ice water, her shivering lips can't say, "I'm cold," for the room is swirling and black.

Through the fringe of her eyelashes a white bulb pulsates. She closes her eyes against the dizzying apparition and touches the gauzy ball. Her eyes smart at the whiteness and smell of adhesive and medication. A blanket keeps her hands from finding her side. Gram's face appears above the swathed nose as she leans close to whisper, "We're going home."

Amy rides down the hallway in a wheelchair, slowing as it approaches Mom, who is standing with the policeman and another man who is a stranger. Mom's pinched face means the bandages are a disgrace. As the wheelchair stops, Mom bends down and says, "Honey," a word dishonest salesladies use, "honey, this is Detective Houghton."

His shoes are the same shiny black ones the officer wore; they glisten as he speaks. "Amy, I'll be coming to see you. We'll talk when when you feel better. But you rest first. Get some sleep. Tomorrow we'll talk about what happened."

There are tiny eyes where the shoestrings come out. Ten on each shoe. Each is an accusing eye; the string holds back the tongue that would lash out and gobble her up if the black twine broke. The toes of the shoes are black mirrors. The white ball between her eyes pulsates, erasing his words.

Home will be safe: if Gram sits by the bed, and the policeman guards outside the window, walking in slow circles in the gravel with his shiny shoes, his hand poised above the holster where the pistol rides on his hip. But when he gets out of the car in front of their house and opens the car door for them, he only walks them halfway up the walk, then he says loudly, "Well, Mrs. Hershey, tomorrow Officer Houghton will visit. He'll be working on your case, and he can direct you to various services if other problems arise." Mom hurries to the house, her shoulders hunched, shutting out her disgusting daughter. The light in her bedroom goes on. She must be with Flossie, the good sister, the one who hasn't brought shame to the family. The policeman is leaving. This could be a time to run, dragging Gram along, but Gram is walking tiredly toward the house. Inside her dark bedroom, Gram will fall asleep, snoring softly, and the man will return and no one inside the house will hear him and know he's taken the girl he raped to live with him.

In the morning, Amy lies curled beneath the covers, pretending to sleep long after Gram leaves the room. Three times the toilet flushes, the water in the sink is run and drained, footsteps creak in the hall, voices murmur in the kitchen. Amy's pulse pounds into the pillow: problem, problem. She counts each sound. The phone screams, so she covers her head with the pillow and her temple throbs: problem, problem. The policeman's shiny black shoes walk toward her with clipped cadence: problem, problem. He must talk to the filthy girl, the one the man raped.

Gram looks into the covers, her lips pursed. "We're going to get dressed." She means, "I'll dress you. You'll do what I say, you dirty, disgusting child."

Gram puts the dress on over a naked body; the panties are too painful to put on. Gram brushes the hair and puts chunks of yarn on each side. Her breath is hot and smells like old coffee as she orders, "We'll brush your teeth. And help you go to the bathroom."

Amy perches on the toilet seat, willing herself to let go, to let the stream of urine flow through the rawness. With the sting of the first release, she cries and tightens the muscles of the passage. But her bladder is full to bursting, so she grasps the edge of the toilet seat and grits her teeth against the pain as the urine rushes from her. She blots the toilet tissue between her thighs. The tissue is a salmon color. She drops the wad into the stool water, which is an ordinary color, flushes the mess away, and washes her hands, careful not to look in the mirror. She will not let her mouth touch the water from the faucets. She will never eat or drink and will never have to come back here.

The voices in the living room mean she's expected to appear. A man speaks. The officer. She will hide in the bathtub behind the shower curtain, or dare to slip along the walls to her bedroom, but he will find her. The front door and the kitchen are the only exits, and everyone will see her slow, crippled attempts to escape. Gram's voice is feathery, the words lost in her secretive tone. Amy will join them before they come to get her.

The man's hands, hanging loose and relaxed between his knees, are massive: big-knuckled, freckled, dotted with golden hairs—but they aren't hands with pale fingers and pink nails. The fingers of this man's beefy hands casually intertwine as they rest on his tightly-sheathed fat thighs, but behind his hands his fly bulges. Shaking the sight away, she hangs her head, his shiny shoes a dark blur at the the edge of the globe of her nose. At the low rumbling of the man clearing his throat, Gram moves from her place across the room. "Amy, let's talk about what happened."

The nose is an igloo; inside she's wrapped in a white fur

suit, a polar bear curled into a ball, sleeping through the long Arctic winter. Her heart moves as slowly as the frozen water beneath the ice where the igloo is built. It is so cold and slow, no one can tell if she is living, and she will dream of falling snow, tiny flakes as pure and cold as silence.

Gram's voice sounds magnified, the way voices sound when they try to pull people out of sleep. Her fingers are reaching out. The man is holding his penis. Amy is falling, and the silent screaming begins. There are freckles on the back of her right hand and her left, her right arm and her left. The policeman is leaning closer. "Amy, I'd like to put what you tell me on a tape recording." There are no freckles on her thumb.

The thumb is covered by Gram's liver-spotted hands, "You'll have to speak up, honey, speak up, or the officer won't hear you."

Amy nods, so Gram will take her hand away and give back the freckles. The officer's face is cut into pieces by the nose. He says, "I'd like you to answer some questions. I'll use my recorder." The first questions are fill-in-the-blank with yes or no. Yes she had been coming home from school. Yes she had waited quite a while before leaving the building. Yes she was alone. Yes it was later than she usually walked home. No there were no other children around. Yes she had spoken to someone she didn't know, someone in an old dusty car. And Gram is angry. Amy did not obey the old rule. But there isn't time to apologize. The officer wants to know the street. Now the man with the mask of sunglasses is leaning out of the dusty car, asking what she can't understand until she walks closer. "The street, Amy, the name of the street."

There is the gravel beneath her feet as she ran and the car behind her, but there is no name of the street. "The one by the school."

Gram asks, "Mabel?"

The officer puts the jumble of scenes scattered within her into a puzzle. The man had made her run to show him the way to a strange little house on Helen Street. She sang the number as she ran, "Five-and-three-and-a-two," or "a two-and-a-five-and-a-three." Turning and running down one block and then another, she stopped in front of the house with the thigh-high weeds. His clothes, his cameras, his water, and . . . "And when you gave him the water—and?"

The officer knows about the dead animal in the man's lap and how it could pound between her thighs until she bled, how the man could smash her face so she'd lie still and not move until he went away. The officer knows how to come home through alleys, so she tells the black box as if it had happened to another girl. Then he pushes the button and the machine stops. Now she can crawl back into the bed and watch the blank, white wall. Gram is silent. It is too shameful to look at her old face, which must be disgusted. Her silence says, "You are dirty, too filthy for words. This could only happen to a girl like you."

The officer is going to leave, talking quietly to Gram at the door, confirming this is a hideous case. And Gram wants to go to the kitchen. The commandment is to eat. But Mom's scrambled eggs fall from the fork. Mom and Gram whisper to one another at the sink. The napkin will hide the goo. The ball is warm in her hand. Flossie stares. She might tell. The women whisper in hisses. God, make them let me go back to my room to hide in the dark.

Daddy is yelling in his drunken voice, "Goddamn it, why didn't you call me? Why didn't you let me know?" Mom whines and Amy digs her fingers into her arm. This might be a dream from years ago. The man ripping her open could've been a nightmare. But rawness tunnels between her thighs and her nose is a bulb. Her throat is dry. Her heartbeat races. The voice of Daddy is now. The tide from the other room laps closer, closer. Gram says, "Michael, don't bother the child. Leave the child alone."

"Goddamn, I'll see my baby, you old bitch, I'll see my

baby." And his footsteps are coming out of the kitchen. Oh, Jesus, he's coming. Lie as still as death. The covers rip away. His face, washed of anger. He looks so surprised, so sick. God, make me disappear, make me disappear. Daddy kneels, unable to look at his ugly child, the white line of his scalp wavers as he rubs his knuckles in his eyes and makes strange hiccuping sounds. Her voice would make a sick, meowing sound, so she tries to hide the tape and to keep her voice inside. She tries to be as silent as possible, so he can forget she exists. Oh, God, I'm sorry. Oh, God, I'm sorry. Forgive me. Forgive me for not remembering the rosary. To say she is sorry for the rest of her life is a penance for her sin. Daddy is tucking the blankets over the body so no one will see. Perhaps the black eyelid will show him how sorry she is. He is going away. She will pull the sheet over her face the way doctors do for dead people.

Amy has lost count of the days that have passed. Gram says, "It isn't good to stay home and just brood about what happened," and looking stern, she adds, "You must go to school." Amy's mouth waters as if she might vomit, so she can't explain her plan to never leave her room, except to come to the table or to go to the bathroom. No one but Mom and Gram and Flossie will ever see her. Daddy has made it clear that no one can bear to look at a raped girl. Gram must look closely at the face to understand it is impossible to go to school. But Gram is looking in the closet, trying to find a disguise for the ugliness. To live under the bed in the dark wouldn't be possible. Gram is coming back to the bed. Oh Gram, not school with its wide halls and noisy children shoving, and Mr. Crandall's room with everyone pointing at the bruises and bandages, laughing at the disgusting girl. And out on the street the man waits. Oh, Gram, listen. But saliva is rushing upward and before she can sit up in bed the retching convulses her, and vomit oozes through her fingers.

Chapter **33**

Paralyzed by feelings of inadequacy, Barbara stares at her child. Splattered with vomit, Amy is being led by Gertrude to the bathroom. At the sink, Gertrude mops at Amy's stained face. The child pinches her eyes closed. The skin of her face is a color chart of the palest shades of nauseous green to the darker tone of bruises, the colors heightened by the white of the bandaged nose and the bloody incrustations of scabs. The bout of violent vomiting is symptomatic of a disturbance far more severe than Barbara is willing to accept. Screaming at Mom, terrorizing Amy, Michael has made Amy sicker than she's ever been. Oh, Jesus, Michael, why couldn't you have helped us, protected us.

Mom—oh, God, she carries on now, even now. As Amy is caught again with a fit of vomiting, Mom waits for the retching to end and looks into the glossy eyes, repeating, "Bath. Would you like a bath?" But her voice is too loud. She fumbles with the tiny buttons on the soiled gown. The buttons defy her old hands; she is off balance. Amy tenses, backing away. Mom scolds, "Hold still," but Amy takes another step backward, so Gertrude reaches out, and Amy begins to scream a throat-tearing cry that rocks Gertrude back on her haunches. The mouth beneath the bandaged nose is a gusher of tearing sounds. Gertrude steadies herself against the sink. Hysteria. People slap hysterics or restrain them. Amy collides with the toilet and crumples to the floor, the scream reduced to muffled sobbing. Gertrude turns an ashen face, "Barbara—Barbara—get help—call the detective, get the number of the crisis center—the rape crisis center."

Tracing the column of P's in the phonebook, Barbara's hand trembles. The palsied movement of the finger can't be hers, the mind looking for police in the P section must be demented; she flips to the front of the book for emergency numbers. She begins to shakily dial, sorting out what she will say, ashamed to make the call but admitting she is too frightened to return to the room without the assurance of another human.

Chapter 34

Gwen weeps in Michael's arms, leaning against him. He seems to support her, yet he fears he would fall without her. Oh, Jesus, my God, my baby, the blue-eyed angel in the communion dress, raped. And who the fuck holds Amy? Not Barbara, that goddamned jerk, so scared she's not worth a shit. Jesus. Raped. Oh, God, this time You got me—fucked me over the worst way You could. My baby. Christ, Gwen must feel this shuddering, this sobbing, this absolute helplessness, this total powerlessness.

He releases her and turns away. But she's waiting, wanting to know what the fuck a man does when his kid is raped. "I'm callin' the cops. The bastards better get their asses on this case. They're not gonna get away with this. My baby's . . . violated. Those goddamned bastards are gonna answer up. Christ! Some asshole assaults my baby . . ."

And it's raining and the Mustang's fuckin' windshield wipers don't work, and Jesus where the hell are the cops in this goddamned dump. Some pervert coulda killed my baby. He did, ah Jesus, he did kill her. Nothin' will ever be innocent again for Amy. She'll always be afraid, always feel dirty, feel like a piece a shit, the rest of her life—scared of her shadow like dopey Barbara or crazy for dope like Gwen. Old Gwen is probably blasted by now, toking away to shut out the world. Ah, Christ, to be in the haze—to lose the world for awhile—to just get out this shitpile for a while.

Amy's destroyed. Her baby face bruised. Her little body torn. Ah, Jesus. Those fuckin' stupid women. They always think they got a handle on life and they let some fuckin' pervert wreck their baby. Ah, Christ, it isn't fair. It isn't right. Jesus, somebody, somewhere has got to pay. Just one fuckin' drink, just a little grease to get you through. Jesus, this fuckin' town is filled with perverts and it's got more churches than bars. Just a drink to get the whole fuckin' thing in perspective, just one little drink to steady the nerves.

Chapter **35**

Waiting for the detective to come to the phone, Barbara hears her raspy breathing bouncing off the mouthpiece and fights for serenity: she must take charge and appear to be calm and in control. When she decides she's been forgotten and is planning to hang up, a strange man answers, explaining that the detective is out but offering to be of assistance. Attempting to sound assertive, Barbara speaks too loudly, "Rape, we reported a rape." The silence on the line means shock, disbelief, a need for further explanation. She rushes on, ashamed to confess her desperation. "You said there is a counseling service, a crisis center."

Steeling herself to be more controlled, she dials the second number. A woman's childlike voice answers, "Rape Crisis Center." The abrasiveness of "rape," spoken so casually, makes Barbara consider hanging up, but she begins her explanation with an anonymous sounding "we." The soft voice slowly draws a noose around the garbled words, pulling out more and more detail until Barbara gives the woman her name and address.

Someone is coming to the house. Perhaps it will be the

soft-voiced person. It would be best if it were, so the story wouldn't have to be told again. Mom will have to be told about the vistor. And perhaps Flossie needs to be warned. But how to deal with Amy . . . She has crept back to her old bed where she must be hiding. Mom sits on the couch. She looks shattered. The reality of her beloved grandchild's suffering appears to be more than the aged woman can bear. To change Amy's perceptions will require a power Gertrude had as a younger woman, the power she'd exerted daily in her home with her husband and daughters, in her classroom, among her friends. But that was years ago. And screaming scenes have never been a part of Mom's life. Her gray exhausted face is almost as frightening as Amy's battering, as Michael's insane rage. The world is coming apart.

The doorbell is ringing. This is too soon. No one from the rape crisis center could possibly be arriving so soon. Michael. Oh, God, he's come back to continue his tirade. Barbara opens the door ready to attack, ready to defend her child against the maniac's intrusion. But the placid face and massive body of Detective Houghton are a wall filling the doorway. "Mrs. O'Connor, may I come in? I have news. Very positive information."

Barbara steps aside so he may enter, oppressed by the power of the man, totally submissive to his command. Mom is approaching rapidly, buoyed by his words. He takes off his hat and nods deferentially to them. "We've found a suspect. A very likely suspect."

Chapter **36**

She holds the cone of melting ice cream to her lips. As the tip of her tongue traces a droplet trickling down the side of the scoop, it touches a wiry hair. She shrieks and thrusts the ice cream from her lips. The cone she holds before her is transformed to the dead animal of the man. He watches her from a chair at the Baskin-Robbins store. His eyes shimmering, he says, "Touch it. Kiss it." She tries to shake his penis from her hand, but her fingers won't open. She screams, swinging her arm violently.

Her eyes open to the pain of glaring light and Gram reaching out to still the flailing arm. "You're all right, Amy. You've just had a nightmare." But Gram doesn't sound sure, and her face has the look it had after the vomiting in the bathroom. Amy shakes her fingers so they are a blur, so the blood will begin to circulate again, so she can be sure her hand is empty. She closes her eyes against the bright light, against the shame of Gram seeing her. Gram is calling, "Amy, Amy, Detective Houghton wants to see you." The light behind her eyelids is dried blood. The detective will want to talk about it. She sees the dark maroon she saw when the man crushed her, pounding the thing inside her, turning her bloody inside and out. To escape, she opens her eyes. Gram's soft bosom is rising and falling because she's alive, because she's breathing. And the whiteness of the bandaged nose bobs like a bleached sun across Gram's face. If Gram isn't obeyed, she'll get angry and the man will return in nightmares.

She lets Gram guide her to sit six steps in front of Officer Houghton, exactly in the spot where the policeman sat. The detective's fat legs are showing his lumpy fly. She strips away the fabric where his thick penis is ringed by golden curls, then quickly looks down, ashamed. She's a whore, someone men rape because she lets them. She stares at the funnel shape of carpeting blocked off by his shoes. If she keeps her eyes on one section of carpeting, she might stay out of trouble. She mustn't let his voice tempt her to lift her eyes to watch his face. Even though he speaks softly and uses her name, she will keep her eyes fixed on the worn shag and try to count how many tufts of carpeting there are, beginning at the top of the funnel. Determining the precise number, she doesn't listen closely to the words he's sending to her in the little balloons cartoonists use. Gram's voice is starting to poke, its stern edge recognizable only to someone who knows her. It is like the secret pinches teachers use on rowdy boys when the class is on a field trip. Amy stares hard at the carpet to mark her place and then listens, tilting her head slightly so Gram can tell when to relay answers to the officer.

He is opening his case, telling her he has some photos he wants her to look at to make an identification. Gram is angry. She wants a polite smile and response, so Amy forces herself to say "yes," just loud enough for him to hear. But her fingers won't unwind from one another to reach for the picture sliding toward her. "I'll show you eight pairs of photos. One is the man we suspect assaulted you." Gram helps the policeman bring the photo closer. In the glossy, gray photo a fat, bored face with sagging cheeks stares at a spot beyond the camera. "Have you seen this man before?" He's a stranger; she shakes her head no. The picture is replaced by one of a balding man with round glasses and a large nose. She shakes her head again. The next photo is a man with glasses, a young man with dark hair standing out from above his ears and tiny white beads in the center of his eyes that seem to look right at her; he looks sort of like a janitor at school. The third picture is the man. Her right hand springs from her left. "This one." She points at the pale, sick eyes. "This one." She almost touches the thatch of dark hair. "This one." She points at the dark lips, which are almost black in the photograph.

"You're sure?" He shuffles the photo beneath the stack and puts another one on top, one of the man's profile, showing his crepey neck with the lump of his adam's apple, his sunken, tiny eyes.

Mesmerized by the image, she says, "Yes."

The officer is pleased. Rearranging his stack of photos like flash cards, he asks her to check a few more. She doesn't want to look at them. But when she sees his photo again and says, "This one," the officer is so pleased he packs up his pictures. She risks shifting her eyes to his knees. It is safe to look at his belt, then the white buttons on his shirt, and quickly, while he's busy and won't see her daring move, she glances at his face, which is sunburned and chubby, fringed with blonde hair. "That'll do it for now." He sounds very happy. "And I thank you, Amy, you've been a big help." He watches her eyes, so she looks at the floor. "You've given us information to help us make an arrest."

She wants to ask if the police will capture the man so he can't come back, but all the grownup voices are talking at once. Even Mom, who's been the shadow, is out of her chair, thanking him. They are moving away, speaking, forgetting to tell her what to do next. Watching them, she sits rigidly holding her hands so they can't reach out to grab the policeman's case containing the photographs, to steal the man's picture, to look into his eyes to see why they weren't kind. She has to study the photo, to see what she did wrong. She had tried to be helpful, holding water for a choking man whose eyes were grateful at first, but then became strange, frightening her so much, even now, that the inside of her mouth feels as if she's sucking a lemon. If she could learn why it happened, she could get out of the chair and look at people, be with people. She made the strange, lost man hate her, beat her, hurt her. He made her dirty and had not even given her a chance to apologize. She has to understand. But the picture will be gone soon. She hears them saying goodbye at the door, and the officer says they'll be in touch.

After he's gone, Gram mutters in a tired voice, "You were very good, Amy. The officer said you were a big help." But Gram doesn't stand close when she speaks to tell her lie. Seeing the picture of the man who Amy got into trouble made Gram ashamed, so ashamed she doesn't even bother to move Amy from her chair, because she's too disgusting to touch.

When the doorbell rings, Gram exclaims, "It must be the counselor from the rape crisis center." Gram will be ashamed again, telling about her granddaughter's ugliness. The woman's brown and sensible looking shoes with roller-coaster soles move silently closer. The mouse-gray cuffs of her trousers look clean and new. Even though she comes from a dirty place like the rape crisis center, her voice isn't nasty-sounding. She must be the person who takes care of bad girls who cause rapes. She cleans up the bad things they do.

She and Gram look down, whispering about what to do with this nasty girl. This woman must come to take raped girls away to a place where doctors make what's wrong with them better, to protect people from them, but first what happened has to be explained. Now Mom comes out of the kitchen. Drying her hands on her apron, she shakes hands with the woman and begins talking in a whispery voice, as if what she had to say is too awful to say out loud. They are talking too fast to find a place to say, "I'm sorry, I'm sorry I made everything so wrong." They're so busy talking it might be possible to quietly sneak away. And then Gram turns and says, "Amy, it's probably best if you go to your room."

When she pushes the bedroom door open, she almost knocks down Flossie, who is crouched by the jamb, listening. Caught spying, Flossie races across the room, bellyflops onto the bed, and whines, "Can I go out now?"

Amy sits on her bed. "No," she snaps, wishing she could say yes so she wouldn't have to be with Flossie, who will start asking questions, but Gram and Mom expect to be obeyed. The bedsprings creak noisily as Flossie's fat body bounces into a sitting position and scoots to the edge of her bed.

"They're talking about the rape, huh?" The dirty word excites her. "The policeman and that lady." She smiles sneakily. "Let's listen. We could go down the hall and listen." Flossie is repulsive. Her plan is so crude. To argue with such an ignorant person is impossible. Sneaking and spying are what criminals do. Mr. Crandall said spies had no allegiance except to their need for adventure. This is all a dirty adventure to Flossie. But Amy is the star of the dirty story. She's even worse than Flossie.

She wants to hide. She slowly crawls onto her bed, a bed that shouldn't be used until bedtime, when normal people sleep. She's sorry to destroy Gram's work and hope. She sits on the bed, too tired to get undressed, and realizes Flossie is staring, waiting for a reply. Her smile has turned down at the corners: in moments, it will become a full pout and then the loud crying will follow. Amy looks at her shoes, too weak to fight, and hears Flossie scramble away, slamming the door behind her.

Chapter 37

Preoccupied with the traumatic visit of Detective Houghton, Barbara has no energy to deal with this rape-crisis person, this Gayle Fabe. Her wiry hairdo and her name mean she's Jewish. A nice enough girl, who must've been in college during the late sixties, which accounts for her wearing slacks to work and using her first name as an introduction to her clients, but there's something maddening about her. She's so totally attentive; her big, bland eyes linger on Barbara, assuming she is the head of the household, so there is no way to relinquish the role, to say, "Ms. Fabe, my mother has been the responsible party here." Ms. Fabe is a sensitive listener, nodding and repeating key phrases, so it is easy to elaborate a fantasy. Barbara spins the tale as if she'd played the role of mother as she should have, as she so desperately wishes she had. Amy and Gertrude are so silent Barbara averts her face as she speaks. Panic at being exposed heightens the fiction of her tale. Mom is murmuring reinforcement of the lies. Her support in this collusion keeps Barbara babbling. Amy is so withdrawn she may not even hear the fiction. And Flossie has sneaked into the room pretending she's invisible, so surely she won't expose the lie. To seal their agreement, Barbara turns a fey half-smile to Gertrude. Her silence is a confirmation; they'll share this secret. But it is painful to look at Mom's exhaustion, which must be an anchor sinking inside her as she acknowledges her daughter lies, her daughter is crazed. To see herself as flawed, as a poor mother, has broken her. Mom is beaten.

Ms. Fabe is explaining in a very soft voice that certain behaviors might be expected from Amy. Sleep disturbances, eating problems, emotional outbursts, fear of being alone are not unusual behavior "under the circumstances." Barbara nods knowingly as though she were prepared to be the ideal mother. Now Ms. Fabe wants to speak alone with Amy, so Gertrude leaves, looking dazed, and Barbara follows.

The silence between them as they step around the cluttered kitchen is as flimsy as the ragged, overbleached sheets stretched taut on the beds. Neither dares speech. When the phone rings, Gertrude doesn't rush to answer it. She seems to have made a decision to do her part by not doing. As the phone jangles, Barbara panics. As if she's unable to speak, Gertrude tilts her head toward the ringing, her gesture for the shift of responsiblity, tightening the old leash of fear that has kept Barbara at close heel with her head hanging to the ground for thirty-two years. The compassionate brown eyes of Ms. Fabe made words tumble out, building a plausible story. But the receiver is so impersonal, Barbara will open her mouth and silence will flow through her, setting her to nodding dumbly, struggling until she can manage, "Just a moment," and hand the phone to Mom. The third ring is interrupted. On tiptoe, Flossie is struggling to lift the receiver from the wall. The pathos of her attempt to accept a responsibility so beyond her touches Barbara. Without putting her hand over the mouthpiece, Flossie calls, "Gram, they want you."

This wouldn't be an easy time to begin a shift of power. Barbara nods to Mom to accept the call. Holding the receiver to her ear, Mom looks dead, yet she must be listening for she's murmuring, "Yes, Officer, yes." When she hangs up, Flossie flaps about her asking, "Wha'd he say? Wha'd he say?" Gertrude stills her with a curt, "He's coming over, He'll explain." And Mom turns to the sink, her shoulders narrow and hunched. Barbara peers into the dusk, resolving that no matter how tired she feels, she'll scrub the venetian blinds first thing in the morning.

Chapter **38**

Mom's voice is fuzzy with sleep. "Gram said she heard you crying and screaming." Amy murmurs, "Yes," careful not to say "yeah," which is rude.

"Did you dream about what happened?"

Because words won't come through her lips, she nods yes, for it was a nightmare, yes, for it was about the man, no, for it wasn't about "what happened"; it was the ice cream nightmare, with the hair and . . .

Mom kneels so close her breath is hot and sour. "What does all this head-shaking mean? Did you dream about the man?" Her staring eyes are monster eyes with little blood-veins spreading across the yellowed whites and black holes for pupils. Amy turns her face on the pillow so she won't smell the sour breath. Mom talks behind her. "Well, we weren't going to tell you this until morning, but maybe it's best to do it now because you're so frightened. The man won't get you. The man can't get you."

"Did the police . . ."

"They got the man. They found him."

These words mean safety; the fear may be over. But of course this is a test. Don't trust joy. She manages to mumble, "He's in jail?" He can't be crouching outside her window, waiting to come inside; he's in a cell behind bars. The policeman has the key and soon they'll put him in an armored car with his wrists and ankles chained to take him to a bigger jail with stronger doors which is further away.

She must see if Mom's lying. Her tiny pupils stare unwaveringly trying hard to be convincing. "He's dead."

The man is running away, his baggy suit flapping, his strange hands held at shoulder height as if he might surrender, but he stumbles along noisily wheezing, attempting to escape. A bullet pierces his shoulder: his body begins to crumple like a burning paper.

"They found him dead." Mom is talking to the igloo on the nose. "He hanged himself at his house." Mom speaks in a rush as if she has to get it over. "Day before yesterday. There was no note. The policeman said the man liked to take pictures of little girls, to touch them, but never as bad as . . ." And now she whispers, as if the others might be embarrassed and only Amy will understand these filthy parts. "As far as they know, he never raped a girl before."

Mom stops talking and sits back on her heels. Her face is a crazy person's. The man can't be dead. He'll never die. Like a monster in a movie, nothing can stop him. He can be cut down, but he'll rise again to rage and rape. She can never escape him. Blood splattered and cracking on her inner thighs, she can never run from him. To make the images go away, she stares unflinchingly into Mom's eyes. It's respectful to pretend to believe the lie. She owes Mom that: she nods as Mom says, "It's over now. We don't have to worry."

When Monday comes, Amy slides deep into the bed, listening, preparing her arguments for why she can't go to school. There's no explanation for her classmates about her bandages and bruises. But Gram doesn't come to lift off the blankets or to try to peer into the tunnel, to coax her up to the light. And from the kitchen, she's only heard one complaint from Flossie. "Amy oughta go t'school." The usual slamming of cupboards and flushing of the stool mean Mom and Flossie are getting ready to leave. Soon Gram and she will be alone and the day will unwind, like a skein of yarn looped across her two outstretched hands, and unfurl and roll into a ball. But the silence of the house can't be filled with sleep. She tries to will herself to dream of summers at the old Hershey house, or the matinee of the ballet, but the red behind her eyelids might turn to the man in the Baskin-Robbins chair, or his face, gray and choked, slowly swinging from the noose. In cowboy movies, the hangman's noose is tightened around the criminal's neck and the blindfold slipped in place, a complicated process with a drumroll and guards and a scaffold. A person could never hang himself. The fleshy neck would pucker where the heavy rope pulled tight, but there's no place to suspend the rope. At school, there is a sickening book, a favorite of Duane Fenton's, about the Ku Klux Klan, with shadowy photos of lynchings. Negroes dangle from trees with their heads flopped to the side, their hands and their feet tied, their faces puffy and twisted, and their clothing torn as if there'd been an enormous struggle. Pink fingernails fumble with the buttons of her shirt. She fights the shroud of the sheets, sits on the edge of her bed, and gasps until breathing comes easily.

At the kitchen table with the bowl of cornflakes before her, she can't fill the spoon to sip the milk. The curling brown flakes are withered fingernails, flaking scabs. Her mouth waters as if she might vomit.

Gram sets her coffee cup down and looks at the sodden mass of flakes. "You can't eat?" Her tired voice is filled with such kindness and love and goodness it is endlessly sad. A sobbing shakes Amy's insides so her teeth chatter, and she snuffles loudly. Gram is touching her, moving closer, her crinkled cheek brushing Amy's filthy cheek. She must not fall into Gram's soft bosom and have the old arms fold around her to make a warm darkness where she'll feel the heart beat, for Gram would be soiled. Gram lets go and whisks the cereal bowl away, speaking in the energetic voice she uses when she becomes too emotional. "Would you like some more milk, or maybe some cocoa?"

Even though she feels sick, Amy manages to drink half a glass of milk so Gram will leave her alone at the table. Since milk is all she can swallow, she'll live on it. She'll put on a dress but never leave this house. Maybe she can learn to sleep. She'll pretend the darkness she sees is the one within Gram's embrace and not the one the man made her see. Maybe Gram will sleep with her. At the Hershey house in New York, when nightmares came Gram let her crawl into the big bed. The bad dreams never returned when she slept in the warm curve Gram formed about her.

Deep in her plan for a new life, she is startled when Gram sets a book before her, *Rootabaga Stories*. Rabbits and children and skyscrapers are crudely drawn on the cover beneath the plastic and the banner, "School Library Book."

"The policeman returned your book. He found it in the house on Helen."

Policeman, house, Helen: the rape day. This is the ridiculous book she'd read on the day as she walked alone. She set it inside his house on a dusty table, so her hands could be free to carry the garments for the man who Mom says put a rope around his neck to kill himself. Amy asks, hesitantly, "Did they find this book when they found the man?"

"Yes, they found it by the couch where . . ."

"And the man?"

"He was dead."

Amy covers the stupid rabbit's face with her arm. "He was hanging?" This answer will prove if he's dead. Gram studies her ugly old knuckles as if silence will make the question pass. Amy pushes at Gram's hands and says sharply, "He was hanging?"

Gram looks up, then back at her fingers, speaking quickly and so softly it's hard to hear. "He hanged himself in the bathroom in the shower with a belt."

"The shower?" The belt loops around the showerhead. "How could the shower kill him?"

"The shower didn't kill him." Gram speaks slowly, making diagrams. "He put the belt around his neck, but he must've attached it first to the rod inside the shower . . ."

"Oh." His pale fingers fiddle with the belt, looping it around his neck. The shower must've been inside of a bathtub. Gram's face is as white and waxy as the lifeless statues in the museum. Her blank eyes mean there mustn't be any more questions now. What has happened has made Gram sick. Staring at the *Rootabaga Stories,* her small irises, which used to be like coffee bubbling up through the percolator, are as flat and cold as coffee left overnight in the cup. The man is hanging in the shower, his face getting gray and wheezing breath whistling through his dark lips. Dead. He didn't want to go back to jail. He killed himself because of what he'd done. Usually he only took pictures of little girls, but he wanted to rape Amy, saying, "My friend wants to visit." Her eyes drift to the side of the bandage and the halo of unfocused light. "Touch it. Kiss it."

She has to erase the pictures of the man. She follows Gram to the sink, walking so quietly Gram turns, her hand on her heart, as if a rapist pursued her. Amy steps back, lowering her eyes, an apology, murmuring, "I want to help." Gram kneels and holds her against her soft bosom.

In the dark warmth, Gram's heart beats, twelve long, slow counts before she lets go.

Gram says Amy can help wash venetian blinds for Mom if she promises to stop when she gets tired. "It won't make me tired," Amy says, and she fixes her face in a little smile to hide her discomfort as she climbs the three steps of the stepstool, being careful not to overturn the bucket. Counting each blade as she slides a sponge along its surface, she builds her rhythm into a hypnotic trance. Gray dust turns black on contact with the sponge and rolls into ribbons, leaving streaks of pale metal. The filth rinses away, making thunderclouds in the bucket. Returning to the bladelike blinds, she wipes the last streaks away, careful not to cut her fingers. Then with an old towel she buffs the tired paint to a dull glow. But she's reaching the last blind, and this ritual must not end. Gram says it's okay to wash the other blinds if she likes. There are blinds in both of the bedrooms and in the kitchen; she hurries as quickly as she can with her bucket and stepstool and bruised body.

After lunch, she'll find another job. Like Mom, she'll get down on her hands and knees to take the wax up off the floor in the bathroom and kitchen, using a Brillo pad and a razor blade. The walls can be washed. And washing windows could be an intricate game. She's lost count of which blind she's on when the doorbell rings. Dizzy with apprehension, she freezes. Gram's sensible shoes clomp through the kitchen and dining room and are muffled by the frayed living room carpet. The door opens and there is silence, then Gram says coldly, "Well, yes, come in."

Drying her hands by wiping her palms on her dress so wetness and wrinkles won't show, she prepares to climb down the stepstool. She looks up. Daddy. This must be a dream. Do not trust joy. Daddy is home. He knows, and he's coming home. Flapping her arms, she catches her balance as he moves toward her and lifts her, encircling her ribcage and swinging her so close to his chest her tiny breasts burn. He sets her on the floor. Her knees feel shaky with the warmth and smell of him so close. His shirtfront is only inches from her closed eyes, and her skirt brushes the buckle of his pants and the fly of his trousers. Behind him, in the doorway, Gram is watching. Even over the ringing in her ears, Amy hears him whisper, "How ya doin', baby?"

"Fine, Daddy," she mutters. She might die if she looks at him any longer or if she touches her cheek to his shirtfront and lets her arms go around his waist and loses herself in him. She closes her eyes so hard she feels the blow that broke her nose. He smells like tobacco and aftershave and fresh perspiration, and his movements have the crisp tension he had before he got so sick. He isn't drunk. She opens teary eyes to stare at his starched white shirt.

Because it's lunchtime, and Gram always does what she's supposed to do, she offers to feed him. He acts like he doesn't hear the invitation, which isn't surprising. He always acted like Gram wasn't around, watching TV when she talked or suddenly picking up a magazine and flipping through it. But when Gram turns toward the kitchen, he follows. The warmth where his hand cups Amy's is so powerful all other sensations are a haze: this is being safe, this is being happy. Hanging onto his hand, so he won't move out of her sight, she follows him through the hallway into the kitchen, hurrying so he won't let go. Their bond is broken when he reaches the table where Gram sits, looking very old and small, and he stares down at her face, which is sick with fear. His voice is so angry he almost yells, "Why didn't ya call me?" His fists smash onto the table. "Goddamn, why didn't you let me know?"

Gram hunches her shoulders as if she's prepared for him to hit her. He leans toward her. "Some psychotic exposes himself, rapes my kid, and kills himself. He coulda killed her too. It's just a fluke the lunatic didn't. There's no reason in hell this had to happen. A pervert can't just pick up a kid. The kid's gotta cooperate. If you took care of Amy, this never woulda happened. She oughta live with me." He's punching his chest with his thumb, but Gram is not watching. "And I want Floss too. Barbara's not fit to be a parent. And you . . . well, you're, you're just too old to keep tracka kids."

Gram's voice sounds so calm it's as if somebody else is speaking. "Leave this house. Our lawyer will be in touch."

When Daddy slams the door, the house shakes. He is very, very angry—so angry he may never come back. Too weak and trembly to speak, Amy sneaks a look at Gram, who is sad and silent. She knows she's lost the argument. Finally Gram says, "I'd better make us something to eat."

Amy can't eat. Her insides are stretched so thin between Gram and Daddy, she might tear. But Gram needs to fill the silence since the door slammed. A peanut butter and jelly sandwich, milk, and cookies will be fine. Sweet, soft foods are the only ones Amy can bear. Gram doesn't scold when Amy sips milk and licks frosting from between Oreos. The grainy sugar melts in her mouth, turning sour in her stomach, keeping her achingly hungry. Tonight in her room, she'll slowly lick the frosting from their centers. But now she sits, letting Gram, who's just a sad woman—"too old to take care of kids"—busy herself. With every ounce of energy, Amy begins to hum softly so Gram won't talk.

So many words Daddy said have to be clearer. She must understand each one to be able to recreate his visit, so she can understand it completely. After lunch, she'll pretend she's tired so she can go to her room and lie down, leaving Gram to methodically and perfectly finish the chores. There will be time alone to remember his words, to look them up in Mom's old dictionary, to imagine what life will be when Daddy comes to take her with him.

Lying in her bed, staring at the ceiling, she tries to recreate each scene of Daddy's visit. Some of his words sounded louder than others: lunatic, psychotic, rapist, exposed, pervert, fluke. She huddles beneath the covers, looking through the dictionary. Every meaning must be considered. She wants to write down the definitions, but Gram might come in and see strange movements under the tent of the bedspread. The words and their meanings will have to be memorized. "Lunatic" is like "lunacy." Her head throbs with the strings of incomprehensible words.

By Tuesday he hasn't called, nor has his lawyer. But Mr. Crandall says the judicial system in America is slow because of its complexity. Wednesday she has an appointment with the doctor, who wants to check her nose and other injuries. She worries about what "other injuries" means, but it's too embarrassing to ask. Mom has to work on Tuesday, and Gram says it's foolish for her to miss. But when Mom calls to find out about the bus route, she is told two transfers are necessary, which she says will take forever, so she's going to get Daddy to take them. Gram's excited as she says, "Oh, Barbara, calling him would be a waste of time." What she said about Daddy is cruel and untrue. He cares. If he could, he'd take them to the hospital. Gram hasn't told Mom about his visit because Mom will cry when she learns her girls are going to live with Daddy. Gram is waiting for the best time to tell her little girl how Daddy will be taking his children.

Amy's glad Mom won't try calling Daddy. Having him in the examination room with the doctor would make her so ashamed. If the doctor pulled down her panties in front of Daddy, she knows she'd die. The hospital smell of antiseptic makes her goosebumpy. Her veins are cold as the shot stretches the room like the inside of a balloon and then turns it black. She flinches at Gram's touch as Gram says, "Amy and I'll get along."

After six days inside the house, the sunshine in the yard is blindingly brilliant. Birds twitter. It's a first-grader's drawing of a spring day, and Gram is holding her hand. Amy follows like a baby. Gram is a charm against lunatics whizzing by in cars. Lunatics' mad spells change with the phases of the moon. The phase of the moon since Friday has changed, but every lunatic might not respond the same. Each might have his own way. Follow Gram, use her plump body as a shield. Don't excite the rapist. Don't lure a wheezing man, to turn him into a pervert who will rape, then kill himself. Keep your head down so the drape of your hair and your bandaged nose are almost a mask. Breathing gets harder with each step closer to the bus-stop bench. Gram plans to sit on the bench in plain view of the cars. Amy's legs shake, making her walk so slowly Gram stops to turn and see. Her sick face stares at the sidewalk turning darker gray in a puddle around Amy's shoes. Streams of urine run down the inside of her legs, soaking her ankles.

Gram hurries as quickly as Amy can walk. Safe in the house, Gram leaves Amy in the bathroom, a dirty chore to tend to later. Gram phones to change the appointment. Her voice is fuzzy calling, "Amy, the doctor will delay the appointment. Your nose can stay in the splint a few more days." The ball of white wavers between her eyes. He wants to see the bandage. She pushes the door open a crack and asks in a tiny voice, "He's not going to give me shots?" Gram is silent. Amy whispers, "He won't make me take off my clothes and get on the table? He won't look at me?" Gram doesn't answer. She's coming to take care of her responsibility. At least Daddy didn't see this.

When Mom gets home from work, her face is tense. She stands close to Gram, asking, "Well, what happened at the doctor's?"

Gram's voice is almost too soft to hear. "We didn't get to the hospital. Riding the bus was a little too . . ."

Looking over Gram's head, eyes squinted, forehead wrinkled, Mom curses the air. "Damn, I told you not to ride that bus—call Michael. He's got to do more than send an occasional check." She dumps her purse on the counter as she reaches for the phone. "Riding the bus is ridiculous. I'll just have to call him."

And before anyone can stop her, she's dialing. Her face flushed, her teeth nipping at her lower lip, she's ready to explode. As she waits for him to answer, she stares at the couch where Amy huddles, trying to escape her angry eyes. He must've answered, for Mom turns her back on all of them, as if doing so will make her conversation secret. "Michael." But her voice is too sharp to be private, "Michael." She clenches the receiver and bites her lip before she presents her case. "Michael, we need your help."

When she hangs up, the skin around her mouth is white, wrinkles bunch between her eyebrows. "That man," she says, wringing her hands as if they might attack the air if she doesn't occupy them. "He says he's got a busy schedule this week. Can't miss a day's work. Never minded missing before. But now he's too busy to miss a day. Doesn't have time to take his daughter to the doctor." Amy looks at the floor, awash with shame for Mom. Daddy can't bear this woman who used to be his wife. Mom will never be able to make him love her.

Gram's voice is as soothing as her cool hand testing for a fever on the brow. "Now, Barbara, we can manage. I can call a cab or . . ."

"Oh, he'll make arrangements." She says "he" as if she's holding a filthy rag at arm's length. "He'll have his 'friend' —that woman he lives with—drive Amy. He gave me her phone number, their phone number, in case I might want to call her. As if I'd want to call her . . ." Her face looks so sick she just might cry. "I should never have agreed—that woman, his mistress, his . . ."

Gram's face is alive with her old energy. "I'll go with them. Let me go along."

"Oh, I don't know, Mom, I—" But Mom will agree. Of course, Gram will go. Gram is as good as a fairy godmother.

The doctor and Gram and Gwen all assumed Amy would go back to school. And after Gram reported to Mom, she hadn't even asked what Amy wanted to do. To try to fight them was as hopeless as struggling beneath the man. Being here in the hallway at school is living a nightmare. Perhaps if Amy closes her eyes, then opens them again, the vision before her will disappear.

Flossie trots before her through the dim hallway toward the door flooded with sunlight from the playground. Rushing to become one of the shrieking children, Flossie doesn't turn or look over her shoulder, for she must play violently until the bell rings. The only escape from this hallway, smelling of chalk and children's lives, is to run back down the broad concrete sidewalk through the gates of the chain-link fence. But then Amy would be on the street alone. She stands near the door of the principal's office, holding the envelope for him that is addressed in Gram's handwriting, as letter-perfect as the charts posted in first grade. Amy desperately wishes she knew its message, but to tear it open is wrong.

Mr. Crandall's voice floats overhead, "Good morning, Amy." She holds the envelope in front of her heart to hide the wild beating and lifts her chin so she won't be rude. The white bandage blends with his shirt; the button by the collar has four little holes where the thread is stitched. But the plastic sheen of the surface makes it difficult to tell if the thread is crisscrossed or parallel. The shirt is moving closer. If she steps back, she'll fall as she had when the man tore at her. "We missed you;" his hand is moving. She turns her chin a quarter turn to tell the hand to stop, and the hand drops. But his voice is unwavering. "Do you plan to go to class?"

She murmurs, "I have to go to the office." He is staring at the bandage, at the scabs. He sees what the mirror saw. And he said, "Mirrors don't lie," when he taught *Snow White*. He sees the scabby place on the chin and the place that looks like a winking eye by her nostril. He sees the bandage covering what used to be a nose. She wants to go with Mr. Crandall and forget about giving the envelope to the secretary.

His leather belt with the nasty-looking metal tongue sticking into the leather is moving up and down with his breathing. "Well, come on to class when you get finished." He's leaving. In class the kids in the room will look and whisper behind their hands.

She speaks urgently, embarrassed because her voice is so loud and crude, "Do you know what happened?" She looks at his eyes, in spite of her horrid face, because she has to know.

Behind the thick lenses of his glasses, his dark eyes do not look away from her face. "About the assault? Yes." He waits for a reply, the prisms refracting light at the edge of his lenses. Who told him? Does assault mean rape? Has he told the class in a friendly Mr. Rogers voice, "Amy was assaulted." They may think she has a broken arm or has been bitten by a dog. "Your grandmother called last week." The belt buckle shifts. He wants to leave. He knows assault is a nice word for rape. He knows she's a filthy girl.

She murmurs, "Okay," so he'll leave.

The secretary tears the seal of the envelope with a long knife. She reads. Amy starts to count: one chimpanzee, . . . When she reaches twelve, the secretary says, "Oh, Amy." Because she is truly sorry for making the secretary deal with a disgusting person, Amy hangs her head. The secretary folds the note and leaves, the click of her heels like little drumrolls, the rapping of her knuckles on the door of the principal's office muffled gunshots as she calls, "May I speak to you for a moment?"

The door clicks shut on their secret meeting. Amy carefully counts, one chimpanzee, . . . On thirty-three, the door opens, and the drumroll begins again. The principal doesn't want to look at her. He has sent the secretary to deliver his message. She speaks softly, so nobody in the office or the principal behind his closed door can hear her. "Amy, you may go to class."

Amy leaves quickly so the secretary won't get in trouble. She's a kind lady who sends stray dogs home to protect them from the dogcatcher. To obey the principal, Amy walks quickly with her head down, moving close to the wall. The halls are almost empty, except for a few preoccupied teachers, grownups who won't be apt to stare and point. The secretary kept the note. She gave it to the principal, who might have thrown it in his trash. The cross janitor, who shouts at children who run on his waxed floors, is pushing a wheeled trashcan around the corner. The note might be in the can. Or the principal could be calling the police right now. When they come to school, the secretary will tell them the raped girl is in Mr. Crandall's classroom. To run from the building is to risk rape. Mr. Crandall's room could not be as awful as rape.

Chapter **39**

Michael needs another drink, right now. All day he's been sneaking beers to take the edge off this razor-sharp anger. Took five beers before lunch to manage a dopey grin at A.J. Bayless. Faking interest in how many fuckin' rolls of toilet paper they need can't be done straight. He ought to be with Amy today, instead of palming her off on Gwen, who called in sick with the cramps to get time off to drive the kid to the doctor. Gwen's great: a woman to depend on. Probably picked Amy up on time and whipped through crosstown traffic to reach the hospital and got the doctor's instructions straight so the kid gets the right care. Amy is a hell of a lot better off with Gwen than Barbara. Sure, Barbara goes through the motions. But everything she does is such a flop, and she works so hard at it. She'd drag the kid around on the bus and sit like a mouse in the waiting room, getting stepped on by everybody. She doesn't have the gumption to get a car, to learn to drive. Christ, her goddamn mother still runs her life. Hard to explain living with wimpy Barbara for so long. If she didn't care, it wouldn't be half as bad, but she mopes around, giving it her all, and still it isn't enough to get her outa the dugout. Everything she touches turns to shit.

He parks his old clunker in the visitors' parking section of Gwen's apartment, a spot he's come to assume is rightfully his. On more than one occasion, he's cursed the owner of a car parked there, a bona fide visitor. Reaching for the six-pack he's carefully stashed on the floor, he glances at his briefcase bulging with papers. Worry about the work tomorrow. Since the rape, beer has been as essential as cigarettes. It isn't like falling off the wagon. Sticking to beer, regardless of the amount, beats whiskey all to hell. It's like a fat guy drinking diet soda. Along with this sixpack and what's left in the case by the fridge, there oughta be enough to last till tomorrow. Hey, Gwen's little MG's already home. Get upstairs, grab a brew, and see her.

He shoves the six-pack in the fridge and checks the inside of the door where he keeps his arsenal. His anxiety ebbs when he sees the case on the floor is half full. Crouching before the open door, looking for a cold one, he speaks loudly into the fridge because Gwen's followed him into the room, and he can't waste a second getting his brew. "How'd it go today?"

"It was okay," she says in a voice as cheery as her yellow shorts and halter top.

He stands, turns toward her, and pops the cap with the bottle opener, sending it flying through the air to clatter on the floor across the room. He'll get it later; now he stands in the frame of refrigerated air, liking the chill wheezing out of the box as he takes a long swallow. It's a waste of electric-

ity, but it's the best way to start the first beer at home.
Phoenix is so fuckin' hot: the beer he drinks in the car gets
warm and tastes like the can.

She stoops to pick up the bottle cap. He regrets having
her pick up after him but doesn't apologize, because he's ad-
miring the contrast of her dark tan with the shorts. It's too
bad she doesn't have more boobs to fill out the tiny halter,
but those lean thighs make up for a lot. She turns to dump
the cap in the trash, and he feels warm when he sees the
little indentations before her buns began their curve up.
Jesus, she's nice. Christ, better ask about Amy. "The doctor
said Amy's okay?"

Her voice floats over her shoulder. "He says she's mend-
ing well."

Jesus, it sounds like she's describing a dress. "That's a
hell of a remark to make. What kind a jerk is this guy?"

Her smile is a warning to cool it. "He's kind of a jerk, but
I think he knows his business. He means her nose is healing.
He took off the splint."

This is noncommittal for Gwen, who's usually so chatty he
has to turn her off or drown in words. Disregarding his beer,
he pins her with, "Well, how else is she?"

Her eyes are evasive; she's a terrible liar, so obvious when
she's trying to twist a situation to fit what she wants. "Well
. . . She's not any better." He sees Amy's sick little face and
body and feels the rage that exploded at his burnt-out mother-in-law. He angrily pitches the empty beer bottle at the
trash and turns his back on Gwen, afraid of how she can
make him feel.

And she's standing close now, close enough he could turn
and be in her arms. The stream of her breath touches him.
"Physically, she's okay. But psychologically, she's . . ."

"She's fucked up." Oh, Jesus, what a sick unconscious
slip. "Shit." The blue-eyed baby in the white confirmation
dress has learned what she'll never forget.

"Well, they're trying. The doctors, the grandmother, I'm
sure your wife . . ."

Michael turns so abruptly Gwen steps back. "Grandmother, wife—ah, Jesus, Gwen, those two wouldn't know how to get out of a wet paper bag." He stops. His voice is breaking. The crap Barbara's taken all these years proves she's not a survivor. Taking care of kids under normal conditions is all she's capable of doing. She's way out of her league.

Gwen is watching so closely she'll detect how close he is to tears. He looks away as she speaks. "You wish Amy could be with us, don't you?"

"Yeah, I've thought about it." He stops. She must not learn about the scene with Gertrude. The threat to call the lawyer was so weak. Jesus, when he's angry, he lays a pile of shit then drags his feet through it. For once, be careful, make sense, do it right. Gwen understands these games, is good at playing by the rules, a college kid who gets things done.

Her eyes move across his face, reading his response as she speaks. "But the way things are, I think these little visits are all you'll get."

"Yeah," he admits softly. It doesn't take a genius to see the hopelessness. But "the way things are" may be an offer to change her status. Gwen's the one who's still married, who's kept that barrier, so it's easy to get together with no threat of commitment as part of the package. She likes getting loaded on her secret stash, likes getting blasted without getting hassled. And she never bitches about drinking. Her eyes glow with compassion. Just hold her, rock her, for a little while, close out the fuckin' mess of the world, shut the door on Barbara, on Flossie, on the godawful fuck-up with Amy. "Yeah, well, I guess you're right," his voice is thick as she moves into his arms. He hasn't held her long before he feels the need to take her to bed, and she goes without any coaxing.

Chapter **40**

Leaving school, Amy must escape Duane Fenton and Johnny Damiano, who follow her. She walks as rapidly as the rawness between her legs allows. But they are gaining on her, their voices growing clearer and more taunting. Their words become a song, "We all know what / you did to him," eight quick steps. "We all know what / you did to him" is eight more. The faster she moves, the faster they chant, until she begins to run. They start to laugh, snickering and snorting as she stumbles through the dusty desert on the shortcut home. Slowed by their laughter, they are falling behind. For half a block, her rasping breath in her throat and her footsteps are the only sounds she hears, so she dares to pause and look over her shoulder to see the empty path behind her.

Now she slows down, letting her heart fit back inside her again, trying to breathe with her mouth closed, wondering if blood has oozed onto the crotch of her panties, smearing between her thighs. Perhaps the boys are acting out the story of the tortoise and the hare and have run ahead to hide in the bushes, to leap out when she passes to begin their chanting again. She breaks into a trot as she tries to decipher their plan. Home: she must get home. Fingers of pain clutch at her side and dig between her legs when she hears giggling and Duane's croaking bullfrog voice saying, "A-m-y," pausing between each letter as if it were a word. Then Johnny says her name, and together the boys say, "We know what happened, we know about you." She increases her stride, afraid to break into a run, remembering how she's been told to behave around strange, threatening dogs: remain calm, don't let your fear show. But the boys are gaining on her, their tone growing more shrill, their words becoming nastier, too filthy to listen to, so her body won't obey the calm advice of Gram. Their laughter begins to bubble and seethe, forcing her forward, gasping and choking on breathlessness and tears. And she runs on even when they are no longer in pursuit, because now she only trusts fear. A stitch in her side slows her. Clutching her side, she hobbles toward home, her breath coming easier now. She checks over her shoulder at every other step. No one follows, no one crouches behind the bushes or cars. But they know. And they will tell, so everyone will chant, "We all know what / you did to him."

When she reaches home, she dashes toward the bathroom, but Gram appears from the kitchen, and her face means she wants lots of answers. Amy steps behind the overstuffed chair to hide her legs in case blood trickles between her thighs. She picks at the frayed upholstery, answering Gram's first question, "Oh, fine." If she rushes to the bathroom, a surge of blood might betray her. Gram would want to know what made the bleeding. From behind the chair, Amy answers questions with a single word in a bored, tired voice. But Gram commands, "Amy, let's go to the kitchen. Come on, hon, let's . . ."

Amy buries her face in the circle of her arms on the back of the chair and gulps against tears, choking on the dust embedded in the fabric. When Gram strokes her shoulder, her hair, Amy lays her cheek on her arms, looking away. As the sobbing slows, Gram says, "You had a bad day."

When Amy speaks, she's surprised by her angry tone. "Mr. Crandall and Elizabeth were the only ones, the only ones who said they were glad to see me." She blots at a tear stinging her wounded cheek.

Gram massages her shoulder, "People don't always say what they feel. Sometimes they can't."

"But everybody looked at me—at my nose and my eyes and my scabs."

"You look different from how they remember you. You've been gone awhile."

Amy whispers into the crook of her arm, "They know."

The kneading of her shoulders stops. "They what?"

By pressing her palms across her nose and mouth, she shields herself as she murmurs into her fingers, "They know." Gram leans forward, so the explanation can be whispered, "I don't know how, but I know they do. They followed me. They said—" And she presses hard on the side of her face to make herself stop crying, but it only makes her hurt, and a tear slides down the side of her hand.

"Come on now," Gram touches Amy's wet cheek, "Let's go to the bathroom and wash your face and see if we can figure this out."

She lets herself be led. Now bloodstains won't matter. Gram knows the worst. Everyone knows what the man did, what she made him do. Her evil has been discovered. She has been punished, forgiven, and she may be redeemed. Redemption must be like the part in the mass when the tiny bell rang, and she woke from the daydream to join the parishioners slowly pounding their fists upon their hearts, chanting sorrowfully, "Mea culpa, mea culpa." Leaving church after mass, she felt a serenity that the nuns said was a state of grace. The nuns said there were miracles beyond human comprehension. Holding Gram's hand is a miracle. It is tranquillity; safety from the demons who know her evil. She never wants to let go of the goodness of Gram. Dreamily, she stands by the sink, letting Gram wash around her eyes and mouth. And her hands are caught in the warm moisture, cleansed by Gram's patient ministrations. Suppressing a yawn, she converses with Gram. Yes, Mr. Crandall had been kind. Each time she'd dared to steal a glance at him, he'd nodded and smiled. And most of the students had not been cruel. They probably thought she wanted to be alone, for as each one entered the classroom, she looked at her desk. When Mr. Crandall said, "Amy's back after a week's absence, she had an accident," she squeezed her hands in her lap until the bones ached. She hung her head so nobody asked for details. Only Elizabeth came at lunch break to say, "I missed you."

Gram pats Amy's face and hands dry. "See, Elizabeth is a nice girl." And she's turning to run a bath. "A very decent girl."

As the water rushes into the tub, Amy starts to struggle out of her clothes. She doesn't want Gram to remember the frightening scene here. Amy will have to try to become a decent person. To cover her disgrace, Mr. Crandall had lied to the class, saying she had an accident. Walking down the corridor, trying to blend into the wall, she'd tried to imagine how to describe her accident if anyone asked. Falling from a ladder or being thrown against the dashboard of a car might account for her appearance. She must keep it simple because Mr. Crandall said, "What a tangled web we weave when first we practice to deceive." But Elizabeth would be shocked if Amy said, "A man raped me," and if she added, "and then he hanged himself," Elizabeth would think it was too dirty to be true. Yes, Elizabeth is too decent to be told what happened to Amy.

Sitting in the tub, Amy lets Gram bathe her and tries not to flinch. All day in class, she'd kept her eyes lowered, making a game of tallying visual detail. And when the visual detail bored her, she closed her eyes and let her nose and her ears tell her about the world.

As if waking from a deep sleep, she is surprised to find herself seated at the kitchen table. Waking and sleeping drift in and out of one another these days, so it's difficult to know what is real. She must force herself to eat the sandwich set before her. Gram is muttering, "But I don't see how the kids could know what happened. I called the office, sent a note—surely your teacher wouldn't tell your class . . ."

Amy pokes her finger into the jelly layered over the peanut butter and shakes her head so Gram will know Mr. Crandall hasn't told on her. He lied to the class about Amy to protect them from the dirty girl she's become. She's preparing an explanation in defense of Mr. Crandall when the kitchen door opens and Flossie appears. Being careful not to look at Amy, and ignoring Gram's invitation to share a snack, Flossie bustles by but pauses at the door to sneak a curious look at Amy. And it's clear why Flossie went to school early. She went to the playground to tell the boys. Duane and Johnny, older boys who usually ignored her, would want to hear a story of rape and a hanging. And if Amy was the nasty girl who caused it all, they'd listen closely, for Duane despises Amy because she hadn't let him kiss her, and Flossie gave him a story to use to hurt her. To tell such a story for their attention, Flossie must be an evil, nasty girl, almost as bad as Amy. The old sickness crawls up from her belly.

Unaware, Gram continues to sip her coffee, turned to the color of mocha with sugar and cream. Gram is so good: old as she is, she is still so trusting. The cruelty of her youngest grandchild would hurt her so. She must not be told. She sets her cup on the table and speaks slowly, deliberately, as if she's untangling snarled string. "Honey, you just might be imagining things. You know how kids love to tease. You know you just have to ignore them."

Amy nods so she won't have to speak, so Gram will understand the boys can do and say whatever they want. Amy will behave, accepting their taunts silently. This is how she'll pay for her evil. Good girls don't cause trouble. They are quiet and sweet and saintlike. So she must try to be very, very good to make up for all the trouble she's caused.

On Tuesday morning Amy purposely dawdles so she won't have to walk to school with Flossie, who is moving more quickly than normal, a sign she's frightened. The nuns said it is good to forgive. And even Mr. Crandall, who isn't religious, says it's good to be forgiving because resentment is a waste of energy. But just being close to Flossie makes Amy's stomach churn. Flossie can never be trusted again. Not speaking to Flossie is the best Amy can force herself to be.

Returning to school is so terrifying, it must be a test for goodness. Martyrs and saints have had to bear more. But surely Duane and Johnny are waiting, and this time they'll tell their friends. As she trudges along the dusty path, she listens for their laughter and chanting and considers safe places to hide at school. As she approaches the school, she decides her journey is blessed, for no boys appear. If Duane and Johnny have told, the story will rage through school, and the perfect spot for such a nasty tale is the restroom. In the smelly room, lined with mirrors, she waits within the stall for the first bell. Breathing shallowly, so she won't sense the smell so strongly, she hopes no girls notice her shoes and how long she's been in the booth. She listens intently, but there is just the silly conversations of the girls who stare in the mirror watching themselves. At the bell, they scatter, slamming doors.

She's able to hang back and enter the classroom attaching herself to a group of giggling girls. But her skin prickles as she walks toward her desk and must pass Mr. Crandall. He rocks on his heels, "Good morning, Amy." And with everyone staring, she must tilt her face as a greeting. Duane and Johnny lounge against the sink, sneering. They cluck suggestively as she passes so close they could reach out and grab her arm, the front of her dress. Her heart beats as if it were a prayer, "please God." And the boys do not tell her story that would strip her naked for the class to see a body raped by a man. Duane snickers and Johnny gasps, sounds which might not have been made if she'd prayed more diligently. Her prayer lost its urgency, and God unleashed evil when she did not ask for His protection.

Crouching beside the shelf beneath her desk, she fumbles about, gathering school supplies, trying to appear normal as the class stares. Thank you, God. This prayer will be perpetual until the lunch bell. On the playground, Duane and Johnny will wait. She is sorry she didn't ignore them. She hadn't minded Gram and refused to take notice, the way the dictionary defines "to ignore." Hail Mary, full of grace, the Lord is with you. Pray for us sinners now and . . . Our

Father who art in heaven. Mr. Crandall expects attention. But the vow to God for perpetual adoration must be fulfilled. And the school prayers have not been spoken for so long they are all forgotten. Mea culpa. Mea culpa. A promise of sacrifice for your blessing. It was very bad to take God for granted. To ignore Him must never be done again.

To stay inside during lunch period would cause a scene. Mr. Crandall would want to know why. She takes her little brown bag out from under her desk. Oh God, make Duane and Johnny go outside. Make them forget about me. They bolt for the door. Oh, thank you, God, for working miracles. The only children left in the room are the odd ones, who spend time alone, drawing circles in the dust or trying to catch insects or singing loudly, bouncing a ball against the building. And she's the oddest of all. God forgive me. Mea culpa. Hail Mary . . .

"Amy." Elizabeth will present a test. "Amy, let's eat lunch." To speak with Elizabeth, pray, eat, and ignore simultaneously—all in the name of goodness—will be a difficult test. Sitting under the ramada, Amy unwraps her peanut butter sandwich. When Elizabeth begans to speak, Amy takes a bite of the sandwich; peanut butter sticks to the roof of her mouth. Swallowing is an act of contrition, a blade in her dry throat. But she continues to silently pray, murmuring "yes" or "really" when Elizabeth pauses. Plot summaries of all of Elizabeth's latest reading fill the entire break. Amy watches an ant stagger beneath a crumb, finishes a Lord's Prayer and begins another. God is pleased.

"Elizabeth," the dull, snotty voice of Duane calls, "Elizabeth." The knee of his Levis is ragged. The urge to urinate burns. Elizabeth's thin, white throat turns toward his voice, straining as she recognizes Duane, a boy who has never spoken to her before. His voice is heavy and sick, as if it comes through a head filled with phlegm. "You know, Elizabeth," oozes in the nasty way his tongue probed Amy's mouth, "you know how she got them things on her face?" His boot toe taps two times. "Her lover boy put 'em there.

He's so hot, he give her them hickies. And then," the toe taps three times, "she fucked him." His face is triumphant. And Elizabeth's face is stunned and pale against her rosy-faced, big-eyed classmates. Amy covers her eyes. Her palms smell hot and dusty. "And she was such a bad piece of ass, he put a rope around his neck and yanked it up tight until he croaked." His laugh cracks, ending in a cry. And in the distance, children call and swing chains groan. It may be this silent always. Our Father.

Soft footsteps through the dust have the sound of a grown up approaching. "What's going on?" asks Mr. Crandall. And Duane runs away. Mr Crandall calls, "Duane!" The sounds of running become more distant. And it is silent. "What happened? Class, now what happened?"

And finally, Elizabeth, who always minds the teacher, murmurs, "Duane said some nasty things about Amy."

"Ah," he exhales as if it's painful: she senses he's nodding, speechless with exasperation, the way he gets when the class drives him "beyond the limit." The bell rings; his voice is very tired. "Let's go in. We'll straighten this out in class." And they scramble to their feet, following him. Her hands won't move from her face.

Elizabeth's hands flutter at her shoulders, and she says, "Amy," as if to waken her. But Amy shakes the hand away. Her classmates whisper as they pass. Oh, God, make my knees bend, let my hands drop, let decent Elizabeth leave. Let her see this is hopeless. Even God has forsaken such a filthy girl. The vacant playground is silent. Her fingers part. Elizabeth is here, whispering to Mr. Crandall, plotting what to do. Be good. She forces her hands onto her lap to show cooperation. Mr. Crandall is approaching. Be good, be good.

Yes, she nods three times. She'll go to the nurse's office. Yes, she'll wait for Gram. She'll get some rest. But she cannot touch his hand that he holds toward her so she can stand. She cannot look at Elizabeth, who waits at a silently safe distance.

In the nurse's office, Amy lies on the cool sheets of the cot and listens to the phone call. The nurse is trying to reach Gram. After she dials, the phone rings and rings, a staccato drill. No one is home. Dear God, please listen now. The scene on the playground might be retribution. Please God, let Gram answer, please. The nurse puts the receiver down with a click. God, make her keep trying. But the nurse is a busy woman.

The nurse is walking rapidly across the office on her tractor-tread shoes that squeak like a machine needing oil. She smells like disinfectant leaning over the bed, saying in her no-nonsense-voice, "Your mother works?"

"Yes." Yes, Mom is at work, not home in the kitchen like Marcy's mom or the other nice kids.

"There's no business phone number given."

Amy shakes her head. The names of the restaurant and the street are lost in her memory. She squeezes her eyes tightly shut to imagine the answers.

"There's a number here for your father."

Amy's eyes open. Daddy is a busy man who doesn't have time to come running to grade schools. He has sales to make. But the nurse is squeaking her way to the phone. Amy pulls her knees to her belly to stop the burning between her legs from pouring from her. God, make his secretary answer. Don't let him be there. Daddy's never in his office. He's in his car with a cigarette dangling from his lips as he angrily whips in and out of traffic. He never thinks of his children except on Saturday afternoon when Gwen speaks for him. The nurse is saying, "Yes, I'd like to leave a message. His daughter, Amy, is in the nurse's office at school. Please call at 721-6320." Daddy will never call. The gray building where he works is too far away: miles of confusion keep them apart.

God, make the nurse call Gram. But the nurse is chatting with a teacher, laughing and joking. Amy's case is closed. The nurse has done her duty. Now there are other problems to attend to before three, when she can go home. The hands on the electric clock on the wall click loudly around the minutes. A boy has a nosebleed. Two girls have skinned knees. The nurse helps each and sends them to class. Now she sits at her desk. God, please make her call Gram. The bell rings so startlingly, Amy almost wets the sheets. It is only two o'clock. She must ask permission to use the nurse's bathroom.

Returning to her tiny cot, Amy tries to become as close to invisible as she can. Her ugly face in the bathroom mirror explains why the nurse is so cold. With her hands beneath the pillow, and her face pressed in to the starchy case, Amy's pulse hammers at the side of her skull. She closes her eyes and arranges her hands beneath the pillow in an attitude of prayer. God, make Gram come home from the endless series of chores she does. Bring her in from outdoors where she hangs hand laundry, or picks up trash from the overturned garbage cans stray dogs attack at night, or pulls newly surfaced weeds from the desert of the yard. God, forgive me for missing church all this year. Even Gram, who isn't Catholic, says church is inspirational, which must mean goodness. Church is where one learns to be good. She will find her rosary and remember the prayers. She will find a church to attend.

The nurse is coming, "Your father called." This is miraculous. "He's coming to pick you up." God answers frantic prayers. "He should be here around two-thirty. As soon as he can drive across town." God's mercy is love.

Chapter **41**

Michael dashes up the steps of the school, not pausing to check his reflection in the glass doors. A phone call to come to school is so unexpected it's spooky. Couldn't get hold of the old broad, or Barb, or even Gwen. Nobody's home when you need 'em. Kid musta freaked out. Knew she was too quiet. What really happened just took a while to hit her . . . This school is a jab in the gut: no place smells like school, thigh-high drinking fountains, crazy drawings by the kids all over the place—but all the little fuckers are gone. Nothin' as lonely as a school after dismissal. The door marked Nurse's Office is only yards away.

Amy docilely follows Michael out of the building. Their ride to the seamy neighborhood is tense with silence. The little fuckers cut her down so bad she went to the nurse. Jesus, kids are cruel. The boys are real bastards. Now the kid's sitting so close to the door of the Mustang she just might fall out. She's keeping her head down. Hasn't said two words in a row since the rape, and she looks like she might never speak again. For once it's a good thing the muffler is so shot it roars. At the next stoplight, when the sucker quiets down, it'd be good to ask Amy to go for a Coke. Her crazy staring has got to stop. Got to lighten her up. The kid's a zombie.

At the stoplight, as he waits for her attention, her head is bowed, her lips moving rapidly, her hands folded in her lap. Jesus, the kid's praying. Michael shifts gears. Damn, this is serious. Sneaking glances, he confirms the praying is continuous: a little nun celebrating perpetual adoration. The kid's gone bonkers, off her nut. She's gone inside to stay. To watch her is to feel a sorrow so deep it's pain. He stares at the light until it changes, then guns the car and flares with anger for Barbara's inadequacy.

He slows as he turns onto the street where he used to live. All the twenty-year-old tract houses look equally destroyed, so it's hard to remember how many blocks from the main artery the house is. Gwen's been the navigator these past months. Christ, it seems like years since this was home, this crappy dump where nothing ever worked out. God, old Amy's really praying away. No chance of interesting her in being a co-pilot. He squints at the house numbers painted in fading letters on the curb. This religious stuff is too weird. Why Amy's into this now is a mystery. Shoulda never let Ma put the kids in a school with nuns, but fighting off Etta is like stopping Niagara Falls. How the hell would Gwen diagnose this case? She's had courses in child psychology. She knows about kids. Jesus, she oughta be here now. Or old Gertie. She's supposed to be some kinda super teacher. What the fuck's she doing for her loony granddaughter? These women are screwin' up. They're supposed to make things right. The kid's gone over the edge and they're not doing shit.

Ah, there it is, the little white house, the third from the corner. The windows sparkle—like the old broad has been doing her thing. Christ, she sweeps sunshine off the roof. Like mother, like daughter. Probably out emptying the trash or scrubbing those fuckin' windows when the school called. Just get Amy out of the car and get Gertie to open up a little. Get a cuppa coffee. Make peace with the old doll. Let Amy wander away and ask Gert what the hell's been going on. Old Gert might bury the hatchet if she sees the kid's got big problems, something to talk about, some place to start.

Michael parks the car and fleetingly checks himself in the rearview mirror. Wishing he looked less rumpled to meet her, he strokes his fingers through his hair—maybe if he looks a little boyish . . . He turns to Amy, who looks stone deaf, as he says, "I'd like to visit with Grandma." God, the kid looks terrible, shrinking like she expects to get hit. Oh,

Jesus, seeing Gertrude, maybe even Barbara, what a kick in the nuts. Run, Michael, run while you can. Get sauced and forget. The kid's trying to open the door like all she expects is to get dumped out. Christ, there's nothing left inside her but shame, shame clear to the core. He leans across her to open the door, talking softly so his voice won't break, "Come on, kid, let's go and see your Grandma."

Chapter **42**

With her hand in Daddy's, she trots to keep up, terrified of the impending confrontation. Dear God, make Daddy not yell at Gram. Keep the pee from running down my leg like it did at the bus stop. He is ringing the bell instead of walking in. I'm sorry, God, to have neglected you. Sister Angelique, who swatted the heads of children who weren't praying in chapel, should be here. Hail Mary, Mother of God, pray for us sinners. The tired doorbell rings and rings. And blessed is the fruit of thy womb, Jesus. Gram O'Connor had laughed when Amy said "fruit of the loom" and told Big Mike, who laughed too, saying, "Baby, you got it wrong. It's womb." And finally in fourth grade, the plastic model of the invisible woman had a part called a womb, an inverted bloody pear suspended above her legs, Mary's blessed fruit. And blessed is the fruit of thy womb, Jesus. Blessed is the fruit of thy . . .

Daddy's hand on her bowed head is the priest's at mass. "Doesn't seem to be anybody home." He lifts his hands to peer in the window. Since Gram has lived here, they don't have to wear a key, someone waits for them to come home from school. Amy turns the knob to let them in. Because Gram insists Phoenix is filled with friendly people, she doesn't lock doors or keep a gun; she says, "I'd probably shoot myself trying to shoot the other person."

Daddy's coming home, coming into the room with the sagging couch shrouded with a throw, with doilies crocheted by Gram on the arms of the chairs, a room he might return to, where they will be together. The radio plays softly on Gram's favorite station, NPR, where she gathers facts and sometimes argues out loud with the reporters. Tuesday is ironing day. The laundry basket with its sprinkled clothes that were chilled in the refrigerator overnight is set by the electrical outlet. The rack for hanging ironing is in place, but the rack is empty. The clothes are always completed by the end of school, waiting to be put away after the five o'clock news when they are perfectly dry. Yea, though I walk through the valley of the shadow of death, I will fear no evil. Gram will be in the kitchen. Daddy will wait for her to come to the living room, waiting till she enters to sit down. Thy rod and thy staff comfort me . . .

Passing through the dining room, Amy murmurs, "Thy kingdom come, Thy will be done." In all the churches seen from the bus windows, priests wait to hear confession. God's house on earth is open. Gram is stretched out on the linoleum. The cord of the iron released from her limp fingers is by her hip. On earth as it is in heaven. Gram is dead. The window curtain above her head billows gently into the room, lifts like a parachute and drifts down.

Daddy is coming. He brushes by, stopping with a sharp inhalation of breath. "Oh, Jesus." Then he's kneeling by the body, so only the silver head and the lifeless legs in the freshly-laundered terrycloth scuffs show. His hands cup soft hair, feathering through his fingers like dove wings.

Amy's throat fills with saliva; she swallows hard to keep from vomiting, unable to scream, "Don't touch her," unable to look away from Daddy's hands slowly lifting Gram's head. But he leans further over the body, so the face is blocked by his shoulders tensing as he moves. The gauzy curtain is limp. And Daddy's saying "Amy" like short, swift slaps across her cheeks. She presses her shoulder hard into the doorjamb until her bone aches, her eyes pinched shut against the roaring. Daddy's voice is like sharp teeth, "The phone, get to the phone." His anger and urgency open her eyes with a shudder. From white-ringed lips, he spits, "The phone, the phone!" His power is clenched and punching, rocking her loose: "The phone!" Gram's face is a plaster mask resting in the nest of her cloud-like hair, her lips slack and gasping, her eye staring up at nothing. But the lips move, the lips breathe. Oh, Jesus, oh, God. Oh, Mary.

The ambulance arrives, its screaming siren echoing, so before one wail stops a second begins. Flossie is running up the driveway. Two men in aqua jackets brush by her coming into the kitchen. Daddy follows, staying out of their way. They lift the gray-faced body onto the cot, tucking a starched sheet about it, strapping it with a belt like the ones on film boxes at school. With whispers, clicking, and a whoosh, they turn the cot into a cart and wheel the mummy toward the door. Amy gnaws the side of her thumb, staying a safe distance behind. In the yard, the ambulance has backed into the drive and up on the lawn. The men push the cart inside a freezer. Gram's ash-colored face is part of a white slab. They ask Daddy if he plans to ride to the hospital. The veins in his hands are ropelike as he puts his hand to his forehead, saying, "Her daughter's coming. I'm the son-in-law, the ex-husband." And the red light whirls splashing clots of gore. "Her daughter's coming." He sounds as if he thinks the men don't believe him.

Amy wants to tell the thin man, the one who looks angry, to believe Daddy, who made her phone Mom to tell her to come right away because Gram is sick. And when Mom said it wasn't possible, Daddy heard the silence and yanked the phone away to say, "It's an emergency. Gertude might die," and hadn't waited but half a second to hang up and to fall to his knees beside Gram. The man had to believe Mom was coming, so they'd take Gram out of the freezer into the hospital and not let her die. The ambulance light flashes. Oh, Jesus. It's flashing again, oh, Jesus.

And Mom is running across the yard, her yellow waitress uniform apron bouncing with the lump of the order pad in the pocket. She walks by Daddy, glancing at him as if she's passing a stranger. She stops in front of the ambulance attendants; her breath comes in hatchet-like gasps. The pulse at her throat held so carefully aloof leaps with the wildness of an injured bird in the hand. The attendants lean close as if Mom speaks with great difficulty, her hand on her breast to hold everything inside. And the men help Mom climb in with Gram, click the doors shut, and run to the front of the ambulance. The light is whirling and the ambulance backs down the drive, wailing, and floats by them. Daddy's hand on her shoulder makes her tremble. Gram's gone—alive, at least for now, but so sick she's lost in herself. Mom will be a silent, cold woman. The siren sound is getting softer. And Daddy says, "Let's go on in." He pats Flossie's hair as she clings to his legs sobbing. He strokes her. "We'll talk to Flossie and wait for word from Mom."

The ambulance drives over a hill, so the street is empty against the horizon. And even though it's afternoon, there is one star high in the sky. Star bright, star light, first star I see tonight, I wish I may, I wish I might. This isn't a prayer, but God might hear it.

Chapter **43**

Standing in the yard between the girls, Michael's arms encircle their shoulders as he walks them slowly toward the house. Gert must've had a stroke: her coloring, her paralysis. Christ, the kids—Amy saw the lifeless face, Floss saw the ambulance, her grandma lifted into it, looking like a corpse. Jesus, get them into the house, fast as you can.

Oh, my God, Gert's laundry basket blocks the doorway into the kitchen. Get it out of their sight. Get rid of the fuckin' iron. Wind the cord on the handle, shove the ironing board that's half in, half out of the closet back in. Get everything the way it's supposed to be. Gert would want everything perfect. That clock's gotta be lying. Four-fifteen. Been in this room my whole fuckin' life. Alone in the kitchen with the kids in this house, waiting. They're like little clouds, to shape, to carry. Jesus, it's scarier than hell. It's breaking out of yourself for other people. Want to say, Amy, Floss, kids, we'll get through this in spite of growing old and dying, looking into a fuckin' cesspool, we'll get on with it. But no words come.

He sits at the dinner table, passing the ketchup bottle, the pickle relish, the lettuce, the tomatoes. Slopping ketchup on the charred burger that he fried, Flossie starts giggling, spitting milk and pinching her nose to stop the milk from dripping out of her nostrils. Patting her on the back to stop her choking, Michael starts to laugh too, so hard he's crying. "Come on, Floss. Clean up your act."

"Mom," Amy whispers, a big-eyed bird dog, giving the warning. Barb's at the door, her face a hatchet.

She looks frail as hell, like a breeze could carry her away, leaning on the doorjamb as if she might fall if she tried to stand alone. Her voice is quiet but very sharp. "How can you laugh? Here in my house, making my children laugh, after you saw my mother . . . " She braces her arm against the jamb to turn, to leave. "I want you out. Out of this house. Back, back with your whore."

Michael stands, picks up his plate. The girls are so ashamed they don't look up from the table. No need to stay. Their Mom's back—she does the kids, 'cause everything you touch turns to shit. Do 'em a favor, get the hell out.

Stumbling toward the car, Michael begins to cry. Gert's destroyed. Face frozen—except for the eyes, where some

kinda life exists. Jesus, the strength of that woman. Even
helpless, hate still shines in those eyes. And she's got reason
—hatred 'cause you knocked up her daughter, 'cause you're
a drunk, 'cause you run around. Oh, Jesus, Gert, if you
could see me now. Smoking dope and fuckin' a dope fiend
who sings "Ride a Cock-Horse to Banbury Cross" when she
screws. Yeah, Barb, Gwen's a whore and a dope fiend too.
Making fudge suckers in bed with Kahlúa. Oh, Jesus, Barb,
how the hell will you ever exist without your mother? Barb
and the kids'll be in the poor house in a couple a days.

Squinting, he backs the Mustang into a strong, dusty
wind, barreling out of the driveway. Rain pelts the windshield and the wipers creak, making mud on the glass. "How
could you? My house, my children, my mother . . . " He
swipes at his nose with the back of his wrist, blinking back
tears, peering through the rain-splattered windshield at the
slick pavement. No way to find out about Gert. Oh, Jesus,
life always turns out so shitty.

Chapter **44**

Mom slammed the door to Daddy's room so hard it meant
she might never come out, and then Daddy left, not saying a
word, just quietly going out through the front. What Mom
said caused such shame, Daddy's gone and never returning,
and Mom's disappeared. The juice from the hamburger has
leaked onto the plate and turned into fat. She ought to vomit
up the food, swallowed so greedily when she forgot about
Gram and sat and laughed and ate. Mom is so disgusted
she's gone to her room, so she won't be near people who
laugh when others suffer. "How could you?" she asked, and
it's a good question. The laughter started when they were
fixing the hamburger. Slicing the onions and the tomatoes,

Daddy had started joking, blocking the memory of Gram on the stretcher being lifted into the freezer. Gram might have died or might be dying now, and they had forgotten her. People who laugh when others suffer are evil. Mea culpa.

Flossie kicks the table leg with a solid, consistently rhythmic thunk, the sound of a hammer beating a nail in the lid of a coffin. Amy grabs her chubby wrist. "Stop."

Flossie blubbers, "I didn't do nothin'." She shakes her hand loose from Amy's. "I didn't make Gram sick. You did. You're gonna make her die." Her bee-stung lip pooches as she stares ahead to keep from crying.

Before the tears gush, Amy pushes away from the table and wanders down the hall past Mom's closed door, past the bathroom, where Gram's gown hangs on a hook like a shroud. In the name of the Father, the Son, the Holy Ghost. The Holy Ghost. The Holy Ghost. Gram's gown is Gram's sick face, resting on the cot, rising into the ambulance. Selfish, so selfish, you thought only of yourself. She strikes a blow above her heart, mea culpa, mea culpa. Gram is a saint. The Holy Ghost.

The phone. The phone is ringing. She runs to the sound by the ghostly light of the TV, around Flossie, who doesn't glance from the screen. The screaming ring must be answered; she bashes her ribcage against a kitchen counter and clutches her side. " 'Lo."

The voice crackles, "Amy, Gwen."

"Um."

"Grammy's okay. She's had a stroke. Your Dad and I went to see her."

Amy nods; this must mean Gram isn't dead.

"There are some temporary symptoms. Her left side is paralyzed. Paralysis means she can't move, can't speak."

Amy freezes. Not to move, not to speak, like a punishment in a fairy tale. But Gram has never been wicked. This is a curse for the wicked, whose tongues are torn from their mouths with bleeding roots still flowing.

"Amy, it's temporary. She'll be all right. She'll be okay. It'll take time. It'll take . . . Amy, are you okay?"

Her tongue bumps thickly against the roof of her mouth. "Yes." She whispers, "What shall I do?"

"Go to school. Talk to your Mom. Help her. Get along with Flossie. You might write a note to Grammy. I'll get you the address. We'll see you on Saturday. But please go to school. You'll feel better if you go to school, okay?"

But as Amy tries to do what Gwen told her to do, the image of Gram, paralyzed and gray, rising into the freezer, oozes into her eyes, pushes inside her nose, making her breathing rapid. She must obey Gwen. But Mom doesn't want to leave the cave inside herself. She has nothing to say to her disgusting daughter, who brings unending difficulties wrapped in pain. Helping Mom means not talking, staying out of her way. Getting along with Flossie means being her slave. Attending school is another of Gwen's commands. To protect herself from the savages waiting in the shadows, she will chant on every step of the way, "Help me, God." She makes a vow to pray perpetually, to go to church and make a confession.

Amy comes into the classroom long before the bell, surprising Elizabeth, who looks up from her paper-grading. The corners of her mouth jerk spasmodically, her voice has the twang of a plucked rubber band. "I'm so sorry that the boys were so cruel."

"Oh, it's all right." Their ridicule might be a penance for Gram's life.

"All right? They were very, very cruel." She returns to her marking as if there's no other interpretation, the part of her hair meticulously unyielding above her serene face.

Behavior like hers can only arise from ignorance. She must be made aware. "The stuff they said is true."

Elizabeth stops writing but doesn't lift her face.

"I was raped. The man killed himself."

Elizabeth sets down the pencil, crosses her hands on the paper and speaks, a teacher with something serious to say. "I understand. But the boys were . . . They were very cruel. They shouldn't have done it."

Her dark eyes are blurred by glasses. But her primrose mouth said it understands rape, suicide. Elizabeth doesn't understand. Someone ought to shake her. This girl who believes she knows everything knows nothing of wretchedness. She needs more information to make her understand. Even now she grades papers as if nothing else matters. "My grandmother's dying."

Elizabeth lays down the pencil, her face perplexed. "No."

Amy is silent, building suspense for her victim. But this is not a plot summary, this is real. "She had a . . . a . . . stroke."

Elizabeth nips at her lower lip. "Like a heart attack?"

If she says, "I don't know," she'll humiliate herself by crying. This is more serious than suicide or rape.

Elizabeth leans forward. "What do you know about strokes?"

Amy shrugs. Gram looked dead, riding away in the ambulance.

"What did your father tell you?"

Ashamed to look at her interrogator, Amy hunches her shoulders. To confess Daddy hasn't taken her to live with him as he promised is too shameful. Elizabeth quotes her father constantly; she'll assume Daddy has deserted.

Elizabeth covers her mouth. "We can ask Mr. Crandall. . . . or we could look it up." She is on the trail of discovery, out of her desk on her way to the set of World Book Encyclopedias. Maybe this is a good plan, for Mr. Crandall says, "knowledge can make you free," and Gram kept a set of encyclopedias called the Book of Knowledge. But Elizabeth is leafing slowly through the S book, and the students will be coming in soon. Dear God, I'm sorry I haven't prayed all morning. Elizabeth closes the book and reaches for the A volume, muttering, "The cross-reference for stroke is apoplexy." She locates the boldface type and reads as if she were a talking book, "Apoplexy: a condition of unconsciousness and paralysis caused by a disturbance in the blood circulation in the brain. The word means . . ."

Amy wrings her hands; oh, God, please help, please . . .

The bell rings. Elizabeth stops reading, thrusting the book under her arm. "I'll read it during class, and at lunch we'll talk."

On the ramada, Elizabeth opens her lunch. Amy hangs her head; she hasn't her usual brown bag packed by Gram. Elizabeth puts half of her egg salad sandwich on Amy's lap. She gladly accepts, filling her mouth with the glutinous mass, which she must force herself to swallow. Our Father, who art in heaven, hallowed be Thy name.

Elizabeth folds her lunch bag, setting it aside. "I learned strokes are hemorrhages in the brain. She'll be paralyzed now, but not always, maybe—maybe it's because she's old. Because of too much strain."

Gram's face won't always be gray as concrete, still as . . .

"But your grandmother's not that old." She zeroes in, "It's strain." She fills in the blanks on an examination. "Your parents' divorce, your grandmother's move from New York, your . . . problems."

The rape made Gram sick. Amy's legs tingle as she stands, so she stumbles as she runs from the ramada, loping at a crazy angle, pounding through the dust, breathless as she passes the school, through the chainlink fence onto the asphalt. Elizabeth is dressed in the black robe of a judge. She pounds a gavel: guilty, guilty, guilty.

For the rest of the afternoon, Amy plans to hide in bed. Prayers aren't possible. A priest must speak to God for a person who has committed so many sins. Perhaps the Pope can exchange her life for Gram's. But a good Catholic goes to church, and Easter has come and gone and Amy hasn't gone to confession or taken communion. Her name has been removed from the rolls of the church. The Pope, who is responsible for millions of souls, won't make a miracle for a girl who is no longer a Catholic, and Gram's Lutheran. A priest will have to hear the confession, to right these wrongs. She lies in a pose of Gram. Oh, God, I'm sorry for making everything go wrong—I vow to come back to your church.

The kitchen door closes. Mom is home and no chores are done. Oh, God, I'm sorry for being so selfish. Hurry into the kitchen and help Mom, who sits at the table with her back to the dining room, her shoulders trembling.

Amy touches a shoulder, which stiffens. Mom's bloodshot eyes are glossy with tears. A long sigh seems to pass through her. "How was school?" She dabs at her nose with a crumpled tissue.

"School was okay."

"I've got to go to the hospital. You'll have to take care of Floss."

Action will be prayer until the visit to the priest. Waiting on Flossie is penance for bringing pain to the family. Let her flounce her butt out of the kitchen to watch TV instead of doing her chores. Let her think she's getting away with something. A good person forgives and sacrifices like Jesus. Flossie is a trial to teach worthy behavior.

The entire night seems to pass without sleep. Tomorrow she will visit a church where a priest waits, a guide from this nightmare. Earlier in the year, when she tricked everyone and skipped school for entertainment, it must have been God's plan for her to learn the skills of deception. She will go to school, a model student, with books and papers, leaving in time to avoid being tardy, but never arriving. Yet this deception will be used for ultimate good. It is very late. Her legs ache and her eyes smart, but when the room turns bright with dawn, she'll get out of bed and make the journey to the house of God.

At breakfast, Flossie keeps her face down. Kindness confuses her. She is used to a sister who criticizes her. Flossie's so frightened she bolts her food, and sacrificing her usual second helping, runs out the door to be free to race to school alone.

Amy cuts across the street half a block before the school crosswalk, expecting a policeman to swoop down upon her with his motorcycle, or the school patrol to yell out a reprimand. Chanting "thank you, God, thank you," she passes unnoticed. Please, God, don't let Elizabeth see me, or Marcy or Duane. She skips and jogs to the corner grocery two blocks from school.

Alone in the partially-enclosed phone booth, she hoists the book onto the shelf to look up "churches" in the Yellow Pages. Catholics have a separate listing. Saint, Saint, Saint . . . Joseph is closest. God, I promise to bring back the map if You'll let me tear it from the book. It wouldn't be stealing, God, only a loan.

Amy sits close to the front of the bus, behind the gruff driver, who knows she's a girl cutting school. She furtively checks her stolen map, afraid the driver watches in the rearview mirror. Gram says, "To navigate, use a map and mark it; look for major landmarks." Street signs and numbers coincide with the map. She mumbles, "Thank you, God for this blessing. St. Joseph, God, help me find St. Joseph." She closes her eyes to try to visualize God in His heaven looking handsome like Jesus, but older and wiser.

"Girl, are you looking for the church, St. Joseph's Church?" The black woman is a prune rolled in sugar. "If you was lookin' for St. Jo's then you just missed it. The bus done passed it." Her spidery black fingers points to the window, where a pie shop and a used-car lot flash by. This woman may be Satan, black and evil like rape and suicide and stroke. Please, God.

A man's voice, possibly a representative of God, or God Himself, says, "That's St. Joseph's Catholic Church back there." God is testing. She must see the source of this wisdom. The driver has spoken, staring into the mirror. The black woman's voice floats over her, "Well, he the driver, he oughta know." The driver shrugs, so she stands to pull the chord.

The church is not the mirage it appeared to be from half a block away. The doors are massive. She may not be able to open such mammoth doors. The wrought-iron handles might cut her palms. Beyond the "Bingo Tuesday Night" sign, a long row of boxy buildings serves as a school, where good children, who do what they're supposed to do, watch from the windows. A nun might come scurrying from the classroom to pull Amy inside by her ear, to be punished before the snickering students. Oh, God, let me be cleansed and in a state of grace.

Hurrying away from the staring students, she comes to the side of the church. There is an entrance on the side, a passage into God's house. The door will open easily. But inside, the rows of pews may be filled with kneeling people, waiting for the priest to prepare communion, and she'll be framed by sunlight so they will stare. Gravel crunches; a car is coming. She pretends to study the board by the door. "Masses weekdays 7:00 and 9:00 A.M." This is Thursday and it must be later than 10:00. Confessions are not listed. Today she will not kneel in the confessional to whisper her sins to the screen shielding her from all eyes, even the eyes of the priest. "The Sacrament of Penance, Saturday, 4:30–5:30 and 7:00–8:00."

Penance is confession—but to escape from the house on Saturday and ride the bus: oh, God, have mercy. Don't let me die today or tomorrow, to burn forever, condemned to suffer for these sins. How foolish to believe a simple show of penitence would relieve such grave sins. Oh, God, guide me on the long trip home, get me to the right corner. Give me the strength to live the rest of this day, or the rest of this life. Taking a deep breath, she pulls at the heavy door.

Thank you, God, for letting Your house be empty. Slipping into the last pew, she attempts to genuflect to show rev-

erence but doesn't touch her fingers to the holy water. It
might not be right since there's no mass to attend. Oh, Lord,
make me worthy to be in Your house. If I had been a good
student for Sister Mary, instead of being so silly, giggling
and playing with my friends, daydreaming or wishing the
time away, my soul would not be so damned.

This house for God is very stark: The walls are wooden,
and the colors are the muted shades of the desert. This
church isn't filled with the scents of melting candles and incense like the parish in New York, or stained-glass windows
splashing strange light on the statues of Mary and Jesus
and the suffering saints. A crucified Christ the color of dust
hangs behind the pulpit, but He has no golden halo or skin
streaked with blood. He has no bleeding wounds like the
Jesus in New York. On the wall beyond Him, a green banner
is emblazoned with golden letters, "God is Love." The candles on the altar flicker. She has not crossed herself. In the
name of the Father, who looks like a kindly, elderly grandfather, and the Son, who is blonde like Daddy, and the holy
Ghost, who is Gram's frozen face. God would be pleased to
have his supplicant kneel as she prays. But the bar to kneel
is pushed up. Our Father, who art in heaven, hallowed be
Thy name.

God has provided a *Monthly Missalette*. This little newspaper has detailed instructions for mass. The major concepts
are in boldface type. If she reads slowly, she can construct
the mass, but of course she won't reach God. Only a priest,
who's closer to God than she can ever be, could reach Him.
"Kyrie eleison, Christe eleison, kyrie eleison."

There is a song for the sprinkling of the holy water so the
Lord will cleanse all sins, "so we shall be whiter than snow."
Perhaps the holy water will wash off the bruises and rid her
body of the filth. There are pages and pages filled with confusing words and the names of people she doesn't know. But
every page says, "Thanks be to God," and has meaningless
words with familiar sounds, sounds she'd repeated with her

classmates so they were a song. But these words teach God's lessons, the keys of faith and rescue. "Believe in God, in Jesus, in the Holy Spirit. The Catholic Church and Communion of Saints, the forgiveness of sins, the resurrection of the body and life everlasting . . . "

To take this missalette home would be a major sin. God's possession must not be stolen from His home. Memorize the spelling of communion and resurrection, then look them up. Learn a prayer to have the power to speak with God. But the prayers are hopelessly long to memorize. She is too evil for mercy. Putting the missalette back, she notices a page on the back covered with prayers brief enough to commit to memory. "Prayer of self-offering" is the shortest of all. Forgive me, God, for serving you with what is simple; only the evil would make such a choice.

She reads each prayer, drawn by the invitations to abandon her sinful ways and give her soul to God. The Prayer of Our Lady states, "No one who has ever sought her intercession was left unaided." But "virgin" is too painful to repeat. Beneath the prayer to the Virgin is the Prayer to Jesus in the Eucharist. She imagines Christ, wearing a crown of thorns, watches from heaven. "From the evil enemy, protect me. At the hour of my death call me / And tell me to come to you / That with your saints I may praise you / Through all eternity."

She rises from her knees, crosses herself, and backs down the nave, on the aching legs of a penitent, staring into the dusty eyes of Christ hanging on the cross above the altar. In the entryway she turns, and the flickering votive candles light a display of pamphlets. Placing a quarter in the locked box, she takes a booklet entitled "Prayer: the Key to Salvation."

In the park, she watches pigeons and reads, "The man who prays will be saved; the man who does not pray will be lost." "Men" includes women too; this prayer might apply to her. God and His army should protect her. As she prays, she tries to visualize the dusty Christ at St. Joseph's or the bloody Jesus from the parish in New York: Jesus with His body, broken and bleeding, lying across Mary's lap as He died for our sins. Gram's face rises from the sheet-draped stretcher. Daddy's leaving, silhouetted by the sun in the doorway. "The saints are in heaven because they made use of prayer." But Gram said, "We make our heaven or hell on earth."

The park is filling with children, first- or second-graders. The first shift at school has been dismissed. She must hurry to catch the bus. God is punishing her, making her late, yet she's been praying to Him. "He helps you that you may be able." She must pray more. Continual prayer will reveal to her what God wants her to do and what He will do. She must do her part to save her soul.

Walking down the sun-dappled sidewalk, she feels nauseous and sees dancing stars. She hasn't eaten today. At her last meal, she mashed food with her fork. Oreo frosting, sugary-sweet, would slide down her throat. The bus isn't coming. She dashes for the convenience mart. The junk-food shelf is right by the register, close to the sliding glass doors. There aren't any Oreos, but Ding Dongs and cupcakes with frosting like plaster tempt her. Hurry, pick up the packet of fuschia-colored balls with pale coconut compressed in rubbery frosting. Pay with the exact change and get back onto the street to see the roof of the bus rising over a hill a block away. She tears the cellophane. She'll gobble down the sugary mess before she boards the bus.

A great chunk of the frosting sticks to her finger. The bleached white mass adheres to her skin so she has to lick it off. The crumbs of the chocolate cake are stale, like hair scratching her mouth, her throat. The dead animal stands up, its pink skin flecked with dark fuzz. She retches, spewing crumbs and gummy frosting into the gutter. An old man watches, mildly curious. And the bus is slowing.

Flossie lies in the living room in front of the TV. Thank you, God. Serving God continually will keep evil away. Amy says, "Thank, you, God," for each piece of silver she takes from the drawer. The forks are the stirrups, the knees locked against the doctor, prying to insert strange metallic instruments. "Hail Mary, full of grace."

The kitchen door opens. "Amy!" Mom's voice is a slap. "Where have you been?" Her fingers dig into the shoulders, and limp acceptance makes her furious. Her grip tightens and shakes the shoulders violently. She screams, "Don't you lie to me! That school called me." And now she's crying, her voice harsh from strain, shrieking, "Trouble, you're nothing but trouble!"

Chapter **45**

All week, Gwen has been squirreled away, working on school. Home from work early on Thursday, she starts to rearrange the furniture. Christ, she acts like she's on the rag. She rushes off to the kitchen and starts slamming cupboard doors, doing the Barbara number. To calm her down, better ask her what the hell she wants to do this weekend. "Hey, Gwen."

She screams and drops the hot burner from the stove. She cries uncontrollably as he kisses her fingertips. Brushing away her tears, he smells the unmistakable order of pot. Christ, no wonder she's burning herself; she's loaded. "Hey, you going to be okay?"

She nods, looking ashamed and totally hopeless.

"Well, babe, I was gonna ask you for a date—want to go with the girls to the show? They had a real shock."

"Oh, sure, sure, Michael." She begins to cry again. "I just wanted you to know, I'll do all I can to help with Amy, with Flossie. I have a very special feeling for Amy, I . . .

Michael, can we sit down? Can we really talk about this?"

Armed with a cold six-pack and Gwen's "magic box" with a multitude of colored numbers, they go the living room.

Gwen sits crosslegged on the couch and takes an awkward toke, using her uninjured left hand. She holds the smoke deep in her lungs and exhales slowly, her voice high with tension. "Michael, Amy adores you."

He taps the hollow can and manages a half-smile where bitterness and pride battle. "Yeah?" It's a question. Adores?

"You're the center of her life." She moves closer, looking really loaded. "Michael, I know so. All you have to do is look at her. It's written all over her."

He presses his thumb over the opening so the aluminum edge bites into his flesh. Gwen is so fucked up. Got such a lousy record with men, she's just doesn't know what makes people tick. "How come you could see it written all over her?"

"Well, you see," she says with her hand on her heart. Best to play it cool and pretend not to watch when she gets this way. "I identify with Amy. We're a lot alike. She's a Daddy's girl and I was a Daddy's girl. God, I was such a little crusader, sitting in the den talking to Daddy at the end of the day. Turn-Daddy-straight-and-the-world-will-be-right kept me going. I was such a perfect kid. And Daddy's well now. But Mom's the one who set him straight. Won him over with a massive dose of guilt." She stops, as if this last confession makes her feel sad as hell.

Blasted out of her mind, naked except for her wrap-around bathrobe, she's not exactly a candidate for homecoming queen. Her eyes have that hazy look. Jesus, the only time she really talks is when she's stoned. Then she goes on these crazy tears. "But Amy lost her Daddy more than I lost mine. I just lost my Daddy to alcoholism. And . . . "

He drinks his beer, hoping she's done with her bleeding-heart confession.

"Amy feels she's lost you to divorce. And to me, she's lost

in lots of ways." She stops as if she's considering shutting up but realizes she's already said too much. "You asked what I see when I look at Amy, and what I see is a lot of pain. More pain than I like to look at."

"Yeah." Jesus, he hates looking at the kid, she's a fuckin' martyr. But looking at her got tough to do a long time ago. Ah, Christ.

"It's hard for me to imagine what's happened to her, and how I'd react if it happened to me. I'm supposedly an adult, and I couldn't cope. No way could I handle what she's been handed. And Amy's only eleven, yet we expect her to cope." She's studying her roach, probably considering whether to get out her clip or light another. "Rape. I mean, God, that's every woman's nightmare. And Amy experienced it before she knew the meaning of the word."

He closes his eyes. Jesus, Gwen, cool it.

"I know it's tough, Michael, really tough."

He crumples the beer can. "I know." He speaks to the destroyed can in his hands. "And what the fuck makes you an authority?"

"Michael, I've got eyes. You've got to show her you care."

"Ah, Jesus, Gwen." He punches his chest with his thumb. "What do ya call these weekly visits, my checks, my trips to zoos and Walt Disney movies? It may seem shitty to you, but that's how I show I care."

She says, "Oh, Michael, you know what I mean."

He chucks the can across the room, watching its graceful trajectory. "Jesus, I'm fuckin' sick of women tellin' me what to do."

"Oh, Michael. I know you're trying with Amy, with Flossie, and I think you're . . . you're doing fine. I just think . . . "

He's out of the chair and brushing past her, rushing toward the bedroom. Her fingers brush his shirtsleeve, but he's by her before she can grab him. But she's right on his trail to the bedroom. He stands halfway between the bed and the closet, with his hands in fists on his hips. Just put your shit in a suitcase and split.

.

He continues to stare at the bed and speaks in a flat voice. "Having Amy here won't work." She hugs herself, looking so wounded he has to say it now to get it all out. "Ah, Christ, we're a couple of cripples—I drink and you, Gwen, you seem to forget you're married."

Her shoulders sag with the weight of reality. "Yes, Michael, you . . . "

"I admit it. I admit it. I admit it. But I said somethin' about you. Do you know what I said?"

She looks confused by this little quiz. Married. She's not gonna own up to married. Turning her face to the wall, she looks real pissed, as if her marriage to Sutton is none of his fuckin' business.

"Gwen, I love you." Jesus, this is straight from the heart, just let it pour. "But, Christ, Gwen, I'm your wild card, somebody to play when you're loaded, when you're not lost in your goddamned do-gooder version of a Baptist missionary."

She is sobbing.

He speaks a little louder to make sure she hears it all. "I mean, I'm willing to stay on like it is, but Jesus, get off my back." And the kid looks so loaded, so out of it, so all alone, there's nothing to do but stay.

Chapter **46**

It seems very late, maybe five, when Amy finally reaches the church. The door is so heavy she opens it only wide enough to slip inside, and it closes behind her with a muted thud. The odor of melting candles and insense is so oppressive it's difficult to breathe. The blinding sunlight of Phoenix is freedom. God, help me be comfortable in Your house. Sunlight streaming through the stained-glass windows makes an iridescent path to the altar. At lunch Daddy's sulky silence flared into rage. School called him. Mom called him too. He said, "Amy, you got to go to school," and he looked so angry and ashamed, and Gwen just stared and drank wine. First Gram got sick, then Mom got mad, and now Daddy and Gwen. Oh, God, be my salvation.

She tiptoes to the last row of pews. None of the kneeling women turn to see how she hasn't touched the holy water, nor bowed as she faced the altar. No one seemed to notice how God's door barely opened for a person as strange and evil as she. God must be speaking with the women who are praying, heads bowed, lips moving, rosary beads clicking through their fingers. Her presence isn't noticed while He speaks. Sick with longing for such an intimacy with Him, she sits on the edge of the pew across the aisle from the women. She must learn what they know; it might be possible for her to feel His peace, His love. If she becomes a nun, she'd be a bride of Christ. This is a presumptuous thought. She must be committing the sin of pride. She doesn't know exactly how to make a confession, or what to do at mass, yet a nun's life is constant devotion to God. Sister Theresa with her caterpillar moustache used to slap children's hands with a ruler. Amy had laughed when the boys called the Sister "Dog Face." God is not in the heart of a girl who has such unloving thoughts. God is not in the heart of a girl who has forsaken Him.

The women kneel in the pews by the wall because beyond them is a row of doors with little red lights above them. These must be the confessional booths, the place to cleanse a sick soul. God opens a door and an old woman comes out, the light goes off, and a kneeling woman stands.

God will provide the instructions for making a confession in the booklet in the rack. The flimsy pages of the missalette flutter as she leafs through it in search of instructions. She thinks confession begins with the prayer, "Oh, my God, I am heartily sorry for having offended thee . . . " But the booklet only contains directions for the mass. God, let me

remember before it's my turn. Please, God, don't let me wet
my pants. Women are entering and exiting the confessionals
at a steady pace: only three are still kneeling. Oh, God, have
mercy.

Yea, though I walk through the valley of the shadow of
. . . The creaking shoes are worn by an old woman. Her face
is so serene. Her sins must be absolved. The lights above the
doors of two confessionals standing side by side are off. Rising from her knees, which are sore from kneeling on the
poorly-padded board, she doesn't know if her legs will function, but she must hurry. The priest is waiting. It's difficult
to walk quickly down the narrow aisle without stumbling.
She is breathless as she pulls at the door without turning the
knob.

She furtively checks to see if anyone has seen how little
she knows about God's ways. But her humiliation has not
been witnessed. God, let me escape my state of wretchedness.
Let the discipline of religion save me. God, forgive me. I
have sinned. My God, the priest is waiting. He will speak to
God, delivering confessions. She lurches into a room no bigger than a phone booth, lined with white acoustical tile, and
as the door closes behind her with solid-sounding click, a
small light above the entrance illuminates a screen before
her, and in the shadows beneath it is a narrow knee-rest.
This is where she must kneel and beg forgiveness. My God.
She turns, ready to race from the room, and the small perfo-
rations in the tiles melt from the surface, elongating into
staring eyes. Turning from their accusing stares, she gin-
gerly places her knees on the knee-rest and is pleased by the
discomfort she feels. A saint totally submits to pain. She in-
tertwines her fingers and watches the screen to see if perhaps the priest might be silhouetted there: there's no evi-
dence of life beyond the gray mesh, yet she senses someone's
presence. She bows her head in a prayerful attitude, and her
hissing breathing fills the coffin of a room. A muffled growl
jerks her attention to the screen. Someone clears his throat.

She touches her finger to her forehead. Oh, she must hurry. His time is valuable; she must tell, she must tell.

"Forgive me Father for I have . . . " she hasn't bowed her head in humility but is staring hard at the screen. There is life there. God, forgive me my insolence. Posted on the tile is the prayer written in flowery script, the prayer she could not recall. This is divine guidance. This guides the shameful Catholics, who do not know God's prayer. She reads in a rushed whisper, tumbling over the words, "Oh, my God, I am heartily sorry for having offended Thee, and I detest all my sins because of Thy just punishment, but most of all because I offend Thee, my God, who art all good, and deserving of all my love. I firmly resolve with the help of Thy Grace, to sin no more and to avoid the Near occasions of sin. Amen."

Her thumbnails lying opposite one another cross over the knuckles on her forefingers. God gave this prayer. God will permit confession. It is best to list all sins since the last confession. Murmuring to the flesh-colored moons of her nails, she begins, "My last confession was"—the shameful truth must be spoken—"two years ago. Since that time, I have . . . " The priest loudly clears his throat. She waits for the roaring to cease, but as she begins to speak again, she knows she must carefully list her venial sins, beginning with the tiny ones and building until she has told them all. Her soul will not be truly cleansed until she's told not only her venial sins but her mortal sins. He must hear everything. With a quaking voice, she begins, "I have . . . "

"Speak more slowly, more loudly."

She whispers, "I'm sorry," and speaks as directed for half a sentence, then rushes along in a whisper. Again she's stopped, again she begins. The third time he stops her, she starts to cry, her hiccups punctuating meaningless phrases.

"You must control yourself if you expect to receive the grace of God."

She tries to hold her breath against the involuntary hiccups that shake her, but her body betrays her with a loud, peculiar gasping and her tears are an uncontrollable wash. She snuffles in her last effort to control herself, but her eyes burn and the top of her head is seared with grief. She closes her eyes against the discomfort and lets herself go in a shuddering fit of crying.

From the other side of the screen, a throat clears loudly, a warning from the priest to stop the tears and get on with a responsible, good confession.

She trembles and snuffles loudly. Never, never, never can she confess her mortal sin to a priest who growls when she weeps about her venial sins. Turning in the tiny space, she manages to open the door to leave before he has a chance to scold her.

Running and gasping along the street, unable to stop, she wails and tumbles along at a precarious angle, brushing aside staring people. God doesn't want her in His church. It's a place for sinners with venial sins, easily explained, easily forgiven. The priest will never carry her messages to God. As she runs, her face streaks with tears and mucus, her breath comes in razor slashes in her throat, she feels her bladder distend with urine. With a burning contraction of her vagina, she tries to hold back the flood, but acid sparks dribble from her and stream down her legs, staining the sidewalk, marking the trail of her humiliation.

She shrieks and waves at the bus approaching the corner. Climbing aboard, she doesn't bother to mop her nose or eyes. She stares boldly into the driver's curious face as she thrusts her money at him. When he returns her coins and points to the place for her to deposit them, she sniffs crudely, defying him to ask her about her problem. Walking down the aisle, she holds her head high so the passengers can fully witness her ugliness. All the way home, she stares out the windows, rigid with her pose for anyone who will bother to look at her. The priest wouldn't hear her. God doesn't want her; she will not hide her ugliness from anyone. Everyone can see the girl no one loves. The filthy girl. This is what she is. This is what she's become: the filthy girl no one loves.

She deliberately swings the kitchen door wide so it bangs against the wall. Mom turns. Amy poses in the frame of the doorway, giving Mom and Flossie time to stare. Amy will not hide the urine-soaked sneakers and dried streaks on her legs. She won't hang her head to hide her face, glossy with dried mucus, red with scars. The girl who has become evil while living with them won't hide anymore. Before their speechlessness, she parades like an arrogant fashion model. When she reaches the dining-room archway, Mom mutters, "Where have you been?" This is obviously not her only question, but the only one she dares to ask.

"Out." This single word slaps Mom's face: it's electric with anger. Get to your room and pull the door closed; slam it so it reverberates, "Stay out."

Disregarding her wet pants soaking into the bedspread and the smarting of her thighs where they rubbed as she ran, she sits on on her bed. A howling wind inside her ears flutters with scenes from inside the confessional. The picture of God, the kindly, gray-bearded grandfather, is being eaten by flames. And the growling priest is bursting the screen of the confessional, a snarling old dog with bared fangs and iridescent eyes, lunging for the throat. Priests are God on earth. This cannot be God. This cannot be love. They cannot exist. The soul is a communion wafer dissolving on the tongue—it is nothing.

The cruel old priest isn't God, isn't love. Gram is love, was love, is dying. There might be love in seeing Gram. Sneaking into the hospital after the visiting hours for adults, when the lights are dim, tiptoeing through the shadowy halls to sneak by the nurses' stations, Amy will look into every room until she finds the right one. But when she finds Grammy's bed, she won't find Gram. It won't be the lady who read stories and taught how to bake. The face frozen in concrete is Gram. She needs a long, quiet sleep. Mom never says a word

about Gram when she comes home from the nightly visits to
the hospital. Gram's a living dead person with nothing left
to give. Gathering energy to breathe to stay alive is all she
does. Mom never talks about Gram dying because Mom
never talked about sex, or menstruation, or rape. Death is a
word Mom never speaks.

Gram, Mom, Daddy, Flossie, Gwen, Mr. Crandall, Elizabeth: all are figures drawn on a gauzy, fluttering curtain
that always lifts beyond her grasp. Now light streams
through the crude weave of the fabric, so the figures painted
upon it are nothing but splashes of unfocused color. She
bunches the curtain together and pushes it aside. And she
stands before a great, gaping, black hole where wind groans,
where she might fall forever, unseeing, turning head over
heels, fearing yet hoping for an end to the fall. She shivers
in the darkness and hugs herself to keep from falling, rocking and whimpering, gasping for breath through the congestion of her nasal passages, smelling the stench of stale urine.

She falls back on the bed to escape her odor and struggles
beneath the covers to alleviate the cold that rises from
within her. Soon she sleeps, a shallow half-waking state. *A
plump, tanned, blue-eyed woman smiles into the sun. It's Mom,
happy in a way she'd been so very long ago and then so briefly.
Amy and Flossie and Mom lounge in the sun on a white sandy
beach, lolling against the enormous metal freezer warmed on the
outside by the intense sunlight and coated with rosy sand. Mom's
ample body keeps the door of the freezer closed, so none of the
cold air escapes to destroy the Eden-like tranquillity where they
bask as she explains in a low, gentle voice, "Not everyone is as
happy as we are. Not everyone is continually warm and well fed,
cooled by tropic breezes, fed upon sun-ripened fruits. Some people
struggle in the cold and dark and feel pain." Flossie and Amy
don't listen to the ramblings of the sad refrain. They giggle on
either side of Mom's mountainous bosom, their shield as they
flick grains of sand at one another.* A knocking sound tears the
cocoon-like warmth from her. She opens her eyes to the

grayness of early evening. Her mother's leaden voice says, "I'm going to the hospital and won't be back till late. There's food in the refrigerator if you want to eat."

The dream won't return even though she tries to induce it by curling into the precise pattern she'd been in before the spell was broken. Her bladder burns—the way the front of her face feels, behind her eyes, when she has to cry. She bites hard at her thumbnail, trying to ignore the sensation in her lower body, saddened because she has never been on a beach with her mother, or seen her mother's skin colored to that invitingly edible, toasty hue. Amy's eyes tear. She will soil herself and the bed if she doesn't go to the bathroom.

The face in the mirror is not ugly enough. The puffy nose and bruises about her eyes are bad, like a monster mask, but the jagged scabs rippling over the reddened flesh disguise the wounds. She eases her fingernail beneath the end of the hardened skin and lifts the wormlike growth from her cheek. The surface beneath is shiny, thin skin coating a bloody erosion. It seems somehow cleaner than the scab, so she squeezes the edges, and it flushes to a crimson ribbon. The fragile skin holding it together tears. The lips are enflamed eyelids. She adds another eye to her face, one which reminds her of when she'd had pinkeye. She turns her chin slowly to watch the eye wink at her and notes a drop of blood forming at the outer corner, like a tear. It begins to ooze down her cheek. But the other side of her face needs to match this. There are three eyes: two with wide, dilated pupils making her irises as narrow as two aqua breath mints; and her new, diseased rabbit eye. She inspects her other cheek. There's a little scab at the outer edge of her nose. She digs her longest fingernail beneath it, and it pops off, leaving a dimple of blood. This might be the pupil of the eye. She smears the blood outward across her cheek to see if she can achieve the effect of a fourth eye. It needs more work. She drags her fingernail hard across her cheek, but the skin is resilient. Staring hard at her face, she tries to be objective about the mask she sees. It only shows part of the horror she feels inside. She opens the medicine cabinet to search for something to help her carve a mask for herself. Her insides are infected. Her skin must be lanced so the pus can ooze. The demons will leave if she frees them. They will drain from the eyes she slashes.

Mom's razor is on the second shelf. It is pink plastic, and tiny hairs are stuck in the paste of old soap. It would be difficult to use. The blade won't come out. Behind it is a pack of straight-edged razors, the kind Gram used to scrape windows when she washed them.

The blades are so tightly packed, getting one out isn't easy. Each blade is wrapped in a cardboard shield. She eases one from the box and lifts the cardboard flaps on a glittering blade with a grip labeled Industrial Steel. She admires the angle of the end of the razor and tests the blade's sharpness against her palm. It doesn't immediately penetrate. But Mr. Crandall said humans' skin is as strong as the pigskin of a football. After pressing the blade in a number of spots on the surface of her palm, she settles on the pale skin of the inner part and with persistent effort is able to make an incision. The tool will serve very nicely for her purposes.

While she runs a tub of hot water, she quickly disrobes, rolling her nasty dress, socks, and panties into a tight ball to hide at the bottom of the clothes hamper, where its odor will be absorbed by other clothes. She turns to the mirror to complete her face. When she finishes, she'll have six eyes: four in stairsteps down her cheeks beneath her own glossy eyes.

But they don't please her. They aren't uniform: she'd winced as the skin broke and the blade went awry. Her skills improved as she progressed, but the total effect is less than satisfactory. Before she turns to the tub, she attempts to smile at herself to watch the new lids flutter, but the tender flesh smarts, so it trembles.

As she steps into the tub, she glances over her shoulder at her face in the mirror. From a distance her mouth is the greatest gaping hole of all as she gasps at the scalding temperature of the water. Involuntarily, she leaps from the tub. Shaking her hands, she stares at her reddened feet. It will take greater effort to accomplish her goals.

Clutching the edge of the tub, pressing her butt on the cold rim, she forces herself to hold her feet in the water by staring at the wall, counting the black tiles scattered among the white. Her feet are numb. They've given up fighting, or the water has cooled, she isn't sure which. How many eyes can there possibly be in her body? The place she touches in her fur-ringed vagina—a giant cyclop's eye; beneath her knees in the shadow of her kneecaps; the hollows beneath her ankles, where the bulging eyes of her anklebones will shade the bloody wounds.

She steadies herself to stand in the tub and glance at each of her breasts with their embarrassingly provocative rose-colored nipples: albino eyes. And beneath the cage of her ribs, centered in the hollowed-out place of her belly is the eye of a snail. She presses the palm of each hand hard against the opposing upper arm to force herself to remain in the searing water. Her wrist bones whiten with pressure as she lowers her unwilling body into the tub. Watching the blood rush to the surface of her skin, she submerges herself in the water. Hold yourself in the flame. Be cleansed—a burning paper turned to ash to be scattered in the gathering dusk. The guilt, the fear, cease. Burn. Burn. Poisons drain. The body licked by flames to purify. She stretches out full length, submerged to her chin, and closes her eyes. The ritual is not complete. Her arms are still heavy with her infection. Beneath the water, she tightly grips the blade, sawing the inner flesh of her left wrist. She must keep her eyelids closed tightly until the venom escapes. When the task is completed, she will have a new window to cleanse and purify her.

Chapter 47

The curses he wants to speak are locked in by the cigarette dangling from his lips; his hand is a fist clenching the receiver, his knuckles cramping. Oh, Jesus, God in heaven, this can't be true. It's just another one of Barbara's fuckin' hairbrain, dipshit schemes to trap me.

"Michael, are you there? Do you hear me?"

"Yeah," he nods with ashes drifting onto his chest, "yeah."

"Amy's dying. She's dead. The tub's full of blood."

"Yeah. I'll be there."

"She's all pale and bleeding."

"I'll be there."

He turns so Gwen can't watch him, hear him. "Shit, I've got to get out of here. Get over there. Barbara's nuts! But never this crazy—got to get over there now." And he watches his hand groping at his shirt pocket for a cigarette as smoke drifts into his face from the butt in his lips. He shakes his head, coughing. Amy in the tub, her blood, the water . . .

"Michael, Michael, what is it?" Gwen's touching his arm, holding his wrist, her eyes big.

He can't stand to look at her eyes as he mutters, "I don't know," but her face is a halftone on Amy's body. This is too fuckin' sick and sad to tell. Keep Gwen out of it. "Oh, shit, I don't know. I got to go—go and see Barb. She's flipped out. The kids are sick, or some damned thing—I don't know." Jesus, get outa this fuckin' woman's grasp!

"It's Amy, isn't it? I'm getting dressed and coming." Ah, shit, let her wait in the car. There's not enough time and energy and heart to argue.

She has enough sense not to say anything when he's driving tearass across town, running stop signs and red lights as if he's the last man on earth. And Jesus, when they get to the house, the front door is standing open, all the lights in the place are turned on, so the rundown dump looks like a set of a horror movie.

He runs from the car into the house and Barb is coming up the hall, her face pale, bug-eyed, her hands bloody. God, she's really crazy, crazier than ever before. Ah, Jesus, there's something going on in that house, a nightmare.

It's a hell of a lot worse than he'd imagined. Amy's a corpse. Blood. So much blood. Jesus. Looking at her reams his head right out through his gullet. This can't be Amy. But the nostrils, the eyelids: there's life.

He's on his knees, his voice saying what he has to do, his hands doing it. The women obey, whispering. Her pale little body hacked with bloody slashes. Jesus, she wanted to kill herself, wanted to make it hurt a lot.

Chapter 48

The beating of the drums is reaching a frenzied pitch, and the flames are leaping higher and higher, and still she must dance for the old men of the tribe who don't care if the limbs of her body and her skull ache with fatigue. She doesn't dance in this ritual because she has a choice. She must dance naked before all of the tribe until the men decide who shall possess her, then she will go, without a spoken word, into the dark hut and do whatever her master demands. She whirls about the fire as rapidly as her exhausted legs will move her feet across the burning coals, her arms drooping lower and lower, permitting her head to bob beneath the layer of smoke to gasp breaths of fresh air. But still the drumbeats intensify, demanding more of her body than it can possibly perform, and as she thrashes toward the sound to show how desperately she is trying to be obedient, she hears her name, but the

*voice calling her is not the tribal leader from his throne of wild-
animal skins, but the hysterical screech of her mother.* To move
toward the sound, Amy must guide her numb hands, but the
tingling heaviness of sleeping limbs makes them difficult to
lift. She bashes her hand against the side of the tub, sending
a slash of pain through her arm that opens her eyes to her
mother's lips saying, "Oh, my God." But the eyelids are too
heavy, they flutter, blacking out Mom's lips, opening on the
scarlet waters of the tub, closing at the sight of blood.

Someone leans over her and the waters around her begin
to move, draining away. She shivers against the wet porcelain supporting her. Her teeth chatter and her skin prickles
with goosebumps. Then warmth falls upon her, a heavy
blanket drapes her. If she opens her eyes, they will show she
is thankful, but the light holds them closed.

Mom is not alone. She talks rapidly and fearfully to someone about something frightening. Others are approaching
the tub. Huddling further beneath the blanket, Amy moves
her arms to hide her hands between her thighs and feels the
soggy bindings. Someone has wrapped her wrists. She wants
to see the bracelets, to see her blood, but as she begins to lift
her hands, she's so chilled she trembles.

A blanket envelopes her so she shivers into its scratchy
warmth. Gwen says, "Oh, my God, Michael, my God." He is
the dark silhouette through the weave of the blanket.

As the cover is folded back, Amy closes her eyes against
the glaring light. "Oh, baby." Daddy leans over her; she
contracts her torso in shame. He sees her naked. To cover
her breasts, she shifts her throbbing, swathed wrists. Now
the pale skin on her belly and groin with its newly sprouting
wiry hair is exposed. With a slash of pain, her hands sink to
hide herself, but the struggle is hopeless.

His hand slips behind her neck, and her head lolls back,
far too heavy to support by herself, and then his fingers are
on her left forearm, turning it gently so it flops like a dying
fish. He unwinds the towel. Each of his movements pulls her

from beneath the deep water, where sounds and actions are heavy as sandbags, to the surface, where the air on her open wounds is a whiff of ammonia. She holds her eyelids open far enough to view the world through a fringe of eyelashes.

Daddy's quick breathing opens her eyes. His face in profile is tense. As he lifts her arms, she whimpers. He stares into her wide eyes, his wordless apology. And then he lifts her wrists, unwinding the bandages, and she rises to glimpse the red gaping lips, opening and closing. His face pales even beneath his tan as he says, "Gauze, I need gauze," and her eyes are drawn to the sighing and gasping chorus behind him. Above his head, Mom's hands wring one another. Gwen's fingers clench the white fabric on his shoulder. Spots dance before Amy's eyes, so she lets her head loll back on the rim of the tub and watches with detachment when he drops the soggy, bloodstained towel and begins to wind gauze over the wound. "Get her a robe," he commands, as he gently crosses her wrists above her belly and begins to tuck the blanket under her chilled backside.

He carries her into the dark yard. She feels enormous and awkward bunched against his chest with her feet dangling far past his waist and her neck cricked at a painful angle. She tries to breathe shallowly, wishing it would make her as light as she was when she was six and he carried her this way, half asleep, to go home from Gram H.'s. With her ear pressed against his chest, she hears a tiny wheeze rippling within him. His chest contracts as he stops by the car and gathers his breath to speak. "Barb, get in back. Gwen, you drive. I'll hold Amy."

Chapter **49**

In the lobby of Emergency, a nurse blocks the examination-room door, looking at Gwen, who could be a hooker in her shorts cut up to her ass, and her halter top with her tits showin', her hair a frizzled mess, the *Playboy* bunny look-alike. The nurse turns to Barbara and says, "Only the parents can go in." Gwen, who's nobody's mother, just steps out of the picture. Like this hospital is a courtroom. The nurse is the judge, the conscience they need to make rules for decent behavior.

He carries the kid into the examination room. She's breathing regularly against his shirt front, her eyes closed, half awake, half asleep. When he eases her onto the table, cradling her in his arms, he really sees her face. It's a carnival mask, slashed and bleeding where she must've hacked it with the razor. His throat closes to the back of his nostrils. God, she's sick. She's carved her face somethin' awful. Ah, Jesus, what were you doin' at the time? Fuckin' Gwen? Drinking beer? Sleeping in front of the TV? He eases his arms out from under her limp body, and she looks up, her eyes bigger and bluer and more innocent than anybody's. And he gets busy stretching her out on the table, so he can go on. So she won't see his eyes.

Jesus, his shirt was a blotter for her bloody face when he carried her in here. Christ, they keep you waiting forever for a fuckin' doctor, not even a nurse. Somebody ought to press the lips of the cuts on her face together, so they won't scar so bad. God, her face is the worst; she musta been sick for so long to do this, so sick for so long and nobody saw. You were drunk—a fuckin' dick who spends your life drunk. Cross her wrists on her chest, give 'em a little elevation, check the bandages to see if they're still bleeding, and hold her feet up so she gets a little blood flowing in her head.

"Jesus, Barbara, sit down before you fall down. Where the fuck's the nurse?" Ah, Christ, why me? Jesus, baby, what the hell can I do? Just stand here. Just be here. Give up Gwen. None of this woulda ever happened if you just hadn't had to fuck Gwen. Jesus, Christ, where's the damned doctor? Ah, God, let Amy make it. Of course she'll make it. She's not dead. This is a reprieve. A second chance, a colossal fuck-up gets a second chance. And if you blow this one, you might as well blow out your brains and Amy's too.

The doctor's just a kid in a hurry. There aren't a lot of questions. He talks in a low tone to Amy, keeping her calm, working fast. He doesn't seem to think this is out of line. It looks good because of Barbara, who looks as sick as Amy. Looking at the sutures in the wrist, Barb turns pale green and starts to fall to the floor—a total distraction. The doctor's so busy reviving her he hasn't got time to lecture about counseling for the kid and the family. And when the doctor's done with his job, because he's been quick and decent you got to act interested in counseling, take the numbers, take the names along with the prescription for painkillers and sleeping pills.

To hell with the counselor. The answer is go home. Dry out. The kid's so fuckin' unhappy she wants to die. She just chose a faster ride than the slow slide of drinkin'. Well, hell, quit it, even beer. Quit it all: booze, Gwen, pot—go home and dry out and the kid'll be okay. Barb just can't cut it alone. Maybe if her mother hadn't had the stroke. Maybe if Amy hadn't had her problem, or been the kind of kid she is. But it's too many maybes. Go home and do it right. Live straight. Be straight. There's no maybe about it. Barbara's worse than useless. The kid'd be better off alone than with her. There's no question what has to be done.

And when Amy's cleaned up, and stitched up, and sitting in the wheelchair ready to wheel to the car, and he kneels beside her to straighten her robe, to make sure everything's okay, she looks at him. Her face is like some Christian martyr's: the slashes painted with disinfectant, her hair all gold and curly, her eyes so big. Looking into her eyes, he makes an unspoken vow: Go home, be a father. Let Barbara hang onto your arm. Just wheel the chair down the hall past Gwen. She'll know. She already does. Jesus, this is a turning. It's a relief. Christ, to be free of the past. And when the sick need for a drink comes, and it sure as hell will, and when the aching for Gwen begins—and it will; Christ, when pushin' the toilet paper is an endless job, and dealing with jerkoffs is an hourly event and the solitude of some bar looks like heaven, all you have to do is replay the kid dying. Christ, you been born again.

Chapter 50

On the drive home, her head resting on Daddy's thigh, Amy closes her eyes against the dark silence of the adults. Oh thank you for letting me be with my Father, my Father, my Father. *Riding in a helicopter over a snow-covered field where hungry dogs roam, she stands by the open door, staring down at their iridescent eyes and bared fangs. She slips and begins to fall through space toward the mouths of the snarling beasts, but someone catches her hands. She dangles from her father's grasp, her wrists throbbing and aching, her pain as intense as her love for the man who will not let her fall.*